# HUNTED

Also by Abir Mukherjee

*A Rising Man*
*A Necessary Evil*
*Smoke and Ashes*
*Death in the East*
*The Shadows of Men*

# HUNTED

## ABIR MUKHERJEE

Harvill
Secker

1 3 5 7 9 10 8 6 4 2

Harvill Secker, an imprint of Vintage, is part of the
Penguin Random House group of companies whose addresses
can be found at global.penguinrandomhouse.com

 Penguin
Random House
UK

First published by Harvill Secker in 2024

penguin.co.uk/vintage

Typeset in 11.25/16.5pt Adobe Caslon Pro by Jouve (UK), Milton Keynes
Printed and bound in Great Britain by Clays Ltd, Elcograf S.p.A.

The authorised representative in the EEA is Penguin Random House Ireland,
Morrison Chambers, 32 Nassau Street, Dublin D02 YH68

A CIP catalogue record for this book is available from the British Library

HB ISBN 9781787302723
TPB ISBN 9781787302730

Penguin Random House is committed to a sustainable future
for our business, our readers and our planet. This book is made
from Forest Stewardship Council® certified paper.

*For Sonal, Milan and Aran*
'Chirokaal'

'Our most basic instinct is not for survival but for family'
Paul Pearsall

# DAY 1

## *MONDAY*

## CHAPTER 1

*Yasmin*

*Nothing good comes without pain.*

The chiffon scarf dances around her in the breeze. Yasmin shifts it casually to her shoulders while the world beyond the windshield melts: the carboniferous ghosts of trees yielding to the sprawl of settlements and, in the distance, the contours of the city, its dark lines and needlepoints etched out in the smoke-blue haze of the horizon.

*Los Angeles.*

The sight of it prickles the soft hairs on the back of her neck as the fear rises within her once more.

She tries to bolster her courage, drawing on a lifetime's worth of anger. That's why she's here, after all: to make a stand for those who can't.

Beside her, Jack takes a sip of soda – that's what they call it here – and in her head she plays with the novelty of the word. He places the can in the hollow of the armrest between them and she reaches out, touching his bronzed fingers with hers, tracing the faint blue outline of the rough tattoos. Jack glances over; her all-American white boy, his eyes hidden behind Oakleys and his hair under a Patriots cap, but he says nothing. How she wishes he would. A sentence, a word, anything, just to reassure her or . . . to show her that he too might be scared. His glance though sends a shiver through her. An act that feels illicit. She breathes in the tang of his cologne and turns once more to look out at the vista.

The landscape changes. The dead gradually giving way to the living. Taller buildings now, drawing closer to the freeway; packed in tight like matches in a box.

Billboards and yard signs sprout like weeds: Vote Costa and Take Back America; or Greenwood for President and A Better Tomorrow. Make your mark. Take your choice.

Jack signals, and she feels the car lurch across four lanes of traffic, pitching onto an off-ramp before she's even had a chance to read the destination on the overhead sign. The soda rocks in its holster, a splash escaping, falling onto cheap black plastic.

'Slow down,' she says. 'What's the hurry?'

Jack looks over and she feels that frisson again. The power of his stare. He brakes for a red, takes a left when it shifts to green and then just cruises, between golden-stemmed palms along a sun-blessed boulevard that stretches on to forever. If this were a movie, she'd have lit a cigarette. Instead she lets the window all the way down and rests an arm on the door sill, fights her rising fear and tries to lose herself in other thoughts.

*Everything will change today.*

A young mother in faded T-shirt and frayed dungarees propels a buggy along the shaded sidewalk and for a moment Yasmin dreams.

*Maybe a kid one day. Maybe even a house.*

She shakes the thought from her head. In a few hours' time, the world will be different and she and Jack will never see each other again. It has to be this way. Miriam has told them so.

They have hardly spoken this morning. Not since leaving the safe house. She, dumbstruck by fear and the incomprehensible magnitude of what lies ahead, and he? Maybe he is being stoic. Or maybe he is just as terrified as her. Two hundred miles and barely a word between them, but now, from nowhere, the impulse wells up inside her, the urge to ask him: *What the fuck are we doing?*

But it is too late now. They have made their decision; decided it together and reaffirmed it in bed last night. Miriam would freak if she knew.

Jack is already pulling into the covered parking lot, taking a ticket at the barrier, pulling off his shades, driving up the ramp.

*Too late.*

*Eighteen years old and already it's too late.*

Jack drives the car nose first into a space and kills the engine. He looks at her and this time she doesn't flinch. This time it is his turn to place his hand on hers.

'You okay?' the words like balm upon her skin.

'*No,*' she wants to tell him. '*I'm really not.*' But that too is impossible. Where she is from, you learn to keep your demons hidden. Instead she nods and consoles herself with the currency of his smile. She is, she realises, doing this for him. She might have started on this journey out of conviction for the cause, but she is completing it because she's falling in love with him.

Jack slides off his seat belt. He reaches for the door handle and Yasmin follows suit. She gets out and ponderously pushes the door shut. Jack is already retrieving the trolley cases from the trunk. He pulls up the handle on one, passes her the other, and places his shades back on his face.

He takes her hand.

They follow the signs: up stairs, through brushed metal doors, along walkways, passing from parking-lot concrete to the bright, white marble of the mall; crossing the boundary between utilitarian and aspirational. Ahead lie JC Penney, Bloomingdale's, Macy's and myriad other stores packed with shoppers seduced by discounted prices and refrigerated air.

She watches them: the sandal-clad parents, eyes flitting between shop windows and hyperactive kids; the tribes of teenagers – the golden ones and the trench-coated goths – loitering near the fountains and attentively ignoring each other; the leather-skinned pensioners in big shirts and sensible sneakers doing laps of the mall like athletes unable to shake the habit; the small-time political surrogates peddling buttons and bumper stickers and politicised baseball caps. Yasmin watches them all with a pang of perfect regret.

She passes the window displays, barely registering the high fashion or high heels that once she might have gazed at longingly.

Jack squeezes her hand.

'You want a coffee?'

*She wants a vodka.*

What she wants is something to obliterate the doubts screaming inside her. But that isn't about to happen. She purges the thought and instead looks at him and nods, not quite trusting herself to speak.

He smiles back.

'Starbucks?'

The question is irrelevant. Their route and actions have been planned in advance. The question is part of the routine and the routine is for the security guards and CCTV cameras.

He leads the way, as confident in his direction as though he were walking home from the bus stop, through an eddy of kids and into the glass-domed atrium, joining a stream of shoppers ascending golden escalators toward the gates of the food court. He lets her step on first, standing behind her and encircling her waist with one strong arm as the stairs rise, and for the smallest of moments she wonders whether that arm protects or constricts. She turns round, the extra step negating his extra height, and for once they are level. A wave wells up within her, a bitter-sweet rush that encompasses everything from love and exhilaration to pain and pitch-black fear.

She clutches the escalator belt and feels like throwing up.

The landing appears ahead, bright and white. Jack takes the lead and once more she follows him, dutifully.

She wonders what he is thinking.

Does he too have doubts? How could he not?

Jack orders lattes while she waits for a table, loitering close-but-not-too-close to an old couple who sit hand in hand in front of empty cups. They are silent, yet Yasmin senses that a whole world of words passes between those thin, mottled fingers. By the time Jack returns, the table is hers. Instinctively she lowers her gaze, just as Miriam would want it. He places the black plastic tray on the table and takes the seat opposite. A cookie sits alongside the lattes. A gingerbread man with glazed eyes of icing sugar.

*Last chance.*

What was it they said at Christian weddings?

Speak now or forever hold your peace.

But she can't speak. She certainly can't look at him, fixing her gaze instead on the china mugs and the oversized biscuit.

*Too big.*

Everything in this country was too bloody big.

She reaches out, searching for the warmth of his hand and finding nothing but bare table.

*What is he feeling? Surely he too must be scared?*

She feels his touch, his fingers upon hers, and looks up at him and sees the nervous energy in his face, the electric charge ripple across his shoulders.

He is, she decides, dealing with his fear in his own way.

'It's okay,' he says. 'We're nearly there.'

He lifts the gingerbread man from its saucer, breaks it in two and holds one half out to her. She takes it and stares at it: a head and half a torso.

'Jack.'

He looks up from a sip of coffee and her confidence evaporates.

'Do we have to ... you know ... ?'

'Baby,' he says, rising from his chair and taking a seat on the bench beside her. She feels the strength of his thigh against hers. 'You know we have to. It's the right thing to do. And when it's done, we'll be together. Don't matter what Miriam says, we'll make it happen.'

His words soothe her, but they don't silence the screams that swirl in her head. And he's right, of course. They need to keep going. Someone has to. Someone has to strike a blow.

Jack takes another sip and places the cup back on the table. She watches as he clenches and unclenches his fists.

'It's okay to be frightened,' he says. 'I'm scared myself. But it's like Miriam said, we need to hit back at these bastards.'

She looks down, her eyes falling on the trolley case beside her. She thinks of its contents which she has never seen.

She picks up her cup and sips, swallowing hot coffee and registering only the burnt, bitter aftertaste. She contemplates a bite of her half of the gingerbread man but doesn't have the appetite.

'You clear on what to do?'

She nods.

'Good,' he says, then rubs the back of his neck and reaches over. She feels him thread his arm with hers. He squeezes her fingers, then kisses her and she doesn't know what to feel.

'It's time,' he says softly.

The kiss seems to renew her courage. Suddenly she is on her feet, going through the checks as though on autopilot. She knows the drill. They have practised it. Jack is already heading out into the mall. She will wait. Two minutes only. Enough time so that he can lose himself in the crowd. She spends the seconds clutching the handle of the trolley case, wheeling it forward and back.

Two minutes. It had seemed longer during the tedium of the dry runs, but now it is over too quickly.

She pulls the case behind her and sets off, joining the sea of bodies making for the escalator. She heads down, past carefree faces going the opposite way. It hurts to look at them, so instead she stares at her feet.

Three minutes to reach the prearranged location: the landing outside the radio station; the shock jocks broadcasting their poison into a million minds. Odd that the station should be in a mall, but then its positioning is one of the reasons Miriam has chosen it as a target.

'*It'll send a powerful message.*'

Jack will be inside by now, in the reception area. At least that is the plan.

She is not to enter, just plant her bomb in the hall outside and wait among the crowds for him to plant his and return. They will make their way back to the car and drive a safe distance and then phone in the warning.

'*No innocents will get hurt.*' Miriam has been categorical about that, and she has faith in Miriam; *absolute faith.*

But then she triggers the sensors on the automatic doors.

They open. Jack is not there.

She hesitates, hovering on the threshold, peering into a different world from the throng of the mall beyond: a world of white, anti-septic light; of sofas and flat screens and blonde receptionists behind

7

a gleaming desk. She stands there, a stone in a stream, as crowds of shoppers brush past, their voices crashing in on her, drowning her own thoughts. A security guard is already assessing her for signs of threat. But there is no sign of Jack. *Where is he?*

She steps back and collides with an old woman in sunglasses and sneakers. She mumbles an apology but with one eye still scanning for Jack. Her heart is pounding. She needs to keep calm. He must have been waylaid. The mall is packed after all. But long minutes pass and still there is no sign of him.

She tasted salt on her upper lip.

*Is he lost?*

But Jack would never make that sort of error.

*Maybe she is in the wrong place?*

She turns, frantically scanning the floor for another entrance to the radio station, but there is none.

The black fear begins to well up again, threatening to overwhelm her. She keeps looking for Jack, searching for his dumb shades and his stupid baseball cap.

*Has he been arrested? Is it all over before they've even started?*

But she has watched the videos, the clips on YouTube of screaming onlookers and their panicked, herd-like stampede away from trouble. If they have got him, then where is the commotion? Where are the shouts of frightened shoppers, and where are the cops with their guns?

As one thought recedes, another takes root: darker, more pernicious.

*Has he had a last-minute change of heart?*

Has he decided that, after everything, this wasn't what he wanted? But then, why wouldn't he tell her? An electric panic seizes her.

*Where the hell is he?*

Her breath comes fast and shallow. She tries to force those last, terrible thoughts from her mind, but they flood back like storm water bursting a levee. She gulps at the suddenly thin air and feels the stares of passers-by boring into her soul, sensing her fear. Knowing her guilt.

She reaches into her jeans, takes out the phone Miriam has given her and dials his number from memory. No saved phone numbers. They have been strict about that. She waits for it to connect, agonising seconds spent in the hope that he will pick up, but it just keeps ringing till she hears the computerised lilt of the phone company's voicemail, asking her to leave a message.

*Fuck that.*

She cancels the call and slips the phone back into her pocket. Something is clearly wrong. The plan is quite specific: plant the bombs and leave together. She cannot get out of here without him.

*She doesn't understand.*

Frantically she searches for somewhere she can dispose of the case: an exit, a toilet, even a bin for fuck's sake.

Then she remembers the corridor, the concrete stairwell to the parking garage. It would do. She runs, wheeling the case behind her, fighting through the crowd, ignoring their protests as she barges past.

She can see them now, the brushed metal doors just a few hundred metres away. She runs on, closing the distance: four hundred yards, three hundred. She feels her phone vibrate.

*Jack. It must be Jack.*

She slows to a walk, pulling her phone from her pocket. She does not recognise the number, but it doesn't matter. Whoever it was has ended the call and suddenly she knows it's too late. She hears another phone begin to ring. It is inside her trolley case. She doesn't know what it is and at the same time knows exactly what it means. Yasmin Malik drops the phone in her hand. She thinks of her brother and begins to recite the declaration of faith. 'There is no god but God and Mohammed is his –'

And then the bomb in her case explodes.

9

# CHAPTER 2

*Shreya*

Shreya Mistry longed for a cigarette. A nicotine punch to numb the shock of the carnage, but she'd tossed the last pack months ago, and anyway, it was out of the question on account of gas leaks.

There was no logic to it. At least none that she could see. No rhyme. No reason. Just victims dead and dying.

The air tasted of charred plastic and industrial solvent; of sack-cloth and ashes. No more flames now, just smoke that billowed thick and black and impenetrable and mushrooming into charnel-house clouds.

She threaded her way through the cordon of emergency vehicles; lights on their roofs dancing kaleidoscope red and blue, triggering that familiar fizzing in her head. She looked down at the ground and centred herself. Around her the first responders: firefighters, police, paramedics; all just bystanders and stretcher-bearers now, traversing a parking-lot no man's land of twisted metal and crystal-line shards of glass; ferrying the dead like battlefield orderlies.

*She shouldn't be doing this.*

She should be keeping her distance like they were told to, like the others were doing – the ones who didn't obsess the way she did, the ones whose careers were still moving forward.

*Good for them.*

She kept walking, heading for the entrance, past the painless faces of the dead lined up in rows on the ground. As for the injured, the bloodied, the traumatised, she avoided their eyes. Behind her, sirens wailed and people cried. She shut out the noise and filled her head with numbers. Sixty-three dead. A hundred and fourteen injured. Fifteen years at the Bureau. Fifteen years, and four months. Yet this was a first.

*What sort of people bombed a mall?*

A mall, in the middle of the day, when it was full of nothing but old folks and kids and store assistants working for minimum wage. And it *was* a bomb, confirmed now, though obviously she'd antici-pated it from the start – as soon as the alert had reached the Bureau; fears that had festered and brooded, that had sat in her stomach and multiplied as she and half the field office had sped to the scene.

*What sort of people bombed a mall?*

The question wasn't just rhetorical. She listed the candidates. Hard left and far right. The Global Action folks, saving the planet by blowing up bits of it, or the American Redemption fanatics, looking to bomb America back to greatness.

In a sense it didn't matter. The dead didn't care and most every-one else would utter thoughts and prayers and then believe whatever post-truth palliative they wanted.

She donned a mask and latex gloves and approached the entrance.

'You can't go in.' A thick hand, shoved in her face by a sweaty cop. 'Building's structurally compromised. Whole place could come down at any minute.'

She showed him her badge. Held the photo ID close to her own head in case he was one of those who had trouble telling one brown woman from another.

The cop gave a shrug.

'No one goes in till the engineers say so. Don't matter who you are. I got my orders.'

'And I've got mine,' she told him.

*A lie.* It made the hairs at her neck prickle. Lying was difficult, though she was getting better at it. The trick was to shut down your brain and try to look people in the eye as you said it. But then eye contact was another challenge, in its way just as problematic as lying. She steeled herself, then stared at the officer, gazing at him with the zeal of a Jehovah's Witness on the doorstep till he backed down and stepped aside.

'Fine,' he said. 'It's on your own head.'

She hoped not.

The first couple of yards inside, it was hard to tell what had happened. The place appeared untouched; outlets and convenience stalls pristine and desolate as though just waiting for opening time. Only shattered glass and the litter of bags and backpacks – the detritus of the fleeing – pointed to what might lie ahead.

Yellow tape presaged the route. Her colleagues would have been in here already, hot on the heels of the first responders; gathering what evidence they could before being evac'ed out once the structure had been deemed unsafe.

*She shouldn't be here.*

The story of her life.

The noise, the chaos of the parking lot faded, yielding to a singular silence. It struck her as odd that the pain and the grief out there had been born in here, conceived in terror, a malign force that had migrated, leaving behind it a wasteland. She kept going, the only living thing in a world of mannequins, her footsteps echoing on polished floor tiles.

She closed her eyes, savouring the peace for a moment, before abruptly opening them again, reminding herself that *that* was not a fitting reaction.

She turned a corner and everything changed: sharp, ordered white dissolving to chaos and charcoal black and the stench of charred flesh and rubber; a jagged, bloodstained mess of twisted metal and tangled electrical cables; of dust and rubble and the ghosts of lives cut short. She closed her eyes and counted. It often helped. Safety in numbers. *One, two, three . . .* A ten count was normally enough. Today it took close to thirty. She took a breath and opened her eyes to a different world; the Third World. Iraq or Libya maybe, but with sneakers in place of sandals.

*Ground Zero.*

She knelt to recover a child's doll, a Raggedy Anne type thing like the one Nik had told her to buy for Isha years ago, when the girl was still a baby. She turned it over and stared at its charred and puckered face then placed it back on the floor and considered the blast radius.

*Large. A sophisticated device.*

She took her bearings. A service entrance nearby. No stores particularly close, no obvious target, at least not that she could see. A strange place to set off a bomb. A couple hundred yards away, a more central location, and the casualties could have – *would have* – been far higher. Whoever had done this had been . . . inefficient.

Her lungs burned, bronchial tracts constricting from the fog of bomb debris and asthma. She raised a hand to her mask as the coughing fit bent her double; a febrile twenty seconds that felt like life-sapping minutes. She beat back the panic, visualised what was going on in her chest just like she'd been taught, till the fit passed, then straightened to ringing ears and wet eyes and dancing pin-pricks of light. She wiped them away and stared up at the ceiling: at the small blinking light on the black dome of a security camera.

The building groaned. An iron gasp of despair. She should leave now. Before the whole place decided to come down.

*That camera.*

It might have caught something . . .

She found a mall plan – a diagram etched out in happy colours showing shops and levels and stairs – and committed it to memory. The work of seconds. No mention of what she was looking for, but malls like this generally housed their brains in their basements. She made for a stairwell, down concrete steps to a bunker of offices vacated in a rush. Lights on. Laptops running. An office plan taped to a wall directed her along a desolate corridor that fell in and out of sight to the beat of a flickering strip light, past bulletin boards and motivational posters, to a door at the end. A cursory knock and then she pushed it open, stepping into a room that stank of fast food and cheap deodorant.

A bank of screens flickered across one wall; a patchwork of images, twelve inches square, displaying all corners of a hollowed-out mall. In front of them, consoles that looked salvaged from a TV cutting room: all keyboards and knobs and dials.

There should have been agents here. There should have been men and women, checking faces, crawling over camera footage, but there was no one. Dan was playing it safe, waiting for the all-clear from the structural engineers; but then he'd been playing it safe his whole career. That was why he was station chief now while she was – what exactly, other than a pain in everyone's ass? And that's why she was down here now while Dan and the others were outside.

Old security systems like this one were simple enough to operate – just logic and trial and error. She pulled over a creaking office chair and sat down in front of the console. Finding the right camera wasn't hard: it was the one showing an image of stark and absolute destruction. A couple of keystrokes brought up a menu. A few more and the footage spooled backwards, shimmering like mercury. She kept going till the picture changed – the devastation of a bomb site morphing into fog and then fitting itself back into structured reality.

*Order from chaos.*

She pressed a button and the image rippled and froze. In the centre, a girl in T-shirt and jeans and holding a trolley case had just dropped her phone. It hovered halfway between her hand and the ground.

Another key-press and the image shuddered to life, the action reversing like some manic comedy clip: the phone jumping back into the girl's fist before she took off, rushing backwards toward the centre of the mall and out of shot.

*Why was she running?*

Shreya toggled cameras and found another angle, rewinding the footage to the point where the girl came into shot. *Was the girl scared?* Shreya wasn't exactly the greatest at reading facial expressions but even she recognised fear when she saw it.

The girl continued her backwards run across the concourse, past window-shoppers and families and kids before stopping beside the fountain in the middle of the atrium. The perfect place to let off a device.

Shreya bit at her lip.

Dead centre. The girl had stood right there. And yet she'd run for an exit, only to stop and answer her phone seconds before her bomb exploded.

*Why?*

Shreya wound back further, slowly, incrementally, following the girl across screens and back in time; back to outside what looked like an office; back to the food court; back into a Starbucks; back to a table and to some guy in sunglasses and a baseball cap.

*Who was that?*

She felt the floor judder. Metal groaned.

*She should leave . . .*

She looked to the ceiling, then back at the screen.

*She couldn't. Not yet.*

She pressed rewind, tracing the two of them walking backwards hand in hand: back down the escalator and through the mall, back toward the door to the service area the girl had been making for when she'd stopped and the device had exploded. The guy in the baseball cap seemed to know where the cameras were. He walked with his back to them or, when that was impossible, with his face shrouded by his hat. They went back through the door to the service area and Shreya searched for the feed from the camera in the corridor beyond, finding it and once more going through the whole process of reversing time to the point the two passed through.

Her eyes flickered. She pressed a button to freeze the footage. The girl stood motionless, fingers pressed against the steel plate of the door, caught in the act of pushing it open.

*There.*

The merest of smiles crept onto Shreya's face, just as the ceiling cracked and the first of shards of plaster rained down.

She leapt from the chair and ran. Out of the room, back along the corridor as the building roared. The noise . . . it filled her head . . . disorienting . . . Which way was it? Left or right? She chose left. She always chose left.

She sprinted as the dust fell, as the walls around her shuddered, searching for the familiar: the water cooler; the staff chart on the wall with the faces of its employees staring out like mugshots on a wanted poster.

She burst through the doors into the stairwell. The building screamed; the death throes of a wounded animal.

*Not enough time to head upwards.*

So she headed down, running further into the bowels of the building, making for the basement parking lot with its forest of reinforced concrete pillars; down the stairs as the lights flickered then failed around her; taking them two at a time, into the darkness, her breath ragged now, her windpipe constricting.

*She shouldn't have come down here. She should have listened to the cop on the door.*

The edges of her vision clouded. She burst through the doors and into the parking garage as a tsunami of rubble and dust and plaster crashed toward her. And then the world dissolved.

Shreya saw her late mother. Arms folded. Face set in a semi-permanent scowl that was both accusation and damnation.

*'What did you expect, Shreya? A happy ending? After the choices you made?'*

Was this karma? A fitting end. A life crushed under rubble.

*'Why, Shreya? Why the FBI?'*

It wasn't like that, Mom.

What did the woman want? An apology?

*'Shreya?'*

The voice changed, her mother's plaintive tone supplanted by another just as familiar, just as grating.

'Shreya? Can you hear me?'

The voice grew louder in the blackness. In her head she swam toward it, suddenly conscious that she was lying flat, horizontal amid the void. With an effort she wrenched open her eyes to white light. Bright. Uncompromising.

The taste of blood on her lips.

'Shreya?'

The world resolved into focus. Strip lights: harsh, hospital white. She raised a hand against them. The grooved metal ceiling of an ambulance. The sharp tang of disinfectant. Dan kneeling over her, his face contorted in an expression she couldn't fathom.

*Dan.*

She tried to sit. A forlorn effort, swiftly abandoned with a billowing wave of nausea.

'Dammit, Shreya . . .'

The rest she couldn't follow. The words struggling for space and meaning amid the roaring that filled her head; her thoughts muddled, mired in fog. Among them, something important. Something she needed to tell him.

'You could have fuckin' died, Shreya. You're lucky some cop you mouthed off to remembered you, otherwise we wouldn't have known you were even in there.'

She looked up at him, the buzz in her head growing as she made eye contact.

'And you said my mouth would be the death of me.'

'Screw you, Shreya. What the hell did you think you were you doing in there?'

*That was it. That is what she had to tell him.*

'Checking the security footage. I think I found something.'

'What?'

His expression changed to one of . . . surprise, she guessed. It was gratifying. She liked it when she confounded him. It made up for nearly getting killed.

'The bomber,' she said. 'It was a girl . . . a young woman. She came in with some guy but carried out the attack alone . . . And she left prints on the door from the parking lot. The exit nearest the blast site.'

She had to show him. But things had changed since she'd watched the security footage. Half the building had collapsed.

Would that door even be there now? She needed to get her bearings; tried sitting up, but her ears pounded and the world began to spin and then she collapsed into darkness once more. In her mind, Shreya saw the girl: running across the mall . . . stopping . . . reaching for her phone . . .

Dying.

# DAY 2

## *TUESDAY*

## CHAPTER 3

*Shreya*

*Why had she been running?*

The shrill tone of the telephone shattered her introspection.

'Shreya. Get in here.'

Dan's voice, rough as a Mexican cigarette.

She rose gingerly from her chair and walked from her cubicle – *temporary, just till they could find her something more appropriate, but it might take a while* – crossing the floor to the clamour of an office animated by crisis. A twinge in her back almost stopped her in her tracks: a memento mori from the mall – a reminder of the constant and casual proximity of death. The doctors had discharged her, insisted she go home from the hospital – and she had done so, for six hours, till the pull of the office and the pang of unanswered questions had become too strong. She had gone in to the Bureau to join caffeine-fuelled colleagues coming off the back of an all-nighter. That's just how it was with terror attacks. No rest for anyone till a breakthrough was made. Add a toxic presidential election into the mix and the situation was, as Dan would say, a shitshow.

That was eight hours ago. Now the man himself stood at the threshold, a brick wall dressed in yesterday's shirt and tie with one solid hand on the door frame like he was steadying it. He ushered her in with a glance and closed the door behind her.

She took a seat in front of his desk, beside his bookcase of heavyweight texts with gilt-etched titles, and looked straight ahead at the bunch of framed certificates hanging on the wall like papal bulls yellowing in penance. Dan retreated to the other side, to a swivel chair that complained under his weight, pressed his palms together and made a show of studying her face, an act which only made her uncomfortable.

'How you feeling?'

*Like crap.*

'I'm good.'

'You sure? You need some time off?'

'*No* . . . boss.'

She threw the final word in, gratis. Dan seemed to like that sort of thing.

'You want a coffee?'

She didn't want a coffee. She wanted to know what they'd discovered.

He sensed the question and answered it with a nod.

'We found the door. We even got prints. Her name's Yasmin Malik.'

Fast work. The door to prints, to an ID, and all in the space of twenty-four hours. Impressive what could be achieved with the director and the whole political establishment breathing down their necks.

'Her prints were on file?'

A shake of Dan's head.

'Not exactly. She's not American, she's British, and a Muslim. They took her prints when she entered the country.'

'We know anything about her yet?'

A grunt prefixing his reply. 'It ain't pretty. A girl with a shitty past. Dad died young. Mom diagnosed as bipolar, suffering from depression, who couldn't cope. Taken into care. A history of absconding, a record of petty theft. Last recorded as staying at a women's refuge south of London. She had one brother, two years older, taken into care at the same time. He ended up joining IS in Syria; reported killed in a US air strike.'

Yasmin Malik sounded like a poster child for radicalisation.

'Homeland Security has her arriving at Portland International on a flight from Dubai about nine weeks ago. She took a flight from London and changed there.'

Nine weeks was a long time.

'Where's she been since then?'

A question answered with a shrug.

'Anyone claimed responsibility?'

'No comms chatter. At least none that the CIA or NSA picked up, but an outfit calling itself the Sons of the Caliphate sent a coded statement to the *Washington Post* claiming credit.'

The name was unfamiliar.

'Some Islamic State affiliate?'

'Search me.'

'Any demands?'

'Just the immediate release of all remaining inmates at Gitmo. Apparently there's thirty to forty of the bastards still being held there.'

Shreya blinked. Twenty years at Guantánamo without a trial. She bristled at the thought, not out of compassion or regard for the incarcerated but because of the contradiction. It was un-American.

'Anyway,' Dan continued, 'the president ain't about to release them, not now, not in response to a bomb attack and an ultimatum from some group no one has ever heard of. It'd be political suicide.'

'So more attacks?'

He gave a nod. 'Look at the timing. Unless we find them fast, my guess is more bombs, more dead Americans before election day. Still, I guess it's nice to have some good old-fashioned Islamic terror again. Makes a change from all the fuckin' home-grown nut-jobs of the last couple years.'

She couldn't see why that might be preferable. Was he making a joke? She never could tell. In any case, she didn't question him. She was too busy considering the ramifications. A Muslim girl carrying out the largest attack on US soil since 9/11, eight days before an election resting on a knife edge. That was a material event, a paradigm shift, or as Dan might say . . . *a fucking disaster*. It had the scope to change the outcome.

Dan wiped a hand across his forehead. 'The AG is having a meltdown. It's the hard right's wet dream.'

This she understood, even if the description grated. From talk-radio jocks and alt-news hosts to evangelical preachers, this would be manna from heaven.

In times of trouble it was always easier to peddle fear than to preach tolerance. And the Dems would respond by doubling down too, falling over themselves to show how tough they were on terrorists – the foreign kind, at least. And that would mean even more pressure on the Bureau to catch – and kill – whoever was behind this.

*Why was she running?*

The question surfaced unbidden once more, a cork bobbing in the maelstrom of her mind.

'We need to consider other options. We can't just assume it was Islamist,' she said, 'not yet.'

He shot her a look that made her brain hurt.

'Don't start, Shreya. Would it kill you just for once to accept things at face value?'

*Face value.* But that's what she was doing. She'd seen the look on that girl's face.

'The girl was scared, Dan. She was trying to get away. You need to look at the footage.'

'And I will, just as soon as we can get to it, assuming there's anything left under that mound of rubble they pulled you from. Right now though, the working assumption is Islamic terror and that seems right to me. She wouldn't be the first suicide bomber to get cold feet.'

'Nor the first to be coerced into something against their wishes.'

He gave a sigh.

'We've been here before, Shreya. Why do you need to question everything?'

She felt the first prickle of heat on her neck. She didn't question *everything*. She just had a problem with people doing half a job. Why couldn't he see that?

'So I should just shut up?'

He shook his head in that way that people did when they thought she was being difficult.

'Why can't you just accept that your colleagues aren't all idiots? Based on the threats received and the proximity to the election, we've got to assume the threat is jihadist and that another attack is imminent.'

'I don't think they're *all* idiots.'

'I've told you before, Shreya, you need to learn when *not* to speak. Discretion is the better fuckin' part of valour. Or hadn't you heard that?'

She nodded.

Of course she'd heard the expression. People had been saying it

25

to her in one form or another for as long as she could recall. It sounded like cowardice.

'So what do you want me to do?'

He stared at her, just a moment too long. His voice suddenly softened. 'Shreya, this case is not going to be your concern. You're being transferred to San Diego.'

'What?'

'Orders from on high.'

There had to be some mistake.

'But I just spent eighteen months down there.'

'Maybe they thought you were doing good work.'

Once again she couldn't tell if he was joking.

'Is this because of yesterday?'

He gave a grunt.

'Look, Shreya, I guess they need the manpower. Drugs and immigrants floodin' across the border like it isn't even there; and if Costa gets in, well, you can bet he's gonna head down there every chance he gets for a photo op. Fuck, we're lucky he hasn't suggested declaring war on Mexico just for the bump in the polls.'

She couldn't help but think there was more to it. That was the problem when you spoke your mind. You pointed out some hypocrisy, some double standard of the folks who ran the place, and suddenly *you* became the problem.

She looked back at Dan.

'The girl, Yasmin Malik, she was South Asian. If there are more attacks coming, then you need me on this. Who else is gonna give you the kind of insight I can?'

He spat a laugh. 'This ain't 2004 any more, Shreya. You think you're the only South Asian in the Bureau? There's plenty of others and most don't come with your . . . baggage.'

'Or my experience.'

'Experience that told you to walk into a building that was about to collapse? You know how much fucking paperwork I'd have had to deal with if you'd died?'

'I got a result.'

'You still shouldn't have gone in there.'

'But we *needed* to find out what happened.

'We? Or *you?*'

'Dan, let me stay on this case. I'm expendable. I can get things done for you. If it works out, you take the credit. It all goes to crap, you got someone to blame.'

He should have gone for it. He should have thanked her. She felt he would. It was the logical option after all.

'Fuck you, Shreya. I don't need credit, and I don't need to be pulling your ass out of the rubble of a building.'

He gave a sigh.

'It's out of my hands. Take the rest of the week off. Just make sure you're down in San Diego by Monday.'

Outside the world reduced to smears of movement in her peripheral vision.

*San Diego. Again.*

They might as well have handed her a gun and a glass of brandy and told her to do the decent thing. It was hardly fair on the San Diego Bureau either. They weren't exactly going to be throwing her a welcome party. Shreya Mistry – *Shreya Misfit* – an agent without a home; a problem without a solution.

She should have told him to take San Diego and all his patronising BS and shove it up his ... She left the sentence unfinished. Profanity was difficult, even within the confines of her own head. Another agent might have resigned there and then. Maybe she should have. But what else did she have besides the job? A broken marriage? A teenage daughter she hardly ever saw?

No, it was better to sit there and take the crap; to listen to the man in authority. That's what the smart woman always did, wasn't it? Defer to the man, even if it was just the right side of mediocre.

She stared at her reflection in the door's plate glass. She looked tired. She looked *old*. What had happened to her? Hadn't she once been the face of a new, improved, multicultural Bureau, tipped to be fast-tracked to the top?

How did it all go so wrong?

Dan, in his more bellicose moments, put it down to her personality, her inability to follow orders. It wasn't true. She could and did follow orders, just not the dumb ones.

*Whatever.*

There was no point in dwelling on it. She'd fought those battles and lost. Been frozen out and forced sideways. In Russia they'd have sent her to Siberia. Here, they'd seconded her to San Diego.

The image of that girl haunted her head once more. That and the guy who'd brought her, who'd kept his face shielded from the cameras. Who'd left her there to die.

*Why was she running?*

Dammit. That wasn't her problem any more. San Diego – now that was her problem.

Her cellphone buzzed.

Her father.

'Dad, what time is it there?'

'It doesn't matter. Old men don't sleep. I was watching the news. You are okay?'

'I'm fine, Bapu.'

Her neck burned. The heat that came from telling a lie. She rubbed it, but it did no good. It never did. Lies were always difficult, and white lies, for some reason, the hardest of all. Best to change the subject.

'How are you? You making friends? How's Mrs Wilson down the hall?'

'Friends? *Jah!* She wants me to do bingo and line dancing. Isn't it bad enough that I'm in this place? Must I also do bingo?'

'She likes you, Dad. She's just being friendly.'

A sigh on the other end of the line.

'It's not our way, Shreya. It's unseemly.'

'It's been over a year. You can't mourn for the rest of your life.'

'Your mother would have, if it had been the other way around.'

That was true, but that was her mom, perennially suspicious of anything not in lockstep with the values and prejudices she'd been raised with. She'd have taken up the role of a widow, wearing white and eating only vegetarian food, with the zeal of a martyr.

Still, her father had a point. The thought of him being cajoled into extra-curricular activities by an old white woman in a retirement home, struck her as wrong, somehow. It wasn't how an Indian man expected his autumn years to turn out. He should be surrounded by family and grandkids.

'Aren't you always telling me to try to fit in, Dad? Maybe you need to do the same?'

'I'd rather be dead.'

She closed her eyes. Her late mother's penchant for melodrama, reincarnated in her father.

'I might have some leave coming up. I'll try and fly over.'

*Not a lie. A half-truth.*

'Will you bring Isha?' he asked. 'She said she might come for Diwali. I haven't seen her since her birthday.'

Shreya could have said the same. Six months since she'd last seen the girl in the flesh. What was it, a month since the last phone call? Why had it been so long? Granted, she wasn't the most loving of mothers – the sort of mother-daughter intimacy of soap operas and the school gates had always been difficult for her – but she could *and should* make sure the girl knew she was there for her. At least she was still living with her dad, even if it was with him and that new woman of his. She felt a jolt of something in her gut, like a stone dropping down a well.

'I'll speak to her, Dad, and see what I can do.'

On the TV screens, helicopter images of the ruined mall played on repeat. A Muslim girl from England, lying low in America for nine weeks before setting off the biggest bomb since Timothy McVeigh. Where did she even get a device like that?

Her laptop pinged. An email marked San Diego: Relocation.

*To hell with that.*

Shreya reached for her phone, brought up a Washington number and pressed call. It would be late evening there. Still, she took a chance.

A voice eventually answered.

'Luca. It's Shreya.'

'Shreya? Oh God. How do you even have this number?'

She cut him off.

'I need a favour.'

# DAY 3

# *WEDNESDAY*

## CHAPTER 4

*Greg*

The truck door stuck halfway open.

Greg punched it with the side of his fist till it wailed shut like a wounded animal. He steadied himself against the flank of the beat-up, twenty-year-old relic with its balded tyres and rusted bodywork.

The air smelled of pine and open country, the black sky holding firm against the first colour of dawn. He waited there for a moment, lost in his thoughts, impervious to the chill, the snap of cold on his skin.

They'd lied to him. They should have told him. They should have been straight with him from the start.

He flinched as a spike of pain skewered through the discordant gang of bone and cartilage and metal of his left knee. Four years on and he still had to sleep with a pillow under it. Most days now it didn't hurt so bad, but on mornings like these, when the mercury dropped and his breath froze, it still felt like a bunch of unoiled gears grinding inside of him.

The injuries he'd come to look upon as divine retribution for his sins; penance for his part in the death of so many innocents in that far-flung country. It was the only way he could make sense of it. And now this.

Miriam had said there'd be no collateral damage, no innocent victims, just those who deserved it. Sell-outs and turncoats and corrupt bastards who'd sucked the country dry. He should have known better, should have worked it out for himself. But he'd believed her. It was naive, he knew that, but when she looked at him and put her hand on his arm and spoke those honeyed words, it was almost spiritual. Like he was in the presence of the great, doubt-dispelling divine. And then, when she spoke, whatever she said became gospel.

And now sixty-five people were dead. Sixty-five more souls on his conscience. What would the Almighty seek in retribution this time?

From the bed of the truck, he retrieved the two tarpaulin sacks. Everything needed for bigger devices. The kind Miriam had asked for.

The wind picked up. Sliced through him like a lance. Brass monkeys. That's what Aliyah had called it. An English expression, she said. Cold enough to freeze the balls off a brass monkey. It still made no sense to him, but right now he didn't care. Right now, all he wanted was to get back inside the house, stand up close to the grate and warm his joints.

The tattoo on his neck itched. The treacherous ink that inched up from his collarbone, with its crudely drawn barbed wire and its swastika. It was all safely covered of course: the mark unseen under T-shirt and thick plaid, but still it burned like it was charring a hole clean through his clothes.

He fingered the small pendant in his pocket. The metal he'd gotten from the old lady down at the general store. Six nights he'd worked on it in the solitude of his bunk or in those few free minutes away from the others after dinner and before lights out. He'd been looking forward to giving it to Aliyah. It was futile now.

Pointless.

He would have to tell Aliyah about Yasmin. About what they were saying on the news.

He shook his head.

Impossible. He wasn't even supposed to know what had happened. Miriam would kill him if she even found out he had a phone let alone that he'd used it to check the news, but the truth is he was curious to see the results of his work; he took a professional pride in his abilities. He hadn't expected to see the list of victims. And he hadn't expected to see Yasmin's name.

Fuck it. He had to tell Aliyah.

He winced at the thought as he carried the sacks across the frozen dirt and up the sagging steps to the front porch. Miriam had christened the place the White House on account of the faded whitewash of its clapboard walls.

The door creaked open, Miriam appearing out of the darkness like an apparition; Miriam, whom they all obeyed, her hair wild and white.

Instinctively he lowered his gaze. It was one of the rules that she set for the girls, and though he wasn't strictly an acolyte, he was expected to follow it too. He set his face, his bored, infantryman face. She mustn't suspect him. The key was to carry on as normal until he could make sense of it all; until he could figure out what had happened and what he was going to do.

She urged him forward now, an agitated flash of a pale hand suggesting he pick up the pace. It was only when he'd made it up the steps that she spoke.

'What took you so long?'

He kept his gaze trained on the floorboards.

'Things take longer in the dark, and that truck of yours ain't the quickest.'

'Any problems?'

'Nope. The stuff was where you said it'd be.'

Not for the first time he wondered just who was supplying the components. The shit was sophisticated. Not the sort of crude, amateurish stuff you could pick up in a hardware store.

'Anyone see you?'

A shake of the head.

'I waited a good five minutes before gettin' close. Place was deserted.'

'You stop off, anywhere at all?'

'No, ma'am.'

His response a split second slow.

'Raise your head, Greg.'

He did as she ordered, focusing on her cold blue eyes. Miriam stared at him as though trying to divine the truth from his face. The power of the stare. The eyes as the gateway to the soul. Maybe she really did believe all that shit. He thought of the phone stuffed into the side of his boot. Another spasm of pain shot through his knee. She must have noticed, because her expression softened and she placed a hand on his arm.

'Good boy. I'll take care of these. Go inside and get some rest.'

*Boy?* Did she forget that he wasn't one of the kids to whom she played surrogate mother? The ones who'd do anything for her. And yet there had been times when her words to him, her small kindnesses, reminded him of his own mom.

*Not now. Not any more.*


He took his leave, headed down the hallway and up the tired wooden staircase, taking the steps one at a time in practised fashion, leading with his right and pulling the left up after him. It wasn't elegant, and sometimes in the company of others it made him self-conscious, embarrassed even, but it worked, and importantly, it kept the pain to a minimum.

*He should have confronted her.*

He should have asked her exactly what the fuck was going on. Yasmin dead, civilians murdered.

*And where the fuck was Jack? Dead too?*

The pictures on his phone came back to him. Shrouded corpses on gurneys. Innocent folks: women and children – they could have been his mom or his friends – all dead because of him.

It must have been a mistake. Something must have gone wrong. He should have asked Miriam, but how, without revealing he had a phone on him? Miriam, who'd given him his life back. He owed her. But there were times, specially when she'd got that look in her eye, when the white hair would fly, the lips would thin to slits and her face would flush red, when he wondered if she really was all there. Truth was, she scared him. And deep down, he knew there'd been no mistake.

*They'd lied to him, because they knew that otherwise he wouldn't have made their fucking bombs. They lied, and he should have known.*

He thought of his mom. He'd never be able to look her in the eye again, that was for sure. He thought of the letter he'd written her. It had been building for months now, the urge to contact her. Maybe, somewhere in the depths of his subconscious, he'd known all along that it would come to this; that people would die and it would be his doing. Maybe he'd just needed to express his thoughts, to try to explain his actions, not that there was any explanation. No justification for any of it. Contacting her had been a risk of course. Miriam had stipulated no communication with anyone, no phones, no emails. Not that there was signal worth a damn out here. The only calls allowed were the weekly ones the girls made to their families, Miriam and Yusuf driving them into town and scripting almost every word they said. And so he'd gone old-school. Paper and pen. He just hoped his mom might understand, and maybe forgive.

He reached the landing and cast a glance toward the dorm room where the girls – where Aliyah – slept. He felt a hollowness in his chest and breathed in. A sharp, jagged breath.

*Aliyah.*

He reached into his pocket for the pendant, running his thumb over its edges.

*What the hell was he supposed to do now?*

# CHAPTER 5

*Shreya*

The plane dropped, her stomach corkscrewed, and Shreya muttered a prayer to a bunch of gods she didn't much believe in. She reached for the armrest, digging her fingernails into its underbelly. Somewhere along the way, calm Californian sirocco had succumbed to wilder stuff coming down from the Cascades, turbulence that only grew stronger the further north they'd flown.

Calling in favours didn't come easy but sometimes you just did what you had to do. Luca Calliveste might be a big shot in the Bureau now, but when she'd first met him, he'd been a rookie agent with a bad haircut that did its best to conceal what seemed a head like a malformed cabbage, not to mention his body odour which put her in mind of dead livestock. What mattered though was that he owed her, ever since she'd pulled his fat head out of the way of the business end of a shotgun.

She'd called him and reminded him that if it hadn't been for her, he'd be in a hole in the ground in a Chicago cemetery rather than behind a big fancy desk in Washington, and that lovely wife of his would now be missing a husband and his two kids a father. It should have made him amenable but he'd refused, point-blank, to get involved in the whole San Diego thing, possibly because that lovely wife of his had apparently left him in the meantime.

She'd kept at him.

'At least let me go up to Portland in the interim. I can be useful.'

And at the second time of asking, he'd agreed.

'I'll speak to the Portland Bureau chief. Get you up there as special liaison – but only temporarily. Monday morning, you gotta be in San Diego.'

Five days. Saving a man's life didn't buy much these days.

The flight was the cheapest: early morning, no frills, no food, just a smile from the flight attendant and accountability to the taxpayers.

A ping of the intercom and then Portland appeared through the clouds. Shreya snapped shut her laptop and closed her eyes as the plane began to buck. Her ears throbbed, air pressure transforming general discomfort into needlepoints of pain. She screwed her eyelids tight. Landings were always tough, but this felt different.

Hundreds of flights, hundreds of landings. Never anything like this before.

*Was it because of the mall? Was the shock beginning to hit home?*

The counsellor had told her she should cry more; that tears were cathartic. She'd been sceptical till she'd researched it and found that crying released endogenous opioids into the bloodstream. *Feel-good chemicals.* The science was convincing so she'd tried it after they'd discharged her from the hospital. Gone into her bathroom and tried to cry, but no tears had come. Not a single, lousy one. In the end, she'd given up and gone back to work.

A jolt of turbulence and she opened her eyes to the slate grey of the city and the black slash of a wide river. She thought of Yasmin Malik.

*Why was she running?*

The plane landed heavily; a thump that jarred her bones. Outside, spears of sleet fell from a sheet-metal sky and splintered on the tarmac. Thirty Fahrenheit, so the flight attendant said.

*And people lived here out of choice.*

The plane taxied, pulling to a halt a distance from the terminal. No sky bridge, just a holding area, a parking lot for low-budget flights and an airport truck wheeling a set of stairs into position.

She gathered her bag and made for the exit, the cold hitting her like an insult. Rain hit the metal stairs like shrapnel and she kept her eyes down, focusing on the slick steps. Only at the bottom did she notice the black SUV.

'Special Agent Mistry?'

A young woman, standing beside the car. One hand struggled to keep hold of an umbrella while the other wiped rainwater from her brow. She wore a waterproof jacket and the kind of smile you only saw on the faces of the young; before the cold, hard world beat it out of them.

Shreya reciprocated.

The woman gestured to the passenger door.

'I'm Special Agent Kramer, your liaison. You best get in.'

*The girl looked mid-twenties. Good to see the Bureau getting its claws into another shiny new generation.*

Nevertheless the advice was good. Shreya headed for the car and got in, reaching for the seat belt as the woman made her way around to the driver's side. She turned on that smile again and started the engine.

'You got a first name, Special Agent Kramer?'

'Susan, ma'am.'

'How old are you?'

'Twenty-eight, ma'am.'

'So you drew the short straw?'

Kramer gave her a glance. Incomprehension in place of innocence. 'Ma'am?'

'Of having to look after me.'

'Not at all, ma'am. I volunteered.'

'And why would you do that?'

'You've obviously never been posted to Oregon, ma'am. Far as the FBI goes, it's a backwater. To paraphrase Luke Skywalker, *if there's a bright centre to the galaxy, then Portland Bureau is the office furthest from.*'

Shreya grunted a laugh. Kramer looked over.

'What, you don't believe me? Even Montana and Wyoming are more interesting. At least they got those alt-right patriot fuckers to deal with. Most we got here are radicalised vegans and a few acne-ridden incels bussed in from inland to stage their misogyny marches. And even those demos have mostly died down.'

'Maybe they found girlfriends,' Shreya said.

Portland didn't sound so bad to her. If only more places were like it. She checked her watch. Her email to Dan, informing him of her little trip up here, would be hitting his inbox just about now.

*Best not to think about it.*

Kramer turned the wheel.

'Is it true what they're saying? That there's more attacks coming?'

'That would be the logical presumption.' Outside the window, concrete sped by. 'Where are we going?'

'Portland field office. Thought you might want to settle in.'

Depending on Dan's response to her mail, she might not be up here long enough for that.

'The airport security footage? You gone through it?'

Kramer grimaced. Nice to see that her repertoire of facial expressions extended beyond smiling.

'Not yet. The request only came through late yesterday. We've located the hard drives, though.'

'They're at the office?'

'No, they're here, at the airport.'

'Then we shouldn't waste time. Forget the office. Let's examine those hard drives.'

The smile returned to Kramer's face once more.

'Yes, ma'am.'

The vehicle slowed and Kramer took a sharp left, accelerating past the glass and steel of the terminal and beyond it the stubby concrete pillar of the control tower. Almost immediately they were on a waterlogged access road into open country. Shreya surveyed a drab, washed-out world of greens and browns. Yasmin Malik had been here nine weeks ago. She'd have seen this same view, or one similar. *Nine weeks.* Where had she been in that time? And why Portland? Why not San Francisco or Vegas, or even LA itself? Why fly into Portland if you were going to attack a mall 850 miles away? There must be something up here, some reason for her coming here.

Kramer pulled up outside a squat prefab with blacked-out windows, moss in its joints and the air of a temporary structure forced into permanency when a better one never came along.

'Offsite backup facility.'

A stream of water sluiced out of a gutter and pirouetted groundward.

'I guess there's little chance of the place burning down.'

Shreya gave a grunt. 'Flooding might be a concern, though.'

She stepped out onto cracked tarmac and followed as Kramer headed for the entrance.

The black lens on a security camera scrutinised them before an unseen hand buzzed open a set of steel doors. Beyond them, a deserted, strip-light-illuminated corridor that hummed to the sound of poorly wired electrics. Shreya tasted stale air, damp and dusty and tinged with the musk of a place forgotten. Kramer pushed on to the end of the corridor, through a door and into an airless cave of a room with racks of servers lined up against one wall and a couple of desks in the centre piled high with monitors and computer hardware. A chair scraped, and from behind the mound, a pale, freckled head with a buzz cut and glasses appeared.

'Zack,' Kramer called out, 'this is Special Agent Mistry. Agent Mistry, Zack Kattowitz. Zack works for airport security.'

'Tech,' he corrected her. 'I work in the IT department.'

'Whatever, Zack. You're a tech wizard. Happy?'

She flashed him a smile and the boy's face flushed red. If Shreya didn't know better, she might have thought Kramer was flirting with him. Not that she *did* actually know better.

Kramer gestured to the room like it was Aladdin's cave. 'All this is Zack's domain. He's king of the security cameras and he's up to speed with what we need.'

The boy gestured to his monitors.

'The flight your suspect came in on landed at 17.07. We have her passing through passport control at 17.46. Here, let me show you.'

He pressed a button on his keyboard, his glasses slipping down his nose.

'The immigration hall.'

On-screen, two snakes of people shuffled forward before finally breaking, hydra-like, in front of a line of perspex booths. A digital readout at the bottom of the screen blinked the time: 17.35.

Zack nodded to a corner. 'She should enter the hall soon.'

Shreya watched. The seconds ticked into minutes and then, finally, she saw something.

'Pause the tape . . . please.'

Zack pressed a key and the image froze. A figure, face shrouded in shadow. The camera captured a wide arc: good if you wanted to see as much of the room as possible; less useful if you wanted to examine a particular face.

'Is that her?' Kramer asked.

She wasn't sure.

'Go on with the footage, Zack.'

The picture resolved itself, the girl moving once more, out of the shadows and into the light; a glance up removing all doubt.

The same girl from the security footage in the mall. Yasmin Malik, wheeling a trolley case behind her. One scene echoing the other.

She was about to tell Zack to speed up the tape when another girl entered the frame.

*That face . . .*

Shreya caught her breath.

*. . . she'd last seen it blood-smeared.*

But it was impossible. That girl was dead.

*Wasn't she?*

She lifted a hand to her face, tried to hide her shock. Kramer would only ask questions, and she had no answers.

Her stomach somersaulted.

That other girl, the dead one, she'd been from London too; the details fresh in her mind as though she'd just lived them. A month before the end of her secondment to Diplomatic Security. The crowd outside the building. The girl falling to the ground. She remembered the blood. She remembered running to her, screaming at the police and protection agents to clear a space. She remembered holding the girl's hand, even as the feeling left it. And then the paramedics scrambling across. The ambulance to the hospital and the rush to ICU. Too late. Always too late.

*Munira.* That had been the girl's name. Munira Begum.

She needed to get a grip. It was coincidence, that was all. So the girl bore a resemblance to someone Shreya'd once seen. It meant nothing. Dammit, wasn't that what white folks did – mistaking one brown woman for another as though they were interchangeable? Hadn't she complained about it more than once? And here she was doing the same thing.

In her defence, the video feed was hardly razor-sharp.

On-screen, the girl who looked like Munira Begum joined the lines heading for immigration a few bodies behind Yasmin Malik. The two didn't acknowledge each other; didn't act as though they'd ever met before. But why would they?

The line inched forward, other travellers arriving behind them.

She tapped Zack on the shoulder.

'Speed up the tape.'

He did so until the girls reached the front of the queue, a security officer directing Yasmin to a booth. She walked up, looking no different from any other tourist, followed soon after by the second girl. Now that she looked closely, there were subtle differences between this one and the girl she remembered from London. This girl's hair was longer; her face thinner.

Both Yasmin Malik and the other girl passed through without a problem. The camera watched them: retrieving their passports; picking up their trolley cases and walking out of shot, all within minutes of each other, never talking, never even looking at each other, yet their actions oddly synchronised like a pair of swimmers. Zack stopped the feed and clicked on another file: the baggage hall this time. It took a few minutes before Yasmin Malik entered the shot, followed dutifully by the other girl. They queued for suitcases, one apiece, Yasmin having trouble pulling hers off the carousel before heading for the exit. Another click from Zack, a bit more searching, and Yasmin Malik emerged into arrivals, the other girl three or four minutes behind.

There they waited, looking around like tourists expecting a guide. After a minute of nothing, Zack sped things up, the girls' movements taking on a comical air: checking their phones; Yasmin wandering off, then returning; all in double-time. Then both suddenly turned as something caught their attention.

'Slow it,' she ordered.

Zack returned the playback to normal speed as a man in overalls appeared from the left of shot. He walked over to Yasmin as the other girl looked on.

Shreya leaned forward.

On-screen, words were exchanged before he picked up her case. Then he turned to the other girl and repeated the process, taking her case too before leading them out of the shot. No more than thirty seconds from appearance to exit.

'Pause the footage,' she said and turned to Kramer.

'You got the full passenger manifest of that flight?'

Kramer was already hitting dial on her phone.

'On it.'

Within minutes they were staring at the full list of names, nationalities and dates of birth of everyone who'd been on the plane with Yasmin Malik. It didn't take long to whittle down the list by sex and age. One name stood out: another South Asian girl, another British citizen. DOB 04.08.2006.

The passport image confirmed it.

Another girl. Another potential threat.

Shreya reached for her phone. She should call Dan. Tell him what she'd found; tell him this wasn't over. But that would entail a degree of explanation she currently didn't have time for. Instead she typed out a message.

*Dan. There's another girl. Came in on the same flight as Yasmin Malik. Her name's Aliyah Khan.*

# CHAPTER 6

*Sajid*


Sajid Khan stepped off the Piccadilly Line and followed the signs for Terminal 2. Outside the heavens were weeping. A seven-hour shift ahead of him and already his feet were soaked; the plastic bags lining the innards of his cracked shoes proving worse than useless.

He flashed a faded pass at a slab-faced security guard who pointed him to the metal detectors. Security had been tightened after that bomb had gone off in America and a small line of workers had formed, waiting for clearance to the airside of the terminal. Sajid, his face set in an expression of grim resignation, joined the queue and waited silently for his turn. He had reacted to the news of the terror attack the way he always did, a way which had, over the years, become depressingly second nature. First came the shock, as scenes of carnage rolled on the news loop; then came the dread and a plea to Allah that those responsible weren't Muslims.

Given that the dead were dead, he had learned that the best

outcome would be for the attacker to be identified as a disgruntled white man. The press would then comment on his mental issues, and after tears had been shed and thoughts and prayers uttered, the memory would fade and things would invariably return to normal. But with suicide bombings the chances of that were slim. It was taken as fact that the attackers would be Islamists, and suddenly a few hundred extremists with a death wish were taken as proxy for a billion people, and as a brown man, everything became more difficult. People on the Tube looked at you differently, the security staff stood up straighter as you approached and scrutinised you harder as you passed. Even Mrs Braithwaite's permanent scowl grew somehow deeper.

Two decades and he'd almost grown used to it.

He tried to focus on the positive. He had his health and a dry pair of socks in his bag, and that was enough to be getting on with.

He trudged through departures, past the glitter of shopfronts to the bureau de change. His place of work: two ersatz rooms at the ebb-tide end of the concourse, one with a gloss plastic fascia, a sign that read FASTCASH, and two screens with icons of foreign flags and their exchange rates to the pound, and the other a bigger, shabbier back office where they kept their belongings, their lunch, and of course the cash.

He was five minutes early for his shift but as usual Mrs Braithwaite was already there.

*Did she live in the back office?*

He greeted her with an affable 'Good evening', and she responded with a terse nod of her grey head and the bald statement of his name.

And that was as warm as Mrs Braithwaite got. At first, he would wonder whether her brusqueness was on account of his skin colour, but it transpired she was just as cold to the Poles, Czechs, Romanians and other folk from the less fortunate half of Europe who also worked there.

As if on cue, his phone buzzed. He took it from his pocket. A text from Rumina:

*Don't forget to take your tablets.*

She would send the same message every day, though the words sometimes varied depending on mood.

From her attitude one would think it was she, rather than he, who had spent five years at medical college, but bringing up such a fact would only expose his flank to counter-attack. 'Five years wasted.' Everything sacrificed for asylum in a land that did not even recognise his degree.

With fresh socks donned and his shoes hidden by a bag under the radiator, he took his seat behind the desk out front and smiled at the first of his customers.

The evening shifts were interesting. Suited and booted corporate types stocking up on cash before catching their last-minute flights to Paris, Frankfurt and Geneva. They were on expenses and hardly ever baulked at the rates Sajid offered them. Then there were the long-haul holiday flights. There were fewer of them at this time of year, but they still offered their tensions. He would usually face a few indignant pensioners querying the conversion rates and a smattering of multi-tasking, frantic-faced parents converting eleventh-hour holiday cash while filling out forgotten travel insurance forms on their phones and herding several screaming infants.

He had finished with one such family when *they* showed up; at first just an amorphous mass in his peripheral vision. Then came shouts. He turned. People were screaming, dropping to the floor. Six, maybe seven figures, hulking brutes bigger than men had any right to be, in black boots, helmets and body armour with machine guns at their chests, all sprinting down the concourse.

Sajid told the family to get down then ducked behind the counter and found himself face-to-face with Mrs Braithwaite whose look suggested she found the situation deeply objectionable and that somehow the whole thing was Sajid's fault.

He felt like apologising. It was generally easier to apologise than to point out that none of this was his doing, but he never got the chance. The sound of boots grew louder, then died suddenly, replaced by the sight of guns in his face and shouts for him – *him!* – to lie down, face first, on the floor with his hands behind his head.

Sajid heard the words but could not make sense of them. He lay there, the barrel of a gun against his skull as his brain refused to believe what was happening. A long-dead memory floated into his consciousness, of armed men and a black, jungle night many thousands of miles away. A hand reached down, grabbed his collar, brought him back to the present and flung him against the wall, his head hitting it with a crunching thud.

And then everything stopped.

# CHAPTER 7

*Shreya*

'Go back to him.'

Zack scrolled backwards and hit pause. The image froze; the man side-on to the camera. Late thirties/early forties, she guessed, and thin, like he was short of a meal or two. A beard, but that meant nothing these days, especially not in Portland, and lank, dark hair, combed back and reaching to his collar. The image was black and white but the shading suggested tanned skin, possibly Latino or Middle Eastern or South Asian. The overalls seemed free of oil stains, which suggested he wasn't a mechanic. A handyman maybe? Or a janitor? Whatever his occupation, he was the sort of man you wouldn't recall a second after passing in the street.

He had recognised the girls, not the other way around.

Shreya turned to Kramer.

'Get a screenshot of him and get it to CJIS.'

'You think it's clear enough?'

She gave Kramer a stare. Yes, the woman was a rookie, but this was Suspect Identification 101. Contacting CJIS was the first thing you did when you wanted someone ID'd. You sent their photo to the facial recognition boys so they could match it against the mug-shots in the Interstate Photo System. It wasn't perfect of course; only as good as the photos held on the system, and if the suspect had never been in trouble with the law, well, then the IPS would return a big fat zero, but now wasn't the time to quibble over the quality of the image.

'This isn't Instagram, Kramer. For now it's the best image we've got. We need to send it; and if we get a better one later, we'll send that too.'

She turned back to the tech guy.

'Can you trace them further?'

'Depends where they were heading. Could be anywhere in the airport, or they might've made for the exit. If they were leaving, then it depends if they were making for the parking lot or the city bus or the shuttle to the Red Line for a train.'

Shreya turned back to the image on-screen. The guy in the overalls. There was something about him: a spareness; an economy of action. He'd spent a total of ten seconds talking to the girls before leading them off. *A man in a hurry.* Probability suggested he'd be heading for the exit. And transport? The obvious choice was the lot. A man who could organise explosives of the kind used in the attack on the mall in Burbank would not be using public transport. It would be a car, or, judging from his attire, more likely a truck.

'Show me all the parking.'

Zack shrugged. 'Where d'you want to start? There's about a dozen cameras over four floors: Concourse West, Level 1, Concourse East,

Mezzanine . . . It'll be trial and error and they might not even show up at all.'

'We better get started then.'

It took ninety minutes to find something. The entrance to a parking level, a wide-angle view of distant cars and concrete pillars. A black-and-white image, grainy and shimmering like a 1950s TV show, but still clear enough to spot the two girls and their chaperone pass by.

'Show me where they went.'

Zack shook his head.

'Cameras only cover the entrances.'

'What about at the exits?'

The tech guy shook his head. 'No actual ticket booths. There *are* cameras at the ticket barriers but they just read the vehicle licence plates.'

Kramer came forward.

'What time did they get to the parking lot from the terminal?'

Zack wound back the footage till the trio were in shot again. The time came up at the bottom right of the screen: 18.14.

Chances were, they'd have left within ten minutes of entering the lot, but that wasn't a certainty.

'Can you get a list of the licence plates that left in the hour after this?'

Zack scratched at red skin on his neck. 'We should have that data. It'll be on a different database, but I can get it. Might take a while though, and it might stretch to five hundred vehicles. That's peak time. Lots of flights getting in.'

She patted him on the shoulder.

Shreya assessed the numbers. Five hundred vehicles; five hundred registered owners. Most likely the vehicle they were looking for wouldn't even be registered in janitor guy's name. Nonetheless it was a thread that needed pulling.

'How long will it take?'

'An hour . . . maybe two?'

*Dead time.* Every minute that passed allowed this girl, this Aliyah Khan and her bearded friend, to further disappear under the skin of America and into its bloodstream.

'Do it,' she said. 'Do it fast.'

# CHAPTER 8

*Shreya*

'What the hell, Shreya? You think it's okay to just go over my head? What strings did you have to pull? Shit, I'm surprised you still got strings left to pull.'

She'd been dreading this moment, when her phone would buzz and the screen light up with Dan's name, but now that it was here, it was almost a relief. He'd already signed off on her exile to San Diego. What else could he do to her?

Still, it had made sense to leave the room and take the call in private. There was no benefit in having an argument with him within earshot of Special Agent Kramer or the tech guy.

'You gave me till Monday to get to San Diego. You didn't say anything about what to do before that. I thought I'd make myself useful.'

'Useful? I've had three missed calls from the Portland office asking what the hell is going on and why was I sending agents up there without informing them.'

'What'd you tell them?'

'I told them it was classified. Hell, I could hardly say I knew nothing about it, could I? I can't even order you back here without looking incompetent.'

She tried to utter something reassuring about his competence but he cut her short.

'I don't want to hear it, Shreya, but *you* better hear this. If you're not in San Diego by 9 a.m. on Monday morning, you're history. I'll see to it myself.'

She gave the phone a nod.

'Yes . . . boss.'

'And?'

The question threw her. Did he want an apology?

'Sorry?'

'Shreya, you conned your way up there. At least have the courtesy to tell me what you've found. Tell me about this other girl, Aliyah Khan.'

She breathed out, then kept it brief.

'We've been going through CCTV footage from PDX. She was on the same flight as Yasmin Malik. We identified her from the passenger manifest and her passport details. Both girls were met at arrivals by a man – we're now trying to identify him and the vehicle the three of them left in.'

Silence on the line.

'You talked to *CJIS*?'

His tone suggested the bawling-out was over, temporarily at least.

'They're on the case.'

'Keep me posted.'

'Yes, boss.'

'And, Shreya, one last thing. Why'd you go to Portland? The local team could have found all that out.'

She wondered what to tell him.

'Because the girls came to Portland. There must be a reason for it. You don't just fly into Oregon if you plan on attacking LA or anywhere else. There are easier, cheaper and quicker ways of getting into the US from Dubai. And what were they doing for the nine weeks before the attack? Where were they staying? Whatever's going on, this is where the trail starts. This is where we'll find the breadcrumbs.'

'You didn't think to tell me any of this before heading up there and stirring up a ton of shit?'

'You'd just taken me off the case and ordered me to San Diego, Dan.'

She heard a sigh.

'That wasn't my call.'

*Not his call? So who the hell's call was it?*

In truth, that sounded like BS; just Dan covering his backside, but there was no point in her saying so. It was better to just get on with things. Her dad, and her therapist, would be proud of her.

'I better get back to it,' she said. 'I'll call you as soon as we find something.'

She hung up and returned to the room where Zack, the tech guy, was still peering at a monitor. Kramer gave her a look she found hard to decipher.

'What is it?'

'CJIS has come back.'

Her stomach lurched.

'And?'

'It's not good news. Initial search has returned no potential matches with a confidence interval of over ninety per cent.'

No solid matches. A damp squib of a revelation.

'But there were some potential matches falling between seventy-five and ninety. They've sent through the mugshots.'

Seventy-five to ninety per cent. Statistically it sounded positive, but in reality it was shaky ground to build one's hopes on.

'How many matches?'

'Seven.'

'You got the images?'

Kramer gestured to her laptop. 'Right here.'

They went through the mugshots together: several non-starters - two with square heads, no hair and thick features, compared to janitor guy's longer face and angular nose and cheekbones; and a third too well built to be their man in the overalls. Another had a tattoo on his neck creeping out from under his collar. Their guy from the airport didn't seem to sport any ink.

The final three needed more careful examination. Shreya took her time over the details, the curve of the mouth, the creases around the eyes. She stared at one in particular – a man called Mohammed Elyounoussi – his stats suggesting the same height and build as the man at PDX, decent facial resemblance too; but Elyounoussi had been arrested two weeks earlier in his home state of Michigan for petty theft, the latest in a litany of minor offences according to his file, mostly in and around Dearborn, and while there was no shortage of religious terrorists who'd started out dealing drugs or committing robberies, once they'd found their cause, they tended not to continue with their old criminal endeavours. A jihadi might once have been a pimp or a pusher but, once a jihadi, they tended to leave the old sins behind. Would this guy Elyounoussi join an Islamic group, turn up in Portland, two thousand miles away from Dearborn, to meet Khan and Malik, then a few weeks later, head all the way back to Michigan to resume a life of petty crime? Shreya was a studier of patterns; this didn't fit.

She turned to Kramer.

'What do you think?'

The young woman looked eager.

'Pretty good resemblance. You grow out the hair and it could be our man. You want me to get on to Detroit? Ask them to follow up?'

*The exuberance of youth.*

Shreya stalled her with a hand.

'Look at his file though. It's all just petty theft and a couple of other misdemeanours. Nothing that points to any religious extremism.'

The agent's face fell.

'Still worth checking out though. It sure looks like him . . . and, well, it wouldn't be the first time a guy with no prior history suddenly discovered his strong religious convictions and decided to blow something up in the name of Allah.'

And it wasn't the first time Shreya'd heard that particular anecdote. Funny how no one ever seemed to make the same remark about white guys. No one ever saw a regular white guy and said, 'Yeah, that guy's got no priors, but let's check him out anyway because other white guys have bombed Black churches or gone on incel-inspired killing sprees.' It was the notion that being non-white somehow made you less worthy of the benefit of the doubt; somehow less American.

She remembered an English girl she'd been at school with back in Auburn. The girl's parents were British. The girl had been born and raised there till she was six and yet, to the kids and the teachers she was more American than Shreya who'd been born in a hospital five miles up the road.

'Agent Mistry?'

She snapped out of her thoughts.

'D'you want me to contact Detroit?'

She wondered if, had the suspect been white, Kramer would

have been quite so convinced that this was their guy when the CJIS assessment only put the likelihood of a match at between seventy-five and ninety.

She gave Kramer a nod.

'Do it.'

Another attack was imminent. There'd be time to hate herself later.

# CHAPTER 9

*Sajid*

'Where is she, Mr Khan?'

Sajid was bleeding, again. His world had contracted; morphed into unreality. The pain though, that was real enough. The pain and the fear and the stink of his own sweat.

He sniffed, wiping at the bruised, swollen flesh of his nose with one shoulder, even that innocuous movement sending a wave of pain through him. The men in black who had turned up at his place of work, who had wrestled him to the ground and beaten him and cuffed him and trussed him like meat before throwing him shoeless into the back of a van, they had all but wrenched his arm from its socket.

They had brought him here to this place, read him his rights, searched him again and then thrown him into a cell without a word of explanation. He had sat stunned on a cold, hard bench, until the shock had lifted and the fear descended.

What did they want with him?

He had heard the tales told by the angry young men outside the mosque, of the way the police treated Muslims, but he had not believed it – he had not *wanted* to believe it. And yet, here he was: abducted, beaten, brutalised. And for what?

He did not know how long he had been in the cell. They had taken his watch and there was no access to daylight. At some point they had hauled him out again, introduced him to a lawyer – *his* lawyer, so they said; an Asian man like himself, dressed in a blue suit and silk tie; his accent as polished as his shoes. On second thoughts, a man nothing like himself.

'Why am I here?' Sajid had asked.

The lawyer's expression had hardened.

'They think you're a –'

*'Where is she, Mr Khan? Where's your daughter?'*

He was in a room with no windows, just a steel table surrounded by four chairs – all occupied: the two facing him by a man and a woman, both in grey, whose names, though they had stated them for the record, he now struggled to recall. He was still shoeless. They could have given him footwear: plastic sandals or cardboard slippers, but they had not. It only added to his humiliation, his vulnerability.

He was here, the man told him, *to assist with inquiries.*

He had inquiries of his own. He asked why the men in black had beaten him.

'Because you resisted arrest,' the woman told him, which came as a shock as he could not recall being afforded the opportunity to resist anything.

And then she opened a manilla folder and showed him the photographs: the charred, disfigured bodies. The bloodied remains of adults and children. Shops in the background, their windows blown in.

He recoiled.

Why were they showing him these pictures? Did they expect to shock him? If so, they would be disappointed. He had seen worse. He had seen bloated, fly-infested corpses rotting in the heat of his homeland. And not in photos but first-hand, as close as these two officers were to him. He still lived with the horror: the stench, the fear, the shock and anger of seeing his brothers and his sister, lying lifeless.

They asked him what he knew of the bomb attack in LA and he told them.

'I don't know anything.'

But it did not seem like they believed him.

'Where is your daughter, Mr Khan?'

The same question, spat at him this time by the male detective. It confused him. He assumed they meant Mia. They knew where she was: the same place she'd been for almost three years now.

It was why he had not answered them at first. The anger had welled up within him as soon as he heard the question; trumping his fear and his confusion.

'Lying in a hospital bed,' he now told them. 'Where your colleagues put her.'

But they did not mean his elder daughter. They meant his younger one. They meant Aliyah.

'Tell us where she is, Mr Khan.'

He turned to the lawyer for guidance. The man told him to say nothing, but that was not possible. Exasperation had loosened his tongue; and saying nothing, absolutely nothing, would only make him seem guilty. And so he resolved to speak, though he had nothing to say.

'Where is Aliyah, Mr Khan?'

He shifted in his seat.

'She is . . . overseas.'

'Where, exactly?'

The question came from the woman.

'Japan. Tokyo. She is teaching English there.'

His interrogators exchanged a glance.

'And you're sure of that?'

Sajid felt the bile rise in his throat.

What sort of a father did not know where his own daughter was? But then, if he had known where his elder daughter had been, she would never have ended up –

'Mr Khan?'

'Yes.'

'How long has Aliyah been there?'

'Maybe two months now?'

'And she went there directly from the UK?'

He nodded. 'That is correct. From Heathrow.'

'When was the last time you spoke to Aliyah, Mr Khan?'

His head spun. Why did they care about Aliyah?

'Has something happened to her?'

'When was the last time, Mr Khan?'

He thought back, and for the first time a shred of doubt crept into his mind. Fear pricked at his temples.

'I don't know, six, maybe seven days ago? She sends WhatsApp messages. I would show you if I had my phone, but it was taken by the men who accosted me.'

'And when you spoke to her, she was definitely in Japan?'

Sajid nodded. Where else would she be?

'I bought the ticket myself.'

'You bought her ticket?'

'I paid for it. Emirates, via Dubai.'

The male detective wrote something on a sheet of paper and passed it to his partner. Sajid strained to read it.

'Was she travelling with anyone?'

He began to sweat.

'As far as I know, she travelled by herself.'

'You expect us to believe that?'

'It is the truth.'

A partial truth at least.

The detective looked at him as though he were worthless. Did he consider Sajid just another treacherous Muslim? *Guilty until proven innocent.* He wondered if the man had a family. Did he go home to a wife and children?

The woman spoke.

'What are you not telling us, Sajid?'

'I am telling you everything,' he implored her, his voice breaking, and immediately he felt disgusted at his own wretched state.

'You're sure?'

'Please, just tell me what this is about.'

'Aliyah didn't fly to Japan, Mr Khan.'

'What?'

His temples throbbed.

How could they say such nonsense? Why were they trying to confuse him with these lies?

'I took her to the airport myself. I watched her walk to departures. I have spoken to her half a dozen times since she left.' He leaned forward, closing the distance across the table and held out his hand. 'Give me my phone. I shall call her right now. You can speak to her yourself.'

He half expected an unseen hand to restrain him, to pull him back into his seat, but instead the male detective reached down to a briefcase at his feet and retrieved a clear plastic bag with Sajid's phone inside. He opened it, extracted the phone and passed it over.

'Please,' he said. 'Call her.'

It was the look on the man's face which perturbed Sajid, for while his tone suggested that this was a most sensible and reasonable course of action, his eyes spoke of someone who already knew the conclusion.

Sajid picked up the phone. It came as a shock to see his own hand shaking. He scrolled for Aliyah's number. In his head he requested Allah's divine and benevolent assistance and pressed call.

From the phone came the silence that preceded a possible connection. He felt his heart thump. One, two, three, and with every additional beat, his hopes faltered.

Too long. It was taking too long.

Aliyah might have been on the other side of the world but he had phoned her before. It should not take this long.

Then, suddenly, Aliyah's voice. His heart leapt, then fell just as rapidly.

'Hi, it's Aliyah. I can't take your call right now. Leave a message.'

He pressed cancel, then tried again.

'Hi, it's Aliyah. I –'

Sajid shook his head. There had to be an explanation for it.

He grasped at the first straw he could. 'She must be asleep. It is probably the middle of the night there.'

Like an automaton, he pressed call once more.

'She isn't going to answer,' said the woman, almost kindly. 'The phone has been switched off for over a week now.'

'Hi, it's Aliyah –'

'When it was last activated,' she continued, 'it was in the vicinity of Portland, a city in Oregon in the United States.'

Sajid dropped the phone, deaf to the clatter as it hit the table. He shook his head at them. This was insane.

'Why would Aliyah go to this place, this Portland? Where would she even get the money for such a journey? I had to buy her ticket to Tokyo. I watched her check in.'

'Aliyah did fly to Dubai, Mr Khan,' said the woman. 'But she didn't catch her connection to Tokyo. Instead she took a flight to Portland International. The Americans have her on CCTV arriving there. Her passport details are recorded at immigration. She arrived with another young woman, Yasmin Malik. Do you recognise that name?'

Of course he recognised the name. The whole world recognised the name.

The woman continued. 'She's the girl who carried out the suicide bombing of the mall in Los Angeles two days ago.'

The bottom fell out of Sajid's world.

# CHAPTER 10

*Greg*

The rain was coming down hard, roaring, battering the roof and pitting the yard and turning dirt into mud. The noise was good. It helped drown his thoughts. The barn felt like a cold store, his fingers frozen, numb and clumsy, hardly able to perform the delicate operations required to get the new devices ready.

He blew on them; rubbed them together like he was sparking a fire. There was work to do and time was short and so far he'd achieved next to nothing.

It wasn't just the cold. It was the turmoil, the confusion in his head.

He reached into his shirt pocket for the stub of a pencil. In itself it wasn't exactly incriminating – he could say he needed it for calculations – but he wasn't supposed to have it and he certainly hadn't declared it to Miriam. What he went for next, though, there was no doubt, if they found it, he'd be in trouble. He bent low under the workbench, pushed aside a few crates, dug deep into one at the back and pulled out a beat-up tin box, the metal smooth and cold under his fingers. He creaked it open and stared at the folded sheets of paper. It was stupid. He knew that.

*'Never put nothin in writing 'less you absolutely have to. You jus handin folks a loaded gun to point at you.'*

Just about the only advice his dad had ever offered him without the added emphasis of his fists. Maybe that's why he'd begun writing down his thoughts in the first place – a middle-fingered salute to his old man – but the truth was, writing helped him take the tangle of threads in his head and straighten them out into thoughts. Writing helped him make sense of his confusion.

It was all there, in that tin. His fears, his turmoil. His feelings for Aliyah. And everything he wanted to say to his mom in case he didn't make it out of this alive. He needed to write. Needed to get his thoughts about Yasmin down on the page.

The barn door creaked behind him. Instantly he shut the tin, threw it into the crate and pushed it back into the shadows, then straightened, snatching up a soldering iron and holding his breath.

'Greg?'

*Aliyah.*

His stomach leapt. A collision of emotions. The joy of seeing her; the thrill of a few clandestine moments, tempered this time by anguish, by guilt and a fear at what he might say.

He placed the soldering iron back on the bench and turned. Slowly he raised his eyes to her face. The sheer illicitness of it was intoxicating. Once more he was struck by its beauty; struck too by the amount of time it had taken him to perceive it. She, however, avoided his stare, just as Miriam had taught her. The eyes were power, the eyes were a window, and the eyes were treacherous. Eye contact was frowned upon, rationed, savoured.

'Anyone see you?' The question was superfluous – she knew better than to take risks.

For a second she hesitated.

'No. What is it with everyone this morning?'

'What d'you mean?'

'Miriam all but bit Rehana's head off at breakfast. All she did was ask about the bloody timetable.'

He held his tongue. He needed to tell her. But not now. Not yet. Not until he'd worked things out for himself.

She walked over to him and took his hand, peering at the device on the bench in front. She'd taken an interest in his work. Wanted to know how things functioned, how the components fitted together, and he'd explained things to her in rudimentary terms: the battery, the initiator, the explosives, and the switch – the cellphones that she and Yasmin and Rehana would, from a safe distance, use to set off the bombs.

*Except Yasmin was dead now.*

She squeezed his fingers and he felt his heart pound.

'How's it going?'

'Good.'

'How long before they're ready?'

The anticipation in her voice riled him. Why did she have to ask about the bombs? Didn't she care that once they were ready, their time together would be over? She would have her mission, handed down from on high by Miriam, sold to her as some noble crusade no doubt: striking a blow against fascists and racists and religious bigots or some such bullshit. It was all lies, of course, Miriam playing her games within games, but Aliyah would believe it, and she'd carry out her mission and that would be the end of it.

More than once, he'd tried to broach the subject, tried to tell her that Miriam wasn't all she seemed to be; that maybe she wasn't being entirely honest, but she'd shut him down. It was like a switch flipping. One minute she was warm and open; the next she was cold and shuttered. There was no point rehashing it.

'We're on schedule,' he said and she leaned into him, resting her head on his shoulder. He put his arm around her.

From outside came birdsong. He didn't know what type of bird it was, and he didn't care, but for an instant, that bird singing its heart out like it was midsummer seemed the most important thing in the world. It was life. There was always life.

He reached into his pocket and felt for the small metal pendant, running his fingers over its smooth surfaces and its hard edges as though he was rubbing a charm for luck.

'Aliyah?'

She turned toward him and lowered her gaze.

'How you feeling? . . . I mean, about all of this?' He searched for a gentle way of putting it. 'About leavin'?'

He felt her stiffen and instantly felt a pang of regret. If life was about soaring in those few, fleeting moments of happiness, he had in one sentence managed to bring them both back down to earth. Aliyah bit her bottom lip. Funny how so simple an act could be so completely disarming.

'What choice do we have?' she said. 'Like Miriam says, someone's got to *do* something. If not me, then who?'

His heart fell.

'It don't bother you that once you leave, we'll never see each other again?'

She flashed him a smile and this time she did look up at him.

'I told you already. Doesn't matter what Miriam says, we *will* see each other again. I'll make sure of it. It might take six months or a year, but I'll find you.'

It was true, she *had* told him already, and he'd allowed himself to believe it might be possible, that they might both somehow meet again, but that was before Yasmin and Jack and LA. Now he saw it for what it was, for what it had always been: naive fantasy.

*He needed to tell her.*

'We'll do what they do in the movies,' she said. 'Let's decide on a place to meet. One year from today.'

'What?'

'Choose a state capital. Topeka? Baton Rouge? Carson City?'

State capitals. She knew them all, revelling in the obscure ones. She liked capitals, claimed to have memorised those of all the countries in the world, and he for one hadn't been able to catch her out. It was one of her quirks, picked up from her sister, she said, like the stupid English phrases she was always teaching him. 'Or maybe somewhere further? Where have you always wanted to go?'

He couldn't tell if she was joking.

'There must be somewhere, Greg. Somewhere you've dreamt of going.'

'As far away from here as possible. Somewhere warm.'

She looked down at his damaged knee. A glance, nothing more, then raised a hand and caressed his cheek with soft fingers.

'An island somewhere? The Indian Ocean. How about Mauritius?'

He smiled and shook his head.

'It's settled then,' she said. 'Mauritius it is. A year from today.'

'What's the capital?' he asked.

'Port Louis,' she said without missing a beat. 'We'll meet and we'll find a place to live. A hut on the beach and we'll play chess.'

'I don't know how to play.'

She smiled.

'Well then, I'll teach you.'

'Mauritius then. And chess,' he said, knowing it would never happen. He should have told her. There and then. About Yasmin. But he didn't want to destroy the moment or the way he felt in it.

He reached into his pocket and pulled out the pendant. Encased in his fist, he held it out toward her.

'I made you something.'

She stared at his fingers: blue ink scarring white skin.

Slowly he released his grip, unfurling calloused fingers like crooked petals, revealing the tiny bird-shaped sliver of silver in his palm, a small loop of wire above its head. Looking at it now, it suddenly seemed so inconsequential, so amateurish, so ugly. She would hate it.

'It's beautiful.'

Blood pounded in his ears.

'I love it.'

'It's a dove, I guess,' he said, holding it up so it caught the light, and realising that it might have just as easily been pretty much any other bird. She took it from him, examining it, marvelling at it, before reaching for the thin chain around her neck. She unfastened it then gently threaded the pendant onto it. He watched as she slipped it back around her neck, the little bird glinting silver against her skin.

From the window, he caught sight of Yusuf, walking down the steps from the front porch. She must have seen him too, as she quickly unfastened the chain, removed the dove and squirrelled it away in the pocket of her jeans. She turned for the door.

He couldn't leave it like this; couldn't let her just walk out. He caught her by the hand. 'Aliyah,' he said. 'Why wait a year? What if we just left today? What if we just got in a car and drove? All the way to the other side of the country. We could disappear. We could catch a plane to Mauritius or wherever and start again. Let's go. Tonight. We can slip out after dark.'

She pulled free from his grasp. It felt like she was pushing him away. She shook her head.

'You know we can't.'

The words hit him squarely in the gut.

'I've got to go, Greg. If Yusuf finds me here, we'll both be in the shit.'

She was halfway out the rear door before he could recover. He watched her disappear, down the hill, out of sight of the house. He turned back to the bench; to his work; to the assembly of the constituent components of death. But his focus, his concentration had deserted him, fleeing with Aliyah out the door and down the hill.

He heard the telltale creak once more.

'Greg.'

He set his face to neutral and turned, focusing on the man's mouth and not his eyes. *Seeing but not seeing.* It was easy once you got the hang of it.

The Afghan stood at the threshold, fists clenched.

'Yusuf. What can I do for you?'

'Miss Miriam wants to know how long for you to finish.'

He sighed.

'This ain't like fixing a flat. It's fucking complex. You can tell Miss Miriam I'm going as fast as I can.'

The Afghan cracked his knuckles.

'How long?'

Iron in his voice this time.

Greg picked up a cloth and made a show of wiping his hands.

'Ten, fifteen hours. Maybe less if there were fewer distractions.'

The man stared at him and Greg made sure to look at the dirt. He turned back to the bench and reached for a screwdriver as behind him he heard the door close.

*Fuck you, Yusuf. Fuck you and Miriam and all the others.*

# CHAPTER 11

*Sajid*

The questions had lasted several hours: the same ones, again and again and again, checking his story, twisting his words, tripping him up. New ones, thrown at him, attempting to catch him unaware.

'Tell us about the mosque you attend ... Tell us about your imam ... Tell us about the men outside, with their leaflets. What's your relationship with them?'

And then back to Aliyah, and Oregon, and her flight there; back to Yasmin Malik whom he did not know.

He was like a boxer on the ropes defending himself out of sheer instinct and his belief that whatever else she might be, his daughter, Aliyah, was no terrorist. He held on, he told himself, to protect her.

And yet they knew he was holding something back. Once or twice he had come close to telling them his secret but he hadn't. It was a trivial thing, he was sure of that. Indeed, its triviality is what made it worth holding on to. If it was truly important, he might have told them, but it felt as though they were trying to humiliate him. As long as he held that one piece of information back, they would not have broken him.

In the end, they had let him go; given him a pair of plastic shoes without laces and sent him packing.

Out of the front door.

Out into the rain.

To contemplate his fears.

*Aliyah.*

Had she lied to him? Was she really involved with ... with all this ... it was too painful to even utter the words. It was a lie. It had to be. The police were lying. Just as they had in her sister's case. They had beaten Mia, put her in a coma and then claimed they hadn't. How could you trust anything they said? And yet ... Mia had not told him where she was going that day. She had disobeyed her mother's instructions and Rumina had blamed him. Of course she had. He had nurtured the girl's political spirit. He had wanted to help open her eyes; to help her see the world.

And Aliyah? Something had changed in her too that day, her childhood terminating prematurely upon the cliff-edge of her sister's injuries. But this? This was inconceivable. He felt as though he was falling, spiralling uncontrollably. His daughter was no Islamist. It was hard enough persuading the girl to fast during Ramzan, and now the police wanted him to believe that she would die for her religion? It was madness. And yet. Where was she?

He could not bear to lose another child.

Shoulders hunched and head bowed, he walked in a daze toward the Tube station.

He had not expected the cameras, nor the scrum of reporters with their flashbulbs and their flood of questions. They stood under an acreage of umbrellas, each emblazoned with the logo of their particular news outlet. They reminded him of strutting peacocks.

'Mr Khan. What did the police ask you?'

'What do you know about the attack in Los Angeles, Mr Khan?'

'Mr Khan. Did you help the suspects leave the UK?'

'Mr Khan –'

'Mr Khan! –'

His name, hurled at him from all directions. Who had told them? It must have been the police. How else would these jackals know to turn up here and lie in wait for him? But he would not answer their accusations. What was it the angry young men that stood outside the mosque said? 'They always twist the words of a Muslim. To them we are all guilty.'

Well, the bastards could go to hell. He was not going to give them the satisfaction of a cheap headline or a celluloid sound bite they could play on a loop. He would keep his head down and his mouth shut, and when they saw he would not answer, hopefully they would give up.

But it was too much. His mind closed down. He walked, like the bombed-out, shell-shocked refugee he had once been, no longer hearing the questions or sensing the flashes.

He was almost there. He could see the red halo of the Tube sign, could almost feel the sanctuary of the station, when it happened.

'Where's your daughter, Mr Khan? Where's Aliyah?'

He did not see who had launched it, but the question found its mark, striking him squarely in the heart.

He felt his blood rising. 'Let the devil take you,' he thought. 'Let the devil take all of you vultures.'

'Is your daughter responsible for the LA bombing, Mr Khan?'

Something inside him splintered.

Sajid stopped and turned. His accuser was a slim, blonde woman, sheltering under an umbrella while Sajid stood head-bare to the rain.

She could not be much older than Aliyah.

'Was your daughter behind the LA attack?'

Sajid felt his fists clench. Every fibre in him wanted to shout 'You do not know a thing about my daughter!'

But then, it seemed, neither did he.

He shook his head. 'Aliyah is not mixed up in this. She is not the girl in the TV footage. I do not know who that is or what she has to do with my daughter. Aliyah was supposed to be in Japan, but the police say she is in Oregon. Aliyah knows no one in Oregon. This is all a mistake.'

And even as he said the words, in his heart, he knew he was wrong.

# CHAPTER 12

*Shreya*

She'd wanted to keep going, but fatigue and Kramer's counsel convinced her it was time to stop. Zack, the tech guy, had left ninety minutes earlier, citing childcare needs for kids he looked too young to have.

Kramer had driven her to a grey box of a hotel somewhere in the suburbs south of the city, a neon sign on its roof radiating cobalt blue against the night. Her phone buzzed: the Bureau's Detroit office; the search for Mohammed Elyounoussi, the guy whose photo-fit bore a resemblance to their man at the airport, was *ongoing*. Her stomach twisted. It meant they were having trouble finding him. It meant she might be wrong and that he might be here, in Portland. Then again he might also be in one of a thousand other places.

The room was on the third floor, the last door at the end of a hallway of soft uplights and thick carpet. She touched the plastic card to the lock, waited for the click and then entered a room that felt like a refrigerator. She punched buttons, switching lights on and air con off, then reached for the TV remote and searched till she found CNN and Wolf Blitzer opining on the latest polls that put Costa closing the gap to three points.

Too close. How he was even in with a chance? What the hell was wrong with this country? How was it that a guy who was quite possibly deranged, whom you wouldn't trust to look after your pets, whom half the populace saw as an egotistical nut-job who'd run over his own mother to get into the White House, could yet be so revered by the other half, who'd no doubt view that matricide as an act of selfless patriotism. And it cut both ways, of course. If you believed the press, a good forty per cent of Costa's supporters believed Greenwood was a Communist, which was still better than the sixty per cent who thought she was covering up for an international paedophile ring.

How did it get to this? How did the country get to a position where the dictator in the Kremlin was seen by half the country as less of a threat to America than a woman advocating for a return to Roe v Wade?

She ordered pasta on room service, opened her laptop and began going through her emails. Her phone vibrated, dancing on the desk beside her. A number with no name.

'A-Agent Mistry? It's Zack here. I hope you don't mind me calling, but I thought you'd want to know. The ... ah ... the list of licence plates you asked for? The vehicles leaving the parking garage in the hour to 7.15 p.m. It's come through.'

*Impressive*, she thought. The guy was working overtime. An example to those kids of his.

'I-I'm sending it now.'

Moments later the mail pinged into her inbox: the briefest of intros and an Excel file which she clicked on. A list of over 450 plates. A lot of cars, and yet the sight of it was encouraging. Somewhere on that list was a plate that belonged to a vehicle driven by a bearded guy and which contained Yasmin and Aliyah.

She unlocked her phone and dialled the office. Chances were, the guy she wanted would still be at his desk.

'Mike Raven's line, please.'

Raven was a surly old bastard with a penchant for electronic systems and punk bands and little time for the social niceties that led to career advancement or indeed much of a social life. And yet, along the way, he'd managed to find a beautiful wife, a patient one. How he'd done it was one of the universe's great mysteries.

'Yeah?'

She breathed a sigh of relief.

'Mike. It's Shreya.'

'Shreya. I heard they're sending your ass back to San Diego.'

'Don't believe everything you hear down the dog track.'

A snort of derision came down the line.

'You saying it's not true?'

'I'm saying I need a favour, Mike. I'm sending you a file: a list of licence plates. I need you to run them through the databases: ownership details, stolen vehicles, wanted persons, revenues and fines, even the sex offender li—'

'Don't tell me how to do my fuckin' job.'

'Please. I need it as soon as possible.'

'You know how busy we all are? Dan's got the whole office working double shifts till further notice. Which reminds me: where the fuck are you?'

'Portland. Working an angle. One that might pay off a bit quicker than whatever Dan has you working on.'

'How many licence plates?'

'About four hundred and fifty.'

There was a pause on the line.

'It's late, Shreya, and that's gonna be a lot of data.'

'Well, you'll have my respect and gratitude, Mike.'

'Yeah, no offence but I'm gonna need something more.'

'Shit, Mike. I'll get you tickets to Nerd-con or a Black Death concert or whatever you're into. You name the gig. Will that do?'

'Yeah . . . and your chair.'

'What?'

'Your chair in the office. Mine's busted and HR won't sign off on a new one; and seein' as how you're out the door anyway . . .'

'Fine.' She sighed. 'Take it. Just run those plates.'

'Deal. But it'll take a while.'

'Okay, just prioritise, then. Get the list of registered owners first: names and addresses. Send it to me, then check if any belong to vehicles registered as stolen. Flag up any registered to known felons.'

'What you looking for exactly?'

She hesitated. Hell, there was no harm in telling him. It might even spur him on if he knew what was at stake.

'The girl, Yasmin Malik. She and another girl were met by a guy at PDX. I think the vehicle they left in is one of those on the list.'

Raven called back within the hour.

'List of registered owners is on its way to you and I've started the checks. None listed as stolen or registered to wanted persons.'

*So much for the low-hanging fruit.*

'Can you start on the other databases?'

'Doing it now.'

Shreya checked her mail.

'Got the list. Thanks, Mike. I'll put in a good word with Dan for you.'

'Wow, a commendation from you. Be still my beating heart.'

'When will you have the rest of the information?'

'I got a wife to get home to, you know,' he said.

'Relax, Mike,' she told him. 'She'll probably appreciate the break.'

She hung up and clicked on the file he'd sent. Four hundred and fifty-three vehicles and their registered owners. She scanned the list, resisting the temptation to focus on the *unusual* names. Yet she couldn't deny that something inside her, the darker part of her nature perhaps, reacted with a jolt the few times she found a Muslim-sounding one. In the end she decided she had no choice. Time was slipping away. Another attack might be imminent. She would investigate the Muslim names first.

The voice of her younger self rang out in her head.

*'Racial profiling? What happened to you?'*

She swallowed down her shame and scanned the names, one after the other till she had a list of six: five male, one female. She discounted the woman. It was possible she might have been the partner of the guy on the CCTV footage, but that felt like a step too far – a pyrrhic victory for her conscience.

She called Mike again. Told him she was emailing him five names. Told him to run them through the DMV database and to send her their driver's licence photos. He'd notice what she'd done, of course.

Once more she told herself she was just doing her job. And in a sense, she was doing those folks a favour by eliminating them quickly. Not a lie, she told herself, a mental contortion.

The response came through in only fifteen minutes, its arrival heralded by a ping that set her heart thumping. She opened the first attachment. A driver's licence filled the screen. An Arab face. Nothing like the one in the footage from PDX. She moved on to the next one, clicked it open and waited for the licence to appear, then almost breathed a sigh of relief.

*Another one down.*

She cleared the screen, then clicked on the third. It took a moment to open. Shreya took a sip of cold coffee then almost dropped her cup. She sat up straight, peered closer. There he was, her man from the airport, staring up from a California driver's licence.

*Shit.*

She read the name, then grabbed a pen and wrote it down on a pad in large capital letters.

## YUSUF GHANI

A wave of exhilaration washed over her. The ends, it seemed, justified the means.

She studied the picture. Yusuf Ghani: dark hair, dark beard, skin pitted by the after-effects of acne or some pox. There was a weariness to the eyes, or maybe a wariness. The tired, lined face of a man just looking to get through the day. The soul of a terrorist hiding behind the face of a janitor.

# CHAPTER 13

*Greg*

Greg lay on the bunk and stared, not quite seeing the outline of the ceiling. Two in the morning. Pitch-black and bitter cold. Cold that toyed with his joints till the torment made it impossible to sleep. Words and images from his phone played on a loop. The flames, the gutted wreck of the building, the corpses.

Because of him.

All day he had battled to keep them out of his head; tried writing down his thoughts on those pages in his tin box, but the words had been difficult, coming slow like molasses. The work had helped: the concentration on the complex, on the mechanical, yet it was a losing fight. He might concentrate for as long as ten minutes at a time, but then the images would rise up once again. The urge to find out more, to check the internet or find a TV screen, was overpowering, but there was no signal down here at the White House. It was probably one of the reasons Miriam had chosen it as a base of operations. More than once during the day he'd considered concocting some excuse to take the truck and drive into town, just so he could check the news. Too risky. The last thing he needed was for Miriam to suspect he was having second thoughts.

Miriam; that soldier masquerading as messiah, with her clothes from another time; Amish with a hint of assault rifle. The white hair. The barely perceptible scar down the side of her face. The commandments forbidding technology, pride, pleasure, dishonesty and of course eye contact. How much of it was theatricality and how much of it about control? And yet there were times when even he couldn't help believe it was real. That she had the answers. That she was divinely ordained. She was Deborah, from the Book of Judges, empowered by the Almighty to redeem them all. She was the sun at the centre of their system, offering light and life to all and exerting a pull from which it was impossible to break free. She was their alpha and omega, giving each of them what they needed, what they craved, whether it was the love of a mother she offered Yasmin, the strength of purpose she gave Rehana, or even the chance at redemption he'd believed she'd offered him.

That, he realised, was her gift. The ability to get into your head and your heart. To understand where your hurt lay and tell you what you needed to make the pain go away. And all she asked for in return was trust. And absolute obedience.

It was a seductive bargain. Better to believe her words than be cast out. Better to do her bidding than lose what she gave. Lying in the dark, Greg smiled bitterly to think of how most folks wouldn't understand. It only worked if you were busted and with nothing left to lose. Her greatest trick wasn't how she controlled them; it was how she chose those ready to be controlled, ready to believe. And desperate enough to act.

All of them were caught, even Jack and Yusuf, and he

understood their reasons. The only enigma was Aliyah. What did Miriam offer her? What did *she* need? If he had to guess, he'd say it was something intellectual. Miriam made a point of singling Aliyah out, praising her insight, her understanding of the currents and the subtexts of what went on in the world, and she, like a prize pupil, basked in her mistress's praise. But surely there had to be more to it? Something in Aliyah's soul that cried out for the salve that Miriam offered. He wished he knew what it was. Only then, only when he understood Miriam's hold on her could he begin to counter it. And now, with Yasmin dead and Jack missing, how much time did he even have left?

*Jack.*

'No one's going to die,' Jack had told him. A lie told by a man who might be dead himself.

His thoughts returned to Aliyah. He should have left her well alone. He should have focused on the job he was being paid to do. And yet he hadn't. And now it was too late.

Where his feelings for her had come from, God only knew. Maybe it was as simple as the fact that she listened to him without judgement or pity. Whether he told her of Florida or Kandahar, she listened to him and it felt like she understood. Maybe it was because she'd suffered too. Her sister in hospital. As good as dead. Or maybe it was her contradictions: that hard-as-nails exterior hiding a fragility within. He thought of her wish to teach him chess; her fascination for maps and flags and capital cities that she'd coyly admitted to and that even now he found dumb, but oddly endearing. This was the girl who wanted to plant bombs?

Minutes or maybe hours later, from outside, came the low growl of an engine.

He rose from his bed and hobbled to the window and shifted the curtain a crack – enough to catch a sliver of the world outside.

A car door creaked open and there he was: Jack, his face illuminated in the low-watt glow of the car's interior light, duffel bag slung over his shoulder, sneaking home like the prodigal son.

Greg breathed a sigh.

Jack was alive. That was something at least. The car was different. Not the one he and Yasmin had left in. He wondered where Jack had gotten it. Didn't matter.

The car door closed and once more the darkness took Jack. Greg shut his eyes and concentrated. Footsteps on gravel, the creak of the porch stairs. The click of the front door. He opened his eyes again as jaundiced yellow bled into the crack between the curtains. *Too fast.* The door had opened before Jack had reached it. Miriam must have been expecting him.

Greg turned for the door, his footsteps as light as he could make them, wincing once or twice as pressure went through his bad knee. The landing was still. Empty. Blue-black. He listened for voices but heard nothing. Not at first. Not from the hallway. He inched forward then, conscious that the siren song of a single floorboard would be enough to give him away.

A glance at the corridor that led to the girls' room. Aliyah and Yasmin and Rehana's. Just Aliyah and Rehana's now; the hallway cavernous black. From below, finally the sound of voices, no words audible from where he stood, just vibrations that spoke of a conversation behind a closed door.

He took the stairs silently, in his usual fashion: sideways; left foot first with right leg trailing after.

Miriam's study. That's where they were – a sliver of light creeping from under its door. He inched forward, eyes trained straight ahead. The voices grew distinct. Jack's baritone and Miriam's contralto, jumping in, breaking up Jack's monologue, peppering it, he assumed, with questions.

He moved closer, concentrating on the voices.

Jack was talking again.

'. . . what was I supposed to do, tie her to the spot?'

Miriam cut him off; her words fainter, harder to decipher.

'. . . at least a week before they identified her . . .'

And then came another voice, one he didn't recognise, uttering a statement rather than a question.

'It'll be taken care of. Get the others ready.'

Greg sensed something. Not a noise, more like the exhalation of a breath; a change in the air that set the hairs on his neck on end. He swivelled on a dime, wincing as his left knee screamed in protest. All he saw was a glint of something coming down at his head. Instinctively he raised his hands, but it was too late. The blow struck cold and hard. His head exploded in a thousand sparks. His legs buckled. The door to Miriam's study opened as he hit the floor. His vision blurred. Jack was at the threshold with Miriam's white hair further back, and behind her a third figure. Face hidden from view.

Yasmin?

But that was ridiculous. Yasmin was dead. He tried to rise, tried to get a better look, levering himself off the floor with his arms, but another blow came down upon him and the world went black.

*

His head was somewhere else: back in the past, three months previous, a different lifetime; back on that feverish afternoon in the Hog's Back Bar outside of Long View where Miriam had found him keeping his own beer-soaked company. The door had opened and in she'd walked, encroaching on his misery like the ghost at the feast; at first no more than a silhouette, a haloed outline in a doorway. But then she'd crossed the room and he'd seen her face; *that face*, with its hard, blue, diamond-drilled eyes; the iron-white hair, old before its time and worn long over the left side of her face, hiding the thin white line of a scar, faint like a crack on a vase.

She'd walked up and sat down opposite, Jack behind her, hovering in the background, making sure no one paid them too much attention. She'd known his name, and his service record, and the time he'd served in prison shortly thereafter. It hadn't surprised him. She looked ex-military in her own weird way. He guessed she was still connected.

'Greg?'

'Greg?'

He opened his eyes to yellow light and a pounding in his temples. He was lying on the sofa in Miriam's study. Hushed voices came from somewhere beyond his field of vision. He raised a hand to his head and recoiled as a crack of pain shot through him. The voices stopped. Footsteps on the wooden floorboards and then Miriam was standing over him, her expression almost beatific.

'Greg?'

He tried to sit up, fighting back a wave of nausea. She reached out to steady him.

'Please tell me you're okay.'

He looked up, even though he knew he shouldn't. The look in her eyes, the concern in her voice like he was the only person in the world who mattered to her. Just like that day in the Hog's Back Bar.

He took in the depths of the room: Jack at Miriam's shoulder; Yusuf by the door. No sign of anyone else now.

She took his hand in hers, her touch colder than he'd expected.

'What were you doing outside the door? Yusuf thought you were an intruder.'

He shot a glance at the Afghan who stared back without a flicker, then at Miriam who still looked at him as though she were Mother Teresa. Part of him wanted to just tell her the truth: that he'd seen the footage of LA; that he knew of the victims and of Yasmin. Part of him just wanted answers. To be told there was some other explanation. But would those answers be worth dying for?

'Heard the car. I thought maybe Jack was back. I wanted to come ask him how the explosives performed.'

'In the middle of the night?'

He gave the smallest of shrugs.

'I didn't want to wait.'

He turned to Jack, focusing on his mouth. Seeing but not seeing.

'How'd they do?'

The grin said it all. There had been no mistake. Greg fought for equanimity.

'And the girl?'

Miriam remained inscrutable.

'You don't need to worry about Yasmin.'

'I'm not.' The words slipped from his mouth rather too rapidly.

'Look at me, Greg.'

He did so, into those blue eyes both piercing and seductive; at once burrowing into his soul and persuading him to trust her.

'You're not having second thoughts, are you?'

'No, ma'am.'

'Remember the point of what we're doing here.'

He nodded and yes, he even understood. Games within games. Enough to change the course of history.

'Okay,' she said. 'How're you coming along with the new devices?'

'I'm . . . I'm getting there. Another day and they'll be ready.'

# DAY 4

## *THURSDAY*

## CHAPTER 14

*Sajid*

He awoke the next morning to the sound of rain. The curtains were drawn but Sajid could still hear it, lashing against the window like the wrath of God. He should probably get up, but what was there to get up for?

He lay prone on his half of the bed with the duvet pulled up almost to his ears against the chill. Rumina lay with her back to him, separated by a gap of inches and a chasm of miles. He thought of the nights he had listened to her breathing as she slept. He listened now for her breath but heard nothing, which suggested that she too was awake, lying sullenly in the darkness.

The journey home the previous evening had been a descent into hell – territory he had traversed before, the night Mia had failed to come home from her protest march. He'd recognised the landmarks: the panic of not knowing; the sickening, paralysing abyss of fear of what might have befallen her. Now he had both Aliyah and Mia to fret over, and it was only as he'd reached the small courtyard in front of the block of flats that the realisation of having to break the news to his wife had hit him like a punch to the stomach.

He had sat Rumina down, held her hand, told her what had happened, what the police had said. She had balled her fists and flung them at his chest. She had screamed he was wrong, and through her tears asked why he would say such things. He'd tried to hold her, to comfort her, but she had pushed him away and accused him through reddened eyes.

'It is *your* fault! *You* let her go, overseas, by herself. I told you it was a mistake!'

And it was true. All of it. He *had* let Aliyah go, over Rumina's express objections.

'*She's only eighteen. Travelling alone to the other side of the world . . . What will people say?*'

It was that last barb which had made him take his daughter's side. His wife had lived her whole life as hostage to other people's opinions and he would be damned if he let his children grow up the same way. He'd had his doubts – what father wouldn't? – especially after what had happened to Mia, but should Aliyah have to suffer for that? He had let her go because she needed to discover the world beyond east London, beyond the confines of the small, suffocating, claustrophobic Bangladeshi community with horizons limited to the mosques of Whitechapel and mores of 1970s Sylhet. She deserved the opportunities which her mother had never had, the chance to live a life without restrictions, without the worry of who would think this or who would say that.

He had paid for her ticket, and now she was gone. Not to Japan but, if the police were to be believed, to America, with a girl who had blown up a shopping mall.

Rumina blamed him because she needed to blame someone simply to make sense of it all. *But who did he have to blame? How*

96

*was he supposed to make sense of it?* Rumina's anger would subside in time, but the hurt? The torment would leave her broken.

He got up, stumbled to the window and moved the curtain a fraction. In the street, the pack of reporters had disappeared.

*Finally. Washed into the sewers by the deluge, hopefully.*

He looked up to the heavens and uttered an Alhamdulillah, *thanks be to Allah*, though more out of habit than conviction.

Slipping on his cardigan, he ventured into the hallway and made sure the door was closed before checking his phone's screen. A dozen missed calls and God knows how many messages. His instinct was to delete them all, but as long as there was the remotest chance that one might be from Aliyah, he knew he couldn't. Instead he steeled himself and listened to them all, each one a knife to his heart, deleting them as quickly as possible to cauterise the pain.

He shuffled his way through to the kitchen, hardly registering the sting of ice-cold tiles on his bare soles, and filled the kettle. The morning's first cup of tea was a ritual. He used to enjoy making it. Rumina might brew every other cup during the day, but that first one he always made himself. And on days when he wasn't working the early shift, he made two cups: one for her as well.

This morning too, he brewed two cups, taking one through to the bedroom and leaving it on the table on her side of the bed as a first small gesture of reconciliation. In twenty years of marriage, he had lost count of the times that the offering of a cup of tea by one to the other had signalled a willingness to draw a line under their squabbles. But this time felt different – he corrected himself – *was* different. As he placed her cup, Rumina had stirred only to turn her back to him. There was no point in trying to speak to her about it, and anyway, what was he to say? Instead he wandered back to the kitchen and his own rapidly cooling cup.

He took a sip and reached once more for his phone, pressing call and listening, but now without much hope that Aliyah would answer. The call failed. Automatically he tried again. It was easier to go through the motions of trying to call her than to think about her out there somewhere.

In less than a day, the remaining pillars of his life had cracked and crumbled. His daughter was a stranger, his wife had retreated behind a wall of accusation, and his boss Mrs Braithwaite had left a message informing him his employment was suspended.

His thoughts kept returning to the police and his interrogation. *'What are you not telling us, Sajid?'*

Why had he not told them of Najmah? The girl who should have been on that flight with Aliyah; the one whom Aliyah had set up the Zoom call with, to put his mind at ease, to reassure him that she would not be travelling to Japan alone. The one who, in the end, did not go with her.

He had to find her. He had to know what she knew, but how?

Finally the turmoil drove him from his home, out the back and through the estate so as to avoid any still lurking reporters, and onto cold, hard streets. He did not consider himself religious, certainly not by the standards of his community, where ostentatious piety was worshipped almost as much as ostentatious wealth, but if there was solace to be found, it would be at the mosque, at the feet of an imam.

He considered making for the one at Whitechapel. It was large and anonymous and offered less likelihood of a chance encounter with anyone he knew, but in the end, settled for his usual mosque. He regarded the imam as a friend and, just as importantly, it was closer.

The walk was tinged with fear. His skin itched. Every car windscreen, every curtained window, seemed to have a figure behind it, watching. The world knew of him now; it knew of his shame.

The imam received him into his office and plied him with tea and sympathy and the word of God. Sajid nodded along in time, though any advice washed over him, his mind straying to Aliyah and Oregon and what he might have done differently.

Part of him had switched off. Unreachable. It was as if he were an observer, looking down with a curious detachment upon his own life.

*Why had he come?*

Clearly the answers he sought were not to be found here.

He got up, thanked the imam and made for the door, conscious that the man too seemed relieved at his departure. As he left the office, others came up to him – faces that he recognised but whose names he could not recall – offering condolences laced with questions, the answers to which, he was sure, would be whispered gleefully to others over the coming days.

Finally, and in a bitter irony, even the angry young men outside the mosque looked at him differently, ceasing their chorus of vitriol as he exited. One even had the gall to pat him on the back.

Sajid wanted to shout: '*I am not one of you! I am the same man I was last week.*'

But what would be the point? It would only be one more thing for people to gossip about.

It was raining once more. He hurried home by the shortest route, taking roads best avoided.

*A mistake.*

A gaggle of white youths were huddled under an awning outside a pub, the King's Arms he believed it was called, lunch-time pints held casually while cigarettes burned between knuckles. Big men, in thick boots and olive-green bomber jackets with a sheen of satin to them. He knew the type. Tattoos and close-cropped hair and hard laughter. When he had first arrived in this country, similar youths, maybe even the fathers of these boys, would throw taunts and slurs at him, and sometimes, if the drink had flowed and their blood was up, they would graduate to fists and boots.

There was less naked aggression these days – maybe attitudes had changed; or maybe they just preferred younger prey – yet he could never quite shake the feeling that these men would, if given an excuse, gladly beat him to a pulp; and what better pretext than his face on the news, pilloried as the father of a terrorist?

One of them spotted him and suddenly, wordlessly, like wolves picking up a scent, their behaviour changed: conversation stilling; laughter dying.

They watched him now, sizing him up, and he watched them back, from the corner of his eye, sensing their thoughts. Any moment now, they would recognise him.

And there it was: that flash of realisation on the face of one of them; a turn toward the others for corroboration; the whispered discussion. He felt the heat rising within him; felt their eyes upon him. The weight of their stares. A determining of their course of action.

His feet faltered under him. What had he been thinking? He should never have ventured out of the flat. He should turn back and take his usual route home, or at least cross to the other side of the street. He made to step out onto the road and then stopped.

*No.*

He would stay on this pavement. He would walk past these men, and if they attacked him, so be it. He lowered his gaze and continued walking, every step bringing him closer to the men till he could smell cigarette smoke and taste the tang of warm beer.

He was abreast of them now, trying not to let his fear show. He held his breath and focused on his movements – forward – one step at a time – a few more and he would be past them. He did not see the arm reach out, but he felt it, the electric shock of the shove at his shoulder sending him slipping on slick kerb stones, over the edge and onto the road.

He fought for balance, heard the blare of a car horn, the screech of tyres. He saw the shock on the face behind the windscreen. It happened too fast. Not enough time even to close his eyes. The car swerved, missing him by inches.

The driver didn't stop.

His heart thumping, Sajid looked over. The boy on the kerb could not be more than twenty. His pale skin flecked shaving-rash pink at the neck. He seemed as shocked as Sajid. A moment more and his mates had surrounded him, shielding him from view. They sneered at Sajid.

What was he supposed to do? Challenge them? Report them to police who didn't care? The same dilemma he and those who looked like him faced every day. He felt the anger swell within him, more at his own impotence than at them. There was nothing to do except turn, swallow another humiliation and head home.

He walked off to the sound of their jeers.

'Yeah, go on! Fuck off, you Paki.'

# CHAPTER 15

*Sajid*

He had not been home thirty minutes when the buzzer sounded.

*Bloody reporters.* Could they not give him some respite?

He ignored it, the ringing continued. Rumina surfaced from the bedroom. Her face was censure enough.

'Are you going to let them wake Tariq?'

Sajid made for the small hallway and opened the front door.

'This is bloody harassm—'

The words died in his mouth.

The woman did not look like a journalist. With her jeans and jumper soaked through, and lank blonde hair dripping on his door-mat, she looked more like a drowned rat.

'Please,' he said. 'We are not answering any questions. Now please leave my family alone.'

He went to shut the door but she stuck a hand in the gap between it and the jamb. Sajid stopped millimetres from her fingers.

'Please, Mr Khan,' she said. 'I need to talk to you.'

She sounded foreign. American, he thought.

'I told you, we are not speaking to reporters. Now please leave.'

He inched the door forward, hoping she would remove her hand, but she didn't. He felt the door make contact with her fingers and froze.

'I'm not a reporter. My name's Carrie Flynn. I saw you on the news. I think your daughter is out there somewhere with my son.'

*

'*Ké?*'

Sajid ignored Rumina's question and the stare which accompanied it and headed for the box room. The question only followed him, this time with greater force and the formality of English.

'Who *is* she, Sajid?'

He turned abruptly so that Rumina almost ran into him.

'*Darao.* Let me find out.' And then a whisper: 'She says her son is with Aliyah.'

Rumina raised a hand to her mouth.

'With Aliyah?'

He found himself oddly satisfied at her reaction.

'So she says.'

'*Kothai?*'

'*Arré* – let me speak to her.'

From the cupboard, he grabbed a towel, returning to the sitting room past his bewildered wife teetering on the cusp of the kitchen doorway. The woman, Carrie, sat dripping on the sofa, hands knotting and unknotting together in her lap like a scolded child.

She looked up as he entered.

He passed her the towel.

'Please. Take. It might help a little.'

104

*What sort of a person travelled halfway round the world without a coat?*

And then he remembered his own arrival in this country, shivering in only a shirt.

The woman towelled rainwater from her hair. Nervous, energetic movements. 'Look, I know it seems crazy coming here, but I had to. I think, I think your daughter and my son, they might be mixed up in the same thing.'

Sajid pulled a chair from the dining table and sat down facing her. 'What do you mean?'

Having finished with the towel, she seemed unsure what to do with the it. He took it from her and she thanked him with a weak smile, then reached down for the rucksack at her feet. Unzipping it, she rummaged before pulling out an envelope. She opened it and extracted the letter within.

'This came the day of the explosion in the mall in LA. It's . . . it's from my son, Greg.'

She thrust the pages at him.

'Please, read it. It'll explain some things.'

He took it from her hesitantly. Correspondence between a parent and child was close to sacred. It felt wrong to share it, and yet, here was this woman offering it freely to him, a stranger. He scanned it, the roughly formed letters of an unsure hand, then read it quickly: the talk of a job; of a fresh start; *and* something else, something he could not, or would not, discuss.

'. . . *they got me making stuff. Doing things I thought I'd left behind in Afghanistan, but the boss – I can't tell you her name – says it's for the good of the country . . .*'

And then, at the top of the second page, he saw his daughter's name.

'. . . *I've met a girl. Her name's Aliyah. You'd like her. She's from England. She's interesting. Different from the others here. Different from pretty much anyone I ever met. I think she might like me. I can't tell you what she's doing here any more than I can tell you what my job . . .'*

Opposite him, Carrie seemed to fidget. He looked up and she was staring at him expectantly, as though he was judge and jury of her sanity; as though everything depended upon his assessment of this letter that had impelled her to travel so far.

*'. . . I have my doubts though. I think they might be setting her up. I'm not sure I could live with another victim on my conscience . . .'*

He turned to her and pointed out the lines.

'What does he mean by this?'

She looked at him guardedly.

'I-I don't know.'

He'd seen the expression before, most recently on the faces of his interrogators in that police station. There was something she wasn't telling him.

'Do you know where it was posted?'

The woman shook her head. 'The postmark just says Southeast Portland. But from the letter you'll see that they're not in the city. He talks about some house out in the wilderness.'

He read on, searching for anything that might point to where Aliyah might be, or what she might be doing there, but there was nothing. Just a request for the forgiveness of his sins.

*What sins?* he wondered, but despite the circumstances he could not bring himself to ask such things.

'Have you shown this to the police?'

The woman knotted her fingers together once more.

'No.'

'Why not?'

'Greg's had problems with the police before. You saw the explosion in LA. The police think they're Muslim terrorists. Whatever they're involved with, the police ain't gonna give them the benefit of the doubt. Hell, telling the police would be as good as giving both our kids a death sentence.'

Sajid closed his eyes. The image of Mia came unbidden to his mind, lying in that bed at the Royal London, sustained by drips and kept alive by ventilator. And all for committing the cardinal sin of attending a protest. *Head injuries – exact cause unclear – that is what they had said – caught in the stampede; a victim of the general lawlessness.* But people who had been there had said it was the police – a baton to her head, sending her crashing down, to be crushed by the panicked crowd.

He understood this woman's reluctance to contact the police. Indeed, a part of him felt grateful she hadn't.

He looked at her.

'So what, then? Why did you come here?'

She raised her hands and he saw a parent at the end of her rope, recognised it.

'I think we should go to Portland, get to them before the police and the Feds. Together, maybe we can convince them to give up on whatever they're planning.'

His stomach lurched. Had he misheard? Was she really asking for his help? Did she honestly think he might know anything that might help her to find Aliyah and her son? Who was this woman anyway, this American, brazenly turning up at his door with tales of her son and a letter that might have been written by anyone? Maybe she *was* crazy. Maybe she had written the letter herself.

But what if she was not mad? What if she was telling the truth? Could he afford not to listen?

She seemed to sense his turmoil.

'If we can't find them, who knows what'll happen?' *He could answer that.*

He would lose another daughter, and with it, any chance there was of once again making his fractured family some semblance of whole.

He turned to Rumina and spoke softly.

'*Oh-goh, ektu cha boshao.*'

He turned back to Carrie.

'Will you have some tea?'

\*

A thousand questions shouted in his head; a thousand questions he was not yet ready to ask. He mumbled an apology.

'I should help Rumina in the kitchen.'

It was an excuse to leave the room, to find quiet sanctuary and gather his thoughts. He headed for the bedroom but stopped instead at the door to Tariq's room. He turned the handle and pushed softly, hoping that the hinges might not creak. The little boy lay asleep in the cot which took up almost half of the small room; the same cot in which Aliyah had once slept, and Mia before her. There was such a strong resemblance between all three. Indeed, at a glance, he could almost fool himself into thinking it was not Tariq lying there, but one of his sisters.

He thought now of the woman sitting in his living room. His doubts surfaced once again. Who was she? Had she honestly come all this way because she thought that he might be able to help her find their children? And the letter she claimed was from her son? It was ridiculous. Maybe she was just another reporter trying to trick him.

In his cot, Tariq coughed. Weak and wet and fragile. It set Sajid's heart on edge. The boy stirred before stilling once more. Sajid pulled the thin blanket to cover his narrow shoulders.

He returned to the hall, closing the door softly behind him. The room opposite he did not venture into. It was silent now, empty of the two souls who should occupy it. Their laughter, their squabbles, their vibrancy leached away. It was still partitioned; Mia's half all but untouched since that day. The bed made and remade but never again slept in.

It was Aliyah's half that had changed; altered beyond recognition, scrubbed clean of all colour and life, as though in permanent mourning. More than once he had offered to paint the room, to redecorate it, but she had declined. Even her chess set – her pride and joy – now sat untouched. She had excelled at the game (she insisted it was a sport) long ago, learning to beat him and almost anyone who cared to play; always two, three, four moves ahead. It was Mia who had taught her, and since the accident, she had not played a game. Now the pieces stood forlorn, stuck in their rows, never to advance again.

*Aliyah*. She pulled at his heart just as strongly as Tariq; she commanded his care in just the same way. He could not pull a blanket over her shoulders but he could help the woman in his sitting room. As a father, what other choice was there? He would answer her questions, provide what assistance he could, and then she would leave.

In the living room, it was warmer now thanks to the glowing coils of the electric fire. Rumina brought tea: mugs, milk, sugar, biscuits, all balanced on the time-worn plastic tray bought a decade before on a day trip to Brighton. She placed it upon the low coffee table. He noticed that she gave Carrie a half-hearted smile and then took a seat on the sofa beside her. Close but not too close.

He took a sip of tea: warm, sweet, comforting; prepared the Bengali way. Fragrant, loose-leaf Darjeeling tips, brewed till almost stewed. Amid all of the upheavals and sacrifices of his life, tea had remained constant and uncompromised.

'Did your daughter know the girl who set off the bomb?'

The woman, Carrie, was staring intently at him. Sajid coughed. He looked to Rumina.

His wife's answer was forthright.

'She never mentioned her to us.'

The woman waited, hoping Rumina might follow up with something. *Well, she would be waiting a long time*, Sajid thought. *Izzat* – family honour – was too important to Rumina. She would not volunteer anything that even tangentially might taint her daughter with the tag of terrorism.

He filled the silence. 'What about your son? Did you know he was in Oregon?'

'Not till that letter landed in the mailbox. Haven't seen him in over six months, not since he got out of prison.'

She looked at him, searching his face he thought, assessing his reaction. But he had seen enough of life to know not to rush to judgement. Rumina, though. She would have no such qualms. He turned to his wife, half expecting to see the curdling of her expression, the censure in her eyes, but her face was a mask.

'Look,' she said. 'The only lead I got was your daughter's name. I wouldn't have flown all the way here if I had any other option. Now is there anything you know which might help? Anything Aliyah might have said before she left? Something she might have mentioned about where she was going?'

He glanced at his wife. She would not approve of what he was about to say, but they were past the point of Rumina's approval.

'Aliyah never mentioned anything about Portland. She said she was going to Japan. Naturally we were reticent, but Aliyah introduced us to an older girl, a girl called Najmah, whom she said was also going. Aliyah organised a call so that Rumina and I might speak to her, to reassure ourselves that all was as Aliyah had told us.'

He avoided his wife's glare. Carrie's eyes, however, seemed to flicker.

'And where's she now, this Najmah? Did she get on the plane with Aliyah? Do the police know about her?'

Sajid shook his head. 'The morning of the flight, Aliyah told us Najmah had caught Covid. She was isolating and would catch a flight in a few days. I decided against mentioning any of this to the police.'

'So Najmah might have never gone? Where is she?'

He shrugged. 'I've asked the imam at the mosque, but he professes not to know, and the police have taken Aliyah's computer.'

Across from him, Rumina reached out a hand.

'If she's still in London, I think I might know where to find her.'

# CHAPTER 16

*Greg*

*Infatuation.*

He hated the word, but how else was he to describe the urge to see her, to be with her, the hollowness in his gut, the constant gnawing within when she wasn't there? It was dangerous, and pointless. And yet, he couldn't stop, even when his brain told him he had to. Even Jack had noticed it at one point. Caught him staring at Aliyah. Fortunately, he'd jumped to the wrong conclusion. Assumed all Greg wanted to do was fuck her.

*'Not worth the risk, man. If Miriam finds out, she'd put a bullet in your head. No fuck is worth dying for. Certainly not with some moslem chick.'*

Good old Jack. Always thinking with his dick.

But he had a point. Aliyah wasn't his type; she should mean nothing to him. And yet all of that paled into insignificance in the face of one salient, undeniable fact.

She got him.

After so long being alone, to be able to speak with someone about what he'd seen – *what he'd done* – it was like being able to breathe again. She got his pain – he didn't know why – but she understood.

*Really, Greg?*

His feelings were based on what, exactly? The fact that she'd displayed human kindness? That she'd listened to him spout off about his life? It meant nothing. And yet she *had* listened, and asked questions, and *empathised*.

Truth was he'd no idea how she felt about him. He was too scared to ask, but she'd taken risks to spend time with him: a stolen half-hour; a whispered conversation. The looks, the hints of smiles, the *glances*. Things that, if spotted by Miriam or Jack or Yusuf, would have been dangerous.

*Surely that all meant something?*

At times he was sure that she felt something for him; at others he was just as convinced that it all meant nothing. At times he fantasised a shared future for them: a house and kids or just a car and the two of them simply driving, free of all this.

It was ridiculous. It was pathetic. He'd assumed he'd never see her again, not after she'd carried out whatever mission Miriam had in store for her. Of course he'd wondered what that was, but Aliyah never spoke about it, and he hadn't pressed her. There hadn't been any point till now. He guessed she'd carry out her mission and disappear. She'd be given a new identity, but that hadn't stopped him dreaming.

And then his bomb had gone off, killing innocent people – killing Yasmin – and the scales had fallen from his eyes. There would be no future. For either of them.

The ringing of the alarm clock shut out his thoughts, the thing hammering out its tinny monotone until the clockwork wound down and the noise slowly died.

Six a.m. Fatigue weighing on him like a slab, compounding, magnifying the pain in his skull.

He fought through it and followed his thought on Yasmin to its conclusion. Whatever had happened at the mall in LA had been no accident. The grin on Jack's face last night had been enough to confirm it. And that meant the other deaths too had been part of the plan. *All of them.*

And if Yasmin had been marked to die, then why not Rehana? Why not Aliyah? It stood to reason. The girls were pawns, he'd known that from the start; sold a dream by Miriam: of being loved and understood and accepted and told that they were going to change the world. And they *would* change it – just not in the way they expected. Once they'd set off their bombs, Miriam would have no further use for them. Shit, after that they were just potential problems; kids who knew too much. Logic dictated they be silenced. Miriam's genius, he realised, was in figuring out a method of execution which only added to the impression of terror she wanted to create.

But if Miriam was willing to kill the girls, to murder civilians, then what about him? Instead of cash, would his reward be a bullet in the back of the head, or a knife in the ribs?

Across the room, Jack grunted and turned over.

'*The less you know, the safer it is for everyone.*' Jack's words, before he'd left four days earlier; before he'd headed off with Yasmin.

Greg sat up. Slowly he went through the usual rituals, massaging his left leg, starting with the thigh, up near the groin, and working his way down, assisting the circulation till he reached the dead area around the knee, where they'd cut him open and only half fixed him, damaging the nerves so that when he touched it or even stabbed it, he felt nothing. He kept going, working his way further south: the diminished calf, the tight skin around the Achilles, and finally the heel and the arch of the foot.

Gradually the warmth entered his leg and the pain ebbed. Like thawing a hunk of meat, that's what it felt like sometimes, especially on the black days; not something that was part of him but dead weight he'd be forced to carry for the rest of his life. Well, at least he still *had* his leg. He knew enough guys . . .

He repeated the process with the right leg; not because he needed to, but because there was a certain satisfaction to the symmetry, like an athlete's cool-down routines after training.

Finally he stood, stretched his upper torso and shivered. The room was an icebox, the thin curtain frosted to the windowpane. With effort, he made his way to the door and out of the room, the smell of coffee carrying him forward, down the stairs, one leg at a time, and to the mess hall.

Aliyah and Rehana were already there, huddled and half asleep on one of the benches of their usual table. Aliyah looked over as he entered and his stomach flipped as he caught her glance.

*He had to tell her about Yasmin.*

He gave her the merest of nods – enough for her to register; fleeting enough so that no one else noticed – then lowered his eyes and headed for the empty table in the corner.

Yusuf brought him breakfast: a plate of eggs and hash browns rather than the usual thin porridge. Miriam must've given the order. The Afghan's face was set, a mask of indifference betraying no sign of what had transpired between them during the night. The plate though, he let fall some inches above the table, landing in front of Greg with a clatter.

He still didn't understand why Miriam kept Yusuf around – something to do with her time in Afghanistan, according to Jack – but surely there were others who could do what he did? Others who weren't Muslim. Or was he just another pawn? A convenience to be disposed of when the time came.

Mumbled conversation drifted over. Rehana and Aliyah.

*Did they know Jack was back?*

He wondered what Miriam would tell them. Whatever it was, the girls would swallow it – he'd no doubts about that. She'd given them every single reason to trust her.

He didn't understand it, and yet he did. Deep down, it was as though Miriam understood everything. She'd already asked every question you'd thought of and had worked out the truth. And when she explained something, it was as if she was putting into words something you knew in your gut to be right, but which you'd never been able to formulate.

Hadn't he too been enraptured by her when she'd first found him? Hadn't he been seduced by her words, displaying the same passion – the same conviction – the same pure certainty that what she was saying was good and true and right and that, through her, he could attain both a purpose and redemption?

Only the message she'd preached to him was different. The problems were still the same: the country going to hell; the world burning. Only the causes and the solutions that she proffered with such conviction were disparate. *'We need to take back what's ours, Greg. It's our birth right.'*

The door opened and Miriam walked in looking like a force of nature made flesh, snow-white hair falling like a curtain over the left side of her face. He hadn't seen her in here before. She normally took her meals in her study. Then he noticed the battered steel coffee pot in her hand. At this hour it normally sat on the sideboard. The conversation between Rehana and Aliyah seemed to die in their throats.

'Eat up,' Miriam told the girls. 'You deserve it. The work you've put in over the last couple of months, all you've learned, you're going to put into practice. You're going to do to wonderful things and I'm proud of you.'

She walked over to them and dispensed hot coffee and quiet words of encouragement, and for Aliyah a supplementary hand on her shoulder.

Greg felt a twinge of something. A memory long-forgotten. A Sunday-school sermon, Jesus or a saint, maybe, washing the feet of his disciples. He looked at Aliyah, but her attention was consumed by Miriam. In that moment, he knew what she was feeling. The power of Miriam's presence. That feeling that when she was near, all your doubts just faded away.

It dawned on him then: the better food, the breakfast pep talk; it was part of a plan. As if on cue, the hallway door opened once more and in stepped Jack. He felt the electric charge pass through the room: Rehana staring; Aliyah on her feet, peering round into the space behind Jack.

Greg watched her as the seconds passed and the realisation dawned that Yasmin wasn't following Jack in. He watched the hope in her eyes succumb to confusion. He watched as she turned to Miriam in search of reassurance and received in return a smile of measured determination.

'Our first mission was a success.'

'And Yasmin?'

Miriam's lips thinned.

'Yasmin . . . is safe. She's in good hands, already halfway across the country. In another day she'll have a new life and a new identity.

'Now the authorities, as they always do, will try to con the people. They'll put out fake stories; they'll claim terrible things – about casualties and suicide bombers. They'll stop the media from publicising our statements taking responsibility; they'll try to drown out our message by blaming foreign terrorists and Muslims; they'll try and whip up the right wing. But they will fail, girls, because none of it is true. And they will fail because when we launch our next attack, the media will have to report the truth.'

*Except he knew it was lies.*

It was impressive how well she played it. Looking at her face, or at least the half that was visible, it would be impossible to detect anything but righteous anger and complete sincerity. Looking over, it was clear that Rehana had bought it. Every single word. And Aliyah, she'd accepted it too, not as zealously, but quietly, tacitly. And why not? Even now, part of him *wanted* to believe it – he might have discounted the pictures of the dead, believed her story of government lies – if he hadn't overheard what was whispered in the study last night, or if he hadn't seen the look on Jack's face when he'd asked about Yasmin.

Miriam walked over and he felt his stomach drop. She stared at him for uncomfortable seconds, then poured coffee into his empty cup.

'How're you feeling, Greg?'

He gave her a nod and mumbled something.

She placed a hand on his arm and this time he felt her warmth permeate his shirt.

'After you're done here, I want you to come to me in the study.'

He gave another nod but she was already turning and heading for the door, and in her stead, Jack was pulling out the chair across the table from him. His mind buzzed. Trip wires setting off alarm bells in his head.

'You look like shit, man.'

He grunted and blamed his leg and all the while his brain raced to work out why Miriam might want to see him.

'Not hungry?'

Jack was gesturing at his plate with his fork and Greg realised he'd hardly eaten a thing.

'Ah, no appetite.'

Yusuf brought over Jack's plate and handed it to him. Jack ignored him.

He pointed to the hash browns.

'You mind if I . . . ?'

He left Jack to it. To the greasy eggs and hash browns and wondered how he had the stomach for any of it.

The door to Miriam's study was open. Still, he knocked gently and waited for her to grant him permission.

She turned from the window as he entered, the woods in the distance just a shadow through the rain.

'Greg.' She greeted him with the sort of smile she generally reserved for her girls – full and wholesome and reassuring – which immediately put him on his guard. She directed him to the sofa on which he'd found himself the night before and then sat next to him, hands clasped in her lap like some fourth-grade schoolteacher.

For the longest of moments she said nothing, merely looked at him, staring at him in that way she did and that made you feel like she was reaching inside your head and grasping into every corner. He fought back the urge to open his mouth, to speak first just to fill the silence.

'I'm concerned, Greg.'

He felt fear spike in his chest.

'If it's about the bombs, they'll be ready.'

'It's not about the bombs, it's about you, Greg. That business last night. I need to know I can rely on you. There's something more I need you to do.'

The fear swelled. His lungs seemed to constrict.

He should lie. He should make some protestation of fealty to the cause. But she was too smart, too perceptive, to be taken in by something like that. If anything, it would only heighten her suspicions.

*A half-truth, then. A half-truth was more credible than a lie.*

'Yasmin's dead, right?'

For a moment she was silent, her face impassive, her eyes locked on him. He concentrated on her mouth. *Seeing and not seeing.* He saw the flicker, the inhalation of breath.

'She is. It was an accident. Jack did what he could to avoid it.'

But Jack's face last night had told him otherwise.

*A half-truth then. To match his own.*

'I know about your time in Kandahar, Greg. You were 18C in an SFOD-A. Not many guys can say that.'

And not many folks even knew what that meant. Engineer sergeants from Special Forces Operational Detachments didn't exactly grow on trees. But then Miriam obviously had connections; he had been the right guy for the job she needed done.

'I need you, Greg. I know what you went through in Afghanistan and I'm promising you, you'll get the help you need just as soon as this is over, but right now I'm counting on you. You know what's at stake. The country can't take another four years of this shit.'

He knew it all. He believed it too: the American dream was over for someone like him. And really, what choice did people like him have but to turn to a man like Chuck Costa? He might be a son of a bitch, but at least he understood the anger. At least he listened.

And he would win. If the bombs went off and the Muslims were blamed, the gap in the polls would close and then reverse, he was sure about that.

'Yasmin's death,' she continued. 'Is that a problem for you?'

'You told me no one would get hurt.'

He felt her stiffen.

'It's one life, Greg, set against millions of others. American lives, people like you and me and Jack; our families, who've sacrificed, who've bled for this country. People like your mother, good, honest, hard-working folks. They've been sold out, Greg. We all have.'

He nodded in time to her words while the voice in his head screamed. *His mother.* Why would she mention his mom? He'd never spoken of her to Miriam, or to Jack or anyone else out here except Aliyah, and yet Miriam spoke like she knew the woman. He tried to change the subject.

'You said there was something else you wanted me to do?'

'Look at me, Greg.'

He did as she commanded, raising his gaze to meet hers and instantly feeling the power of her eyes boring into him, searching his face, his head, his heart. Dissecting him. Laying him bare.

He blinked.

Miriam gave an almost imperceptible shake of the head. 'We'll discuss it later.'

# CHAPTER 17

*Sajid*

It was an unforgivable error. He should have remembered, as Rumina had done, that Aliyah had introduced the older girl, Najmah, as a teaching assistant at her school. He should have remembered, and he should have already tried to find her. Now he sought redemption in haste. With the briefest of words to Rumina, he ushered Carrie out of the door and down the street, rushing for the bus stop, turning the corner onto the main road just as the scarlet outline of a double-decker came into view.

'Come,' he said. 'Quickly.' The bus slowed, rumbling to a stop a dozen yards ahead. He waited for her to board, then climbed on, nodding thanks to the driver.

Carrie sat down and gestured to the seat beside her, something which made him feel faintly uneasy. It was ridiculous of course. Had he not sat beside countless women on countless buses before? In this city it was impossible not to. But other than Rumina, those women had been strangers, anonymous to him, and this one, while he hardly knew her, he already felt a responsibility to. She was here *with* him; *because of* him.

He cast aside his reservations and sat.

Outside the East End flowed, raw and shabby and vibrant. Victorian brick and council concrete; shopfronts and curtained windows; the Bow Road and the Mile End Road and signs in both English and Bangla. And everywhere the mass of humanity, white, black, brown. The city in all its variegation. Countless lives continuing. Oblivious to his pain.

Thoughts of Aliyah tormented him, consuming his focus until, with a start, he realised where they were.

'This one,' he said, rising and making for the exit. Carrie was only a step behind.

They alighted onto damp pavement.

At least the rain had stopped. He and his shoes – returned to him in a plastic parcel by Mrs Braithwaite – were grateful for that. He watched the road, divining a break in the traffic that slashed westwards, toward that other London, the one of banks and business and skyscrapers of glass and steel, a mere mile away, yet utterly foreign to the likes of him.

He spied a gap.

'Now,' he said.

A break in the traffic and they weaved between vehicles, then slipped down a side street of rusted railings, cracked pavements and dilapidated concrete flats, their balconies festooned with laundry.

The school was up ahead, a squat, grey, sixties edifice; walls adorned with technicolour murals as though overcompensating for the brutal nature of the building, its thin-paned windows patched up as best as a council budget would allow. How old had Aliyah been when he had last come here? Fourteen? Fifteen? The building was unchanged.

He stopped beside the intercom and peered through the gates.

'This the place?' Carrie asked him.

He nodded. 'Aliyah studied here until last summer. There is a chance Najmah may still be working here.'

He sensed her impatience, her desire to push forward. It was admirable. She had come five thousand miles on a hope. Wasn't that what a parent did for their child?

He took a breath, pressed the discoloured button on the intercom and spoke into the static.

\*

'I'm looking for Najmah Hussein.'

The woman seated behind the glass window of the reception desk looked up. She gave him what felt like a genuine smile. You could tell a lot about people from their smiles.

'She'll be in class right now, my dear. Is it urgent?'

'A family matter,' he said. A half-truth.

The woman checked the clock on the wall.

'There's a break in a few minutes. Sign the book and I'll put out a message for her.'

Register and plastic pen were pushed through a gap beneath the plexiglas. Sajid scribbled an illegible signature into the book as the speaker reverberated to the sound of the woman's voice.

'Najmah Hussein, please come to the reception desk. Najmah Hussein, to reception please.'

She directed them to a row of plastic chairs across the corridor and told them to wait.

The seconds ticked by to the buzz of the overhead strip light and the tang of industrial disinfectant. While he sat, Carrie preferred to pace the floor, wearing out, he thought, both carpet tile and shoe leather. Finally he felt the soft quake of a thousand chairs shifting. Voices rising. Sajid looked to the receptionist. She volunteered another smile.

Swing doors burst open under the pressure of a wave of trainer-clad students. Bright faces. Carefree faces. The way Aliyah's had been not so long ago.

*Where was she now?*

He prayed that she was safe.

The rush of bodies subsided until only the occasional straggler troubled the doors. No sign of Najmah. Maybe she wasn't even in the building? Maybe she had seen them from a window, had recognised him and was even now fleeing from an alternative exit.

But then the doors opened once more and she appeared: the girl from the Zoom call that Aliyah had arranged; tall, thin, her hair covered by a pink hijab and a folder clasped tightly to her chest.

Instantly he was on his feet, moving to intercept her.

'Najmah.'

The girl turned toward him. She stopped dead, the folder falling from her arms, spilling to the floor. She turned and bolted for the exit.

'Wait!'

He called after her, but the girl was already through the doors.

Carrie set off in pursuit. He followed but not before offering the receptionist an apologetic smile.

He pushed through the doors. Najmah was at the gate, pulling frantically at the bars before remembering the release button on the wall, diving desperately for it, smashing it with her palm.

*Too late.*

Carrie grabbed her wrist, pulling her back from the gate.

'Not so fast, missy.'

He caught up with them.

'Najmah,' he said between breaths. 'Please. We need to speak to you about Aliyah.'

She tried to push past, but Carrie held firm, twisting the girl's arm behind her till she cried out.

Sajid winced at the sudden violence.

'Please. Don't hurt her.'

Carrie loosened her grip a little and brought her face close to the girl's ear.

'Why you running, Najmah? We just want to ask you a few questions.'

'I don't know anything!'

He tried to calm her; placed a hand upon her shoulder, but only felt her stiffen.

'A few minutes of your time. That's all we're asking.'

'Leave me the fuck alone!'

Once more she tried to shake herself loose. Once more Carrie tightened her grasp.

'Maybe you'd prefer we told the police about you? Do they know you were meant to be on that plane with Aliyah? They might even think you set her up. Is that how it was? You some sort of jihadi recruitment pimp? Did you persuade her to go?'

The girl's expression changed, the shift from anger to fear as sudden as the arrival of a monsoon shower.

'It wasn't like that!'

'So tell us what did happen.' Sajid's voice as soothing as he could make it between his ragged breaths. 'Aliyah called you her friend.'

The girl looked around.

'I can't' Sajid begged.

'Please, Najmah. Our family is broken. I can't survive the loss of another daughter.'

The girl looked at him. What was that in her eyes? Disbelief? Doubt? Pity?

'Okay,' she said. 'But not here.'

*

She led them to a cafe somewhere up a side street, a board outside touting lunchtime specials for £4.99. Inside, a single customer, a hijab-sporting young mother hidden in a corner, sipping from a mug and rocking a buggy. Carrie made for a table beside a window streaked with long fingers of condensation. While she and Najmah sat, Sajid approached the waitress behind the counter.

'Tea is coming,' he said as he returned, then consciously placed his chair between Najmah and the door. Carrie nodded and turned to the girl.

'What do you have to tell us?'

Najmah looked at her.

'You still haven't told me who the fuck you are.'

The question met with a non-committal smile.

'I'm a friend of Aliyah's parents.'

The girl snorted.

'Really? You live round here?'

'No.'

'Well then. What has any of this got to do with you?'

Sajid answered for her.

'Her name is Carrie and, as she says, she is a friend to my family. *As are you . . .*'

The girl shifted in her seat, her knuckles white against its edges.

'Look, I don't know where Aliyah is. She never contacted me after she left.'

'But you *know* where she went,' Carrie said. 'You *knew* she was going to America.'

The girl gave her silence in reply.

Sajid tried again.

'Was there ever any teaching job in Japan?'

She bit her lip. 'It was just a story she told you so you'd let her go.'

'Why would she do this?'

'It's not that easy to expl—'

She stopped as the waitress walked over, a black tray balanced on one hand with three white mugs sitting atop it like tombstones.

'Maybe you should start from the beginning,' Sajid said, after the waitress had left. 'Do you know the people who . . .'

The sentence died in his mouth. *The people who . . . what exactly? Recruited her to go to the United States with a girl who blew up a shopping mall?* It still made no sense to him.

'. . .the people who Aliyah became involved with?'

The girl picked up the mug in front of her and took a sip. Sajid picked up his own cup. The tea was pale. Almost anaemic.

'Well?' Carrie asked.

The girl took a breath.

'It's not what you think. All that crap on TV, the shit about her being some jihadi fundo. It's all bullshit.'

Najmah leaned back in her chair. Crossed her arms tight. 'Aliyah was never into any of that. Whatever this is, it ain't about Aliyah suddenly finding Allah.'

Sajid felt his stomach turn over. Myriad emotions in milliseconds. *He knew it.* His girl was no fundamentalist. The police, the press, and their gullible white readers and viewers, might think so, but he knew his daughter. And yet that soaring relief, that vindication, that feeling that maybe all was not lost, was pitifully brief and tempered by fear and confusion and the dawning realisation that nothing had changed.

*Aliyah was still out there; still a fugitive.*

He exhaled. He had not even realised he had been holding his breath.

Carrie leaned forward impatiently, hands on table, ignoring her tea.

'So what *is* this about?'

The girl turned to her.

'It wasn't supposed to be like this.'

'Like what?'

'She never said anything about any violence.'

'What *did* she tell you?'

Carrie leaned closer still, closing the space between them. The girl instinctively shying away, pushing back in her chair.

'Please, *ma*,' Sajid said softly. '*Ma*', the Bangla word for mother, also used as a term of endearment toward a daughter. He hoped it might signify a bond of sorts. 'Just tell us what you know.'

The girl hesitated.

'Aliyah was into politics. You knew that, right?'

He knew that. He knew because he had been the one who had instigated the politicisation of his daughters, who had started the whole damn process, pushing first one, then the other, to take an interest in such things, wanting his daughters *to think*, to be empowered, to take an interest in the world.

Najmah's voice wavered. 'I . . . I was helping her with university applications.'

He knew that too. Another family battle: Aliyah wishing to study away from home and Rumina reacting the way she always did, with quasi-apocalyptic complaints of '*what is the world coming to?*' and '*our girls don't leave home to study*' and of course the ultimate and arbitrary '*what will people say?*'

Aliyah had appealed to him against her mother's verdict. He was head of the household after all. But after Mia's *accident*, his willingness to engage Rumina on such matters had evaporated. There was no further debate. College would be in London. A taste of the wider world but home by seven.

'Anyway,' she continued, 'Aliyah wanted advice researching a paper she was writing for social studies. Something about pressure groups and online radicalisation. I agreed to help. Some of it was just contacting environmentalists like Extinction Rebellion.' She gave a snort. 'You know the sort: middle-class white folk who think supergluing themselves to railway tracks or going without avocados is going to save the planet. But she wanted to contact other groups too.' He watched as she gripped the handle of her mug tightly. 'Religious ones; political ones. Caliphate wannabes and ISIS sympathisers. Antifa radicals too, and Alt-right crazies.'

'Alt-right? In America?'

The blood seemed to drain from Carrie's face.

'Yeah, all sorts. She got talking to this guy online, part of some group based in the States. Said his name was Jack. She didn't mention his politics but *Jack* don't really sound Islamic, does it? He told her he'd lost a sister. I guess it must have hit a chord with her, on account of –'

Najmah stopped, choking back the sentence. It didn't matter. He had already made the connection.

'Please,' he said. 'Go on.'

The girl lifted her mug, her wrists so slender that he could see the hard nub of bone and a discoloured outline, the birth of a bruise where Carrie had gripped her. She took the briefest of sips before returning it shakily to the table.

'She started spending more time online, speaking to this guy, and then he put her in touch with a woman. Some kind of guru. That's when Aliyah seemed to change. She said the woman had answers, whatever that meant, and that she insisted Aliyah come to America. Course she knew you wouldn't let her go if she told you the truth, so she lied. She made up that story of teaching English in Japan.'

Sajid's head spun. Agreeing to the Japan trip had been his sop to her. A small taste of the world, he'd hoped; the sugar that sweetened the pill of college from home.

'She said you'd be more likely to say yes if I said I was going too. Course, I told her I didn't want to get involved but she said I wouldn't need to do anything. On the day of the flight, she'd say I'd caught covid and that would be the end of it.'

He sat there, trying to comprehend; the revelation turning him inside out. He struggled to control his voice.

'Why would you do such a thing?'

Najmah looked at the table. 'I ... I thought I was helping her. She told me it was only for a month or two. She wanted first-hand insight into these people. I never thought –'

Carrie's voice cut through the confusion.

'Where? Where did she go?'

Her voice seemed to crack with emotion and for a moment he worried that she might scare the girl back into silence. Yet Najmah took a breath and continued.

'Portland, via Dubai, with that other girl, Yasmin Malik.'

'Was she a friend of Aliyah's?'

The girl shrugged. 'Not really. I think they met online.'

'And then? Where would they go from there?'

The girl shook her head. 'I . . . I don't know.'

Sajid reached out a hand and placed it on her arm.

'Is there something you are not telling us?'

'No.'

Her hands gripped the mug on the table, her knuckles white.

'I think you are not telling me something,' he told her. 'Just as I did not tell the police about you.'

He locked eyes with her, precious seconds passing. He wondered if she would call his bluff. He hoped not. Aliyah's fate hung on what this girl knew; he was sure of it. He needed to know what she knew. *Everything* she knew. And he needed to know it now. Carrie looked as though she was about to speak, but he silenced her with a glance.

Finally she spoke, stammering, slowly summoning the words.

'Aliyah . . . she mentioned a place . . . the place the woman wanted her to go . . . out in the forests somewhere . . .'

Anticipation rose in his breast.

'Where? Where was it?' Carrie said.

'I . . . I can't remember for sure . . . Something to do with a river.'

'Please try. You might save Aliyah's life.'

He watched as the girl screwed her eyes tight.

'I think . . . it was . . .'

She opened them again, and the confusion was gone.

'It was called Ripplebrook.'

# CHAPTER 18

*Sajid*

The screen glistened: a fractured, pixelated haze crystallising into a landscape of velvet green, and at its centre, a cluster of geometric shapes: the slate greys and blacks of a few dozen roofs of a settlement. *Ripplebrook*. Najmah's gift to them. Hardly a place at all. After that, she had upped and left and he did not feel he had the will nor the right to stop her.

Sajid's phone was perched on the table between them. He zoomed out in search of landmarks – towns, rivers – anything from which he could take his bearings, but at this magnification there was nothing. Ripplebrook was an island in a sea of trees. He zoomed out further still, and more isolated hamlets came into focus: Dodge, Elwood, the merest of places connected to the outside world by the umbilical of a few twisting, filigree roads.

A pinch of the screen and the camera panned out once again, its locus now encompassing larger towns: Molalla, Estacada, names he didn't recognise; and then one that he did.

*Portland.*

They were south of Portland, just as the postmark on the letter from Carrie's son had intimated. It was corroboration; proof if he still needed it, that both Najmah and Carrie were telling the truth.

Carrie had seen it too. She slammed a hand on the table.

'That's it! That's where they are!'

Sajid struggled to maintain his composure. Not every glimmer of light meant the sun was rising. Najmah's information was at least two months old. Even if Aliyah and Greg had been in this Ripplebrook, by now they might be anywhere. Yet he could not wholly maintain his equanimity. Ripplebrook was a light in the darkness, a lodestar pointing the way to their children. Ripplebrook was hope.

The image on his phone darkened and died.

'So, what now? Do we tell the police?' The words falling tentatively from his mouth; wary, he realised, of whatever answer Carrie might give.

'Not unless you want to sign our kids' death warrants.'

'So what then?'

She stared at him as though he were an imbecile.

'We have to go there, Sajid. We need to find them.'

'We?'

'Yes, *we*, before the police do, or before they do something stupid.'

He spat out a laugh. The woman was mad. Did she even know what she was asking? He was a Muslim whose daughter was on the run. He had as much chance of getting into America as she did of walking on the moon.

'You don't understand. You think I can just waltz into your country? *You* can go to Portland, but I can't.'

He watched the emotions play out on her face. Americans, he thought, so different from the buttoned-down, stiff-lipped

British. In her eyes he saw the change. Exasperation yielding to determination.

'No. That's not good enough. There has to be a way. A fake passport?'

'I'm not James Bond.'

'We can change yours.'

He shook his head.

'Steal one.'

'From where?'

'Don't you work in an airport? There must be plenty of people just leaving their documents lying around.'

'So you want me to steal a passport, fake an identity, and enter your country illegally? I am not sure that would be such a good idea.'

Carrie's face reddened.

'So you're just gonna give up on them? Give up on your own daughter? Doesn't she matter to you?'

He flinched. Of all the things that had been thrown at him these last few days, from the humiliation of his detention to the cold, silent fury of Rumina's censure, how strange that it should be these few words from this stranger that should cut him to the quick.

He felt the urge to argue back; to put this woman in her place; to make her understand that in the real world he simply did not have the option of running off to America in search of Aliyah, however much he should wish to.

And yet he said none of those things.

His response, when it came, was measured.

'I have a son and a wife and another daughter in hospital. What happens to them if I am arrested? Do they deserve a father and husband who cannot care for them because he is sitting in an American jail for the rest of his life? Because believe me, your people won't just charge me with theft of a passport, they will say I was involved in whatever terrorist bullshit they think Aliyah is mixed up with.'

For a moment she said nothing, then suddenly she sat up straighter. There was a certain look in her eyes which made him apprehensive.

'What if you didn't have to steal a passport?'

*

'*Have you lost your mind?*'

Rumina's face suggested that she certainly thought so.

The conversation had started in the kitchen as the kettle boiled, the tone hushed, as appropriate for an argument between spouses with a stranger sitting in the next room, but quickly degenerated into heated, increasingly vociferous accusations – at least on his wife's part.

He had expected nothing less. Her grief, her anger, both of which had so far manifested as icy silence, now erupted.

How could he be so stupid? How could he be so arrogant to think that *he* and that American woman sitting in their lounge, *that whatever-she-was*, could find Aliyah before the police? And what of his wife? What of his daughter in hospital? What of Tariq – the son she had given him years after both of them had given up hope?

What was he supposed to tell her?

With his hands he pleaded with her to lower her voice.

'*Oh-go, shōnnō na.* I have to *do* something. You said that this was my fault; you said *I* let her go. Then it is up to me to bring her back.'

He saw her tears. Their slow trickle down the sides of her face. He moved forward to embrace her but her iron hand pushed him away.

'This is madness, Sajid. Simply madness. Haven't you done enough harm already? *You* . . . always *you* . . . putting ideas into our daughters' heads. "*Do this; think that; see the world; fight for what is right.*" Everything *you* wanted but never had the courage to do yourself. And now? See? Where are my girls? Where are they, Sajid?'

He could say nothing. She was right.

He poured scalding water from the kettle over the leaves in the strainer and watched as the water stained brown. And with that, the weight came into him. He wasn't a bad man. He wasn't a bad father. He had played his role in these tragedies and he would do so again.

'*Decision-ta final.* I am going.'

He turned, leaving her to finish brewing the tea. As he reached the door, she fired one last barb.

'You always made me look like the villain, Sajid, the one holding them back, when all I wanted to do was protect them. They are gone and now you are going too. You will get caught or they will kill you, and then it will be up to me to gather what remains . . . without you.'

# CHAPTER 19

*Shreya*

The scream of engines heralded the arrival of the Gulfstream; the early-morning rain coming down like it was in a hurry and the plane's wheels kicking up a wall of spray as it touched down and hurtled along the tarmac. Kramer had parked the SUV thought-fully, or maybe recklessly, close to the runway, but Shreya still waited to the last minute before stepping out to the sting of the wind.

The cabin door thudded open and Dan's head appeared. He took the stairs carefully, holding the pneumatic strut for balance as the gale whipped his hair into a bird's nest.

He gave her a grimace that was quickly lost to the rain.

'All set?'

She gestured to the SUV. 'Car's waiting.'

She got in the back beside him, close enough to smell the damp-ness of his clothes. It made her uncomfortable. The smell of clothes always did. She introduced him to Kramer, who gave him a nod and started the engine.

Dan turned back to her.

'So what you got, Shreya?'

She caught Kramer's gaze in the rear-view mirror.

'Yusuf Ghani. Afghan. Forty-six. Came to the US in '21 when it all went to shit over there. No relatives or next of kin, at least none we've found so far; immigration records are sketchy, though he was issued with a Green Card – category EB-4. It's given to certain special immigrants: religious workers and current or former US government workers.'

He knew all this, of course. She'd emailed him everything before he took off, but this was as much for Kramer's benefit as his. She hadn't exactly given the girl chapter and verse, restricting all mention of the Ghani breakthrough until a call at 5.30 a.m., less than three hours ago. Judging by her silence, Kramer was in a sulk, but that was her problem. Shreya wasn't about to play nursemaid or apologise for hurt feelings.

'The vehicle he used to pick up the girls at PDX is a Toyota Tacoma,' she continued. 'A 2009 model, registered to him at an address in San Diego.'

'It's not a fake?'

'Licence plate and VIN check out. It's his last known address. Social security records place him there till about twelve months ago, employed in a series of low-end jobs: everything from washing dishes in a diner to cutting grass for the county. Nothing else on file after that. Looks like he just upped and left. Agent Kramer has the Portland office running the licence plates, checking for traffic violations, security cams and patrol car sightings, but it'll take time.'

'Any more?'

'We pulled his bank records: about eight grand in a checking account and no deposits made for over a year.'

'He's living day-to-day then?'

She gave him a nod.

'Payday to payday, most likely. What's interesting though is that he has made the odd withdrawal, most recently two months ago, at a Union Bank ATM in a place called Estacada, about thirty miles south-east of here.'

She waited for that to sink in before continuing.

'The previous withdrawal from his bank account was about three months earlier. Same town, same ATM, same amount. Ninety dollars.'

'So our guy's been up here for a while.'

'That's why I thought you should come up.'

'How big's the town?'

'Small. Thirty-five hundred residents, give or take.'

Kramer took a left, the view outside changing from airstrip service road to highway. Dan reached into his bag, pulled out a thin file and passed it to her.

'Courtesy of the Pentagon. Yusuf Ghani's record of service for the US Military.'

There wasn't much to see inside – the bare bones of a life typed out in double space and redacted with solid black strips. *Heavily redacted*. She scanned it, quickly committing its few facts to memory.

Yusuf Ghani. Born September 1978 in a place called Kameh, outside of Jalalabad, Afghanistan. Recruited as a contractor for the US Army in 2004, ferrying supplies and equipment to American bases. Then came details of the insurgency, and with it the redactions: a whole lot of half-obscured pages. What was left told a fragmentary tale: Ghani had shifted to driving fuel tankers – a job akin to travelling around inside a massive bomb. *That took guts*, she thought. *Guts, or a lack of any alternative.* Then came an ambush by the Taliban, the where and when redacted. He'd been injured and evac'ed then invalided out and sent home to Jalalabad. The visible record stopped there. There were a couple of pages more, but every word had been blacked out, making them look more like a piano keyboard than a document and leaving her to guess at what might have been underneath. All that was certain was that in 2021, amid the chaos of the international pull-out and with the Taliban at the gates of Kabul, someone had issued Ghani with a visa getting him onto one of the last flights out of Dodge and to the US where, with exceptional speed, he'd gotten a Green card.

Outside, the hilly sprawl of Portland passed under a sleeting sky, the city fading as Kramer swapped interstate for roads that twisted between ramparts of trees. Shreya's stomach lurched. She opened her bag and reached for a blister pack of Dramamine, extracting and dry-swallowing two tablets from their foil before closing her eyes and waiting for her stomach to settle.

Kramer pulled onto a side road close to a flag-festooned car dealer-ship and a sign that welcomed them to Estacada. A nice place, all picket fences and trim lawns. Middle America among the pines. *Wholesome*, her dad would have called it. Even after thirty-odd years in the country, he was still a sucker for these postcard towns.

'*This* is America, Shreya,' he would tell her. 'The *real* America.'

Three black Cadillac Escalades, identical to the one she was in, sat alongside Main Street. Kramer parked outside a squat building that proclaimed itself a branch of the Union Bank. Smoked-glass windows looked out onto a bed of withered flowers. She braced herself against the cold and got out, following Dan toward the entrance, Kramer a step behind.

The interior was a couple of degrees too warm, as though feeling the need to compensate for outside, and empty save for a few anxious-looking tellers peering out from behind the bullet-proof, Covid-proof windows of their booths. Kramer's colleagues were already here: big men sporting raid jackets with the FBI crest stamped on the breast like jocks from some school that majored in intimidation.

Kramer sidled up to one of them. He didn't seem to recognise her but she struck up a conversation as naturally as if they were neighbours. That was a skill in itself, Shreya thought; one she'd never been able to master. Kramer walked back with a shake of her head.

'Seems none of the staff recognised Ghani from the photo. He's not a customer of the bank, just some guy who used the ATM outside. They're looking at the security footage for when he last visited, but it was a while back. They're not sure if the recordings still exist.'

Dan rubbed at his temples.

'What about nearby stores? We started door-to-door yet?'

Door-to-door; needle-in-haystack stuff. It might work, might lead to something, but it was hit-and-miss, and with five days till the election, time was running out. What was required was a shortening of the odds. Shreya headed for one of the windows, its smoked glass lending the world outside a dirty, yellowish tint; the sort of filter Hollywood movies added to foreign countries to make them look like shitholes. She thought of Ghani; pictured him driving down the road outside, parking up in front of the bank, getting out of his pickup, walking up to the ATM, putting in his card and withdrawing his cash; not once, but twice.

*Ninety dollars each time.*

Odd amount . . . no, not odd . . . *specific.*

Ninety dollars, twice in a row. The hint of a pattern. She liked patterns. They made sense of the world. She thought of Ghani once more. He would've come to America with pretty much nothing. In that sense at least, he wasn't that different to her dad, coming here from India with little but a degree and an overstuffed suitcase full of dreams. The memories had made him frugal; never spending more than was necessary. Never taking out a dollar more cash than was needed.

*That was what Ghani was doing.*

A specific amount for a specific transaction. More than fifty, less than a hundred. An amount you had to key in by hand. In her mind's eye, she pictured him: walking back to the truck, getting in, reversing out of his space and driving off . . .

*Driving off.*

It was fifty bucks and change to fill up the tank of her Honda. The tank in Ghani's Tacoma would be larger, maybe by seventy per cent or so. It would cost around eighty-five dollars to fill.

But those were LA prices. Around four twenty a gallon.

She turned around and called out to Kramer.

'How much does a gallon of gas cost around here?'

The agent looked at her curiously.

'Round four fifty. Why?'

She didn't answer, just did the math in her head.

Seven per cent more. Add seven per cent to her estimate and it was back to a figure of around ninety dollars for a tank of gas.

*Close enough.*

She pictured Ghani driving off from the bank, down the road, turning into a gas station, filling the tank, handing over ninety dollars, maybe getting a little back in change. He had to pay in cash.

She headed back to Dan and Agent Kramer.

'We should try the gas stations,' she said. 'I think he was getting money for gas.'

# CHAPTER 20

*Shreya*

Kramer followed her out the door and into the storm, her words half lost to the wind.

'Why'd you think he was looking for a gas station?'

*Good question.*

She should explain it to her; lay out her thinking, but sometimes, in the heat of the moment, the words got tied up in Shreya's mouth. The act of spelling out her thoughts to another person became a challenge in itself, like wading through quicksand or pushing water uphill. More than one teacher had thought her stupid because of it. Sometimes it was easier to just state her opinion and be done with it, even if people thought she was being rude.

'A calculated gamble.'

She leaned into the elements and battled back to the SUV. Kramer unlocked it, the turning lights twinkling as Shreya scrambled into the passenger seat and pulled the door shut.

Kramer brought up a map of the town and pressed an icon. On-screen, all the gas stations in the vicinity blinked red.

'Where'd you like to start?'

Five gas stations in town. Another two further out. Once more Shreya pictured Ghani in his truck, the needle on the fuel gauge slipping below the red line.

'We'll start with the ones nearest the bank.'

A couple of blocks to the north-west, the sign of a Shell station glowed scarlet and yellow in the rain. Kramer pulled into a spot so deep in standing water that a rat might drown if it put its mind to it. By the time she'd killed the engine Shreya'd already jumped out, heading past a row of pumps toward the minimart of a payment booth. An electronic bell chimed as she entered and made for the counter, pulling up Ghani's photo on her phone. She brandished both it and her badge at a scrawny kid behind the plexiglas. The name-tag on his chest read *Kurt*.

'You seen this guy? He might have come in to buy gas over the last couple months.'

The kid stared from the photo to the badge and back again, then shrugged an apology.

'No, ma'am. But I'm only here part-time.'

The bell chimed and Kramer entered, accompanied by the north wind. She held back, making for the coffee machine. Shreya looked back to Kurt.

'How many others you got working here?'

The kid scratched at his neck. 'I dunno. You'd have to ask my boss.'

'He here?'

'She,' he corrected. 'Not at the moment.'

'You got her number?'

'Yes, ma'am.'

He gestured to a faded yellow Post-it tattooed with a bunch of

146

numbers and taped to the counter. He pointed to the topmost, circled in red, the name KELLY scrawled beside it.

Shreya punched in the number and waited while it rang, then went to voicemail. She hung up, then brought up the number again, this time typing a message and attaching the photo of Ghani from his driver's licence. Kelly'd be receiving a text instructing her to forward the pic of Ghani to all of her employees. If any recognised him, she should call Shreya immediately.

She turned back to the kid.

'Your security footage stored here?'

'Yes, ma'am. In the back room.'

'Good,' she said. 'My colleagues'll come round later to take a look. In the meantime, make sure no one touches it.'

She turned and found Kramer behind her, holding a cup of coffee.

'You want one?'

'No,' she said and headed for the door.

The storm outside had lulled somewhat with the rain now having the good grace at least to fall vertically. She stood and waited under an awning for Kramer to finish her coffee and join her. Finally the door chimed once more and the agent came out.

'You took your time.'

Kramer seemed startled.

'Sorry. I was just . . . talking to the guy behind the counter, trying to find out a little about the place. Checking if there was anywhere out-of-towners might congregate.'

There it was again. That ability to talk to strangers like they were old friends.

'And?'

'Nothing. Ain't really an out-of-towner kind of place.'

Shreya couldn't help feel a little frisson of satisfaction.

'Right.' Kramer sighed. 'One down, six to go.' She patted the pockets of her coat. 'Mind if I have a cigarette?'

'I didn't think your generation went in for smoking.'

Kramer nodded, reaching into her jacket pocket and extracting a pristine carton. 'Yep. Filthy habit. I picked it up in the army.'

Shreya looked at her.

'You were in the army?'

'Uh-huh. It was the quickest way out of Montana. Seemed a good idea at the time.'

'Small-town girl, eh? Where in Montana?'

Kramer laughed. 'Place called Conrad. Nowhere you'd ever have heard of.'

That much was true.

The girl tore at the cellophane wrapper.

Shreya raised a hand.

'Maybe wait till we're not standing in a gas station.'

The agent waited only as long as it took to get back in the car, taking out a lighter and the pack of Marlboros and offering one to Shreya. Six months without a drag. It was tempting.

'No . . . Thank you.'

'Got it.'

Kramer lit up and exhaled blue smoke.

'So where next?'

The map proclaimed a couple more nearby: a Chevron a half-mile away, and some place called Unity Gas near the turning for the highway.

The Chevron, she figured, wouldn't be much different to the Shell they were sitting outside. The same set-up, probably: five or six staff, maybe more, doing shifts. Unity Gas, now that might be different. It sounded like a mom-and-pop sort of place; the kind her uncle Prashant had back in Auburn, he and Sheila auntie putting in ten- to twelve-hour shifts between them. And the kids helping out in the evenings and on weekends with their schoolbooks in tow. That was the thing about independent places. The folks who ran them lived their lives pretty much tied to the register.

*Unity Gas it was.*

\*

It wasn't much to look at, just a couple of pumps slowly getting on with the business of rusting in front of a low-roofed convenience store with an ice dispenser outside the door and sacks of logs and kindling stacked up against the length of its red-brick wall.

Inside was stocked with everything from fishing tackle to engine oil, piled on to shelving that might just have been erected when JFK was in the White House. The woman behind the counter certainly looked like she might remember those days.

She peered up from the pages of a fat, yellowing paperback and welcomed her with the sort of smile you mostly saw on the faces of white grandmas in ads for baking products.

'Can I help you?'

Shreya walked up to the counter and took out her badge.

'I hope so, ma'am. My name is Agent Mistry.'

On her phone, she brought up the photo of Ghani and slid it over the countertop.

'Can you tell me if you recognise this man? Maybe he's come in for gas recently?'

The woman creased the corner of a page and closed the book. She placed it slowly on the counter and picked up Shreya's phone, adjusted her glasses and took a long hard look at the photo.

'I've seen him,' she said, nodding before handing back the phone. 'Foreign gentleman. As you say, comes in for gas every now and then.'

Shreya struggled to maintain her composure.

'He's not in any trouble, is he?'

'I just need to find him, ma'am. You wouldn't happen to know where he lives?'

The woman shook her head.

"Fraid I can't help you there. Reckon I've only seen him in here a couple of times.'

*She should have known. Nothing ever came that easy.*

'Do you remember when he last came in?'

The woman chewed at her lip.

'Three, maybe four weeks ago?'

She rose slowly from her seat like an ocean liner leaving its berth. 'I'm not here all the time, you understand. If you wait a moment, I can ask my husband.' She called out to the open door behind her. 'Al . . . could you come out here a minute?'

Al appeared, preceded by a shuffling of boxes along the cement floor, a rake of a man in a plaid shirt and corduroy pants, loose skin hanging at his neck like a Thanksgiving turkey. The woman turned back to Shreya.

'Could I see that photo again please, dear?'

Once more Shreya passed over her phone, and with an unsteady hand, the woman held Ghani's picture in front of her husband's nose.

'This young lady's from the FBI, Al. You remember seeing this man? You know, the foreign gentleman?'

Al took the phone and lifted a thick pair of glasses hanging from a chain around his neck.

'I remember him. Must've seen him, what, maybe two weeks ago? Paid for gas and a coupl'a Hershey bars.'

Shreya gave him a nod. 'D'you know anything else about him?'

The man shook his head. 'He ain't local, which is to say I doubt he lives in Estacada.'

'You wouldn't happen to keep any security footage of outside, would you?'

"Fraid not. Camera broke in 2007, maybe '8. Never quite got round to gettin' it fixed. Anything else we can help you with?'

Shreya thought of the girls, Yasmin and Aliyah. 'He ever come in here with anyone else?'

Kramer was waiting with the engine running, on a call as Shreya opened the door.

'Gotta go, Mom.'

Shreya felt a stab of guilt. She should call her own parent. Tell him she was up here. She knew how he worried.

Kramer turned. 'Any luck?'

'He's been here. More than once. Old couple inside both ID'd him.'

Kramer's eyes widened.

'Woah! For real? So you were right!'

Shreya returned her stare.

'You sound surprised, Special Agent Kramer.'

'I'm not! I'm . . . impressed! What else they tell you? Do they know where he's staying?'

'Not much . . . 'cept that they don't think he lives in Estacada . . . and that he always came in alone.'

'Shit.'

Shreya recoiled at the sound of the word. Kramer must've noticed. She must have thought Shreya'd taken some sort of offence, for her next comment was more upbeat.

'It's still positive though, right?'

Shreya nodded.

She looked up at the board advertising the gas prices. Almost ten cents a gallon cheaper than at the Shell station. She'd been right – about the reason for the stop at the Union Bank ATM and the gas station he favoured. She was beginning to understand the man. That was a step forward.

She looked to the distance, to the trucks cruising down the highway.

'What road is that?'

'The one we came in on. The 211.'

Shreya pictured Ghani driving down it.

*Why get gas here?* The couple inside didn't peg him for a local, so why was he coming to buy gas in Estacada? Was it because there were no gas stations closer to him? Or was this on his route somewhere?

She reached for her phone and called up a map. Route 211 – a white line cutting through a green background. To the north it changed to the 224 and ran pretty much to the outskirts of Portland. And to the south, it forked just outside of Estacada, with the 211 looping to the west and the 224 branching off and heading south-east following the path of the Clackamas River.

She typed *gas stations* into the search bar and a number of red dots appeared on the map. As she zoomed out, several more dots appeared, most to the north of Estacada, increasing in frequency like a rash the closer you got to Portland. To the south though, the dots were fewer: a couple on the 211; and on the 224, nothing. Not a single gas station on a twenty-five-mile stretch until it joined Route 22 at a place called Detroit Lake. Shreya zoomed in on the road, tracing it gradually south, making sure she hadn't missed anything.

She turned to Kramer. 'We need to go see Dan.'

# CHAPTER 21

*Sajid*

The wheels hit the tarmac hard, jolting him forward. He rubbed at the pain in his neck and stared at the windswept, rain-lashed new world beyond the porthole. Five thousand miles and yet the place looked no different from Heathrow. He checked his watch: it would have been early in the morning back home, which meant it must be . . . he had trouble with the calculation. He marvelled at the speed of it all. Sixteen hours in total, from ticket purchase to arrival on the other side of the world.

The plane began its sojourn toward the terminal. Other passengers were stirring: waking their children, gathering possessions, performing all the rituals that preceded disembarkation. *Not Carrie, though.*

He looked two rows ahead to where she was sitting, her blonde hair visible like a halo around the headrest. His stomach turned. *What was he doing?* How had he allowed her to talk him into this?

Rumina was right. This was not going to work. They would check his passport, they would realise who he was and they would arrest him.

*Rumina.*

Guilt welled up within him as he thought once more of her and their parting shots at each other. And yet, she had paid for his ticket. From her savings, for he had none of his own. Her money, squirrelled away for emergencies. Despite her words, she had given it to him, and he had taken that as a sign.

Outside, the elements echoed his turmoil, the wind gusting, smashing a sheet of rain against the acrylic of the windows. He leaned back, closed his eyes and uttered a prayer, hoping that the rhythm of the words might bring him some calm. Was Carrie, he wondered, doing something similar?

He ended with an *Ameen* and opened his eyes. Carrie was on her feet now, like the others, ignoring entreaties from the voice on the intercom requesting they remain seated.

Sajid rose, opened the overhead locker and brought down his trolley case. It was miserably light, but then the few possessions he had brought – underwear, a couple of jumpers; toothbrush – they hardly weighed anything at all. The only other thing in there was the cheap pair of binoculars he had bought at a market stall near the Mile End Road. If anyone asked, he was here for a few days of birdwatching. The cover story had been Carrie's idea. To him, birdwatching was an alien pursuit. His people did not watch wildlife through lenses. In his homeland the immediacy of flora and fauna made such things irrelevant.

He had made a few other purchases: a disposable smartphone, the hiking boots on his feet and a Gore-Tex jacket which had cost more money than any coat had a right to, but again Carrie had insisted upon it and Rumina had paid for it and he had worn it throughout the flight.

He joined the other passengers shuffling toward the exit. Carrie was somewhere ahead, but that did not matter. They would not speak, or even acknowledge one another, until they had both passed through immigration and were safely out of the airport. *Assuming he made it that far.*

By the time he stepped off the plane, she was gone. The fear returned, radiating from his gut like an ember. He stumbled forward, just another traveller, part of the herd along the air bridge, then through the terminal and toward the line at passport control. In his head though, he was back in Bangladesh, back in that *other* line, on that night when ... He pushed the memories back, down into the wretched basement of his soul, and forced himself to focus on the present.

The immigration hall was thick with bodies and disparate voices, like the story in the Quran, where Allah had brought all the people of the world to the plains of Babil so that He might give them their languages before scattering them once more. The Jews and the Christians had a similar story, of course, and like different men recalling the same event, they differed in the detail, but the message was the same.

He took his place at the end of the line, now and then shuffling a few paces as it stuttered forward, snaking between metal poles and elastic cordons. He fought the urge to look up at the security cameras or to the other queue where he expected Carrie to be.

Once more his mind drifted to the night, also wet, back in the Chittagong hills. The line had been longer, the guns of the guards antiquated compared to these ones here, but lethal just the same. His father had sent him further up the line, his mother discreetly tucked in a few bodies behind him. He did not look like he had a paisa to his name, and that was probably what had saved him. They had inspected his papers that night, but in a hurry. They had failed to make the connection. Had not realised who his father was. They had missed the familial tie that would have condemned him, and they had let him through the cordon. After that, he had waited. Waited for his mother, who never came. And then he had run, out of the stadium and into the roar of the monsoon. In his mind, the noise of the storm mingled with the sound of gunfire behind him, and its water turned red with the blood of his family.

Later they would tell him it had been a miracle. Allah had preserved him. But if so, why him? And why not his mother, or his father, or any of the others? He had never been able to make sense of it, and in the end wondered whether this miracle had in fact been his burden, to be borne by his conscience for the remainder of his days. Or maybe it had not been divine intervention at all but simply dumb fortune. *May he be just as lucky this time too.*

The closer he got, the more he doubted. The check would be more thorough this time. It would be methodical and meticulous and computer-assisted. They would take his passport, scan it, watch their screens and then realise who he was. His heart pounded within his chest.

'Next!'

A gun-toting guard directed him to a counter with a gesture of his bullet-head. Sajid fumbled in his jacket for his passport and handed it to a stone-faced woman behind the glass who barely glanced in his direction, preferring to assess him from the details in the document. She flicked to the last page, examined it, then finally stared at him for confirmation. He could not meet her gaze. He felt his throat tighten. He looked around. A bored-looking guard sat a few feet away, beyond the line of booths, machine gun slung under his shoulder. Sajid felt cold sweat trickle down his flank. The woman in the booth pressed his passport to the scanner. He counted long seconds, bit his lip and watched her impassive face. She pulled out the passport and closed it.

'Mr Khan,' she said, placing the passport on the ledge between them, 'welcome to Canada.'

*

He could not quite believe it. He had expected sirens, flashing lights, armed guards rushing forward and pinning him to the floor, just as their black-clad brethren had done in London days earlier. Instead he had received a half-smile and his passport pushed back at him. Yes, this was not America, but Carrie had assured him that passport control in Vancouver would be the critical stage. *'After that it's plain sailing,'* and for the first time he allowed himself the glimmer of hope that it might be so.

He walked through baggage claim in a daze, ignoring the suitcase-laden crowds and conveyor belts, and wheeled his small trolley case toward the Green walkway. A uniformed official sat lazily by the entrance. The checks were ostensibly random but he had spent enough time passing through security at Heathrow to know how often random chance just happened to end with a brown man being stopped and searched.

He controlled his breath, fixed his expression to what he hoped was innocent neutrality and made for the corridor, turning his head to avoid the man's gaze. In front of him, an elderly white woman was fighting a trolley laden with suitcases. Behind him the shriek of a klaxon pierced the air. His heart leapt.

*Keep calm, Sajid.*

From the corner of his eye he noticed the guard rising from his seat.

*It could be anything. Keep walking, Sajid. Slow, steady steps.*

He entered the Green hallway, a winding corridor between sterile walls. His legs shook, as though his bones were dissolving.

*What was happening behind him?*

He felt panic rising within his breast as the wail of the klaxon drowned all thoughts from his head.

*Keep walking, Sajid. Keep walking.*

He heard the first shouts behind him. Ahead and to one side, a group of uniformed officials manned a row of tables.

*Customs officers.*

He had nothing compromising on his person, but if they questioned him it would all be over. They would see through him; sense his fear. Up ahead, the elderly lady continued to struggle with her trolley as though she were navigating a tanker through a canal.

He had one chance.

He upped his pace till he was level with her, then quickly hoisted his case on top of her bags and took control of the trolley.

She made to object, but he placed a gentle hand on her arm.

'Madam, let me help you.'

Directing her forward, he held his breath as they approached the tables. Discreetly he positioned her between himself and the officials.

The thing to do was to strike up a conversation. Make it appear as though his acquaintance with the lady had lasted at least the length of the flight instead of two seconds, but his mind was blank.

'A-are you here on vacation?' he asked softly.

She gave him an uncertain smile.

'I was in London for medical treatment. I'm on my way home now.'

He tried to keep his voice level.

'What treatment did you have?'

'You're a doctor?' she asked.

'Yes,' he said. And on a certain level, it was true. What's more, it seemed to put the woman at ease. They crept forward, the woman explaining a build-up of something in her pancreas, past the gaggle of customs officials who barely gave them a look. Sajid felt his jaw relax a little. When it came to random searches, the company of an old white lady seemed to act as a cloak of invisibility.

The doors to the arrivals hall were mere feet away. He should leave the woman and make haste. But that, he decided, would not be honourable. He would accompany her at least through those doors.

They kept walking, closing the distance, *ten feet, nine, eight* ... the doors remained closed. Surely the sensors should have detected them by now? Surely they should have opened? *Five feet, four, three* ... he closed his eyes, wondering if he should simply ram the trolley into them. Just as he decided he had no other option, he heard the pneumatic hiss.

The arrivals hall was busy. Not the anonymous throng of Heathrow or the anarchy of Dhaka, but a sizeable crowd, large enough certainly to get lost in. He deposited the woman beside a row of chairs, giving her the sort of ingratiating smile which he had found senior citizens tended to appreciate, then grabbing his trolley case, quickly made his way to where the crowd was thickest. He looked up. A hundred signs pointing the way to everything from coffee shops to car hire. It took a moment to find the one he was looking for: the SkyTrain.

The doors he had just passed through opened again, this time disgorging not travellers but police. *There was no doubt now.*

He dropped his head and began to move quickly, not looking back and keeping among the crowds. He found a ticket machine and purchased a single to downtown Vancouver. Cash only; Canadian dollars, acquired in London. Taking a wool hat from the pocket of his jacket, he slipped it on and hurried to the platform.

A train was waiting. Two minutes before departure according to the electronic board overhead. He boarded the closest compartment and made his way through the train till he found a sparsely filled carriage. He took a seat and pulled his hat lower.

It could not be long now. A minute at most and the train would set off. He counted long seconds. The speaker above him scratched to life; a voice, metallic and static-heavy, announcing scheduled stops. He might have listened if it were not for the sight of a police officer running the length of the platform outside. He looked to be checking the windows. Sajid bent down feigning a search for something in his case.

The speaker came to life once more, this time emitting an intermittent beep as the doors slid shut. He felt the jolt of forward momentum and looked up. The carriage was unchanged; the same tired faces, the same few bodies in the same seats. Outside, the platform slid away. No sign of the policeman.

He risked a glance through the window of the door into the next carriage and froze. There, standing at the far end, talking into a radio was the officer.

The heat rose at his collar. He considered his options: stay where he was and hope for the best, or risk getting up and moving down the train. A choice between the devil and the deep blue sea as his adoptive countrymen would say.

Action was preferable to inaction.

Beyond the rain-streaked windows, the outskirts of Vancouver were reduced to a constellation of street lamps and bulbs in back bedrooms. Very slowly, he got to his feet and began to walk down the carriage.

He was halfway along when he stopped short. There, through the door to the next compartment, the outline of another uniformed torso: thickset, a gun at his hip, and heading in his direction. Sajid dived for the nearest seat, his heart slamming inside his chest. He pictured the officer bursting through the door with his gun raised. He ventured a glance. The man was still making his way methodically through the adjoining carriage. He let out a breath. A stay of execution. But for how long? Thirty seconds, a minute at most, and then the officer would most certainly come through that door.

The vibrations under his feet changed. He looked out of the

window as the train passed over a bridge; felt the sudden drag of inertia, the train slowing, pulling into a floodlit, elevated platform. *Too early.* This was not the station he was supposed to alight at. The doors slid open. An iron wind assailed his face. Sajid held firm, waiting long, painful seconds. The connecting door at the far end of the carriage opened and the thickset officer entered. His gaze fell immediately on Sajid. For an instant they locked eyes and then the man reached for the gun at his belt. Bells began to ring. The doors began to close. Leaving the trolley case, Sajid leapt from his seat, off the train and began sprinting down ice-cold concrete.

# CHAPTER 22

*Shreya*

'You're sure about this?'

Kramer's voice echoed off wood panelling. Shreya marched on, along scuffed linoleum and under the painted gaze of dead white men.

'Yes.'

Swing doors creaked as she pushed through them. Base of operations. A set of commandeered rooms in the Estacada courthouse: tables and laptops and wires and agents, all set down amid small-town civic decor, and Dan sitting like a spider at the centre of it. He saw her enter but continued his conversation with some agent. She cut in anyway.

'Dan, we've got a sighting.'

He turned to her.

'What?'

'Of Ghani. Old couple who run a place called Unity Gas. They ID'd him.'

He looked at her with confusion.

'Why didn't you call it in?'

'Because I needed to speak with you. We got to move the locus of the search.'

'They gave you a fix?'

'What? No. They don't know where he's based.'

Her ears began to sing. He was asking too many questions. He needed to stop and listen to what she had to tell him.

'So why should we change the search area?'

'Because of the gas stations . . .'

'What?'

'They're missing . . . south of Estacada . . . that's where he is . . .'

The words weren't coming; panic rising in their stead. She had to explain. Had to make him understand. She looked round.

*There.*

'You need to see.'

She made for the widescreen monitor on a desk, a contoured map of the town and its surroundings spread across its face. She pointed to Route 211.

'This is us here. This, this is the road through town . . . the one we came in on. See here . . . it splits in two . . .' Her lungs emptied. She fought for air, short, shallow breaths between half-sentences. '. . . into the 211 and the 224 . . . here, just outside town. And this,' she said, placing her finger on Unity Gas, 'is the last gas station on the route south . . . There's no others for about thirty miles.'

Dan's brow creased. 'What are you getting at?'

*What was she getting at?*

Her head clouded, her train of thought obscured in fog.

'I think . . . I think Ghani is filling up at Unity Gas in Estacada because there's nowhere else . . . nowhere better for him . . . I mean it's the closest for him . . . the closest gas station to wherever he's living; and that –' she stabbed at the monitor, to the area between the southern loop of the 211 and the 224 winding along the Clacka-mas River, south of Estacada – 'would mean that he's somewhere down here . . . He might be staying somewhere along the 211, toward Sweetwater and Colton maybe . . . or maybe along the 224 south of town. It might be coincidence, but I don't think it is. This is the area we need to search.'

*Coincidence? Why had she offered him that?* It was nerves and adrenaline and the urgency of the whole thing and she needed to focus.

Dan stared at the screen, blinking.

'Run that by me again.'

*Hell!* She wanted to scream. She wanted to grab him by his shirt collar and tell him they didn't have time for this. He had to trust her – had to believe her – but he wasn't the type to respond posi-tively to that sort of approach. Instead, she took a breath and started over, explaining once more about Unity Gas and the 224 and the 211; those ribbons of road south of Estacada.

Dan rubbed a thick hand over his neck.

'So all you have is a sighting at a gas station?'

'Yes. No.'

'You're reaching, Shreya.'

'I'm extrapolating.'

'From what? The bank and this gas station? Both of which are in Estacada.' He shook his head. 'It's too early to change tack. We have to focus on the town.'

She could hear the blood clearly in her ears now. The sound of her hopes rushing away. Dan wouldn't get it. Wouldn't ever get it. Another attack could be hours away and he wanted to waste time with a blanket search of the town. To hell with that.

'You gotta listen to me, Dan. Logic dictates that he's –'

He silenced her with a gesture of one hand.

'Don't argue with me, Shreya. Not here.'

If she had to guess, she'd say he sounded upset. But she was upset too.

'For fuck's sake, Dan!'

She stopped, shocked by her own words. It was as though she was no longer in control. Anger and frustration had hijacked her judgement. And still the blood sang in her ears.

She tried again. Lowering her voice. Pleading.

'Dan, you have to listen to me. There's another girl out there. Another potential bomber. We don't have time to waste searching based on protocol.'

It was too late. Even she could recognise the expression on his face. 'Enough,' he growled. 'I've got everyone from the director down demanding a breakthrough. You want me to tell them I stopped searching Estacada because an agent who's not even supposed to be here had a hunch?'

Kramer was waiting outside, leaning against the metal railings beside the courthouse steps, smoking a cigarette as though the cold and the wind were someone else's problem.

She straightened as Shreya came bursting through the doors.

'How'd it go?'

Shreya gestured at the cigarette in Kramer's hand.

'You got a spare?'

Kramer reached into her coat pocket, extracted the packet and held it out.

'That bad?'

Shreya fished out a cigarette and Kramer clicked open her lighter.

She took a drag. The first one in months. It was like slipping into a warm bath. She exhaled blue-grey smoke. The tension she felt began to wane like the tide going out.

'He's not going to move the locus of the search.'

'What? Why the hell not?'

Shreya took another drag. The cigarette trembled between her fingers.

'He said I was reaching. He said I hadn't given him enough to justify moving the focus to south of town.'

Kramer shook her head.

'But you were right about the gas stations.'

'Apparently that's not enough.'

She wondered if it might've been enough for Dan if someone else had suggested it to him, someone who wasn't Shreya. Someone he didn't feel threatened by. Someone he wasn't sending to San Diego.

Kramer flicked the stunted remains of her cigarette into the grass.

'So we gotta carry on with door-to-door?'

'Yup.'

'Jesus.'

'Some residential areas on the north of town.'

Kramer's mouth fell open.

'*North?*'

Shreya exhaled smoke.

'I may have pissed him off a little. I'm not always good at explaining things.'

'Maybe next time you should let me talk to him.'

Shreya gave a bitter laugh.

'You're a rookie. He won't listen to you.'

Kramer fished the keys to the SUV from her pocket and smiled.

'Men tend to listen to me. I might surprise you.'


The night was clear; the mercury falling like a stone. A grey moon shone behind muslin clouds and glinted off the first frost on the grass. It was a nice street. Trim two-storey homes in shades of blue and yellow and brown; small lawns, big garages; every third house with a pickup in the drive.

She headed back along the last driveway, another door closing behind her. The same responses every time. No Yusuf, no Yasmin, no Aliyah. Kramer mirrored her actions on the other sidewalk. They met in the middle of the street.

Shreya cupped her hands and blew into them.

'This is pointless.'

Kramer nodded.

'Yeah. Needle-in-a-haystack bullshit.'

'What haystack? We aren't even in the right field.' Her feet felt like ice. 'How many more houses?'

Kramer checked her phone.

'Four more streets here. Another six 'bout a mile away.'

They walked on toward a solitary street lamp on the corner. Kramer pulled her pack of Marlboros from her pocket.

'You want another?'

She still harboured the residue of guilt from the last one.

'No. Thanks.'

Ahead stretched another street of neat, double-storey cookie-cutter homes. This time the houses lined only one side of the street. The other was open country, wilderness fast dissolving into night.

Kramer exhaled smoke.

'Start at opposite ends and meet in the middle?'

She gave a nod, and headed down the road. The walk would do her good. As it was, she couldn't feel her feet. From behind her came the ring of Kramer's phone. She turned, hoping against hope that it might be a reprieve; someone calling them with news of a breakthrough. Kramer waved her on.

It took another twenty minutes to reach the last house, to ask the same questions and to receive the same answers. *Nothing.* Just like she expected. Two and a half hours of door-to-door and all she had to show for it was sore feet and frozen bones. She headed back up the street as the clouds broke, revealing the pinprick of stars and the pattern of constellations slightly off-kilter. She walked stiffly to where Kramer stood, silhouetted in lamplight, the tip of a cigarette glowing gold against the dark.

'We should call it a night.'

Kramer nodded and proffered another cigarette like Eve offering the apple.

Shreya fought against temptation and the junior agent gave her a smile.

'Fair enough. I'll drive you to your hotel.'

The outskirts of Portland were hued in white and amber electric light; the streets frostbitten and empty under a black sky. Kramer drove slowly, lost in her own thoughts. Shreya left her to it and stared out the windshield at the city. Her own thoughts turned once more to Ghani and to Aliyah Khan. They were to the south somewhere. She felt it in those aching bones.

Kramer turned to her.

'D'you drink, Agent Mistry?'

The question came out of nowhere.

'Occasionally.'

'There's a decent bar near here. You fancy a beer?'


The basement bar was called O'Riordan's, if the neon sign fixed to an iron railing was to be believed, and was reached from street level down a set of old stone stairs that was a lawsuit waiting to happen.

Inside was warmth and the fug of spilled beer. It took her a moment to adjust to the lights; slightly longer to come to terms with the country tunes. The clientele sported plaid shirts and denim, nursed their beers and stared up at a flickering flat screen showing football with the sound off. Not too busy, thankfully. A couple of tables where they could sit in relative privacy and without the world knowing their business. A few heads turned as they entered, as men's heads always did at the sight of unaccompanied women.

She found a booth while Kramer made for the bar, some guy attempting to strike up a conversation as she ordered. Kramer smiled, indulging him right up to the arrival of her drinks and then not a second longer. She walked back to the booth, handed Shreya a bottle and sat down opposite. She raised her own beer in a toast. 'To better luck tomorrow,' and took a swig.

Shreya reciprocated, took a sip of her own and shuddered. Cold comfort from cold beer.

'It won't be any better unless Dan lets us move the search locus.'

Kramer set her bottle down on the table and sat back.

'Please. No more work talk. I need to switch off.' She looked up at Shreya. 'Don't you ever need to, you know, decompress?'

The question caught her unprepared. It wasn't something she liked thinking about because the answer scared her. Truth was, she lived for the job each case consuming her, crowding out everything else until she got to the bottom of it.

It was unhealthy, so her shrink said, but what was the alternative? She'd tried switching off, tried focusing on family and self-care and all the other nice things the therapist had suggested and it just made things worse. How was she supposed to focus on anything while there were questions to which she needed answers?

She gave a shrug. It seemed to unsettle Kramer. Her face reddened.

'I'm sorry. It was a stupid question. You've probably got family and other stuff to take your mind off things.'

Shreya raised the bottle to her lips and thought of her dad. A couple of missed calls from him since she'd got to Portland. A few voicemails which she hadn't been in the right frame of mind to listen to. She thought of him, in that nursing home, being slowly suffocated by the kindness of strangers. She should call him. Isha too. But that was even tougher than listening to her dad's messages.

'I've got a daughter,' she said, suddenly filled with a need to talk about the girl. 'Her name's Isha. She's sixteen.'

Kramer smiled.

'Sixteen. Dangerous age. At least it was for me. You got a picture?'

Shreya reached for her phone. Scrolling till she found the one of Isha dressed up for junior prom. Shreya hadn't taken it of course. Nik had sent it to her, but she was smiling and looked beautiful in it. She didn't seem to smile these days when Shreya took her photo.

She held the phone out for Kramer who assessed and nodded appreciatively. 'She looks like you.' The words providing Shreya with a validation she didn't know she needed. 'You close?'

Shreya blinked. The room seemed suddenly too warm.

'Yeah, maybe not as close as I'd like. It's kinda tough, what with her being in Auburn and me in California. And these days, ever since she started getting into politics, she's not exactly ecstatic about having a mom who works for the FBI. What about you? You got much family?'

Kramer begrudged a laugh.

'Not outside of Conrad, Montana. There I got Mom, Dad and two shithead brothers who I see 'bout twice a year.'

'No boyfr—' She caught herself. 'No partner?'

'Not at the moment.'

She lifted her bottle and took another swig.

On the TV above the bar, the picture had changed. Sports giving way to news. Images from the election campaign. A mass rally for Costa in Columbus – a sea of red hats and blue placards. A handful of protesters being led from the scene, arms twisted into stress positions by security and jeered by the faithful. A cut to Chuck Costa onstage, fist pumping, one finger jabbing at the air, speechifying, preaching from the patriots' playbook. The ticker at the bottom of the screen spelling it out in capitalised chyron:

COSTA VOWS TO TIGHTEN ENTRY RULES. RED LIST OF COUNTRIES TO BE DRAWN UP. ACTION TO BE TAKEN WITHIN FIRST HUNDRED DAYS IN OFFICE.

*Dog-whistle politics.* Nikhil's parents would approve, blissfully ignorant to the fact that where Muslims were banned today, Hindus might follow tomorrow.

Shreya downed her beer and turned to Kramer.

'Time to leave.'

# CHAPTER 23

*Greg*

Jack was snoring. It had taken him long enough. An hour or more Greg had waited, listening to the sound of his own heart. An hour, with the adrenaline and the pressure building like steam in a kettle.

Gently he massaged his bad knee then slipped out of his bed. From under his bunk he pulled out his duffel bag, the sum total of his possessions within. Clothes, toothbrush and the pages from the tin box in the barn. He raised it silently to his shoulder. It was unwieldy. No way could he carry it and also do what he needed to. He'd thought it through, though. Planned it out, leaving as little to chance as he possibly could. And yet all the planning in the world couldn't counter that one unknowable variable. *Aliyah*.

Jack stirred.

Greg froze. Slowly he lowered the duffel bag to the floor.

'Greg? What you doin', man?'

He had to stay calm.

'Need to visit the john. Stomach's a mess.'

Jack gave him a nod and turned over. Greg breathed out. He lifted the bag, then pulled gently at the door. With luck, Jack would fall back to sleep. If he didn't, Greg figured he had five minutes, ten at most, before the guy got suspicious.

The landing was funereal; wreathed in silence. Weak, milk-grey light seeped in from the window at the far end; the one he'd left unlatched earlier. *Planning.* It's what he'd been trained to do.

He made for it and pushed it open. From his shoulder he took the duffel bag, then leaned out the window and lowered it as far as he could, before letting go and hearing it land heavily on the grass.

He turned and took a breath.

*This was where it got complicated.*

Silently he headed for the girls' room. His tread, he knew, was treacherous. Controlling the weight he placed on each foot was an inexact affair these days. He couldn't risk landing too hard on a floorboard. Yusuf wouldn't miss a noise like that. *Did the guy ever sleep?* Instead he shuffled forward, lifting his right leg only slightly and his left leg not at all. As he approached the door he reached into the pockets of his overshirt, pulling out a knife and the thick pad of wadded cotton.

*There was no other way.*

He turned the handle, hearing the soft click as the latch retracted. From now on he'd be working blind. Which was Aliyah and which Rehana? In the dark both girls were just silhouettes: prone, all but indistinguishable. Rehana though was taller. He picked out the larger frame. He'd deal with her first.

Rehana lay on her side, facing the wall and with her back to him. That was good. It made things easier. He stowed the knife – seemed he wouldn't need it – and slipped his arm under her neck, his elbow pointing forward and squeezed, hard. He counted the seconds: *one, two, three.* Ten seconds he needed. Maybe less. He'd knocked out big men in under fifteen. The carotid arteries were wonderful things. It'd be thirty seconds, maybe a little more before she regained consciousness.

*Long enough.*

He stuffed the wad of cotton in her mouth, then reached for the bandana round his neck, untied it and refastened it around Rehana's mouth, making sure her airways remained clear.

*Ten seconds.*

From his pocket he brought out four plastic cable ties – useful for separating the wires in the explosive devices Miriam had wanted. Handy as restraints too. He placed the first around Rehana's wrists and zipped it tight.

*Seventeen seconds.*

The next went round her ankles.

*Twenty seconds.*

The third he looped round the bed frame then around the tie securing her feet.

*Twenty-three seconds.*

With the final one, he secured her wrists to the bedpost.

*Twenty-six seconds and all done.* Good to see he hadn't lost his touch.

He waited.

Rehana began to stir, her eyelids flickering, then opening in alarm. He saw her fear, and almost regretted his action – regretted hurting her – but it was for her own good. She screamed, a wild silent cry; the cotton pad dousing all vestiges of sound till her lungs emptied. The bed shuddered with the struggle of her limbs. There was too much slack in the third set of ties. He tightened them and the movement stopped. He leaned over and placed a finger to his lips. He hoped she would forgive him, then realised that the bigger sin was not in tying her up, but in leaving her behind.

*One minute since he'd entered the room.*

He made for Aliyah's bed.

It was the first time he'd seen her sleeping. For a moment he was floored by indecision. This was the part he couldn't prepare for. He placed a hand on her shoulder and shook her gently till her eyes opened.

It took a moment for her to focus, serenity succumbing to confusion and then fear.

*Shit.*

He placed a hand over her mouth, his face imploring her not to scream; felt her nails dig into his wrist, scratching at his flesh, drawing blood. He hadn't wanted to do this, but he had no choice. He leaned in close to her.

'Yasmin's dead,' he whispered. 'Miriam's planning the same for you. I'm gonna get you out of here.'

She looked straight at him, every feeling flashing through her eyes. Her grip on his wrist loosened.

'You've got to trust me. Aliyah, you scream and we're both dead.'

Slowly he pulled his hand back.

*This was it. This was the moment of truth.*

Silence.

He hadn't realised he'd been holding his breath. Now he breathed out in relief. Aliyah sat up and stared at him. She kept her voice low.

'What the fuck are you talking about? Miriam said –'

'Miriam lied. I'll prove it. But we need to go, *now.*'

She was too confused to argue.

'Get dressed,' he told her. 'Pack some clothes.'

As she got up, he turned his attention back to Rehana, still struggling uselessly in the old iron bed, not from any hope of freedom but because it was instinct.

'Miriam's lying to you,' he whispered to her. 'She wants you dead.'

*Five minutes since he'd left his own room. They needed to move.*

He took Aliyah's hand and headed for the door, pausing at the threshold, listening, his senses attuned to any vibration, then peered out. An empty landing. No sign of life. No sign of Jack, or Yusuf. He ventured forward, Aliyah a step behind, squeezing his hand.

'Where are we going?'

He didn't answer.

A creak from the floorboards as they reached the stairs; echoed by another sound somewhere in reply. There was no time to look back. He gritted his teeth and hobbled on, down the stairs, the pain knifing through his knee.

They reached the hallway; level ground at least. Aliyah pulled at his arm.

'Greg. Where are we going?'

He didn't have time to explain. He offered her a look that he hoped would persuade her to trust him, then led her through the mess hall and into the kitchen.

Floorboards shrieked behind him. He turned to see a figure rushing toward them. Aliyah screamed. He pushed her out of the way, reaching for one of the two drop-point knives at his waist, flicking it open; flinging it at his assailant. It glinted as it spun, striking its target before he knew what was happening.

A yell.

Jack's voice.

Served the bastard right.

Grabbing Aliyah, he flew toward the back door, bursting through it like a dog out of the traps, dismissing all recognition of the pain, stumbling across the gravel, snatching the duffel bag from its resting place under the window. Lights were going on in the house now, banishing the darkness and with it all hope of an unremarked exit.

He reached the car – the one Jack had returned in. Two rucksacks in the back. The half-completed bombs Miriam had made him build – the bombs for Aliyah and Rehana. He pulled Jack's keys from his pocket. Fuck him.

He turned to Aliyah.

'Get in.'

He threw the duffel bag onto the back seat and jumped in himself, turning the key and saying a prayer as the engine growled to life. Yusuf was in the rear-view mirror, painted infernal red in the tail lights and looking like the devil himself, and Jack a step behind, one hand clasped to a bloody arm.

Yusuf raised his hand. Metal glinted in the moonlight. Greg gunned the engine, sending the rear wheels spinning and dust and dirt flying. A shot rang out, and the side mirror exploded. He pressed hard on the gas, momentum knocking him back as the car roared forward, clipping the skirting on the front porch, fishtailing, straightening, then diving down the asphalt to the main road. Two more shots, one somehow pinging off the back bumper. Another curve in the road, then he accelerated and turned to Aliyah.

'You okay?'

She stared straight ahead like she was catatonic. He tried again. 'Aliyah!'

The dirt on the road behind them lit up.

*Yusuf*, he guessed, *in his truck.*

Shit. He should've slashed its tyres. He'd thought about it and dismissed it as too risky. The turn onto the main road was coming up fast. He braked early and hard, felt the seat belt bite into his chest. Twenty or so feet from the turn, he killed the lights, then hit the gas again, spinning the wheel and taking the corner sharp, bracing himself against the G-force of the turn and hoping Yusuf wouldn't have seen which way he'd gone. With the lights still off, he slammed down on the accelerator.

'Greg, stop, this is crazy.'

Aliyah's voice, frantic. Maybe she was right, but any judgement would have to wait. Right now he was driving blind, without lights. The road twisted; he saw it late; he couldn't brake – it would give them away. At the last second he spun the wheel, sending them slaloming across the asphalt, tyres crying out for purchase. Branches scratched at his window, clawing at the paintwork, beckoning him into their clutches. A few inches more and he'd collide. He braced himself for the worst, just as the wheels finally gripped. Once more he gunned the car. A straight road for a couple hundred yards, then a left and a right and a few more random turns and then he'd turn the lights back on. Even if Yusuf was following, the truck would be too slow to keep up with them.

'Greg.'

Aliyah's voice. Louder this time.

'This is wrong, Greg. I want to go back.'

# CHAPTER 24

*Sajid*

From behind him came shouts. Commands to stop. Threats to shoot. Sajid ignored them and ran for the escalator, taking the saw-toothed steps two at a time, reaching the ticket barrier as behind him the sound of boots rang out on steel. He vaulted over, then sprinted for the stairs to the street.

His lungs burned. His breathing twisted into ragged, wheezing gulps. He coughed up sputum. He was too old for this. His pursuers could not be more than a few hundred feet behind him and were probably a decade or more younger, fitter and stronger. Soon they would be upon him like hounds, or they would just shoot him in the back of the head.

He fell into the street, all but colliding with a woman, pushing past her and out into the embrace of the night. The rain was coming down in sheets, as it had done that night back in Chittagong. Once more he ran, not into all-devouring jungle this time but into urban wilderness – eschewing neon-lit roads for a concrete wasteland of dilapidated buildings and construction sites. He didn't look back, just kept running, through mud and broken rock, with his heart thumping and his lungs rasping until his legs buckled under him, sodden earth rising to meet him.

A splinter of something pierced the flesh of his left palm. He felt it enter, but the pain hardly registered. He was too busy thinking of Rumina, and of Tariq in his cot, of Mia in her hospital bed, and Aliyah, lost in the world. The police were only seconds behind him. They would reach him before he could even make it back to his feet. And then it would be over.

Yet the gunshots did not come, nor the hands on his shoulders. Instead he heard them run on; run past him into the night until once more there was only the sound of the rain. He lay there, panting, before finally pulling himself into the lee of a building – as dark and unobtrusive a corner as he could find – and waited. He listened again for his pursuers, but heard nothing save the rain and his breathing and the hammering in his chest.

How long had he sat there? Long enough for the rattle of the breath in his throat to diminish and his heart rate to calm. Long enough to staunch the cut to his palm and bandage it with his handkerchief. Long enough for his clothing, even the Gore-Tex jacket Carrie had made him purchase, to be soaked through.

*Carrie.* He needed to get to her. He had to keep going.

He rose slowly to his feet, limbs aching in protest. Silently, he walked back toward the road, keeping to the shadows. In the distance, the station's elevated platforms took form, their lights strung out like pearls against the night. Carrie. He was supposed to meet her at the next station. He needed to follow that track even though it meant leaving the sanctuary of the darkness.

He reached the roadside and began walking, following the concrete ribbon of the track as it twisted its way downtown upon its pillars. The streets still. That at least was something, but he clung to the shadows nonetheless, the dark spaces beyond the reach of orange lamplight.

A few cars sped past throwing up muddy spray. *Let them*, he thought. *The faster they went, the better.* It was the slower ones he worried about. The ones that might be looking for him. Somewhere in the distance, sirens wailed. He didn't turn. Just kept walking, shutting off his mind to the cold and the wet and the fear.

It was twenty minutes before he saw the next station, like a sunken city in the ocean of night, little different from the one he had fled earlier. Identikit stations, he thought, created from the same massive building blocks. At one of its platforms stood a train. He pulled the sodden wool hat down over his forehead and picked up the pace.

His senses heightened: the station bathed in its halo of electric light; the traffic speeding past; the pavement empty ahead of him.

*Something felt wrong.*

He slowed, checking for police – checking for Carrie – but there was nothing. Only the lights of the station drawing him on like a moth to a flame.

A few hundred yards now.

*Carrie would – should – be waiting somewhere close by.*

Sodium light glinted off stationary vehicles: canary-coloured cabs with yellow lights on their roofs, waiting stoically for their next fare. Except no one seemed to be exiting the station to hail them. He looked up at the platforms. The train he had noticed earlier still sat motionless. It must have been several minutes already. Why had it not continued its journey? He peered up at it, hoping to make out the silhouettes of passengers, but there were none.

He stopped.

It might be nothing. Simply a train failure. Or it might –

He didn't have time to finish the thought. From out of the darkness, bodies materialised. Two men, black uniforms, black boots and black weapons; standing close to the station entrance. He should not have stopped. He should have kept walking. It was his hesitation that attracted their attention. His vacillation that betrayed him. One of them noticed him, and then both were looking at him, assessing him, and then they moved, the first halting traffic, then both crossing the street toward him, hands reaching to belts, releasing catches, extracting guns.

A shout from one of them, ordering him to lie down and put his hands on his head. He ignored it, turning and breaking into a run.

They were shouting at him. Telling him to raise his hands. He hazarded a glance over his shoulder. They were getting closer. Hyenas closing in on their prey. Suddenly the roar of an engine drowned their shouts and a car leapt forward, racing toward his and coming to a screeching stop. A door flew open.

'Get in!'

He reacted on instinct, his brain playing no part in it. It was a strange feeling, one which he experienced almost as an onlooker: rising to his feet; diving into the car; the force of momentum closing the door as the vehicle accelerated away.

He should sit up.

'Keep your head down!'

He obeyed.

'You okay?'

He glanced up. Carrie, driving with the raging determination of a djinn, fearlessly and without regard to circumstance. She could simply have left him. She could have crossed the border by herself and tried to find her boy, but she had waited, and then she had rescued him, and in so doing, she had bound her fate to his. They had crossed the Rubicon together.

'Are you all right?'

Well, they had not shot him. That was a good thing, he supposed. Yet mentally? He did not need to burden her with that.

'I am ... fine.' Somewhere sirens wailed. Dopplered tones shifting from base to alto. Flashes of red and blue reflected on the windscreen.

Carrie flung the car round a corner, almost throwing him into her. She turned to him.

'What happened?'

He did not know quite how to answer.

'I think my passport must have tripped some alert somewhere. I was already through immigration by the time they realised.' The vehicle swerved, before Carrie threw it round another corner.

'Shit,' she said. 'Still, you got through. That's the main thing.'

He winced at her words. Yes, *got through*, but by the skin of his teeth and with only the clothes on his back, and only as far as Vancouver, a whole different country from where they needed to be.

And now they knew he was here. They would assume he was some damn fool jihadi. They would hunt him down and hand him over to the Americans who would ship him off to some black site and he would never see Rumina or any of his children again. There was no alternative now. He would find Aliyah, he would show the world that she was not a terrorist. He would prove them all wrong, or he would die in the process.

'I think we lost them.'

He turned and sat up in the seat. His limbs ached as though he had just run for miles; as they had done that night as a boy. He prayed to Allah for the strength to continue.

Outside, the night passed at ninety miles an hour. Highway

signs sped by, pointing south, toward the border. It was not far. Only twenty-some miles, apparently. He had memorised the route, its contours etched in his mind. She had forced him to, insisting in London that he pore over internet maps and satellite shots of the border, convincing him they had a fighting chance.

He was sure now that they did not.

# DAY 5

## *FRIDAY*

## CHAPTER 25

*Sajid*

They drove south-west, to a sleeping town called Abbotsford. Up ahead would be the turn for Huntingdon and then a long straight road toward the border. He had viewed the whole route online, but now, in the midnight hour, the desolation of the place came as a shock. Just black asphalt between dead winter fields and warehouses of industrial grey.

In the distance the arc lights of the border crossing beckoned, threatened, illuminating a gantry and a customs point with trucks lined up along the roadside like a queue of supplicants outside a mosque.

*America.*

So close now. Sajid felt his pulse quicken. He knew the plan, of course, but he was in the hands of this woman, Carrie, who, to be honest, he hardly knew. A fear welled up, inciting panic in his breast. What if this woman was not who she claimed to be? What if she were an American agent, sent to lure him to the US? Was this a trap he had walked straight into? What if even at this very moment she were delivering him to the American authorities?

The checkpoint drew ever closer. He tried to shake the thought from his head, but it was impossible. He could make out figures, now. Armed guards at the border. He looked over. Carrie's hands tight on the wheel, her shoulders shaking slightly. She had hardly spoken a word since rescuing him outside the train station.

'Carrie.'

She didn't answer.

'Carrie!'

At the last moment she swerved left, along a road parallel to the border. The lights of the crossing receded. For several miles she followed it west through farmland, Sajid's relief growing with each minute. Carrie turned off south, and down a road that twisted through the darkness along the edge of a wood which, he knew from the maps, straddled the border.

He had not believed her when she first told him, that so much of the border would be like this: unfenced and unguarded. The idea that people could cross into America at will; how was he to fathom it? The people who were building a wall in Texas, did they not care who came in from Canada? But she had shown him the photographs on Google. Mile after mile of border, marked only by fields and the odd, waist-high wire boundary. It was extraordinary.

Carrie had chosen the spot: a wood, sixty square miles or so, straddling the frontier and tucked in between farmland. She pulled over to the side of the road, tyres on gravel, crunching to a stop.

'Okay, this is it. You know what to do. The border is about a mile away. The trees'll give you better cover than those fields.'

She reached into her pocket and pulled out a small envelope.

'Chip for the phone,' she said. 'Check you can use the map on it. Once across, I'll drop you a pin with my location. Just head for it.'

He took it and fumbled with his phone: inserting the chip; switching it on; checking the map till he was sure it all worked. Then he undid his seat belt and took a breath. The rain lashed the roof of the car.

'How can you be so calm?'

Carrie gave the merest slip of a laugh.

'Calm? I'm fucking terrified, Sajid. But I'm more scared for our kids. We got to get them out of whatever they're mixed up in. So as long as they're out there somewhere, I'm gonna push my own fear as far down into the pit of my stomach as I can and keep going. And you got to do the same. Because we got no choice. Now, sun'll be up in an hour.'

It was his prompt to leave. His prompt to strengthen his resolve here in the darkness. Aliyah. He could not, *would not* lose another child. He had to save her. And then the quiet, pernicious voice in his head sounded once more.

*To save her, or to stop her?*

Carrie's voice broke the spell.

'Sajid. You're gonna be okay.'

'Yes,' he said, and reached for the door.

He set out into the teeth of the rain, climbing over a wire fence that separated slick tarmac from sodden mud, his boots instantly sinking into the morass on the other side, ice and mud and water, soaking his feet. Not so different, he told himself, from those rainy London mornings.

The border was not far. Across a field and a twenty-minute hike through the trees, he estimated. He moved off as the wind whistled a lament: a song, he felt, sung solely for him. Back on the road, the car started. He turned to see its headlights sweep in an arc, the white beams picking him out for a second before continuing their path, throwing him back into darkness. And then the tail lights, casting their crimson glow as Carrie headed back toward the border crossing. Once more the night descended, whatever moonlight there might have been, strangled by storm clouds. He stumbled on, his feet sodden, chilling rapidly to the bone, toward the treeline.

It took longer than expected: ten minutes where he had estimated five. The mud had been the main culprit, clinging to his boots, sucking him down, miring him in its grip; and the rain, now turned to sleet, had hardly helped. The forest, he hoped, would offer a degree of respite: shelter from the elements and firmer ground.

Already his legs felt like lead, yet there could be no let-up. Even now he sensed a change in the heavens, the hues of the sky lightening all too quickly. He kept on, into the thickness of the wood, stumbling blindly at times, against the slash of branches, against the stumble of roots and undergrowth at his feet.

The enormity of his predicament suddenly hit him. On television, he had once seen a man struck by a bull. What had surprised him was the sheer force of the impact, the distance the man had been thrown. And yet it had been the man's choice, his decision to run with the bulls, just as it had been his own decision to come here, to throw in his lot with a desperate stranger, to break laws, to risk his life, to grasp at the thinnest of reeds – the hope that he might find Aliyah before the sands ran out. His courage began to waver. How foolish, how arrogant he was to think that he, *he*, might be able to find her! And even if he did, *then what?* Rumina had been right. He would get caught or he would die out here. He should have listened to her. He was no hero.

But he was a father.

*A final effort*, he told himself, a matter of minutes and he would be across the border and halfway to meeting Carrie on the other side. He raised a hand and wiped water from his eyes, groping his way forward like a blind man until he stumbled into an obstacle he had not expected. The ground rose suddenly before him: a wall of rock. The darkness had rendered it invisible, both from the road and from five feet away.

And then it struck him. The reason why this few hundred hectares of forest, boxed in by fields and farmland, even existed. It was here because the terrain was too mountainous for anything else. He cursed himself. He should have realised it when they'd pored over the images back in London.

After a yawning second of delirium, he simply decided he would need to find another route. He reached for the phone in his pocket. Shielding the screen from the rain, he tapped for a map. The screen changed: a blue dot flashing in the middle of a grey grid. He waited but the image failed to resolve itself.

*No network coverage.*

A shiver coursed back up his spine.

He stumbled backwards and lost his footing. The phone went flying from his grip and he landed heavily on his backside. Pinpricks of light clouded his vision.

Shaking his head clear, he rose to his knees and began groping frantically for the phone. He searched in vain for its telltale glow. He scrabbled through mud and leaves, to left and right, and found nothing. He reached further, fumbling in the dark with fingers stiff as twigs, until finally, just when he thought it was hopeless, he felt something.

Smooth, plastic, its screen face down in the dirt.

How could it have fallen so far? He picked it up, cleaned it with his palm, then jabbed at it with one finger. The thing began to glow. And then he saw it, praise be to Allah. One small bar of coverage.

He unlocked it. The blue dot appeared once more in its grey grid and then slowly images emerged.

He would need to skirt the cliff face. It would take him further east than anticipated; a mile or two at least before the terrain levelled out. From there he could head south once more to the border, to a point several miles further than he had planned and, more importantly, further from the rendezvous point where Carrie would be waiting.

The sky flickered with lightning, as it had done that night long ago in the hill tracts of Chittagong, when he'd run through the monsoon, away from his home and into the arms of the jungle. He'd had no map then, no compass, no plan for where he might go; just the light of a pale moon to orient him and the stamina of youth to sustain him. Then, as now, his fear had been all-consuming. Then, as now, his thoughts were of his family.

It took an hour of groping through the trees before the ground levelled. Every sinew in his body cried out for rest, their entreaties silenced only by the logic of his predicament. The authorities had identified him. They would know that he was heading for the border. They would inform the Americans who would begin their own search for him. Every moment wasted here was a moment more for his pursuers to organise and to close in.

The phone vibrated. A message. He pressed on it. Carrie's pin. Her geolocation on the other side of the border. Further away than he had expected. He pressed on, turning south this time; heading toward the pin; another long slog through wind and rain and the detritus of the forest floor until he reached a point that the phone told him was the frontier. There was nothing on the ground to prove it. No sign or fencepost, no line in the mud; just a fallen tree, its trunk straddling the border like a bridge across an invisible stream.

The sky above was shale grey now, revealing the contours of the land in front of him.

*America.*

Ahead stretched a clearing, a hole in the forest that looked about half a mile deep and the same again wide. Beyond it, more trees and the rendezvous point where Carrie would be waiting. The pin so near now. Tantalisingly close. Less than ten minutes, he felt, if the map and the technology were to be trusted. And yet, there was the clearing to be negotiated. He should have reached here almost an hour ago, when he was still shrouded by the night. Crossing it now meant exposure. He could find a safer option – walk further east – but that would mean more time and more distance. It came down to a straight choice: another hour in the wilderness or a dash across open country. He was already late. How long would Carrie wait before deciding he'd been caught or worse, came out here looking for him?

He had a thought. If Carrie could send a pin, then he could too. Except he could not. He had never done such a thing before and the mastery of new technology did not come naturally to him these days. He tried and failed and in the end, he simply took a screen-shot of his own map, the blue dot marking his position, and sent it to her, hoping she would see he was close.

His limbs ached. He was not sixteen any more. He could not carry on forever. He was forty-nine and all but at the limit of his endurance.

A message flashed on his phone. The icon of a hand with a raised thumb.

It was hope. And it made his decision for him.

*Shorter was better.*

He took a breath, inhaling the scent of damp moss and pine forest, then burst across the open ground. His heart pounded. With every step across the naked terrain, adrenaline and nervous euphoria coursed through him. He could see it now, the treeline and with it safety, drawing closer. Another minute and he would be there. A few minutes more and he would make the rendezvous.

He didn't even hear the gunshot over the sound of his own breath.

# CHAPTER 26

*Greg*

Aliyah was sleeping, his jacket draped over her. Dawn was knocking on the horizon now and in the half-light he saw on her face the tracks of tears – salt-stained channels – like he remembered on his mom's face once his father finally gave his fists a rest and staggered up to bed.

The car was arctic, the windshield silvered with frost, the metal of the doorsills burning ice cold to the touch. A shiver passed through him; an electric, uncontrollable tingling. He folded his arms, tucking his hands into his armpits and felt the warmth slowly thaw his fingers. His knee growled, the muscles cramping in protest at the cold and the memory of the agony he'd heaped upon it during their flight from the White House.

He'd no clue of where they were exactly: stopped halfway up a dirt road somewhere among the pine and enveloped by forest. He'd driven hastily, erratically, lefts and rights at random, whatever had felt correct, whatever had felt like it was taking them further away from Yusuf and Jack and Miriam and the White House. And all the while he'd had to deal with Aliyah.

She'd screamed at him. '*Greg! This isn't right! We need to go back.*' And he'd told her, '*We go back now and we're both dead.*'

He was sure about that. Certain as the sunrise.

Still she hadn't believed him. Accused him of lying.

Jesus, the irony in that. He had rescued her, saved her from those who would kill her, and *he* was the liar? He had looked her in the eye – there would be no more of that lowering your gaze bullshit – and he had told her everything. But in her arrogance, she couldn't see the truth for what it was. That was the thing about folks like her: so smart they often failed to see what was obvious. Always looking for a complicated answer when the truth was staring them in the face.

She didn't believe him and it hurt.

In the end he'd pulled over, pulled out his phone and shown her: the pictures of the flames and the smoke and the dead and the dying. And then he had shown her the photo of Yasmin and watched her world collapse.

He had looked on as she buckled, crushed under the weight of evidence. It made him feel bad thinking about it. He told himself he hadn't wanted to do it, but what choice did he have?

If he was being honest, though, a part of him felt, not good exactly, but vindicated – satisfied at having punctured her illusions about Miriam. And yet, any such satisfaction was swamped by the weight of his own guilt.

She'd come round eventually, slowly at first, with silent sobs and flying fists and limpid tears, and then, as grief and exhaustion grew, a gradual, fatalistic acceptance of the truth: that Miriam, the lodestar by which she'd set the compass of her life, had lied to her.

She'd sat there in silence after, just staring out at the night as he drove. Eventually, she'd spoken.

'Why can't we just disappear?' she'd asked. 'Why can't we just drive somewhere and disappear. There must be somewhere you know well. Some part of the country far from here where we can hide, at least till we can figure things out?'

He could have laughed at her naivety.

She knew he was from Florida. It was on the other side of the country.

'They've already identified Yasmin. How long d'you think it'll take them to work out that she arrived here with you? And then what? The best thing to do is to give yourself up. Hand yourself in to the police and tell them what happened.'

She'd stared at him as though he were crazy.

'I'm not doing that.'

The girl was as stubborn as his own mother.

'Why the fuck not? You tell them you had nothing to do with LA. Tell them you were taken in by a cult. That they kept you locked in a house in the woods; that they tried to brainwash you. The sooner you do it, the more chance the Feds'll believe you.'

'I just can't.'

He stared at her. Why couldn't she understand? Why couldn't she see that it was all a set-up?

'Whatever Miriam told you is a lie, Aliyah. There is no happy ending here. Our purpose was just to die, along with many others.'

'You don't think I'm prepared to die?'

She didn't understand. What did she know about death? Had she ever faced it? Had she seen it up close? Witnessed it on the face of friends . . . of family? Course she hadn't. She was just some stupid girl brainwashed by Miriam into thinking she was gonna change the world. But he couldn't tell her that. Not in her current state.

'Fine,' he said. 'You're prepared to die. But don't die for Miriam's sake.'

The sky was lightening now. He pulled out his phone and touched it into life. The battery was dying. Might last an hour or so.

With a few taps he pulled up CNN in search of any update on the bombing. He read the lead headline: oversized red letters above a picture of a snarling Chuck Costa pumping his fist at the faithful at one of his rallies.

## COSTA CALLS FOR REINSTATEMENT OF MUSLIM BAN

He gave a bitter laugh. Three months ago he'd have had no problem with that. Hell, he'd have cheered the man on to the goal line. Funny how things changed.

Actual news of the bombing had been relegated to the third item on the home page. He read it but it told him little he didn't already know. Tucked in between was a piece on the presidential campaigns: of Costa rallying in Cincinnati and Greenwood stumping in Cleveland. The polls were tightening; within the margin of error. Miriam would be pleased.

He thought of Rehana, the girl he'd left behind. He thought of the bombs in the trunk. That at least was something. It would take time and expertise to make new ones. Long enough maybe that it might be too late to use them before the election. Long enough maybe to save Rehana's life.

The sun was coming up, its reddish hues melting into an indigo sky. Time to move on.

He started the car, its rumble jolting Aliyah awake. For a moment her face recaptured the terror of the previous night and he feared he might have to go through the process of explaining it all to her again.

He gave her a gentle smile. Just looking into her eyes felt fresh and new and invigorating.

'Where are we?' she asked.

'I don't know. Maybe twenty or thirty miles from Ripplebrook?'

He passed her his phone and asked her to check the map – a sign they were in this together. She showed him the screen: they were only seven miles from Ripplebrook. Somewhere to the east, toward Kinzel Lake. A lot closer than he'd hoped.

'What now?' she asked, though she must have known the answer. He'd told her last night. The only question was where to do it.

The road beneath them blistered and crackled as he reversed the car and headed back down the slope toward the blacktop.

'Portland,' he said. 'We head to Portland.'

The road snaked between walls of pine. Sometimes the trees and the mist would break and beneath him he'd see a patchwork land-scape: the arboreal green scarred by slashes of brown and swathes of black – death from parasitic blight or summer wildfire.

Aliyah hardly said a word. He wondered what she might be thinking but didn't ask, fearful of where the question might lead. She was smart, too smart for him. Better to let her work out what she needed to and come to terms with it all.

In the meantime he kept one eye on the road and the other on the mirror, fearful that at any moment he might spy Yusuf's old blue pickup, or worse, another, faster vehicle driven by Jack or maybe someone else working for Miriam. Who knew how big her network was? There were the ones he never saw: the ones who supplied the explosives and the bomb components; and the ones he caught the occasional glimpse of, like the guy who'd dropped off the vehicle that Jack and Yasmin had driven to LA. Who knew how many people might be out there right now, looking for them?

The land changed, pine yielding to pasture and then to signs of habitation and the traffic that went with it. He knew this place, had driven this road before. Estacada would be up ahead. Estacada with its police station. It gave him an idea.

He pulled off their route and navigated frozen streets, where ads for tractor parts and realtors competed for attention with posters for the man who now wanted to ban Muslims from the country.

Aliyah looked up.

'I thought we were going to Portland?'

'Change of plan,' he said. 'This is closer.'

He felt her stiffen. Maybe she'd expected a little more time to get used to the idea of talking to the police. But she hadn't committed any crime yet; the sooner she handed herself in to the authorities, the safer she'd be.

As for his own position, well, that was more complicated. Yasmin, those innocent folks at the mall, they were on his conscience. He deserved to go to hell, and sooner or later he probably would. Maybe saving Aliyah would go some way to balancing the books – a credit against the many, many debits. What was it the Bible said? It was never too late to start atoning for one's sins. In time he would hand himself in. Right now though, he needed to think it through.

Estacada, he told himself, was a better bet than Portland. There'd be fewer security cameras. He could pretty much leave Aliyah in front of the police house, be out of town in minutes and just disappear.

*Leaving Aliyah.*

Something in his soul fought against that. Maybe it was just fear of being alone again.

*

He parked up a few blocks north of the police station, outside a boarded-up burger joint called Brady's. He killed the engine and for a moment they both sat in silence, looking out the windshield at the restaurant's faded signage offering lunchtime discounts and Sunday meal deals to a clientele, he guessed, that never came back after lockdown.

'You ready?' he asked.

She looked up at him and he felt the power of her eyes.

'I don't want to do this, Greg.'

He reached out for her hand, surprised once more by the slenderness of her fingers.

'It's the safest way. The only way.'

She leaned in toward him and he inhaled the scent of her hair and her skin and felt the touch of her lips upon his cheek. It was over in an instant, though the feeling would linger in his memory.

He got out and surveyed the street: the mom-and-pop stores; the dispensary and the church; the bar and the 7-Eleven; and everywhere the Stars and Stripes on their flagpoles, hanging limp above locked doorways.

*No sign of trouble.*

No sign of Jack or Yusuf or anyone else paying them the slightest attention.

He signalled to Aliyah and she joined him on the sidewalk. He gestured south toward the highway.

'Station's that way. 'Bout five or six blocks down. Remember what I told you. Walk fast and keep your head down till you get inside. Ask to speak to the sheriff or whoever's in charge.'

The rest he didn't reiterate. She knew the fiction by heart: her solo escape; running, hiding, then hitching a ride into town from a stranger. By the time they looked into it, he'd be long gone.

She took his hand.

'Come with me, Greg.'

It was stupid. He knew that. He should have gotten right back in the damn car and put as many miles between him and Estacada right there and then. But he didn't. He held on to her hand like he was drowning and she was the lifebelt and said, '*One block,*' which became two.

The streets seemed to get busier the closer they got. A row of black SUVs sat parked up along the kerb like armoured Rottweilers. Men and women dressed in city clothes milled around the intersections. Aliyah squeezed his hand tighter.

His heart thumped in his chest. At least these weren't Miriam's people. These were government people: FBI or ATF or a half-dozen other acronymed federal agencies. They must've worked out that Yasmin had been up here. Were they already looking for Ripplebrook?

*Shit.*

Suddenly coming to Estacada felt like a mistake. He needed to get out of there.

He stopped on the corner and turned to her. He wanted so much to hold her, to tell her what he felt and how hard this was, but there was no time and no words.

'You need to go on by yourself.'

She looked up at him and it felt as though her gaze might knock him off his feet.

'What about you?'

'It's not your problem,' he said, and she only stared intently. 'I'll be okay.'

And then she was turning from him and walking away. He had to get back to the car. Every moment he hesitated was a moment Miriam or the Feds got closer; and yet for the longest minute, he stood there, rooted, listening to the sound of nothing, nothing in his head, and watching her walk off and out of his life.

It was then, out of the corner of his eye, that he saw them. He turned to get a better look. A bunch of figures, official-looking, going door-to-door and heading toward him; maybe two hundred yards away. He needed to get the fuck out.

He took one last glance at Aliyah.

Something was wrong.

She was across the street now, half a block ahead. But she was turning, crossing the street, heading the wrong way.

*The hell was she doing?*

He stifled the impulse to call after her, to shout her name; nothing was more guaranteed to attract attention.

*Shit!*

He lurched forward, moving as fast as he could, the pain stabbing through his bad knee with every step. He dodged a truck and made the far sidewalk. Aliyah was less than a hundred yards away. He kept going, closing the distance. She stopped at a kerb, looking for traffic, then stepped out onto the road.

Fifty yards . . . forty.

Sweat broke out on his back. He looked over his shoulder and checked for any sign of pursuit. The road behind him was still clear. Thirty yards, twenty. He reached the crossing, stepped out only to hear the blare of a horn. An SUV, black like a missile, shot past him.

He hobbled across the road. Aliyah was so close now; individual strands of her hair visible, blowing in the wind. Fifteen yards . . . ten . . . five.

'Aliyah!'

He reached out and grabbed her arm.

She turned in shock, and twisted her arm, fighting to break free. He held on; felt her other hand, pulling at his collar, tearing at his shirt.

'Aliyah, it's me.'

She stopped struggling.

'Aliyah, where are you going? I thought we'd agreed?'

And then she was screaming something, trying to pull away from him again. He didn't understand.

'Aliyah,' he said. 'It's me. Greg.'

But she wasn't looking at his face. She was looking at his neck. At the crude blue swastika wrapped in its nest of barbed wire.

Instinctively he loosened his grip. He pulled at his shirt, covering the traitorous markings, the branding of a previous life.

She stepped back, away from him, shaking her head.

'You're a fucking Nazi? A bloody fucking Nazi?'

It was all happening too fast.

'It's not like that,' he told her. 'But we need to go now. It's not safe.'

But she wasn't listening. Instead she turned and ran, flying across the road in the face of a pickup truck and down a side street.

He needed to follow her. He needed to explain. He hobbled after her, stopping an oncoming car with his hand. As he reached the side street he heard a commotion and looked back. Federal agents were running toward him. He bolted, ducking into the alley, closing his mind to the pain. He had to lead them away. The car was three blocks back. If he was lucky, if there were a couple more alleyways, he might be able to double back and reach it before they caught up with him.

He took a left, down another side street and kept running. His lungs burned. He couldn't shut out the pain in his knee for much longer. With every step the pressure increased. If he didn't stop, it would buckle under him. He had visions of the joint, the bones and cartilage and metal all giving way, collapsing, cutting through the skin. He had to stop.

He spotted a doorway up ahead, the graffitied back entrance to a derelict shop. The paint was peeling and the wood looked rotten.

Beside it, a low window now boarded with plywood. Whoever had done it hadn't cared much for the job; one corner of the wood was loose. He pushed and it gave way easier than he'd expected. He guessed he wasn't the first to have sought access: thieves possibly; junkies more likely.

He bent it open, slipped through, then pushed the wood shut behind him, his heart pounding as he fought for air. From outside came the sound of boots on rubble; the baritone growl of voices. He screwed his eyes shut.

# CHAPTER 27

*Shreya*

It had only been for a second. An apparition out the corner of her eye. A girl, running from a guy. A flash of dark hair. A glimpse of brown skin. And then she was gone.

Shreya was already turning, running.

'Agent Mistry! Where you going?'

Kramer's voice, shouting behind her. Shreya kept moving, drawing her gun.

'It's her.'

A moment more and Kramer was at her shoulder.

'Where?'

'A couple of blocks that way.'

She pointed at nothing. An empty intersection. No sign of the girl, or the guy.

'You sure?'

She didn't answer, just kept running, making for the spot where the couple had stood, her breath teetering on the edge of ragged. The first rasps of asthma playing in her throat. She scanned the area.

*Deserted.*

She tried to work out what had happened.

*The girl was trying to get away from the guy.*

*Why?*

*Why was she running?*

The same question she'd asked about Yasmin.

Kramer was beside her once more.

'There's no one here.'

'*She* was here.'

'You see where she went?'

She tried to think like an eighteen-year-old girl: lost, frightened, running. She looked around. *There.* An alley off Main Street.

'That way.'

She set off, sprinting for it, the breath now rattling, closing the distance to the mouth of the alley and then reaching out to a wall for support. Her lungs burned. Kramer pulled up a moment later; she hadn't even broken sweat.

The alley was empty, a wasteland of garbage bins and broken bottles . . . and back doors.

A couple more agents drew up.

'Try the doors.'

They ran past her, heading for different entrances: checking padlocks; pushing against wood and glass and metal; searching for anything that wasn't battened down tight.

She got her breath back and headed for the next door.

'*This one's secure.*'

Kramer's voice, finding its echo from the others.

'*This one too.*'

Shreya tried another, then another. Locked doors; bolted windows. They couldn't have just disappeared.

She turned to Kramer.

'Search every building that backs onto this alley.'

'Don't we need clearance for that?'

She shook her head.

'There's no time. We've got to do it now.'

Kramer stared at her. Shreya found it hard to decipher the look, but it made her uncomfortable, like there were ants crawling down her collar.

'We can make a start, Shreya, but there's only four of us. We're gonna need more manpower.'

She was right. Shreya took out her phone and called.

'Yeah?'

'Dan. It's Shreya. We might have spotted Aliyah Khan.'

'Where?'

'Off Main Street. A few blocks north of the town hall. She was with someone – male, early to mid-twenties. We lost 'em in an alley. I'm with Kramer and two others. We need to search the houses backing onto it.'

She waited, cracking her knuckles as Dan thought it over.

'You sure it was her?'

The sighting had been too brief, from too far; the girl could have been Hispanic just as easily as South Asian. And what had she seen? A girl and a guy talking – *arguing?* – in the street. They could have been anyone – siblings, friends, lovers.

Shreya blinked.

'I'm sure.'

The lie was easier when she didn't have to look at him.

# CHAPTER 28

*Greg*

The sounds grew: louder, closer, till he felt they would fall on top of him. His head crowded with black thoughts. They would see the broken pane and they would know he was inside. They would break in and throw him to the floor. They would twist his arms behind his back and cuff him. They would stomp on his knee. They would break his leg. They would drag him out of there and to a cell or maybe a basement somewhere and they would torture him and wring him out like a sponge. He pressed his whole body against the plywood that covered the window he'd accessed and steeled himself. From the other side came a tap, and then a greater, more forceful pressure. The wood budged and he pushed back. He winced against the pain. Another, stronger push from that side and his leg would give way. He braced himself. Whoever was out there was bound to push again.

But they didn't.

Instead he heard a voice, muffled through the wood.

'This one's secure.'

He closed his eyes, slid down a wall and gave thanks for his deliverance. And then he waited, eternal seconds as the voices outside faded and the hammering of his heart stilled. Around him, the decaying husk of what had once been the back room of a store, now reduced to a rancid rathole of flattened cardboard, discarded syringes and charred foil. He'd been there himself; half expected to find a junkie or two lying on the floor somewhere.

His knee spasmed. Even as the stab of pain passed, the panic started. He had to get out of there; had to find Aliyah. *His knee though.* He pressed down on it with his fingers and winced.

Slowly, he placed his weight on his good leg and pushed himself up, back against the wall for balance. He tried putting a little weight on the bad knee and gritted his teeth against the pain.

He surveyed the room and eventually he saw it. An old broom, its bristles black with dirt. He hobbled over and grabbed it. From his belt he retrieved his remaining knife and quickly filed down the bristles till the brush-head was just a stump. He placed the thing under his arm and tried walking. Not perfect, but it would do.

He made his way back to the boarded window. Slowly, carefully, he shifted the plywood curtain: first an inch, then some more. He peered out then quickly brought his head back in.

*Shit.*

They were standing there. Four of them, at the end of the alley, two of them with their backs to him, one on the phone, the fourth checking a doorway.

His heart raced.

He took out his phone, switched on the camera and stuck the top of it out the gap to one side of the plywood. The image stabilised.

The four figures, silhouetted against the light, still standing where he'd spotted them. He let out a breath.

They must have stood there for some time before the one on the phone ended the call.

*South Asian*, he thought. *Like Aliyah.*

He watched as they turned the corner and disappeared from sight. Every second he waited was torture. He needed to find Aliyah.

Two minutes was all he managed. Two minutes and a few seconds. Once more he used his phone to check the surroundings. The alley outside was empty now. He squeezed through the gap and started walking back the way he'd come.

The street was busier now. Mainly locals, he figured, going about their business. He thought about ditching the crutch, conscious of the attention it might attract, but in his present condition that was a non-starter. Aliyah could be anywhere by now. He had to keep going. If he was to find her, he needed to get back to the car and start searching.

He pulled his hoodie tight over his head and set off, hugging the shadows. In the distance, a patrol car appeared, rolling slowly down the street toward him. He thought of turning round, of finding cover in a shop or an alley, but that would only draw their attention.

The car drew closer, stopping at the red light of an intersection. He could see the figures inside now; he could make out the moustache of the cop in the passenger seat. The guy stared back at him and Greg dropped his gaze to the sidewalk.

*Shit.*

The lights changed and the patrol car growled. He didn't risk a glance, just held his breath and kept walking. A man was coming toward him. An old guy, wrapped up against the cold in a scarf and a fur-lined hat with the flaps pulled down over his ears.

Greg stretched out his free arm, beamed a smile and greeted him like a long-lost nephew.

'Hey! How long's it been?'

The old guy looked at him, smiling, trying to place his face. He mumbled something and Greg laughed like it was a joke between buddies.

The patrol car trundled past, the cop in the passenger seat with his eyes trained on him.

'And the family?' Greg asked.

The old guy stammered something non-commital.

The cop car kept going, picking up speed and heading away. He gave the old guy a smile and a pat on the arm.

'Well, it's good to see you.' He smiled. 'I guess I should get going. Say hi to everyone.'

He didn't wait for a response, just started walking, leaving the old guy floundering in his wake.

The car was where he'd left it, untroubled by interest from the police or anyone else. That at least was something. He got in, stowed his makeshift crutch on the back seat, started the engine and reversed out of the bay.

He cruised the streets, hoping against hope that he might spot her. He guessed the chances were slim. She was confused, scared, on foot and with nowhere to go. He just hoped he'd convinced her that heading back to Miriam and Ripplebrook would be a death sentence.

He cursed himself. He should have told her about the tattoo, about the depression and the PTSD and the anger; about falling in with the wrong sort of folks and prison. He should have told her all of it. He told himself that he'd never had the chance, but that was a lie. He hadn't even tried. He hadn't because of his own shame. And how much shame did he feel now?

He took a left onto a quieter road, then another so that he was running parallel with Main Street. A block or two up he spotted something. He stopped dead, the blood in his veins turning cold.

Yusuf's blue pickup, parked by the entrance to a backstreet. There was no mistaking it. He knew pretty much every dent and rusted scrape on that damn thing. He drove past slowly. The cab was empty.

*Fuck.*

The voice in his head counselled he cut his losses. Forget about Aliyah and just get the hell away. He'd done his best. He'd gotten her out of there. He should worry about himself now. He had a car and a head start. He could be a hundred miles away before they started looking for him.

He turned the corner and pressed down on the gas.

And then he spotted them.

Two blocks away. Coming toward him. Aliyah. With Yusuf at her back.

# CHAPTER 29

*Sajid*

The bullet had not missed by much. A few inches? A foot? Splintering the bark of the nearest tree to shrapnel. Sajid threw himself to the ground.

Another shot. This one echoing across the forest. Shouts carried on the wind.

'*Armed Border Patrol officers! Do not move.*'

It was probably good advice, he thought as he rose to his feet.

And ran.

Running was what men like him did. It was the only course of action the powerless had in the face of the strong. *Running*, from their homes, their villages, their countries, not because they were weak or lazy or cowardly but because the only alternative was to give up, to surrender and die.

And so he ran, reaching the treeline, disappearing into the gloom beyond. He ran, as branches lashed his sides and thorns lacerated his hands. He ran, blindly, until suddenly the ground beneath him fell away and he was hurtling out of control down a slope. His foot caught on something and he fell head first, momentum carrying him on, over and down and over again, his eyes struggling with the frenzied, dizzying tableau of blurred images, his nails, his fingers, scrabbling in the mud for purchase, until – *wham* – a blinding crack, and everything stopped.

For a moment there was nothing: no sound or light or cold or pain, and then, like a wave breaking, the world crashed back down upon him. He lay there, fighting for breath, his body doubled around a tree stump. Somewhere dogs were barking; men were shouting. Above him, at the top of the slope. *They had seen him.* He had to get up. He had to run.

His ankle burned. His ears rang from the sound of another gunshot. He needed to head west. *Keep the light behind him. Run into the darkness.* Were the trees starting to thin? Was this the forest edge or just another clearing? Oh God, had he simply doubled back on himself? He prayed that Carrie's pin was accurate; that she might be nearby. He would not last two minutes in open ground. They would catch him. Their dogs would maul him. Or they would shoot him in the back.

*The forest was safer than open country.*

With a cry of anguish he turned, arcing round to what should have been south. He kept running, racing for his life, flying past skeletal trees as the pain in his ankle seared and his chest burned.

Voices in his head mingled with the shouts of his pursuers and the barking of dogs. Rumina, Aliyah, Carrie.

*Carrie.*

*Her voice.*

Except it wasn't in his head. It was somewhere out there, in front of him. The voice called again. And this time it called his name.

He stumbled forward.

'*Sajid!*'

He saw her blonde hair coming toward him. He pushed himself on. Toward her.

'Sajid!'

He barely had strength to speak.

She grabbed him by the hand and pulled him forward. Behind them, the bark of dogs, clearer now. They kept on, past the trees and into the light and then they were clear, out in the pelting rain, running down a grass bank toward the blue Ford.

One of the dogs was closing.

'Get in.'

Numb fingers, slick with rain, fumbled with the handle. Finally the door opened and he collapsed inside, closing it just as the animal reached it, jumping up, clawing the window. Carrie was already in the driver's seat, turning the key in the ignition. Behind them, uniformed men at the tree-line, racing toward the road. The dog barked as though wild. Time was running out.

And then he felt the blessed force of momentum. The men receded, too far away, he hoped, to have got any good look at the car.

It was only a minute later, as his heart stilled, that he saw the blood.


'Carrie. You're bleeding.'

On the sleeve of her right arm, a growing, blossoming flower of crimson.

She did not even take her eyes off the road.

'I'm okay.'

'You need to stop. You need to let me see to your arm.'

She turned and gave him a look. Already her face seemed grey.

'What? You're a doctor now?'

'I was,' he told her, 'at least I was training to be.'

She gave him another glance, as though she were reappraising him. He checked the side mirror. No cars, no flashing lights; no sign of pursuit.

'Carrie, you must stop the car and let me tend to your wound.'

To his surprise, she pulled off the road and drove down a dirt path until they were screened by trees. The car jolted to a halt.

'I'm fine.'

'Let me be the judge of that.'

She looked at him as though he were wasting her time.

'Okay. Do what you need to do.'

There was no time for niceties.

'Unbutton your shirt.'

She did as he commanded and gently he lowered it off her right shoulder.

The flesh around the tricep was lacerated, weeping blood. He needed to see what he was dealing with.

'Pass me the water bottle.'

He unscrewed the lid, first washing the mud from his own hands then gently pouring the liquid over her arm.

Rivulets of blood and water flowed, revealing splinters of bark. No bullet wound. Just shrapnel. Small mercies.

'How bad is it, doc? Will I live?'

He did not care much for the witticism, but he understood her need for it.

'That depends,' he said.

'On what?'

'On exactly how much of my medical training I can remember.'

Gently he pulled at the fragments with his fingers, one by one dislodging them from her flesh, letting the bloody slivers fall to the earth. It would have been simpler and safer with tweezers but for now he had none. The final, smallest fragments were the problem. His hands, once so steady, these days seemed possessed of a constant tremor; his fingers, once so nimble, were now blunt, clumsy tools. Carrie winced as he tried to fish them out.

'Jeez, Sajid. Are you trying to kill me?'

'Not on purpose.'

Eventually he was satisfied he had extracted them all. Once more he washed her arm with the water, then taking a clean shirt from her bag in the boot, he ripped off a length of fabric and wound it round her arm as a bandage.

He took over at the wheel, slowly at first, adjusting to driving on what undoubtedly was the wrong side of the road then speeding up, but still driving carefully, avoiding any unnecessary jolts that might hurt her. As the first buildings passed, she stirred.

'Where are we?'

'Sumas,' he said. 'I need to find a chemist. A drugstore.'

'There'll be police here, Sajid.'

'There will be police everywhere,' he told her.

'You're soaked through and covered in dirt. You get out of the car looking like that and we won't get another mile before we're caught.'

She was right. And so he drove on, through Sumas, with its chemist and petrol station and a dozen Main Street convenience stores and then headed south again, through a land of low cloud and tall forest.

\*

'Make for Seattle,' she said, and he obeyed. A vast commercial shopping mall on its outskirts. She made him stop in the parking lot of an aircraft hangar-sized store, where she left him temporarily and went to buy food and the medication and bandages he'd stipulated and the clothes she said he needed.

As he waited in the stillness of the car, he had time to think. He was a wanted man. A fugitive, just like Aliyah. He imagined that even now, urgent, panicked messages were traversing the Atlantic. The police in London would be raiding their flat, looking for him, looking for Rumina and Tariq. Well, they were with friends. Safe, at least for now. Rumina. He missed her. He desperately wanted to call her, but that was out of the question. He did not know what these Americans were capable of, but if the conspiracy theorists at the mosque were to be believed, they recorded all telephone conversations everywhere. They had computers which could identify you by your voice patterns. They could find you within minutes. He had never believed it, of course, otherwise it would not have taken them a decade to track down that idiot, that destroyer of worlds, bin Laden; still, he wouldn't take the risk.

Carrie returned bearing gifts held in paper bags: sandwiches – '*Not halal*,' she apologised, as though that mattered now – and a thick sludge of a soup that smelled of nothing.

'Did you get the iodine and the antibiotics?'

She gestured to another bag.

'It's all in there.'

He took it from her and set to work, first removing her tourniquet, wiping clean the wound with the iodine, then applying Neosporin and the bandage.

'There. Good as new.'

She reached for a third bag, extracting blue jeans and white vest, a button-down shirt and a zip-up jumper, then socks, and what she called *pants* and *sneakers*. For him. All for him. So that he might change out of his mud-soaked rags.

It was shameful.

'How much did you spend?'

'Doesn't matter. You can pay me back after we find the kids.'

And yet, even as he changed, and she turned her back to afford him at least a modicum of privacy, his disgrace felt compounded. She acted as though it were nothing, as though he, a virtual stranger, undressing in front of her, putting on clothes which she had bought him were no matter at all. How would he explain the mores of his culture? How to explain that enormous, amorphous concept, *izzat*: honour, reputation, prestige – those things that his people clung to even when they had lost everything else?

And yet, who was he to talk of honour? He who had been unable to protect not one, but two of his daughters? He who had smuggled himself into America like a thief in the night? When it came to *izzat*, his had already been forsaken.

He disposed of his rags in a dumpster and then they were on the road again, heading south along an endless highway, through wilderness empty of life and colour.

With every mile he felt himself closer to Aliyah, and yet the land was vast. Even this journey from the border down to Ripplebrook was akin to traversing the entire length of England. And when they reached Ripplebrook, what if they could not find Aliyah and Greg? What if they were no longer there? What then? For now, though, it was enough that they were still free, still in the hunt. Still in with a chance of finding their children.

# CHAPTER 30

*Shreya*

'Three hours, Shreya. Three hours of roadblocks and door-to-door and you found sweet nothing.'

Dan's face was puce, the colour statistically favoured by white men flirting with a heart attack. It was to be expected, she guessed, the stress he was under.

'And now this!' He gestured to a bank of TV screens tuned to the news channels. Another statement from the Sons of the Caliphate in capitalised chyrons running across the screens like it was Times Square. A new demand: the immediate closure of all US bases in Arab lands – Kuwait, Saudi, Oman, Bahrain, the UAE, Iraq, everywhere.

Demands that would never be met, certainly not now they'd been made public. Almost ninety-six hours since LA. The clock was running down on another attack. More bombs, more dead Americans, and the election just four days away.

They needed to find Aliyah. They needed to crack this, and she'd just wasted three hours of time and resources chasing ghosts in the streets of Estacada.

'Dan,' she said, 'we *need* to move the locus of the search to south of Estacada.'

He sighed. 'No, Shreya. Not again. We've been through this.'

'You have to trust me on this.'

He looked at her as though she were crazy.

'After the last three hours? Do you understand at all who you work for?'

There was no point arguing. It was better just to show him again. Maybe this time the message might get through.

From a desk she picked up a marker. She walked over to the map of Estacada on the wall, a couple of locations already ringed in black. She sought out Unity Gas and circled it. From there she traced out the paths of the 211 and the 224 and pointed to the area around the two roads: sparse country, forests, farms and a few hamlets.

'*This* is where they are, Dan. Somewhere between Sweetwater on the 211 and Detroit Lake on 224. Gas stations are the key. Ghani's filling up in Estacada because it's the closest filling station to wherever it is he's based. And he's filling up at Unity Gas because it's the cheapest.'

Dan rubbed at his forehead.

'You got one sighting at a gas station, Shreya.'

'Not *one* sighting. Several. A pattern; itself part of a larger pattern of behaviour.'

'I told you, it's not enough.'

She felt her blood rising. She was right about this. He needed to trust her. She wanted to argue. She wanted to stick his big face right in the map until he got it. But the former was too difficult – the words were drying up in her throat – and the latter would be counterproductive even if it were possible. He wasn't going to listen to her. But maybe he'd listen to someone else. What was it Kramer had said? *Men tend to listen to me.* It was a long shot, but in the absence of any better options . . .

'Ask Agent Kramer.'

Dan shifted his gaze. 'Well?'

Kramer squirmed, looked at Dan's face, Shreya's, then back at Dan's.

'Agent Mistry was right about the gas station. Maybe she's right about this?'

Dan waved his hand at the map. 'So you also think we should focus on this area south of town?'

Kramer puffed out her cheeks. 'It's a large area. Almost a hundred square miles. Diverting all our manpower, it'll still take days to comb the entire area. We should get started.'

Dan shook his head. 'Word of advice. If you want a long and successful career in the FBI, don't hitch your wagon to Agent Mistry. All of our sightings of Ghani at the bank; at the gas station; even this supposed one of Aliyah Khan today; all have been within Estacada, and you'd *both* like me to just forget that and move the locus of the search to a hundred square miles of forest?'

Shreya knew she should keep quiet, just let Dan blow himself out. But that was never going to happen.

'You're being an ass, Dan! Course they're more likely to be in the forest. Dammit, how many terrorists set up a base of operations in the middle of a town?'

The room around her stopped: agents, police, civilians – all suddenly staring at her. She felt the sweat break out on her neck. Dan loosened the knot of his tie.

'You're supposed to be in San Diego by Monday. I want you there by tonight.'

She took a step back.

'You're not serious?'

'Deadly.'

She couldn't quite believe it.

'But you need me on this, Dan. You need me up here.'

He turned from the map and headed back to his desk.

'No, Shreya, I don't. And in the hours you have left up here, you'll do as you're told.'

She trailed Kramer out to the parking lot in silence, the cold hitting her like an insult. Kramer stopped halfway, lit a cigarette and took a drag.

'You okay?'

She wasn't, and for want of a better target, she unloaded on Kramer.

'Did you have to tell him that the search area would be a hundred square miles?'

Kramer took a step back.

'It ain't much smaller. I did my best, Agent Mistry, but you just dropped me in the shit. Now I'm fine backing you up with your boss, you know, but when he asks my opinion, I'm gonna tell him the truth, and the truth is we might spend weeks chasing shadows in the forests round the 211 and 224, and we don't have that sort of time.'

'So what now?' Shreya asked. 'You happy just going door-to-door round Estacada?'

'You telling me I got a choice?'

'No,' she sighed, 'but it's pointless.'

'So what do you suggest, Agent Mistry?'

Shreya felt her anger subsiding.

'I think you know,' she said. 'If it makes you feel better, think of it as my last request.'

# CHAPTER 31

*Shreya*

The next flight to LA left in just over three hours.

Kramer stubbed out the cigarette.

'Let's try the 211. It's shorter. We can check out the length of it and be back before anyone gets too suspicious. Two hours, tops.'

Two hours. Two precious hours to find Ghani or something else that might offer her a stay of execution.

She googled a map of the route, tracing its path through Sweetwater, Elwood, Colton and Cedardale, all the way down to Molalla. But once past Sweetwater, there were quicker and shorter routes to Portland than coming through Estacada. She put herself in Ghani's head. He was the sort of man, probably, who took the shortest route between two points because he had neither the time nor the cash to take the scenic route. If he was living near the 211, it wouldn't be somewhere much further south than Sweetwater. What she needed was a better view of that particular place. She clicked on Street

View. The main roads lit up in fluorescent blue like strands of a spider's web, but the roads through Sweetwater remained stubbornly grey, the place not important enough to merit a drive through by Google's cameras.

She switched to the satellite view and zoomed in. There was precious little to identify – a dozen houses, a general store, a church – Presbyterian – not much else. What she was looking for was a store, somewhere Ghani might have stopped to buy food and water and life's essentials. Frame by frame, she searched for one on the roads around town, and then she saw it. A small shack of a general store.

She clicked on it and a list of photos appeared: a white clapboard building with a Bud Light sign in the window and Ole Glory above the door. The image was close-cropped. No hint of what lay either side of the shopfront, but it was enough. She pictured Ghani again, stopping at the store, picking up provisions. If he was living somewhere off the 211, he'd have gone in there.

She turned to Kramer.

'Sweetwater.'

Kramer started the car and floored it, Estacada soon just a blur in the rear-view, the blacktop twisting snake-like through sodden pine forest. Shreya tried to picture Ghani travelling this road; tried to see what he saw. Finally, *finally*, she felt they were on the right track. Someone down in Sweetwater would know Ghani, she was sure of it. Someone would know where he lived and who was with him.

Thirty minutes till the front yards of Sweetwater appeared, with the general store a few minutes further on, brooding by the roadside as rainwater sluiced off its tin roof, the Bud Light sign unlit in the window and the flag above the door twisted round its pole like a rag on a stick.

Kramer pulled into the dirt lot out front and killed the engine. Shreya opened her door, made to get out and stopped.

'You coming?'

'Thought I'd make sure no one's looking for us,' Kramer replied, reaching for her phone. 'Unless you want me in there?'

Shreya stepped out into the mud. She headed for the steps to the door, crossing the threshold to the sound of an electronic buzzer. She made for the counter, past shelves of provisions and fishing tackle and hunting gear.

A man appeared from a back room. Big guy, in his fifties she thought, gone to seed and with the sort of hard, weathered face she'd come to expect.

'Help you?'

His tone suggested he wouldn't care either way.

She pulled out her ID and the picture of Ghani; held the former up for him, and put the latter on the countertop.

'You recognise this man, sir?'

The guy glanced at the image and sniffed.

'What's he done?'

'We just need to talk to him.'

'He got a name?'

'Yusuf Ghani.'

The man pursed his lips and stared hard at the photo. He looked up.

'Don't recall seein' anyone like that comin' through here.'

'You're sure?'

She pointed at the photo.

'Please, take your time. It's important we find him.'

The man shrugged. 'S'mostly locals come in here.'

She glanced around, as though the shelves might offer her a second opinion.

'Anyone else work here?'

'Sure. There's my nephew.'

'Can I speak with him?'

A slow nod of the head. 'I guess, if you come back Thursday. He ain't around till then, but he'll tell you same as I did. If this guy of yours came in here, I'd'a seen him.'

Her stomach lurched.

This was wrong. Ghani *was* down here. He had to be.

The nausea began rising within her.

If she was wrong about this, then what else would she have been wrong about? Sure there was the land around the 224, but Sweetwater and the 211 had been the more likely locus. A calculated gamble, she'd said, but one she'd expected to win. Now it was her last and only play. The buzzer was sounding. Time was up.

She trudged out of the store and into the rain. Kramer got out of the car as she approached.

'Well?'

She shook her head.

The journey back was solemn, Kramer keeping the questions to a minimum.

'You want me to drop you back at the hotel?'

'Not an efficient use of your time,' she replied. 'You got terrorists to find. Just drop me in Estacada and I'll borrow one of the SUVs and leave it at the airport.'

She looked out the window, at the cold, green country.

'Make sure you check out the 224. He's gotta be down there; the girl too.'

*Aliyah Khan.*

She had failed her. Just like she'd failed that other girl in London, Munira Begum.

Kramer turned to look at her for a moment. 'What makes you so sure?'

'Belief,' she said. Sheer belief in her own powers of deduction;

her ability to think like Ghani. Or just arrogance. There was no reason why her hunch about the 224 should be any more accurate than her belief she'd find him in Sweetwater. As for getting inside Ghani's head – well, didn't that take empathy, something that so many people, including her own daughter, had assured her she completely lacked?

Outside, tail lights glowed.

'Sometimes you just got to take a chance.'

Kramer dropped her a block from the courthouse. Shreya got out, turned and looked back through the open door.

'Take care of yourself, Agent Kramer. You're a fine agent and you've got the potential to be a great one.'

The woman gave her a nod and mumbled her thanks. Shreya closed the car door and watched as Kramer sped off northward. The goodbyes had been short and awkward. Appropriate, she felt, for their brief and ultimately fruitless time together.

She walked slowly back toward the centre of operations, oblivious to the rain. Maybe it was worth having one last go at Dan, throwing herself upon his mercy, appealing to his better nature, and failing that, his vanity. Wasn't there even a certain virtue in doing so? Showing him the lengths she was prepared to go to, just to stay on the case?

She tried. She pushed through the double doors, marched into his inner sanctum and, under the gaze of the town's former mayors looking down from their portraits, she made one last plea for a stay of execution.

'It's out of my hands,' he told her. Which sort of begged the question of whose hands it was in. 'Why don't you try calling your pals in DC?' he said. 'The ones who got you sent up here in the first place?'

She did just that, but Luca Calliveste didn't pick up and his PA couldn't say when, or even if, he might call back.

Dan had disappeared by the time she ended the call. That was good of him.

She negotiated the keys to an SUV from a fresh-faced agent who, if he didn't much appreciate her pulling rank and taking his vehicle, at least had the good sense to keep his thoughts on the matter to himself.

She got in, leaned back against the headrest and closed her eyes.

This was it then. End of the road. No finding Ghani or Aliyah. No happy ending, just a flight back to LA and a drive down to San Diego for ... what exactly? She could bust a thousand narco traffickers and the next day a thousand more would take their place. She could take drugs worth billions off the streets and the price would hardly move. What difference would she make? And what difference would it make to her? Would it fill the gnawing void inside?

She reached for her phone.

'Hello?'

He sounded frail; confused.

'Dad.'

'Shreya? Where are you?'

'Portland.'

'What are you doing there?'

'I'm just leaving it. How are you?'

'Same, same.'

'They treating you well?'

Stupid question. She should never have asked it.

'They treat me like an idiot. Are you still coming? You said you'd bring Isha for Diwali.'

Diwali. Their first without her mother.

'I'm doing my best, Dad. I'll speak to Isha. We'll come down as soon as we can.'

'*Oh-ho*, Shreya!'

Irritation in his voice.

'You always do this! You know Diwali has already started.'

*Shit.*

'It ends on Tuesday.'

Election Day. Could the gods *be* any more capricious?

She ended the call as the usual mix of emotions engulfed her: the comfort that came from speaking to him and the guilt of helplessness that hollowed her out.

*I'm doing my best.*

She punched in a different number which rang and rang and then went to voicemail.

'Isha, it's Mom. Hope you're well, baby.'

She tried to soften her tone; tried not to sound *stiff*.

'I was just calling to wish you a happy Diwali. I'm thinking of coming home for a few days. Your bapa is missing you and I thought we might go see him. Anyway, call me back. Love you.'

She hung up and started the engine, then drove slowly southward. Estacada slipped by. The junction with the 224 loomed. Ghani was down there to the south somewhere. He had to be.

She rubbed at her neck. The road south was calling. Leaving a job unfinished – it always felt like her brain rebelling against itself. An itch she had to scratch.

*Not your problem any more.*

She indicated north, back to Portland; and waited for a break in the traffic. Her eyes panned in the opposite direction.

Ghani was down there. Aliyah too, most likely.

*Dammit.*

She cancelled the signal, put her foot on the gas and turned south.

# CHAPTER 32

*Shreya*

The country to the south was forests and farmsteads and the odd small settlement clinging close to the road. She pulled up the map. Far as she could see, the only buildings of note were a couple of churches, a general store about twenty-five miles away at Ripplebrook and a gun shop ten miles closer, near a place called Three Lynx.

She discounted the churches. Islamic fundamentalists were not in the habit of turning up at ecclesiastical coffee mornings, not as far as she was aware, so that left the general store and the gun shop. The latter was closer.

She drove till she saw the turn-off: a gravel road twisting uphill from the 224. A mile along it, a rusting metal sign on a ragged fence post announced the Pine Ridge Gun Range. She pulled up beside a grey SUV. The rain had stopped, giving way to a bitter wind. She made for a prefab with a tin roof and a welcome sign outside held by a rifle-toting, cut-out cartoon bear.

Inside was stuffy. Five degrees too hot. Behind a counter sat a thickset woman in a khaki shirt and a smile that looked like she'd donned it for business purposes. Shreya walked over and went through the motions. She'd barely brought out Ghani's photo before the woman stopped her.

'You from the FBI?'

*For the moment.*

'That's right, ma'am.'

'I ain't seen your guy . . .'

'Maybe someone else who works here?'

The woman cut her off.

'But you know that girl? The one who blew up that mall. The one they say flew into Portland. I think I saw her.'

Shreya blinked. She picked up her phone and googled an image of Yasmin Malik. God knows there were enough of them to choose from. Every news site in the world had her picture.

'This girl?'

'That's her. The one who blew up that mall. I saw her up near Big Eddy. There's a spot for picnics down by the river. Nice too, when the weather's good. My husband and I were out there couple weeks back. Last good day of the year. Anyway, these kids were over at the picnic tables havin' a meal. Earl and I were a couple hundred yards away, so I didn't get a good look, but when we were headed back to the truck, I passed pretty close to the girl.'

'How many kids?'

The woman shrugged. 'Four or five, maybe. I remember wondrin' bout them at the time.' Her face reddened. 'I mean, I'm not one of those . . . you know . . . but out here it's strange to see a bunch of white and black and brown kids all together. And after that business in LA, I said to Earl, "That's the girl. That's one of the kids we saw up at Big Eddy," but he told me it couldn't be. He didn't remember her. But when they said she'd flown into Portland, I *knew* it was her.'

'You mentioned this to anyone?'

The woman shrugged. 'I didn't want to waste anyone's time.'

Shreya showed her the picture of Ghani once more.

'Was he with them at the picnic?'

Another shrug. 'Might have been. I don't recall.'

Shreya brought up a picture of Aliyah Khan.

'What about this girl? Was she there too?'

The woman stared hard at the image.

'I think so.'

'And Big Eddy? Where's that?'

''Bout ten miles south of here on the way to Ripplebrook. Can't miss it. There's a sign for the turn-off from the 224.'

Thoughts ran riot in Shreya's head: theories; calculations. Yasmin and Aliyah had been ten miles south of here, *with others*: white, brown and black.

She thanked the woman and gave her a card with her contact details.

'If any of them show up here, please call me immediately.'

She headed back to the car. The day was waning, the forested hills growing taller and blacker.

She should call Dan.

*And tell him what?* A possible sighting of Aliyah Khan that was vague and a month old at best? He'd ask her why the hell she wasn't on a plane back to LA.

She brought up the map on her phone and typed in Big Eddy. The image zoomed in on another river bend on the Clackamas on the road to Ripplebrook.

She started the car, then turned south on the 224.

The rain started again, falling soon with a vengeance, spearing the windshield. Ten miles along, she turned off the 224, past a couple of ragtag, boarded-up buildings, and followed the satnav toward Ripplebrook.

The general store sat on a rise, overlooking the settlement like a little king on his throne. She parked and killed the engine. Projectile rain pounded the roof. She looked up at the store. No lights in the windows. No smoke from the chimney stack. It seemed dead. But she had to be sure.

She got out and navigated the waterfall of a moss-lined stairway to the entrance. Beyond the window, a faint rush of grey. Maybe the gods had changed their minds. Maybe someone *was* in there. She pushed on the door and felt it give way.

A silver-haired white woman, stick-thin and wrapped in a fraying shawl stood organising cans on a shelf. She turned as Shreya approached.

'Can I help you?'

Kind eyes, translucent skin, a brittleness to her movements. A grandmother, probably. Shreya dispensed with the badge.

'I'm looking for someone.' She pulled out the photo of Ghani. The woman shook her head.

'I'm going to need my glasses.'

She headed for the counter.

'Bring it here, dear.'

A light went on. The woman searched the counter for her glasses.

'There we are.' She held out a hand. 'Now, let's take a look at that photo of yours.'

Shreya handed it over and the woman brought it close to her face, then looked up.

'That's *Ew-sif* that is.'

Fireworks went off.

'You . . . you know him?'

'Comes in here once in a while. Nice man, always courteous.'

'Do you know where he lives?'

The woman paused.

'Relative of yours, is he?'

'No, but it *is* important that I speak to him.'

The woman took off her glasses and placed them down on the counter.

'Lives somewhere up near the Pipeline Road, I think. Just drive straight through town and keep on till you reach a fork; that's the Pipeline Road in front of you. The left turn winds all the way from here to Three Lynx; the right'll take you down to Lake Harriet. Can't say which direction to take.'

'Has he been in recently?'

'Ew-sif?' The woman looked to the ceiling. 'Came in a day or two ago, I think.'

'Anyone with him?'

A slow shake of the head.

'Just him.'

Shreya felt her heart pound. *She'd been right*. Ghani *was* living south of Estacada.

She thanked the woman and headed back out into the elements. The rain lashed as she rushed down the steps. She'd pay good money to see the look on Dan's face when she called it in. He'd *have* to act now. Have to let her stay on the case. He'd have to descend on Ripplebrook like the heavenly host with as many agents as he could muster; throw a ring around the place and strangle it till they found Yusuf Ghani and Aliyah and whoever else was down there.

She got back in the car and stared out the window, back up at the little store sitting atop its hill. Something felt wrong. Why was Ghani using his own name? Why give it out freely to the local storekeeper? Why not give her a fake one?

She would figure it out later.

She picked up the phone, searched for Dan's number and pressed call. It rang once then went to voicemail.

'Dan. It's Shreya. Call me as soon as you get this. I think I've found him!'

The light was fading; Shreya drove slowly, searching for any sign of Ghani or his blue Toyota, checking every driveway and every window behind which a light bulb burned.

She drove on, out of town and uphill. Once more the trees closed in, walls of fir and cedar thinning occasionally to reveal a fence post or mailbox beside a weatherworn road.

*Dan should have called back by now.*

Cold sweat at her collar. She reached for the phone, pressed redial and waited as nothing happened. On-screen, the bars of reception had dwindled to nothing.

*Damn.*

The road twisted like a serpent's tongue and ended in a fork; a forlorn crossroads at the end of the world. The Pipeline Road.

*Left or right?*

She chose left. Always left. The road rose and fell, an asphalt wave between darkening fields. She switched on the high beams against the dusk – a premature, preternatural darkness that seemed to weigh upon her the further she drove. There was nothing here. Just endless wilderness. The thought arose that maybe she should have chosen right. It irritated her.

Another mile of nothing made the decision for her. She braked, slowing and turning the wheel sharply till the car straddled the road. Only as she reversed did she see it, a single spot of light flickering in the forest, a yellow pinprick, dancing between the trees and no brighter than a star in the sky.

*The headlight of a car, or a bike?*

She squinted. If it was, it wasn't moving.

She turned the car forward once more, heading on, searching for a road that might lead to that light and ten minutes on she found it: an anonymous turn-off, half hidden among the trees. She forced the SUV down it, the chassis creaking its complaints as she crashed it through potholes. The light disappeared, lost amid the forest. The frustration rose once more, her skin growing itchy. She *needed* to find that light; needed to get to its source, whatever it might be. To stop – to lose it – was unconscionable. She had to keep going, and she did, carrying on for a mile further till abruptly, the road veered to the left and there it was shining through the branches, dead ahead and brighter than before. The sight of it mesmerised. She put her foot down, the gravel squelching against the tyres. Ahead a building materialised out of the grey. A large, white clapboard house with darkened windows, two storeys high and ringed by a narrow veranda. But it was the rusting blue pickup parked nearby that made her heart stop.

From where she sat, the licence plate was illegible, obscured by dirt and the fading light, but the truck looked the right age.

*Dan needed to know.*

She reached for her phone, checked for signal and found one precarious bar. She hit call. The bar flickered and died. On the line, nothing but silence.

*Dammit.*

She opened her door and stepped out into the punch of hard rain and crossed the dirt toward the vehicle. She pointed the flashlight on her phone at the licence plate. The small sphere of light picked out the letters and the digits of a California plate registered in San Diego County.

From behind her came a sound, the creak of a door opening. She reached for her gun and swivelled on the spot. Jaundiced yellow light spilled out onto the porch as a figure exited. The door closed, the figure becoming a ghostly smudge against the black.

Shreya gripped the gun tight and took a step forward. The figure took shape. A woman. Pale skin, a shock of long white hair and clothes that looked like they came from a different time. In her sixties, Shreya guessed.

The figure called out to her.

'Are you lost?'

She kept her gun hand hidden and made warily for the steps. She reached the porch and took out her badge.

'Ma'am, I'm Special Agent Mistry, with the FBI. We're looking for a man by the name of Yusuf Ghani.'

'Yusuf?' She found it hard to gauge the woman's expression. 'He does a little work for me, now and again. Right now he's probably in the old barn down by the creek.' She gestured behind her. 'It's a ten-minute walk across the fields from here.'

Her stomach lurched. Ghani was *here*. A few hundred yards away. She needed to call this in. *Right now.*

She checked her phone. Still no signal.

The woman smiled. 'Reception comes and goes up here. Landline's the only way to be sure of getting through. You're free to use the phone in the house.'

Shreya considered it for a moment. She needed to get through to Dan, and this was an old white woman. Hardly the jihadi type. She gave her a nod.

'Okay. Thank you.'

The woman headed inside. Shreya holstered her gun and followed, up the steps to the porch and into a spartan hallway of wooden floorboards and stark, whitewashed walls. The woman gestured to a door.

'Phone's through there.'

The room beyond looked austere: a wooden desk and chair, a sofa in the corner; neat like a museum exhibit. The telephone too, a black Bakelite thing. No photographs or mementos or pictures.

Nothing that suggested a human touch. It was more than austere. It was sterile.

She turned back to the woman. In the light of the hall, she looked younger. Much younger. The clothes and the hair were anomalies. The skin of the face was firm, unlined, except for . . . except for a delicate scar running down the length of one cheek. She hadn't noticed it outside in the dark. Shreya took a step back.

A floorboard creaked. She felt the hairs rise on the back of her neck. She turned.

Yusuf Ghani. There. In front of her.

She reached for her gun.

Too late.

The woman brought something crashing down on the side of her head. Pain exploded in Shreya's skull. The ground rushed up to meet her and then the world went black.

# CHAPTER 33

*Greg*

The hell was he doing? He should have left; got in the car and just disappeared. That's what he'd intended to do as he watched Aliyah get into the truck with Yusuf. Screw her. He'd done all he could. It was on her if she still wanted to die.

So why had he changed his mind? Why had he waited for dusk? Why was he now pulling off the highway and heading for Ripplebrook?

He knew and he didn't. Maybe it wasn't a choice at all. Who else did he have? Who else did he have in the world?

He drove in the half-light, along storm-swept back roads, and parked up the best part of a mile away, approaching the house from the rear, through woods and flooded fields. With his leg it was hardly an easy hike. In the dark, in the midst of a storm, it felt like wading through quicksand.

But he took it slow and eventually he emerged from the trees, the lights of the house glimmering faintly in the distance. It was open country now. Dead fields offering no cover. He needed to get closer; needed to reconnoitre the area. The barn. That was the target. From there he could work out where Jack was, where Miriam and Yusuf might be.

He inched forward, alive to any sound, any action that might give him away, suddenly thankful for the howling winds masking his approach. The barn drew closer, growing in the darkness. He slipped through the doorway and out of the rain. The mud yard in front of the house was quiet: Yusuf's truck parked to one side. In the middle, near the steps up to the front door, another vehicle, one he didn't recognise. An SUV.

Lights were on in Miriam's study, shadows in the window. At least two people. Miriam and either Jack or Yusuf? Maybe all three of them. No other illumination downstairs. On the first floor, the only light burned in the girls' room.

He had a choice to make. Wait a few hours till the lights went out or go now, under the cover of the storm, while Miriam, Jack and Yusuf were all together in that room and might not hear him.

A spear of lightning lit up the house before plunging it back into darkness.

*Fuck it.*

He scrambled out and made for the rear of the house. To the back door, the one to the kitchen. It was locked, as he'd expected. He took off his jacket, wrapped it round his fist and waited. Another spear of lightning. He waited two seconds, then punched at the half-pane of glass in the door frame, the sound of its shatter swallowed by the roar of thunder.

Inside, he crouched low behind a counter, letting the seconds tick by till he was sure his entrance hadn't been heard. Voices emanated from Miriam's study.

He stood up, then froze.

A noise. A door opening. Voices in the hallway. Miriam's. Yusuf's. He reached for his knife. Footsteps, yet they headed away from him, toward the front of the house. This might be his only chance. He slipped up the back stairs, the hall in darkness just like the night before, retracing his steps to the dorm.

*Déjà vu.*

He turned the handle and entered.

Aliyah lay on her bunk. No sign of Rehana.

She looked at him, stunned.

# CHAPTER 34

*Shreya*

Her head throbbed. Searing, point-blank, all-encompassing pain. She touched the source and her fingers came away sticky with blood.

She reached for her gun and found nothing.

'Shreya?'

A woman's voice floated over to her across an ocean of fog.

*Her mother?*

No. The woman with the white hair. It came back to her. Damn. She should've seen this coming. Should've been more careful. Should've seen a potential terrorist, but in her haste, she'd seen what she'd wanted to: a harmless old white woman. What kind of agent was she?

She was lying on something, a sofa maybe. She flexed her fingers then her wrists and feet. They moved freely; unbound. Steeling herself against the pain, she opened her eyes. A white ceiling, a naked bulb.

She tried to sit up. A spasm of pain passed through her like an electric shock.

'You better lie back. You don't want to hurt yourself.'

The woman's voice again.

*To hell with her.*

Shreya breathed, counted to three and then hauled herself upright. Stars exploded in front of her eyes. The woman was sitting opposite on a high-backed chair, cradling a gun. The fear began to rise in the pit of her stomach. She needed to calm herself. She counted; prime numbers: *two, three, five, seven, eleven . . .*

'Why're you looking for Yusuf?'

'It's government business.'

The woman sighed, as though the response was tiresome.

'I'll make you a deal. Answer my questions and I promise you'll leave here alive.'

*. . . thirteen, seventeen, nineteen . . .*

The woman was lying. Didn't take a psychologist to work that out. These people were terrorists. They would kill her just as surely as they'd killed those folks in the mall in Burbank.

She rubbed at the base of her skull.

*Twenty-three, twenty-nine . . . What the hell had she been thinking, coming here alone?*

The woman raised the gun.

'It's a simple question. Why are you looking for Yusuf?'

Shreya looked her straight in the eye. 'Drugs,' she said. The lie rankled . . . *thirty-one . . . thirty-seven . . .* 'He's involved in running drugs from Baja into San Diego . . . He murdered a man.'

The woman stared, her eyes burning into Shreya's. She wanted to look away . . . *forty-*

'Murder?'

She felt her skin crawl . . . *-one, forty-three, forty-seven . . .*

'A man called Hector Escarrà . . . part of the Tijuana cartel . . .

found strung up in a warehouse outside of Chula Vista ... twelve months back.'

The case was real. She'd been there; seen Escarrà's corpse hanging from a hook. It helped to ground the lies in as much truth as possible.

The woman's expression wavered.

'Keep talking.'

She fought back the waves of pain.

'Hector Escarrà was the nephew of Alfredo Escarrà ... a member of the Mexican Chamber of Deputies ... He was found dangling from a meathook in a warehouse ... A few hours before he died, he was seen in the company of a man we think was Ghani ... Two days later Ghani disappears from San Diego ... And then he turns up here in the middle of nowhere.'

She couldn't read the woman's expression. Couldn't tell if she was buying it.

She changed tack.

'I don't know what sort of a hold he has over you, but we can straighten this out.'

This time there was no mistaking the change in the woman's countenance.

'Is that what you think?' She turned toward the door. 'Yusuf. Come in here.'

The door opened and a man shambled in. Yusuf Ghani. He looked different from his picture: older somehow. His face gaunt; his hair thinner. Her master terrorist was a middle-aged man in muddy boots and blue overalls with dirt on his knees.

'Yes, Miss Miriam?'

The voice was pliant. The voice of a man used to taking orders. The truth dawned. Ghani wasn't in control here, the woman was.

She gestured toward Shreya.

'This woman claims you killed a drug dealer back in San Diego.'

Ghani looked stunned.

'I have nothing to do with this, Miss Miriam. You must believe me.' He turned to Shreya. 'I never seen this lady before. I swear it.'

The woman walked over to Ghani and placed a hand on his arm.

'It's all right, Yusuf. I believe you. But this woman, she'll bring others here, and *they* won't believe you. You remember what happened in Herat? I need you to do the same thing here.'

Ghani's expression wavered. He turned his gaze on Shreya. Stared hard till she felt her skin crawl.

'It's the only way, Yusuf. They think you killed a man.'

Something flickered in his eyes. He walked over to Shreya and grabbed her by the wrist. She struggled, fighting him till he aimed a slap at the bloodied side of her head and once more the world exploded into agony.

She felt him drag her from the room, along the hallway, out the front door, across the veranda, and into the night. She saw her SUV through the rain, parked only feet away. It might as well have been on the moon for any chance she had of reaching it. She struggled once more and received another blow.

Her head spun. Ghani pushed her forward, down a hill and around the back of the house, across open, sodden ground; over mud that stuck to her boots and pulled her down. Down. In the distance, a barn, desolate and decaying, loomed out of the black.

This, she knew, was where she was going to die.

# CHAPTER 35

*Sajid*

The light had leached slowly from the day, the passage of time marked less by the position of an unseen sun than by the particular shades of the sky and the blue digits of the clock on the dashboard.

Sajid hazarded a glance in the rear-view mirror. Carrie was asleep on the back seat. That was good. She needed to rest. And he needed time to think. To process. That they had not yet been stopped and arrested seemed to him nothing short of miraculous.

That his pursuers at the border should fail to identify their licence plate or the colour and model of the car seemed like divine intervention, and indeed at an earlier stage in his life, he might easily have believed it so, conveniently ignoring the fact that those same divine forces had failed to intervene when Carrie had been hit by shrapnel, or had even ordained it. Now, he knew better. Good things, bad things, they just happened, because the universe was cold and capricious, and if there was a God, He'd long since had the good sense to stop playing any part in the affairs of men. It didn't stop him praying, though.

He decided that they had been lucky so far, but luck, by its very nature, always eventually ran out. By now his details would be known to the US authorities. The Canadians would have passed them over. The border patrol would have made their report. Someone somewhere would be putting two and two together. And then how long would it be before his image was circulated to the police? How long before his face was featured alongside Aliyah's on CNN and every news site in the country?

He had avoided the highway in favour of quieter back roads, through settlements with strange yet familiar-sounding names; through Harper's Falls and Leaming, Rayford and Billings, and other places whose names passed him by as quickly as the towns themselves. These others seemed hard places, shuttered places, the places of people with nothing, who had lost what little they'd ever had. He knew places like these. Was his homeland not littered with them: the places of the powerless? He had not expected to see them here, not in America, not among whites, not in the richest country in the world.

But there was a difference, of course. The poor in his country had always been powerless, since the beginning of time. It was their lot, their burden, their inheritance and their bequest, handed down like a blood curse. But this poverty, American poverty, was not the same. The people that inhabited these places? Their fathers and grandfathers had bestridden the earth. There had been prosperity here, wealth unimaginable in the villages of Bangladesh, and yet it had gone. What, he wondered, did that do to people? To be masters of the world and then reduced to poverty? Would it engender anger? Fear?

The further they travelled the more he wished for the speed and directness of the freeway. Time was of the essence. Every minute wasted on a meandering back road was a minute Aliyah might be found and caught, or, just as likely, head further from Ripplebrook and his one chance of finding her. He had to take the risk. Somewhere near the border between Washington and Oregon he joined the freeway heading south.

As the miles fell, his spirits rose, and yet, each sighting of a patrol car sent his pulse racing. He wished that somehow they might find another vehicle. A car that the authorities would not be looking for, but that was not an option. He had never stolen a car before and had no idea how one would go about it. On TV shows, he remembered, it was as simple as rubbing together some wires under the steering wheel. Did that really work? He doubted it. Things were never that easy, not for him anyway.

Daylight, what there had been of it, faded and he welcomed its passing. The night had always been his friend. It was under cover of darkness that he had fled his village and it was under darkness that he now drove through Portland. Ripplebrook could not be much further. An hour at most.

*And then?*

The voice in his head was growing persistent.

'Turn off here.'

Carrie's words pierced his introspection.

He did as she commanded, and the freeway fell away, the slip road twisting into a black highway that threaded through dark, pine-seeded hills. Road signs rose, startling green and brilliant white, materialising amid the void like ghosts shaken awake by the harsh light of the headlamps and heralding the imminent arrival of Estacada.

*The last town before Ripplebrook.*

'What's that?'

He craned his neck to see what Carrie was pointing at. A beam of light in the sky, piercing the night like a beacon from the heavens.

He felt his chest tighten.

Once more he felt the panic rise within his breast.

'What is it?' she asked again, her tone betraying an anxiety he had not heard in it since she had stood rain-soaked on his doorstep in London.

Sajid said nothing; merely accelerated.

# CHAPTER 36

*Shreya*

Ghani kicked open the barn door and dragged her to a bench against a wall.

Shreya screamed. The numbers wouldn't come.

'You don't have to do this.'

Ghani ignored her.

'The girls,' she continued, 'Yasmin and Aliyah.'

She felt him pause.

'You met them at the airport. You brought them back here because that woman, Miriam, told you to. Is that what happened? You didn't know she was going to send Yasmin off with a bomb.'

She felt his grip loosen.

'Where's Aliyah?'

For a moment he stared out of a filthy window, back up at the house. He gave a bitter laugh.

'She's gone. They have *all* gone.'

What had the woman at the gun range said? '*A bunch of white and black and brown kids all out together.*'

'Who else?' she asked. 'How many more are there?'

'It doesn't matter. They've all gone. They cannot be stopped.'

He reached out toward the workbench.

'You don't need to do this.' She heard the shrill desperation in her own voice. She didn't like the sound. 'It's not too late.'

'It *is* too late.' His voice was little more than a whisper, hardly audible over the sound of her own desperate heartbeat. 'They have people everywhere.'

She felt him take her hands and pull them behind her. He held her wrists; tied them together with an extension cord.

She turned to face him, but he was already a few paces across the barn, picking up something dull and metallic and heavy.

*A hammer.*

Her legs buckled. She fought to stay upright.

'You do this and the FBI will hunt you down and kill you.'

The threat bounced off him.

'Please, turn around,' he said.

She stood her ground. If he was going to kill her, he would have to do it while she faced him. Let the image of her broken face be seared into his conscience.

He aimed another slap at her head and the pain erupted. She felt him dragging her into a corner, spinning her round, forcing her to her knees. She could sense him behind her, silent, unmoving. She struggled against the cord that bound her wrists. It was no use. She closed her eyes and waited for the blow to fall. She thought of her father, and of Isha. She thought of her life unlived, of her regrets, of the futility of this death.

*What was he doing?*

A rumble came from somewhere outside.

*What was he waiting for?*

The noise outside grew louder: the roar of engines; the crunch of gravel.

'Yusuf,' she said gently, 'you don't have to do this. I promise you, we will sort this out.'

She heard the sound of his breathing, heavy, laboured.

'Yusuf . . . just let me go. I'll make sure you're not harmed.'

Slowly, she got to her feet.

'Untie me.'

From outside came shouts.

She felt the tips of his fingers on her wrists, the cord rubbing against her skin.

*Loosening.*

The barn door crashed open.

She turned to see Kramer burst in, gun raised. Ghani too turned toward her, the hammer still in his hand. She struggled to read Kramer's expression. Shreya shouted to her, tried to get between her and Ghani. Two shots rang out. Deafening. Disorienting. Shreya fell to the dirt-packed floor and saw blood.

# CHAPTER 37

*Sajid*

'A searchlight,' he said.

An incandescent pillar reached down like a summons from Allah. Except its point of origin was not the heavens.

'A helicopter.'

It could not be a coincidence.

Carrie was at his shoulder.

'You don't think . . . ?'

He did not want to consider too deeply what it meant. For now, the only course of action was to follow it.

The sparse lights of Ripplebrook sped past, only to be replaced once more by the blanket of night. The road forked. He turned left, toward the light and the thrum of the rotors. They crested a ridge and he saw it: the searchlight, trained like a laser on the roof of a house, the area around it turned from night into day. Close by, a kaleidoscope of lights circled, flashing red and blue like a fairground ride.

Carrie let out a cry. He knew that pain. He knew the despair. He felt it too. *This* was the place they had risked everything to find.

*All in vain. All maybe just an hour too late.*

'We should stop here,' he told her.

'What? We can't. We need to keep going! Greg's down there. I know he is. Your daughter too!'

He understood her anger. The frustration, the rage born of impotence, all of it. He shared it, yet his fury was tempered by experience, by years of helplessness, a life of being subject to the arbitrary caprices of others. He gestured to the scene.

'It is too dangerous to venture any closer. If we are stopped, no one will believe we were simply passing by.'

He braked sharply and pulled over to the roadside. In the silence, the pitch of what he assumed was the helicopter's engine changed: rising, increasing to a roar. He looked up through the windscreen as a second helicopter buzzed directly overhead.

'What now?'

He heard the fear in her voice.

The new arrival seemed to dance around the first, circling wider, its own searchlight fanning across a wider area. He reached for the radio, pressing seek and scanning the frequencies, ignoring the music stations and concentrating on those broadcasting the spoken word until he found it: the breathless cadences of a news reporter, shouting to be heard over the sounds of rotor blades.

Carrie slammed a fist against the car door.

'This is your answer? We sit here and listen while they arrest our kids?'

He did not know what to say. And really, it was his answer, by dint of there being no better alternative. What else was he supposed to do?

The road behind them lit up. Headlight beams filled the car. He turned in his seat, shielding his eyes. His entrails turned to ice.

*Police.*

They would surely stop; would surely question them: *what were they doing sitting out here in the dark in the middle of nowhere?* They would ask to see their identification and that would be it.

The headlights drew nearer, brighter, mesmerising, filling his field of vision.

He turned to Carrie.

'I need to open the bonnet.'

'The what?'

'The hood!'

He was already bending forward and reaching for the lever.

Even as the thick, metallic clunk of the release reverberated, he was pulling at the door handle and climbing out of the car. He darted forward and lifted the bonnet.

The lights were almost on top of them: full beams, blinding white. The vehicle drew level. He held his breath. It sped past spitting gravel, in seconds just a smear of red tail lights in the dark. Another followed it, then a third. He recognised a logo painted on the side. The same logo as had graced the umbrella of the young journalist who had confronted him outside Paddington Green police station in the rain.

He waited until the convoy had passed, their lights dancing and disappearing into the distance, then stepped back and pulled down the bonnet. He took a breath and walked slowly back to his open door.

The voice on the radio was still pouring forth: agents had entered the house, were searching the grounds, entering a barn. And then the tenor changed.

'*There's movement . . . they're bringing someone . . . it looks like a body on a stretcher . . .*'

An overwhelming hollowness took hold of him, as though his chest might cave in.

Carrie seemed to read his thoughts.

'It might not be either of them.'

'Yes,' he said automatically.

But what if it was? How would he explain that to Rumina? That he had come so close, risked so much, and still failed. In his breast it felt as though his heart might tear asunder. A gasp of despair ripped through him, escaping as though it were part of his very soul.

He felt suddenly embarrassed, ashamed of showing such weakness in front of Carrie. It was important that he maintain at least the pretence of strength despite the anguish in his heart. Had life not taught him as much: when he had lost his parents; when he had fled his homeland; when Mia had first been hospitalised? He supposed it was simply the duty of a decent man: to show equanimity so that others might be allowed emotion. So that they might grieve, safe in the knowledge that he was there, a rock against the storm.

# CHAPTER 38

*Greg*

Aliyah stared at him.

Before she could rise, he walked over to her and placed a hand over her mouth.

'Aliyah, listen to me.'

And then he heard the scream.

Not from her. From outside.

He stumbled to the window; saw Yusuf dragging a woman across the dirt toward the barn. Aliyah was on her feet now, rushing for the door. He lunged after her, caught her arm and dragged her to the window.

'I'm your only hope. You need to trust me.'

He saw the emotions play out as she stared out of the window.

'But this isn't . . . Miriam said . . .'

'Miriam's lying. We gotta go, *now!*'

She turned to him, and in that instant, he saw something change within her: a flicker of the eyes, a stiffening of her shoulders. Maybe she finally got it. Whatever it was she was thinking, it buoyed him.

She gave him a nod.

'Okay. Let's go.'

He led her down the stairs as from somewhere outside came the growl of vehicles. Fear heightened his senses. There was no time to think. He led her to the kitchen and out the back, running through the mud, breathless till they'd hit the treeline. Now, behind him he heard the shouts of men and then gunshots. He glanced back but saw nothing in the darkness; no one pursuing them. At least not yet. They seemed to be concentrating on the house and the barn. It wouldn't take them long to widen their search, throw a ring around the whole place. He and Aliyah needed to move. Fast.

They pushed on, ten minutes of nothing except the sound of their own ragged breathing, until finally they made it to the car.

'Are they dead?' she asked.

He didn't know. He couldn't believe that Miriam wouldn't have prepared for this, that she wouldn't have some kind of contingency plan. What mattered though was that they drive like hell; as far away from Estacada and Ripplebrook and Miriam and whoever else was after them. He'd figure the rest out later.

'Look, I don't know what's going on, but I do know that Miriam was using you. Whatever it is she told you, it was a lie. She's not some bleedin'-heart liberal goddess. She's fucking ex-military. She's right-wing as they come, and she's got friends in high places. She sent Yasmin to die. And she's got the same plan for you and Rehana.'

*Where was Rehana, for that matter? And where was Jack?*

He asked her.

'They left.' Aliyah's voice deadpan. 'They were gone by the time Yusuf brought me back. Is Jack one, too?'

'One what?'

'A Nazi.'

He turned to her. Her eyes were fixed on his neck, its treacherous ink once more safely covered up.

The fucking tattoo.

'I ...' He struggled to find the words. 'There're some things about my past I ain't told you. I should've told you, but ...' How was he supposed to explain it? It was better just to come out and tell her.

'After the attack ... after Kandahar ... when they shipped me back home ... after the operations, when they told me I might not walk again, I ended up ... in a very dark place. I was freaked, Aliyah. For months I was in a bed, with nothing to do but surf the goddamn internet. Fuck, I don't know. It felt like my life was over. I needed to feel ... I needed someone to blame. Okay? It wasn't just the raghead Taliban bastards, it was the fault of all Afghans. All Muslims. It was stupid, really. They were just fighting us cos we were in their country, but that's not how it felt.'

*Why was he telling her this? He needed to get to the point.*

'Anyway, after my recovery, I ended up back home, at my mom's in Bronson; no job, no nothing, just a whole lot of shit in my head. I fell in with a bunch of punks – doin' all sorts of shit for cash: stealing, mugging, armed robbery. They didn't want me at first, on account of my leg. But I told 'em of my time in the army, and that I hadn't been just some grunt. I'd been an engineer. I had skills. Skills they could use. I don't even know why I was trying to impress them. They were a bunch of fuckin' assholes. I guess it just felt good to be wanted; to be part of something. Long story short, me and two others were robbing a convenience store. The owner must've set off some kind of silent alarm because the next thing we know, there's a cop car pullin' up outside. One of the guys, Big Pete, panicked. He took a baseball bat to the head of the clerk. A minute later, the police were comin' in the front and Pete and the other guy were runnin' out the back. I couldn't keep up of course, on account of the fucking leg, and ended up gettin' caught and sent down for aggravated assault and robbery. It was in the pen that I got this thing.' He tilted his head to the side.

'You became a Nazi?'

The way she said it, the way she looked at him – he felt a hot wave of revulsion well up inside of him. Disgust at himself . . . but that wasn't him. That had never really been him.

'It was about protection, self-preservation. When you're inside, you gotta choose a side. If you don't, you'll end up dead.'

'And you just happened to choose a bunch of racists.'

'You think the blacks in there weren't racist? Besides, I was still angry. Angry at everything, but I . . . I never believed in any of that shit. But that's how I ended up with the ink.'

He stammered into silence, then felt the anger well up inside of him. He wasn't on fuckin' trial here. He'd just saved her life, whether she believed him or not.

'Look, I don't care what you think of me. There'll be time enough later for you to shout and scream and call me a sonofabitch, but right now . . . right now, we got to disappear.'

He felt the needle of her stare, yet kept his eyes firmly on the road ahead. It seemed to take an eternity for her to respond.

'And how do we do that?'

*Now that was a good question.*

He headed north toward a place called Damascus. The road to Damascus. Where Saul had seen the light and become Paul. He might have laughed at the Sunday school simplicity of the irony. It wasn't far. Less than twenty minutes on the 211; a little longer taking the back roads.

How long had it been since he was last here? Five months? Six?

Not that long at all, and at the same time it was aeons. An eternity. A different life.

The rain was coming down again. Not too heavy but uninterrupted. Fine by him. Suburban streets took shape. Familiar like old acquaintances. A few miles more, then a couple of turns and they'd be there.

She hadn't said much since he'd told her about prison. Maybe she was still coming to terms with it. *With all his shit.* Or maybe she was just disgusted. Maybe that fucking swastika on his neck had changed everything between them. Maybe she'd run again, first chance she got.

And if she did, he'd a mind to let her go this time. Let her just do whatever the hell she wanted. You couldn't save someone who didn't want to be saved. And then he was back full circle to Saul and Paul and the realisation that no, if she ran, he'd go after her.

The turn was up ahead, beside the wreck of a blue mailbox that listed at a sixty-degree angle. He slowed and took the turn, following the road till he reached the house and garage at the end of it, then killed the engine.

'Where are we, Greg?'

'A friend's place,' he told her.

He looked up at the house, at the hollow windows, at the screen door rusting on its hinges. No sign of life. Deader even than he remembered it.

'Come on.'

He reached for the handle, pulled his hood up and slowly manoeuvred his legs out. He headed for the garage. The doors were unlocked, as they'd been for the best part of fifty years, he guessed. Slowly, carefully, he pushed them open, making sure not to put pressure on his bad knee, then stepped inside, welcomed by the smell of engine oil and the dust of ages.

He let out a breath.

'She's still here.'

The sound of Aliyah's footsteps behind him.

'Who?'

He flicked a switch on the wall. A strip-light flickered to life.

'Who?' said Aliyah. Her tone stronger this time.

'She hasn't got a name.'

He walked further into the garage and pulled at the corner of the dirty brown tarp, as he had done countless times before, in that other life. The one before Miriam. The sheet slid off and he gathered it and placed it beside the doors.

He turned and gazed at the convertible, its once smooth white paint job now bubbled in places with rust, its roof grey with age. It didn't matter. He would never tire of looking at it. Aliyah too stared.

'What the fuck is that?'

'That,' he said like it was his own child, 'is an Alfa Giulietta Spider.'

'It looks like a piece of shit. How old is it? A hundred?'

He ignored the sarcasm.

'Closer to sixty. It's been in here for over half that.'

'I'm not surprised. It looks like a bloody death trap.'

She walked over to the car and rapped her knuckles off the bodywork. He flinched.

'It's safe. Trust me.'

And it was. Sam Cotter had paid him good money to fix it; good money for the parts and paint at any rate. The work, well, that was a labour of love on his own account. It would have been nice to have finished the job – maybe some new panels where the rust had turned sheet metal into a colander; and he'd a hankering to paint it blue, but the Lord and pancreatic cancer had taken Sam, and he'd crawled back inside a bottle at the Hog's Back and that was the end of that.

Come to think of it, he'd first met Sam at the Hog's Back too.

Just an old man, propping up the bar most afternoons. Beer-handed conversation along the counter which had turned into something resembling friendship, mainly because the two of them had nothing else in their lives.

'What are we doing here?'

Aliyah's voice bringing him back to the present.

'We need a different car.'

'What's wrong with the car we have?'

He headed back out of the garage, Aliyah running to keep up with him.

'Jack was driving it,' he said. 'He'll know the licence plate. And if he knows it, then whoever he and Miriam are working with will know it. Half the damn country's covered in cameras, and most patrol cars got some kind of software that recognises licence plates. Now there ain't supposed to be any federal database that covers the whole country, but fuck that shit. We could be a thousand miles from here and some camera might pick up our plate and the Feds, or maybe Miriam's friends, would know about it. We can't take the risk.'

He opened the trunk of Jack's car and pulled out the brown duffel bag with his and Aliyah's clothes. That battered old bag had been through a lot. Almost as much as he had. He closed the trunk and headed back into the garage. The keys to the Alfa were in the footwell, just where he'd left them. The trunk opened with a squeal of metal and he stowed the bag. He turned to find Aliyah staring at him.

'So this is your answer? This prehistoric heap of junk?'

'It's not junk.'

He ran his hand over the coachwork. He knew every dent, every gnarl, every welt. Aliyah might know books and capital cities and chess moves, but he knew cars, and this one was special. Just as important, it was clean and taxed and no one would be looking for it. And it was free of chips and sensors and all the other shit they stuck in vehicles these days. It was an analogue machine in a digital world and it would get them out of Oregon.

'What matters is it won't show up on any databases as stolen. It'll buy us time.'

'But look at it. It's not exactly inconspicuous.'

He gave her the merest hint of a smile. The car was making him feel good.

'Trust me. By the time we need to ditch it, we'll be a couple of states away.'

'And then what?'

*And then?*

'We'll figure it out.'

Ten minutes later, Damascus and Sam Cotter's place were dots in the rear-view with Jack's car safely under the tarp in the garage. The Alfa, with its skinny tyres and tiny frame, was an anachronism on wheels, but shit it made him feel good.

Even Aliyah seemed to be warming to it; at least that's how it felt as she reached for his hand. He turned and gave her a smile.

'Greg,' she said, 'it's not enough to just run. We need a plan.'

He thought for a moment.

'Only plan is to get as far away from here as possible.'

'And then?'

'We hide.'

'Where?'

'What?'

'Where do we hide?'

'I don't know.'

*Why was she asking so many damn questions?*

'It's like chess, Greg. If we're going to get out of this, we need to think three, four, five moves ahead. We need to work out where

we're going and what we do when we get there. We need somewhere safe. Somewhere you know well.'

He shook his head.

'Only place I know well is northern Florida, but that's a couple
thousand miles from here.'

'Florida it is, then.'

He spat a laugh. 'Are you mad? It's too far.'

'Is there anywhere else? Anywhere closer that's safe?'

Shit. There wasn't, not that he could think of. Florida was better
than anywhere else. He knew the country. And there was even a
place they could hide out, *if* he could get them there.

*Fuck it.*

He shook his head and pressed down on the gas.

# CHAPTER 39

*Greg*

Greg stared up at the screen on the wall: Vice President Green-wood on a tour of some county fair. Handshakes and platitudes and an awkward bite of a burger that made you think she'd never eaten one without a knife and fork before. Even now, knowing what he knew, she still made his flesh creep. The stuck-on smile, the stiff hugs. It was like she felt the White House was her due and that she shouldn't even be having to slum it with the good folks from Bumfuck, Iowa. Shit, she'd have lost to any half-credible opposition candidate. It was her good fortune that she was up against a narcissist who mixed incompetence with a God complex, and still she was contriving to fucking lose.

He scribbled some pencil notes on a scrap of paper. He wasn't sure why. All he knew was the act of writing felt good. Like he was sharing his burden somehow. Letting something leak out. And if the worst happened, if they were caught and killed, maybe the words would be . . . he didn't know. They'd remain for someone.

Aliyah appeared at the restroom door. He stopped writing and returned paper and pencil to his pocket. She walked over and sat down across the table and looked up at the screen.

'Bloody hypocrite.'

'What?'

'Greenwood,' she said. 'She acts as though she's a fucking saint; as though she's nothing like that bastard, Costa, but deep down she's not much different. He might be a racist dick, but least he's honest about his politics. She talks tolerance, but she . . . It doesn't matter.'

He passed her the laminate menu. As she read, he stared out the window, past the cars in the lot to the black sky above the plains of the Snake River. When he looked back, she'd put down the menu and was fiddling absent-mindedly with the chain and the dove around her neck.

He shifted on the vinyl of the booth. At least she was talking to him now. She'd been all but mute since the stop at a gas station on the Oregon border. They'd needed some way of navigating and he didn't trust that the map on his phone was secure, so she'd gone into the shop and bought the best part of a dozen good old-fashioned maps covering their route. He'd have bought just one, but she'd insisted on the set.

'Detail matters, Greg. I want to see every street, every junction.'

And then, on the gas station's TV, they'd seen the images: pictures of the LA bombing; smoke rising from the caved-in shell of a building; ambulances and patrol cars and paramedics pushing gurneys. It was the first time she'd seen them properly. The image had then cut to scenes of a demonstration. Old white women bussed in from the suburbs milling with big, bearded American Redemption guys in camo and armed to the teeth, grinning, or spitting their words into a camera. The sound was muted but you didn't need it to know what they were saying.

And then came the footage of Yasmin's final moments – a grey security camera shot of her rushing through the mall, a trolley case in tow, and then a whiteout, the cameras overwhelmed and the feed cutting. He'd reached for Aliyah and she'd stood there, numb, like stone.

She'd spent the next few hours in silence, poring over the maps she'd bought like they contained a secret; seeing in them something he hadn't.

Now, he reached out again, across the tabletop, and touched her hand. She gave a start, pulled it back and he was surprised at the coldness of her skin.

'Have you decided?' he asked.

For a moment she seemed unsure what he meant. He gestured to the menu on the table in front of her.

A waitress appeared, armed with a pad and a pen and a smile so bright it must have been a requirement of the job.

'How you all doing today? What can I get you?'

Aliyah picked up the menu while he asked the waitress for coffee and a few more minutes. Aliyah began to study her maps before looking out of the window. He followed her gaze; just the endless plain and not even a hint of the Rockies. He didn't much care for it. His home was horizons that stretched only as far as the nearest thicket of trees. Spaces as open as this one made him nervous. *Hundreds of miles and nowhere to hide.*

'Aliyah?'

He pointed her back to the menu and she settled on eggs, then returned to studying the maps, every now and then making an annotation of something.

He tried to coax her into conversation.

'Capital of Idaho?'

She looked up.

'Boise.'

'It's pronounced Boy-zee,' he told her.

The revelation seemed to spark something in her. The joy of unexpected knowledge. She looked into his eyes and he revelled in her gaze.

'Boy-zee?'

'Yup.'

She uttered a laugh: a short thing, tinged with disdain, but he was happy to hear it.

'Well, that's bloody stupid.'

He turned and looked around the diner, hoping to find the waitress. Instead he caught sight of another TV screen. His heart leapt.

Helicopter shots of Ripplebrook. The White House, its tin roof illuminated like the Fourth of July; the yard outside strewn with police cars and black Escalades like the ones cruising round Estacada that morning. And there, to one side, Yusuf's blue truck.

Two figures emerged from the building, paramedics, a gurney between them; a body, covered in a blanket. And there, on the dirt outside, holding a foil blanket, a figure he'd seen before. He struggled to recall. Where had it been? When?

He kept watching. No sign of the living. Just that shrouded body starting its last journey. And then the image changed again and this time it felt like a punch to the gut.

A photograph of Aliyah. A passport shot.

He could barely swallow the spit in his mouth.

He turned back to the table, reached for his cap and passed it to her.

'Put this on.'

She looked at him as if he'd suddenly lost his senses, and then she saw the screen. He watched the colour drain from her face.

'We need to go,' he said. 'We need to go, *now*.'

But she was already on her feet, grabbing her maps and making for the door. He reached for his jacket and hurried out after her into the night, back across the frozen parking lot to the car. She'd headed for the driver's side, the door shut behind her like a gunshot.

For a moment he just stood there.

She started the engine and lowered the window.

'Get in, Greg.'

He made for the passenger side and did as she'd said. She pressed down on the gas *and drove*.

# CHAPTER 40

*Shreya*

Ghani was dead.

She was still coming to terms with it. Kramer's two bullets finding their mark. Missing her by inches.

The woman called Miriam though was alive and in custody; led out of the house, bundled into the back of a van and spirited away into the night.

Shreya had watched from the sidelines, like a spectator at her own funeral, shivering under a silver-foil blanket as helicopters circled overhead and spotlights turned night into day. No sign of Aliyah though, or of anyone else, and suddenly Ghani's words had replayed in her head.

*'They've all gone. They cannot be stopped.'*

And then they'd rushed her to a hospital, shone lights in her eyes, stuck needles in her arms and stitched her head. They'd given her painkillers and the all-clear and sped her to a debrief in a dilapidated factory building on the outskirts of Portland. Dan was there, but the questions came from another guy, bald-headed and wooden-faced, who called himself Sullivan.

*Why had she disobeyed orders? How had she found the house?*

She told them everything ... almost everything ... about the search south of Estacada; about Miriam; about the possibility that there were others involved ... everything save the part about Ghani's hesitation; his loosening of her bonds in the seconds before he was shot. She kept it back because she wasn't sure if it had actually happened. It all went by too fast to make sense of.

And then it was over and they told her to get some rest.

'What about the woman? What about Miriam?' she'd asked. 'Where's she being questioned?'

They told her that wasn't her concern and then they bundled her out the room and into a corridor where Kramer was waiting, looking like she'd run out of cigarettes.

'You okay?' Shreya asked.

'Yeah.'

*As okay, Shreya guessed, as it was possible to be after shooting a man in the head.*

'How'd you find me?'

Kramer gave a shrug. 'Tracker. All the Bureau's vehicles have 'em. We did a search and, sure enough, there you were, hunting for Ghani along the 224.' She smiled weakly. She looked like a student correcting their teacher at the chalkboard. 'Seems you won't be heading to San Diego quite as soon as we thought. Guess I should take you back to the hotel.'

\*

The streets of Portland looked like a scene from an Edward Hopper painting: hues of yellow and orange sodium light reflecting off the dark.

Kramer drove slowly, lost in her own thoughts. Shreya left her to it. She'd killed a man tonight. Something like that took time to process, even if you'd done it before.

Her phone buzzed.

*Nikhil.*

What was he doing phoning her at this hour?

Kramer read her face.

'Boyfriend?'

'Ex-husband.'

Kramer rolled her eyes.

'Take it.'

Shreya nodded and accepted the call.

'What is it, Nik? Is Isha okay?'

Nikhil's voice, all but lost amid an ocean of interference.

'Shreya?'

'Nik. Is everything okay?'

She concentrated, trying to make out his words.

'Where are you, Shreya? I just got a call from Raj. Says he saw you on the news; said you looked like you'd been shot. Some Muslim terrorist place up in Oregon.'

She let out a sigh.

*Nik's cousin, Raj. Damn him.*

'I'm fine, Nik. I wasn't shot. Tell Raj to get his facts straight before mouthing off. And don't go telling any of this to Isha or my dad.'

She listened to static on the line.

'You got to stop this, Shreya. How long before you *do* get hurt?'

'Don't start. This isn't the time.'

'How long before I end up having to tell Isha and your dad some really bad news?'

'This is my job, Nik.'

*And I'm good at it,* she wanted to say, but what was the point?

She'd said it before: to him, to Dan, to half a dozen other people in the Bureau.

'We . . . we worry about you, Shreya.'

*We?*

Poor Nik. Her choices had never been easy on him.

'Your dad said you were coming back for Diwali.'

'I was hoping to. But it's looking unlikely now. This case . . .'

'The Muslim thing? Be careful. You know what they're like.'

She flinched. For a smart guy, he could be awfully closed-minded. Parroting the views of his parents. The politics of the subcontinent alive and flourishing in Alabama.

'I gotta go. Tell Isha I . . . that I'll call her when things are less hectic.'

She hung up and stuffed the phone back into her jacket.

'So the ex is still calling you?'

'It's fine. He was just phoning to make sure I was okay.'

Kramer threw her a glance.

'Nice guy. If my ex heard I'd been shot, she'd throw a party. So tell me about Ripplebrook. You get anything out of Ghani?'

Shreya found herself tensing.

'I don't think Ghani had anything to give. I think he just did what he was told. It's the woman, Miriam, who was in charge.'

Kramer raised an eyebrow.

'The old lady? You talked to her?'

'A little. She wanted to know why I was interested in Ghani. I spun her a story about him being wanted in San Diego. She didn't buy it. Told Ghani to get rid of me.'

'You reckon she was born a Muslim or just a convert? They say the converts are the real nutjobs.'

Shreya shrugged. 'No idea.'

'She tell you anything else?'

'Such as?'

'Where Aliyah might be? Who she's with? Where she's heading?'

The roads began to look familiar. The hotel wouldn't be far away. She suddenly felt hollow. The doctors had told her to rest, but the job wasn't done yet.

'Forget the hotel,' she said. 'Do you know where they're interrogating the woman?'

# CHAPTER 41

*Sajid*

Sajid drove. Slowly this time. Without purpose. Without hope.

No. That was not true. His hopes and his mood rose and fell like a boat upon a storm-tossed swell. One moment he might believe that it was surely over, that Aliyah was dead or the authorities had arrested her and not disclosed the fact. They would charge her and try her and sentence her to spend the bloom-years of her life incarcerated in some American gulag. But then in an instant, he would be just as convinced that she was still free, still out there for him to find.

He prayed – a thousand silent prayers to Allah – may it be that his daughter was still at liberty. That whoever they had found and brought out of that house, that Aliyah was not one of them.

The irony. For the last two days he had prayed that she might be there in that place when he reached it and now he wished just as fervently for the opposite. That she was somewhere, any-where else.

For two hours he and Carrie had sat atop their hill, hiding the car behind a thicket of trees and maintaining a hopeless vigil as SUVs and vans sped past, leaving the scene and heading for who knew where. And in the opposite direction went trucks, unmarked and antiseptic white, heading for the house down in that hollow.

'*Forensics,*' Carrie had said.

They had watched as the news helicopter turned, pirouetting in the sky before flitting off back to the north. They had waited until the other one, the police one, had finally turned off its beam and thrown the scene into darkness.

'What now?' he'd asked.

He drove north, the words of the news report playing in his head.

'*A body brought out on a stretcher.*'

Aliyah? Greg? Or someone else?

It didn't bear thinking about, and in the absence of further infor-mation, it wasn't just futile, it was dangerous. He wondered if Carrie was thinking something similar. She had not spoken since he'd started the engine again.

On the outskirts of Estacada, a dimly lit roadside billboard advertised a motel called the Redstones. He pulled off the highway and followed the directions into town until he saw it. He parked, then watched as Carrie walked to the reception, the shadow of her frame falling long under the orange glow of a street lamp. His body ached.

She came back with a set of keys. One room, twin beds, one night only. The thought of it made him flush with discomfort and embarrassment. He would have purchased a separate room if it had been possible, but his stock of dollars, like his stock of self-respect, was dwindling, and so he would bear this shame, like he had borne so many other humiliations in his life, because he could not afford to do otherwise.

He got out and retrieved Carrie's bag from the boot while she went off to purchase food from a vending machine.

The motel room was musty and furnished in hues of rusted orange and brown, with two single beds that all but touched the floor when sat upon. It reminded him of a bedsit he had once stayed in in Shepherd's Bush. He placed Carrie's bag on the bald carpet and headed straight for the TV, switched it on and turned to CNN. The immediate pictures were of a political rally – or a riot, he found it hard to tell the difference these days.

He felt a sudden need to call Rumina, a burning urgency to hear her voice, even if her words were caustic. Just a text reminding him to take his tablets, or even simply the sound of her breath would be enough – a tether back to *his* life; his normal, quiet, *real* life. But that was impossible. There could be no communication between them, nothing that the authorities might pick up on.

Carrie brushed past him toward the en suite and he heard the whining of pipes and the splash of water. She had left open the door and he saw her lower the shirt from her shoulder, revealing the bandage he had applied to her arm. Here and there, the white gauze was flecked reddish brown. He would need to examine it.

'Don't touch it,' he told her. 'Let me take a look.'

From the bag, he grabbed fresh bandages and iodine. Carrie came out of the bathroom and sat on one of the beds. He took her arm, gently unwrapped the gauze and examined the wound, the lacerated flesh still raw.

'How bad is it, doc? I need to get back to work, once this is over.'

She was a domestic carer, she had told him. A home help, she had said, *'for the old folks and the ill all round Levy County'*, wherever that might be.

'I think we can avoid amputation.'

'Well that's a relief.'

'For you *and* the good people of Levy County.'

She suppressed a laugh.

'Tell me about them,' he said. 'About the people you look after.'

'Not much to tell. There's about three dozen folks, elderly mainly, some younger though, all shut-ins, dotted round the county. I look in on them, do what I can in the one-hour slot the company gives me: cook for them, clean for them, make sure they're okay and that they're presentable. It's precious little time to do anything. I sometimes got eight visits a day and there's the driving in between.'

She flinched as he cleaned her wound.

'It must be hard,' he said.

'It's not so bad. I've known some of them since I was a girl. They're like uncles and aunts to me, and they appreciate the company. Sometimes I'm the only person they'll see all week.'

She fell into introspection for a moment as he silently applied fresh gauze.

'And then there are the bad days. The days when you lose someone. Just two weeks ago, I lost one. Miss Kenny.' She sighed. 'I was the one who found her. She passed away in her bed at least. Poor woman; the good Lord takes some too soon and others not soon enough. Back in 2010, she lost her husband to Parkinson's and her boy to an IED in Iraq. All in the space of six months. The flag on her front porch's been at half-mast ever since. Well, I guess she's in a better place now.'

He found himself agreeing with that. A better place. Even if it was no place at all.

The image on-screen flickered. The picture changed and then

there it was, the house outside of Ripplebrook, its tin roof bathed in helicopter spotlight. Recorded pictures, he presumed. Taken while they had looked on.

The image was larger and clearer than anything he could make out back on the hill. The old house was a ghost of a building with hollow black windows and flaking white timber boards. Beyond it, a set of sagging wooden steps led down to a dirt yard which had now been transformed into a haphazard parking lot with law enforcement and emergency vehicles strewn across the mud.

The helicopter circled; the picture pirouetted, panning in on the rear of the house before turning again. *A 360-degree view of the house which Aliyah had come to. Was she there when the police arrived?*

The same question again in his head. Over and over.

Off-camera a reporter spoke in volatile tones of a corpse stretchered from the scene: a bearded man, in his thirties or forties. He sat down on the bed beside Carrie, the weight of his body enough to alter the centre of gravity, pulling her toward him. Self-consciously, he shifted away, hoping she might not notice.

The helicopter circled around once more. On the ground, a woman, wrapped in silver. He felt his pulse quicken. *It couldn't be . . . Could it?* He did not have time to dwell upon it, his attention caught by movement at the door of the house, the camera rushing in to zoom, a blurred image resolving into focus: agents walking out, a figure between them, head covered with a blanket.

Down the steps.

Across the dirt.

Into an SUV.

He tried to make out the shape under the blanket.

*A woman.* As the agents manoeuvred the figure into the back of the vehicle, the blanket slipped. A shock of silver hair. The face of a white woman: narrow, eyes widely set.

*Not Aliyah.*

He breathed out. 'Thanks be to God.' He turned to Carrie. 'It's not them! They're still out there. We can find them!'

She had her hands held up to her mouth.

'Carrie? What is it?'

'That woman . . .'

'What about her?'

'I think I . . . she looks . . .' Finally she turned to him. 'It doesn't matter. You're right, our kids are free.'

She leaned over and hugged him. He closed his eyes, thanked Allah once more, and hugged her back. Long seconds. The tensions ebbing from his shoulders like the ocean drawing back from the sand. But that woman on the television. Carrie's reaction to her concerned him.

When he turned back to the TV, the image of the house and the woman had gone. In their place, he saw his own photograph.

# CHAPTER 42

*Shreya*

The lights of downtown faded in the rear-view. Ahead of them, a post-industrial wasteland of warehouses and wharves. A distance of ten miles, she reckoned, yet it was like going back half a century, from shining glass and steel to cracked brown brick and rubble.

Kramer pulled into the yard beside what looked like a shuttered factory. No lights visible from the outside, least not as far as Shreya could see, then down a slip road into an underground parking lot. A *black site*. Something the FBI had learned from the CIA. They weren't supposed to exist, and the FBI's lawyers would swear blind that they didn't, just like CIA's lawyers had about their own overseas.

She didn't notice any security, not till Kramer had brought the car to a stop beside a couple of empty SUVs. Then she saw the cameras, small, unobtrusive, all-seeing. No one challenged them as they walked from the car, across the lot to a set of doors and into a stairwell. There would, she knew, be armed agents too, concealed close by, ready to intervene and interdict should the order come through.

They took the stairs up one level, then crossed a cavernous floor that echoed to the sound of their footsteps. In the glare of some strip lights, the lumpen carcasses of heavy machinery loomed like fossils.

And then she saw it: *the tank*. A metal box like a couple of shipping containers welded together, floating above the cement floor on iron struts. A room within a room within a black site. Soundproofed, of course, blocking both electronic signals *and* screams.

Kramer gestured to a nearby door.

'We can watch from in there.'

Shreya followed her into a room with the lights turned low and a gaggle of agents gathered in front of a bank of screens on one wall. The images were pin-sharp: the woman called Miriam shackled to a seat, every flicker of movement recorded, every expression ready to be analysed.

Dan sat the other side of a metal table while the bullet-headed Sullivan prowled the floor, jacket off, shirtsleeves rolled. Miriam looked up: blood on her lip; the scar on her face now joined by a purpling bruise.

Shreya questioned one of the agents watching the screen.

'Anything?'

'Nothing yet.'

On the monitors, Dan shoved a number of photos across the table.

'You know who that is? That's Yasmin Malik ... or what's left of her, after you sent her to kill those people. And here are the results.' He stabbed a finger down on a photo. 'Sixty-five people dead. Kids and old folks. People who never hurt anyone.' He jabbed at the photo. 'That little girl there. She was six years old. What did she do to deserve that?'

Miriam stared at him, impassive.

Dan pushed forward another photo.

'Who's this? We know he drove Yasmin to the mall and that he left just as the bomb exploded. Where is he now? Is he with Aliyah Khan?'

Shreya's phone buzzed. Mike Raven's name.

'Mike.'

'You're still alive then.'

'For the moment. What is it?'

'I'm trying to get a hold of Dan, but his phone's off.'

'He's questioning a suspect.'

'That's why I'm calling. We've identified her. Her name's Maria O'Connor. But, Shreya, there's some weird shit going on. She's ex-army. Her file's classified, and I mean bells and whistles, the whole fucking thing. I'm not even sure the president can access this. For the moment, all I can find is that she served in Afghanistan as a member of the ISA –'

'The what?'

'The Intelligence Support Activity. It's one of the army's spec ops units. They collect intelligence for JSOC, that's the Joint Special Operations Command to you. They're the people who tracked down bin Laden.'

'She's an analyst?'

Mike gave a snort. 'No, Shreya, she's a soldier with a Mensa-level IQ. Most ISA personnel are ex-special forces and fluent in several languages. She could probably kill you with her bare hands while reciting the works of Rumi in Persian.'

She struggled to comprehend.

'You're saying that this super-soldier is working with Islamic terrorists? But why?'

'That's for you and Dan to figure out. I'm sending you an email. You got to show it to Dan.'

She hung up and checked her inbox. Mike's name at the top of the list of emails. She clicked it open and read it.

'I need to speak to Dan.'

Kramer looked at her. 'What?'

'They've ID'd our woman. I need to pass this to Dan.'

Kramer's eyes widened. 'Who is she?'

'I'll tell you when I get back.'

She headed for the door, then across the floor toward the tank, Kramer a step behind her. Out of the shadows a figure appeared. A man: suited, gun drawn.

'Stop there.'

Shreya did as ordered.

'I need to speak with Agent Taylor in there. Urgently.'

'I don't know you. Let's see some ID.'

She reached into her jacket for her badge but it wasn't there. She checked her pockets. Nothing. She must've dropped it somewhere . . . no . . . that woman in there, Miriam, Maria O'Connor, back at the house in Ripplebrook, she'd known Shreya's name when she'd come to on that couch. She must have taken her ID.

'I don't have it. But I need to get in there.' She brandished her phone. 'It's vital he sees this.'

The guy shook his head. 'I'm afraid I'm gonna have to ask you to come with me, ma'am.'

She didn't have time for this.

Beside her, Kramer piped up.

'You know me, though, Steve, and I can vouch for Special Agent Mistry. Here's my ID.' She turned to Shreya. 'Give me your phone. I'll take the message.'

Shreya handed over the phone.

The agent turned to Kramer. 'I'll still need to frisk you.'

Shreya headed back to the anteroom with its bank of monitors while the agent patted Kramer down. She was staring at the screens by the time Kramer entered the tank. The woman was still silent. She watched as Kramer crossed the floor and handed the phone to Dan. He read it silently, while Kramer looked at the woman who called herself Miriam. The woman stared back. Her expression changed, and then she spoke for the first time.

'You're the one who killed Yusuf.' Her voice betrayed no emotion, at least none that Shreya could discern. 'You'll pay for that.'

Dan returned the phone to Kramer.

The woman continued to stare at her.

'You hear me?'

Kramer headed for the door. Dan leaned forward.

'Maybe you should tell us how an ex-ISA operative gets mixed up with Islamic extremists, Ms O'Connor.'

On the bank of screens, Shreya focused on the one which showed a close-up of O'Connor's face. The woman breathed in, a long, contemplative breath, then exhaled just as slowly.

Dan fired a burst of questions into the silence.

'When did you become involved with Islamic extremists?

'During your time in Afghanistan?

'Did you convert to Islam?

'Is that how you were recruited?

'What was your relationship with Yusuf Ghani?

'Where's Aliyah Khan?

'How many others are there?'

The woman seemed to smile, then shook her head slowly.

Dan offered another question.

'What did it take for you to betray your country? Was it religion, or love, or something else? Believe me, we'll get to the truth, and then you'll die for your treason.'

Miriam looked up.

'Treason? Have you seen what's happening to the country? The

Republic is on its knees. The clock is ticking and we're two seconds to midnight, and you think I'm the traitor?'

Dan looked to Sullivan who was still on his feet, circling the room like a boxer. The big man covered the distance to where Maria O'Connor sat, shackled. In one swift movement, he pulled back his fist, then shot it forward. Shreya watched as it connected with the side of O'Connor's face.

'Now I'll ask you again. Where is Aliyah Khan and who else is involved?'

Blood dripped from O'Connor's lip. She staunched it with her tongue and stared at Sullivan.

'Violence,' she said. 'It's a fascinating thing, isn't it? The naked expression of raw power. We say we despise it. We lay claim to higher values. But at the end of the day, it always comes back to violence. Your authority; the authority of the FBI; the authority of the whole US government; all the talk of principles and morals, and in the end, it all just comes down to having the biggest stick. Legitimacy resting upon your monopoly of violence.'

She turned to Dan.

'Have you ever experienced true fear, Special Agent? True fear is when you realise that the power you think you have, the power you think makes you invulnerable, is just an illusion. It's when you realise you don't have a monopoly on violence, and that there's someone out there with a bigger stick. Someone with the power to kill you and whom you can't stop. True fear is when you realise that your perceived strength is built on sand and that, in reality, you're weak and naked and most likely going to die. Would you like me to introduce you to that fear, Special Agent . . . *Daniel J. Taylor?*'

Shreya's ears tingled.

She shouldn't know his name.

On-screen, Dan blinked, once, then again. The woman smiled.

'Let's start from the beginning, then. You brought me here

blindfolded. You chained me to this chair in a box without windows. We could be anywhere, couldn't we? No doubt it's well protected. You probably feel safe here, inside your little fortress. What if I were to tell you that this fortress of yours is nothing of the sort? What if I were to tell you its location? What if I were to tell you that you've no idea what you're dealing with and that in approximately ten minutes, this place will be nothing but rubble and that you, me and Agent Sullivan here will most likely be dead.'

Sullivan grunted and aimed a slap at her face.

Dan raised a hand.

'Stop!'

Maria O'Connor spat a laugh. She leaned forward.

'Would you like me to tell you where we are?'

She whispered something too faint for the microphones to pick up. Shreya watched as the colour drained from Dan's face. The woman was ex-special forces. What was it Mike Raven had said?

'. . . soldiers with Mensa-level IQs . . .'

And then she recalled Yusuf's Ghani's words.

'They have people everywhere.'

A metallic scrape as Dan pushed back his chair and stood.

Shreya turned to the other agents. 'What sort of security do you have here?'

The question met with silence. It didn't matter. She was already halfway out the door.

She met Dan coming down the steps from the tank, looking like he'd been hit by a truck. He saw her and rubbed at his forehead.

'She knows where we are. How is that possible?'

'We need to get her out of here, Dan. Whatever's going on, it's far bigger than we thought. We need to get her to a secure facility.'

'This *is* a secure facility, Shreya. Short of an army base, there's nowhere better. And if she's ex-army, there's no guarantee that even that's safe. No. We call in reinforcements and keep her here.'

301

'And what if she's telling the truth? What if this place is about to be attacked? You read that message – the woman in there was special forces. She knows your name. She knows this location. Whoever she's working with, it's not just some bunch of Islamic terrorists. If they attack this building, they'll do so with overwhelming force. They'll want to get her back or kill her. The only logical thing to do is to get her out of here. *Now!*'

He didn't have time to respond.

The air exploded. Noise and light and dust. Screams, then shouts. The floor beneath her shook. And then the lights went out.

# CHAPTER 43

*Shreya*

'Shreya! Have you got a gun?'

Dan's voice, faint. Her ears still ringing from the explosion. Then another noise. The rat-tat of semi-automatic gunfire.

Dan was shaking her.

'Do you have a gun?'

Did she? She didn't think so.

'No.'

The lights flickered and came on again. A generator must have kicked in. Agents were running in all directions. She saw Kramer running toward her.

Dan grabbed her hand.

'Take this.'

She looked down. A Glock.

'And here's the badge she took from you. I want you to get that woman out of here.'

He turned and sprinted for the tank and she ran to keep up.

'Shouldn't we stay here and wait for reinforcements?'

'What? While the whole place is blown up? Like you said, whoever's out there, they know what they're doing. They're attacking an FBI facility for chrissakes. They wouldn't do that if they didn't think they could storm the place before help arrives. I don't know if they want to kill her or just get her back, but the logical thing to do is to get her away from here.'

'Where to?'

He reached the steps.

'Anywhere, just get her out and keep driving till we know what's happening. Take the rookie with you. She knows the city.'

'What about you?'

'I'm in charge. I gotta get the rest of these agents out. Now!'

Another explosion rent the air.

She followed him into the tank. He gave Sullivan the order to unshackle the prisoner. The chain slithered to the ground. Shreya gripped the Glock, tight. The woman was still cuffed, but it was best to take no chances. As Mike Raven had said, this woman could kill her while reciting Rumi.

She gave Sullivan a nod, then pushed Maria O'Connor out of the tank, down the steps. The lights flickered. The sound of gunfire was louder now. In the distance she saw shadows, approaching slowly.

Kramer was waiting.

'We gotta get to the car.'

Dan and Sullivan came down the steps, guns drawn, running interference. They headed to the stairwell to the sound of bullets. Where was it coming from? She tried to think, failed. Sullivan let off a couple of rounds. Random shots into the flickering light. A mistake. At least eight or ten shots furiously returned. One of them found its target, the left side of Sullivan's face disintegrated. The big man dropped. She wanted to stop. Had to see if there was anything she could do to save him. Dan forced her on. He was already dead. A moment later she was shoving a silent Maria O'Connor through the door to the stairwell.

Kramer looked up. 'I'll get the car and meet you at the door.' She sprinted down the stairs.

Shreya turned to Dan. His face was streaked with sweat.

'You're sure about this?'

He gave a nod.

'I have to stay here, Shreya.'

He gestured to O'Connor.

'Now get her out of here.'

With her gun at the woman's back, Shreya herded her down the stairs and waited till she heard the screech of tyres before bundling her through the doors. She pushed O'Connor into the back of the SUV, jumped in beside her and Kramer hit the gas.

Shreya steadied herself, fighting momentum as the car hurtled up the ramp.

'Keep your head down,' Kramer said. 'We're hitting the street!'

Shreya pushed O'Connor down, then ducked low. They surfaced into a hail of bullets, the thud of projectiles against armour plating and reinforced glass.

The vehicle roared over the exit ramp. Shreya's stomach lurched.

Kramer gave a whoop and accelerated out of the yard and onto rain-soaked streets. Shreya sat up and turned to look out the shattered back window. The warehouse was ablaze, smoke pouring from the top floor, tongues of flame licking at boarded windows. No sign of pursuit.

'Where now?' Kramer called out from the front.

It was a good question.

'Head for the freeway into town.'

Shreya stuck the Glock into O'Connor's ribs.

'Islamic extremists don't attack FBI secure facilities. It might be in your interests to tell me who that was back there, because it seems they'd be happy to see you dead.'

The woman said nothing. Just leaned back and closed her eyes.

Kramer took a left. A main road now. Headlights and tail lights filling the windshield.

'Are we being followed?'

Kramer checked the mirror.

'I don't think so . . . wait.'

She swung the wheel and flung the car round a corner. A moment later, she did it again, another corner, another turn. Shreya held on to her seat as O'Connor fell into her. She pulled the gun clear, just in case the woman should try to lunge for it, and pointed it at her head.

Kramer cursed. 'Bad news. There's at least one car on our tail.' She accelerated, the needle on the speedometer rising.

O'Connor gave a bitter laugh.

'You won't outrun them. They'll hunt you down and then they'll kill you.'

Shreya risked a glance out the back window. Headlights, bright, white, showing no sign of falling back. Then they were flying up an on-ramp, swerving into freeway traffic, car horns blaring behind them. Kramer freed the engine; another burst of acceleration. Neon lights passed in a blur, the car switching lanes and overtaking vehicles. Shreya took another glance behind. Too many headlights now. Impossible to identify their pursuers.

Her phone buzzed. Dan's number. She kept the Glock pointed at O'Connor and answered.

'Dan? You okay?'

'They're after you, Shreya.'

He sounded shaken.

'I know. We've spotted them. Are you okay?'

'At least four agents down, but it's over. Whoever attacked us, they melted away as soon as you and Kramer left the building.'

'That means they knew our friend would be in the car. How?'

'How'd they even know where she was in the first place? Where are you?'

'On the freeway, making for . . . Dan, I'm not saying.'

'Okay. Good. Keep going. I'm sending you GPS coordinates for an FBI safe house. Lose your tail, then head there.'

She hung up. They hit the eyeline of a bridge. The lights of downtown Portland rose to meet them.

'Pull off at the next exit,' she said. 'We need to shake whoever's following us.'

The turn-off approached fast. Kramer kept driving, ignoring it until it was almost too late, then swerving right and crashing onto the off-ramp. Shreya turned. Two cars followed.

*Dammit.*

Ahead of them traffic lights glowed blood red. Kramer doubled down, hitting the gas and roaring through the junction, swerving to avoid a truck. Once more horns blared. Behind them an eruption of noise and the crash and scrape of metal.

'One down,' she said.

Shreya's phone buzzed. Coordinates from Dan.

Kramer hit the brakes and turned the wheel. The car skidded ninety degrees. She hit the gas again, slaloming down a side street. Jesus, she could drive. White light filled the car. Kramer swerved to avoid an oncoming vehicle. Another quick left, then a right and then she accelerated once more, hard. Blue and red lights flashed through the windshield. Sirens blared as emergency vehicles shot past, heading the other way.

It was another few minutes before Kramer spoke.

'I think we've lost them.'

Shreya looked round. No lights behind them. No sign of pursuit. 'You're sure?'

'I think so.'

Shreya breathed out. She turned to O'Connor. 'Looks like your friends aren't quite as persistent as you thought.' She regretted the words even as they left her mouth. They were cocky, but far worse, they tempted fate, and if there was one thing her late mother's brand of Hinduism had taught her, it was never to tempt fate.

She punched the coordinates Dan had texted into the map on her phone and passed the device to Kramer. A red dot pulsed on the screen, twenty miles distant. Fifteen more minutes of survival.

Kramer drove fast, sticking to back roads but still covering the distance with the engine full bore, the dot getting inexorably closer. Outside, the city changed to suburban. The buildings thinned out. The roads emptied. The street lights faded to black.

They were less than five miles away. Another few minutes at most and they'd be at the safe house. She didn't know exactly who'd be waiting, but they'd be well armed. Of that she was sure. Enough firepower to hold off a tank division, hopefully.

The map showed a long street, another ten blocks before a few turns and they'd be there.

She didn't see what hit them.

Kramer let out a cry.

They hurtled, spinning sideways, into the black. The car flipped over, a screeching, wailing mass of twisting metal and flying glass. Airbags exploded. For an instant, Shreya felt weightless, before G-force crushed her against the seat belt.

Her chest burned.

She opened her eyes to the darkness. The world upside down. She was hanging, suspended from her seat. She reached for the belt release and fell to the ceiling. Her ribs ached. Blood in her mouth.

It took far longer than it should have for everything to come into focus. How long exactly? Seconds? Minutes?

She called out for Kramer but heard nothing.

Her eyes focused. The girl wasn't where she should be. She turned, looking for O'Connor, and saw only the passenger door hanging open.

*No.*

She called out again.

'Kramer!'

Once more there was no reply.

She needed to get out. No. She needed to find something else first. Her Glock. Where was it?

Had O'Connor taken it? No. Because then Shreya would already be dead. She searched frantically.

*There! Between the floor and the upended front seat.*

She grabbed it then pulled herself through the wreckage to the open door, emerging from twisted metal to find a truck stopped in the middle of the street, its front grille crumpled and its radiator dripping fluid. To one side were two figures: one standing, gun in hand. The other prone. The one with the gun had white hair.

Shreya raised her Glock and yelled. A cry of anger and indistinct words. O'Connor turned.

'Not another step, Agent Mistry.'

Shreya stood her ground, keeping the Glock pointed squarely at the woman, fighting to keep her arm from shaking.

O'Connor seemed utterly calm, tilted her head as if in deep thought.

'You don't think she deserves to die? She killed one of mine. That comes with consequences.'

Kramer piped up. 'Fuck you. I had no choice. I did what I had to.'

O'Connor shut her up with a savage blow to the head. Kramer jerked forward.

Behind them, a car drew up. Shreya shielded her eyes against the glare of headlights.

'You harm her and you won't make it as far as that car.'

O'Connor seemed to find that amusing.

'You don't think I could kill you both?'

Shreya didn't doubt it, but it'd be a gamble.

'I don't think you want to take that chance.'

The woman gave her a nod. She grabbed Kramer by the collar and dragged her backwards toward the waiting car. The passenger door flew open. Shreya took a step forward, then another, closing the distance between them.

'I won't let you take her.'

O'Connor ran her tongue over her lips. Shreya tensed, her finger slick against the trigger.

'Final warning, O'Connor.'

In one fluid movement the woman pushed Kramer away and dived into the vehicle. Shreya sprinted toward Kramer, reaching her as the car tore into the night.

# DAY 6

## *SATURDAY*

## CHAPTER 44

*Greg*

'Who is this guy?'

He kept his hands on the wheel, his gaze firmly at the darkness outside the windshield.

'Someone who owes me.'

'From your time in prison?'

'From my time in Afghanistan.'

'And we can trust him?'

They had no choice. That was it. He was pretty much out of cash and the Alfa was drinking gas like it was going out of fashion, which he supposed it was. He could steal another car but they'd still need cash to fill it at least a couple of times between there and Florida, and Finn Ruck was just about the only person in a thousand-mile radius who might see his way clear to lending him some. Not that he'd sounded all that happy to hear from him when he'd called.

Idaho had given way to Utah (state capital: Salt Lake City).

'An easy one,' she'd said, so he'd thrown a couple of others at her.
'Missouri?'

'Jefferson City.'

'Delaware?'

'Dover.'

God only knew if she was right or not, but she'd answered without hesitation and sounded certain. He looked over at her.

'You wouldn't lie to me, would you?'

She reached for his hand.

'Not about something so important.'

It was the first time she'd reached out for him since Ripplebrook. That was more than enough for him.

He drove as she studied the road atlas of Utah, now and then making a note.

'You ever wonder why state capitals are so often these weird, shitty little places?'

He hadn't, but now that he thought about it . . .

'I've got a theory,' she said. 'Politicians stunt a place. Too many of them in one town and they poison it with their bickering and their corruption. They're like parasites, sucking the lifeblood out of their host.'

He couldn't help but laugh.

'Well, when we get to Missouri, you can explain it all to the good folks of Jefferson City.'

'Missouri can wait,' she said. 'Right now, I want to know about Utah.'

He shrugged and suddenly felt embarrassed. He knew so little about the place.

'Mormons,' he told her. 'This is where they come from.' He was fairly sure that was right. 'And there's a beehive on the state flag.'

The latter point had made her smile.

*

She was asleep now and they were almost at Finn's.

It wasn't much to look at, just a cinder-block house on a twisting spur on the outskirts of a one-horse town called Clement: a flag above the door, a light on in the front room and a scrap of a yard out front.

Parking nearby was out of the question. The Alfa would stand out like a ballerina at a bullfight. He reached for the maps, picked out the one of Utah and turned the pages till he found Clement and then Finn's road. The map showed a side street close by that wound on out into the scrub. That was good enough. Greg kept on till he saw it; turning the wheel and driving up, past a graveyard of forgotten vehicles: skeletal remains, gutted and rusted like old ships marooned on a dried-up lakebed. He parked up some feet beyond, close to a gnarled, leafless tree and killed the ignition.

He stared out into the void beyond the windshield. The fatigue of the last 150 miles had dissipated. In its place an adrenaline-fuelled energy. The engine block ticked and his thoughts fell in line with its rhythm. This was a big fuckin' risk, no matter what he might tell Aliyah. Five years since he'd last seen Finn. Basically an eternity. People could change a lot in that time. Specially people coming home from war. It was a gamble, with their lives possibly, but right now he couldn't think of a better option.

He felt Aliyah stir beside him. He turned to her as though seeing her afresh, taking in the fall of her hair against her cheek, the curve of her mouth, the rhythmic rise and fall of her chest. He hadn't noticed any of these things when they'd first met. People talked of love at first sight but that wasn't his experience. To him, love was a slow-burn: a sort of gradual awakening. And once you were awake you were helpless.

He touched her hand gently yet she woke with a start, a momentary wariness that subsided only when she saw his face. She began to massage the stiffness from her neck.

'We there?'

He gave her a nod.

'House is about a half-mile down the road.'

He felt her anxiety. Less than forty-eight hours ago she was back in Ripplebrook, trusting in Miriam, confident about, if not the future, then at least of her role in it; unaware that she was being used, unaware that *he* was about to turn everything on its head. He had been right to, though. Right to get her out of there. He knew that, even if he didn't understand what the hell was going on or just how he was going to get her to Florida.

He took her hand in his.

'It'll be all right.'

He opened the door and manoeuvred his legs out, the cramp gnawing at them like starving rats. He flexed the joints, coaxing back the circulation, then got unsteadily to his feet. Aliyah, wearing his baseball cap, was already out and grabbing the bags from the trunk. He took a rucksack from her and his duffel and led the way back toward the house.

The light in the front room was off now. The house just a collection of shadows no different from the others around it, as anonymous as a book on a shelf. The street seemed suddenly exposed: no longer small-town America but a canyon in hostile country; a dozen blacked-out windows behind which a hundred eyes might watch, or a dozen snipers take aim.

The path to the door beckoned. From above, just below the gutter, the small black lens of a security camera watched them. He forced himself to breathe, the breath freezing in front of him.

'Wait here,' he told her, and she took up station beside a tree in the front yard.

He made the long walk up the path, feeling naked, vulnerable, closing the distance to the door. Knocked softly. In the silence, the sound seemed to ricochet. Somewhere a dog howled. He glanced over his shoulder. Nothing there save the chasm of night and the frost-bitten silence.

He waited, dangerous seconds that stretched on without relief. He checked the number on the door. This was the place; this was the address Finn had given him. He knocked again, then stared up at the security camera, his arms out wide. The wind seemed to pick up, an icebox blast that swept through the yard, whistling between barren branches and whipping up an eddy of dead leaves. He shivered.

*Where the hell was Finn?*

From behind him came the rumble of an engine. He turned to see the jaundiced glare of headlights in the distance.

*Aliyah.* She'd be visible from the road. He hobbled back along the path, making it to the tree, reaching for her in the dark, his hands finding nothing. His heart raced. Had she left him again? Had she simply been playing along, lulling him into complacency and then running at the first opportunity? He looked up. The car was drawing closer, the beams of its headlamps like searchlights, seeking them out.

'Greg!'

Her voice. *Thank God.*

'Greg. Over here!'

He followed the sound until he saw her at the base of a low wall. Her hand, beckoning him. He let out a breath and stumbled forward to join her, ducking down low. The dog howled again. The car rumbled closer, the growl of the engine rising as it approached. He chanced a look. On its roof, a light-bar. A cop car. Red and blue beacons dark for now.

'Are they looking for us?'

Aliyah's voice, a whisper at his side.

'No,' he said, but that was for her benefit. He considered the options. The Alfa was too far away to make a run for. Their best hope was to hide. To disappear into the darkness and wait. He reached for the knife at his belt.

From behind him came the sound of a door opening. He turned and made out the front of Finn's house. A slash of light from the hallway.

He grabbed Aliyah's hand and, at a crouch, rushed her to the door as the headlights flooded the air above them. A figure stood in silhouette just the other side of the threshold. He closed the door behind them, locking the deadbolts.

For a moment, they stood in silence, Greg listening, as outside the noise of the engine receded. Light spilled from a room somewhere down the hall.

'Greg.'

*Finn.* Older than he remembered.

He held out a hand, and for a second, Finn grasped it. He turned to Aliyah.

'The fuck is this? You never mentioned anyone else.'

'A friend.'

Finn grunted, then led them down the hallway. In the light of the kitchen, Greg got a better look. A thick orange beard over an XXL T-shirt. His friend had lost hair and gained pounds since Kandahar. Seemed the years hadn't been kind to either of them.

Finn's gaze, though, was fixed on Aliyah, the surprise he'd registered in the hallway changing now to something harsher, more bitter. Greg hoped it was just on account of her skin colour. He could talk his way through that.

Finn's eyes suddenly widened.

'Wait . . . I seen you . . . *shit* . . .'

His bitterness turning to anger. Greg reached once more for his knife.

'What the fuck, Greg? That's the fucking Moslem chick the Feds are looking for!'

One chance. That's all he had to head this off. The alternative was not something he wanted to consider.

'It ain't her, Finn.'

The ex-soldier stared at him.

'What?'

He pulled back the collar of his shirt, revealing the swastika.

He shot a look at Aliyah and prayed she'd understand.

'You think I'd be hanging around with a damn raghead, after what they did to me?'

Finn glanced down at his knee.

'So who the hell is she then?'

'A friend. From Juarez. All you need to know is that she's with me. Or isn't that enough for you? You forget who got you out of Kandahar alive?'

Finn reddened. Greg pressed his advantage.

'Look, I ain't gonna lie to you. There's some messed-up shit goin' on, but it ain't what you think. It's mistaken identity. They're trying to frame her.'

Finn ran a hand through thinning hair.

''There's a price on her head, for fuck's sake. The whole fucking government is out looking for her. Just by being here you're making me a goddamn accessory. Why the hell did you bring her *here*?'

'Cos we got nowhere else to go. And you owe me. Look, we need a place to spend the night and we'll be out of here before dawn.'

Finn paused.

'Six a.m. Be out of here by then.'

Greg gave him a nod.

'I'm also gonna need some cash.'

Finn shook his head.

'You want the shirt off my back too? Just be thankful I ain't calling the Feds right this minute.'

*

He took Aliyah's hand and followed Finn through a door and down a set of stairs steep enough to cause him problems.

'You're in here.'

The smell of mildew and confined dust assailed him. The room beyond was a den of sorts: cheap panelling on the walls, a beat-up couch and a dirty rug on the floor, all illuminated by a dim bulb hanging from a low ceiling. High up on one wall: a slit of a window. Good enough for ventilation but useless as an escape route.

Finn gestured to a chipped door in the corner.

'Toilet's through there.'

Greg put his bags on the floor.

'Thanks.'

Finn ignored him and retreated up the stairs, hardly looking at Aliyah. She closed the door and turned to Greg with that look on her face. He beat her to it.

'I know what you're gonna say. But we need a break and we'll freeze in the car. Besides, they're looking for you now. The less time we spend in the open, the better.'

To his surprise, she didn't argue. The shock, he guessed, of seeing her own face on the screen had knocked the fight out of her. Not that he was particularly thrilled at the prospect of spending the night in a basement. The only way out was up the stairs and through the door at the top. If Finn had second thoughts, all he'd have to do was lock that door and they'd be trapped down here. If he called the cops, the only way they were getting out was in handcuffs or body bags.

But he needed to think. Needed to work out just what the hell was happening. Ripplebrook was blown. Yusuf was dead. But what about Miriam? What of Jack and Rehana? And then there was Aliyah.

He would take her to Florida. The more he thought about it, the more it made sense. It was his country. His home. If he could protect her anywhere, it'd be there. He would take her there because he didn't know what else to do, and because if he didn't, he might lose her for good.

# CHAPTER 45

*Greg*

Greg wasn't sure he'd heard it. Nothing more than a click. In that gentle space between sleep and wakefulness it might have been his imagination, the birth of a dream. Whatever it was, it had jerked him to consciousness, instantly getting his bearings.

*What time was it?*

For the longest second there was nothing, just the thump of his own heart pounding within his chest. His blood pulsing through his limbs. But then he heard it. Footsteps on the boards above his head.

*Aliyah?*

No. She was still on the sofa. He could make out her profile.

He rolled his legs off the camp bed, muffling the creak of the springs as best he could and rose to his feet, wincing as a bolt of pain lanced through his bad knee. He reached out to the wall for support.

From above came muffled sounds.

*A voice?*

And then it was gone.

He reached for his boots. Why the hell had he taken them off in the first place? He should have slept in them, like he had his clothes.

He slipped them on. The laces could wait. He made for the stairs, dragged himself up them and stood with his fingers on the door handle.

He should go back. He should wake Aliyah and they should get the hell out of there. But he needed to know what, if anything, he was dealing with.

He turned it: slow and silent. Pale light filtered from the hallway. He stepped out, following it to the kitchen door, half ajar.

He pushed it open.

His friend was sat on a stool at a countertop. No one else there.

'Finn?'

The guy spun round.

'Greg? What you doin' up?' A hint of something in his voice. Surprise? Fear? Whatever it was, it was gone soon enough. 'Guess you couldn't sleep either. You want some coffee?'

'It's okay,' he said. 'We should really get going.'

Finn's eyes went to the clock on the wall. 'You couldn't have had much shut-eye.'

Greg gave a shrug.

'You were right. We should never have come here. I was tired; wasn't thinking straight. We'll get out of your way.'

He turned for the door.

'Wait.' Finn's voice, calling him back. 'This ain't some case of mistaken identity, is it? That girl down there's no Latina. We both seen enough of her kind to know the difference.'

Greg stopped. Finn sensed his hesitation.

'Why're you protecting her? You know she's the enemy.'

Greg bit at the flesh of his lower lip.

'I thought you believed the government was the enemy?'

'There's enemies on all sides. You know that. World's full of bad people. What you actually know about her?'

Finn was on his feet now, walking over. He turned to meet him.

'I know enough to say she ain't a terrorist,' he said.

'So what's she doing here, then? Sightseeing?'

What was he supposed to say? That she'd been groomed online? Lured here to be part of some plot he wasn't sure he understood any more. And yet . . . Aliyah wasn't some innocent, easily led naif. She knew what she was doing.

He didn't have time for this.

'She's done nothing wrong,' he said, and willed it to be true.

Finn was up close now, a foot or two away at most. Greg turned once more for the door.

'What about *you*, Greg?' Finn's voice, almost taunting now. 'That bomb that went off in LA. Looked pretty high tech to me. The sort of device most ragheads wouldn't know how to create. But you could.'

'Me and a couple thousand others.'

'Yeah, but those guys ain't running from the Feds with a terrorist suspect in tow. What is it? They turn you out there? Or is that girl down there givin' you something else? Can't imagine there's many girls keen on fucking a cripple.'

He felt the anger rising. Finn glanced over his head. *To the clock on the wall.*

Shit.

They needed to get the hell out of there.

'You're wrong,' he said and headed out, back into the darkened hallway.

He heard movement behind him. The sound of a drawer being pulled. He reached for his knife, pulling it from its sheath and pivoting on his good leg in one fluid motion.

Too late.

He stared down the barrel of a gun, his gut turning to ice. Finn gestured to the knife.

'You best put that down.'

He let the handle slip from his grip, the thing thudding to the floor and disappearing into the darkness.

'Turn around.'

He was in no position to argue. A hand on his back shoved him forward.

'Let's go wake wifey.'

'You forget I got this leg saving your ass? This how you're gonna repay me?'

Another hand in the back, pushing him down the stairs.

'Cops are already on their way. They'll be here any minute. Half a million dollars. That's what they're offering for info leading to her arrest. I can't figure why you haven't turned her in yourself. You must have it *bad* for her.'

The stairs were difficult. With Finn pressing him forward, it took an effort to navigate the razor edges of each step in the darkness without pitching forward or wrenching his knee.

He kept going, into the basement. Finn turned on the light.

'Where the fuck is she?'

He looked over, expecting to find Aliyah on the couch. Except she wasn't there. He scanned the room. She wasn't anywhere.

'Don't move.'

Finn began searching, checking the space under Greg's camp bed, behind the table, all the while keeping the gun pointed at him.

Greg's eyes went to the door of the toilet. It wouldn't take Finn long to reach the same conclusion.

Sure enough, a split second later, Finn lunged for it, turning the handle and pulling at it. The thing didn't budge.

Greg weighed his options. Didn't like them. But Finn would have that door open in a minute and Aliyah was in there.

Finn pulled at the handle again, the rattle of the door echoing through the basement. He aimed his gun at the lock and fired. A scream from inside. The wood around the lock splintered. Finn took aim again.

Greg steeled himself.

Finn fired. He flung the door open. Aliyah was crouched in a corner, hands covering her head as though that might save her somehow.

But Finn was off balance. His gun hand lowered. Greg leapt, aiming a fist at his head and using the full rotation of his upper body. His knuckles connected with a startling crack, the force jarring the bones of his hand. Finn's legs went from under him. Greg reached for the gun, and then they were both on the floor fighting for its handle. He got hold of Finn's wrist, twisting it, hitting it off the concrete floor, trying to knock the gun from his grasp.

He didn't see the elbow of the other arm smash into his face, connecting with his cheekbone and the cartilage of his nose. His vision blurred. He tasted blood. Still he held on, twisting Finn's wrist till he was sure it was about to snap. Finn yelled out. It would only be a few more seconds . . . and then Greg's world exploded. His whole body convulsed as if electrocuted.

Finn had twisted and kicked his knee, and kicked it even harder once more. He was immobile on the floor, holding his leg, writhing in pain. Finn grunted as he rose to his feet. Then he raised the gun.

*This was how it ended.*

And then Finn was falling, dropping to his knees, the gun clattering on the ground. There was something in his neck – a stave of wood splintered from the door. He opened his mouth wide, yelling without a sound, clutching at the shard with bloodied hands. Aliyah stood over him.

'Come on,' she whispered.

She pulled him up and manoeuvred him toward the stairs.

Finn, gargling in pain, was getting to his feet.

'Wait here,' she said, propping him against a wall. She went back, retrieved Greg's knife and the gun, and with one swift move, brought the butt down on the side of Finn's head. The man collapsed with a groan. She bent over him, whispered something, then went through his jeans. She grabbed his wallet and their bags and then she was back. He took the bags from her as she put his arm over her shoulder and hauled him up the stairs.

They reached the landing. His head still spun, from the pain, the nausea in his gut and the sight of Aliyah taking down Finn. Where had she found the will or the balls for that? Ahead, blue and red lights refracted through the curtains.

'The back door,' she said. 'This way.'

She dragged him on. He heard voices from the front of the house. Men knocking on the door. One patrol car, he hoped. Any more and they'd be toast.

Aliyah pulled at the back door.

'Fuck! There's no key.'

Greg heard a monstrous sound, a kind of guttural yell. *Finn.*

Aliyah turned. She passed him Finn's gun, then reached for the drawer in the counter beside the door, pulling it open, searching frantically for keys.

*There.*

Shouts from the front of the building. Finn's? *No. The police.* Hammering down the front door. Aliyah twisted the key in the lock; turned the handle.

Finn appeared, staggering, at the top of the stairs, the stave of wood in one bloodied hand.

Greg took aim.

It all happened at once: the front door bursting open; the police with their guns; Finn turning toward them; yells, shouts, muzzle flashes; gunshots; Finn falling backwards; Aliyah pulling Greg down and out the back door, into the frozen air.

Her shoulder under his arm, she dragged him, away from the flashing lights and the sounds, staggering through the darkness toward the trees. The voices behind them faded. How long though, before the police started searching outside? The Alfa was too far away. In his present state, they'd never make it. He told her as much. Told her to leave him and just get the hell out of there. She didn't reply, just pulled him on till they reached the edge of the road. She sat him down behind a clump of trees and then she was gone.

Behind him, in the distance, the night glowed. A halo of light over Finn's house. Bulbs on in every room. Two officers going through it. But in the air the sound of sirens. More cops on the way. How long would it take them to find him? He wondered where Aliyah was. He hoped she'd get away: hide, disappear, survive. The seconds ticked by, so slow that it felt unreal, like he was already dead. He closed his eyes and listened to the sounds of the night. He felt oddly at peace. As though his burden was finally lifting. He'd done his best for Aliyah. It was hardly atonement for all his sins, but it was a start.

He heard the murmur of an engine and the crunch of tyres on dirt. He opened his eyes and was blinded by the headlights of a cop car.

*No.*

*Not a cop car.*

*A truck.*

The driver's door opened. A figure rushed out. Aliyah, silhouetted against the lights. She pulled him to his feet, placed his arm over her shoulder and led him to the truck. She helped him into the passenger seat and then ran back to the other side and got in.

'How?' he asked.

As the truck shot off, she looked over.

'Your friend's keys were in his pocket. Seemed like a good idea to take them.'

# CHAPTER 46

*Sajid*

Sajid recited Fojor, the dawn prayer, then followed it up with one of his own, thanking the Almighty that it had not been Aliyah taken from that house on a stretcher, and seeking His blessing for what they planned to do next.

He came to with a start as the motel-room door opened, Carrie in the doorway, silhouetted by dim light.

'Breakfast,' she said. 'Hope you like it black.'

She passed him a paper cup and he took a sip and avoided her gaze. Seeing his own face on the TV screen had changed something. He felt tainted, worthless. It was as if he now wore a mark that distinguished him; that would cause others to recoil from him. It had somehow affected Carrie too. She seemed aloof this morning, taciturn, more reticent to talk to him than he'd expected.

He thought of Rumina. Just one more ignominy for her to bear. She must rue the day she ever met him; must curse her father for allowing him to marry her. What had he ever given her except insult heaped upon humiliation? She had borne it all, of course, sometimes with stoicism, sometimes with bitterness, but always she had endured. Even Rumina's patience had its limits though.

Carrie had misread his expression, confused his concern for Rumina for their proposed course of action.

'Don't worry,' she said. 'It'll be okay. It'll take a half-hour at most. You just lie low in the car. We'll be in and out before anyone knows we're there.'

*In and out . . .* of Ripplebrook. That was the plan. Going back to Ripplebrook was the only useful thing they could think of.

It all came down to Greg, the one piece of the puzzle they held which the police and the FBI were still unaware of. They would go back to Ripplebrook and Carrie would question the residents. She would show them photos of Greg and ask if they had seen him. If pressed, she would say he had gone missing in the area while hiking. A threadbare plan at best; more hope than strategy, yet hope was not nothing.

Outside, birds circled wide-winged on invisible currents. Gulls, he thought, but he could not be sure, crying their lament into the rain. It felt little different to London. At least there the weather seemed to mirror the cold, grey city itself – *in heaven as it was on earth* – but out here, in God's green wilderness, it was strange to him. Out of place. He loaded their few possessions into the car as Carrie made for the driver's side.

'Your arm?' he said.

She gave him a smile.

'It's okay. Feeling a lot better.'

Estacada, it appeared, woke early. It was, in his experience, the way of rural places, to toil before the dawn. Carrie stopped at a gas station and he slunk low in his seat. She returned with a scarf and a baseball cap with a picture of a bird on it. She passed them to him.

'Put 'em on. They'll help you blend in.'

He put on the cap and turned to her.

'Like a real American, no?'

Ripplebrook arrived soon enough, daylight adding details, buildings and yards to what had only been islands of lamplight the night before. Carrie drove slowly, passing a menacing black Escalade parked at the side of the road. Sajid pulled the scarf close around his mouth. A figure appeared up ahead, looming out of the mist like a ghost. Carrie was already slowing down. A man, grey hair peaking out from under a woollen hat, stood hunched, collar of a navy pea coat up against the rain. He looked on as a dog sniffed its way across a patch of land in front of him. Carrie brought the car to a stop and opened the door.

'Wish me luck.'

The man seemed happy to see her, becoming suddenly more animated in the way men often did when suddenly confronted by an attractive woman. She pulled out her phone, showing him, Sajid expected, a picture of Greg. That smooth, effortless manner she had of conversing with strangers, it was something he lacked, something he marvelled at and envied. Even before this trouble with Aliyah, he had never been comfortable around people – white people at any rate. Their ability to just walk into any situation and expect instant acceptance – it was astounding.

Carrie turned and walked back toward him, the taut lines of her face telegraphing the man's response. Nevertheless, as she opened the door he still asked.

'Any luck?'

She buckled her seat belt.

'Nope, but he said to try the general store.'

'The photo of Greg,' he said. 'May I see it?'

She seemed surprised by his request, her reaction only adding to his guilt. She pulled out her phone and called up a picture, then thought better of it, laying it down on the seat and reaching into her bag. From a compartment she drew out a photograph, its edges frayed but its body remarkably uncreased, and offered it to him.

He took it with both hands as if accepting a gift. It showed a young man in military fatigues, an uncertain smile playing on his lips, a duffel bag slung over his shoulder.

'It was before he shipped out on his second tour,' she said, her words tinged, he felt, with regret. 'Before the attack . . . before it all went to shit.'

He knew of Greg's injury, of course. It was one of the few things she *had* told him. He knew of the year the boy had spent in various medical facilities, the time overlapping with Mia's hospitalisation. That he and she should have been sitting beside their children's hospital beds at the same time had struck him as one of those curious, black coincidences which the fates sometimes took pleasure in throwing up.

'He came back a different boy . . .'

'The world changes them,' he told her. 'Despite our best efforts.'

He handed the photograph back to her and she placed it back in the bag.

'We best get on.'

It was not far away. Nothing in Ripplebrook seemed particularly far from anything else. Carrie pulled to a halt at the foot of a set of stone steps which led up to a tired-looking shop.

She got out, leaving him once more with his thoughts, climbing the steps oblivious to the conditions, her coat unzipped, flying in the wind.

She was, he thought, like a typhoon, unimpeded by the forces that all too easily constrained him. If there was something that needed doing, she did it, regardless of the difficulty. She had travelled three thousand miles to seek him, then five thousand more to this place – all in order to find her son. Without her, Sajid would still be sitting in London, wringing his hands and cursing his fate.

*Unshackled.* That was how she seemed. She was *free.* Had she always been this way, or had it happened over time? A process of erosion maybe, or the opposite, a thickening of the skin, like scar tissue over a wound. Had she once been like him, beholden to others? He knew so little about her, had made so little enquiry. In the beginning, in the midst of his own grief, it had been easy not to ask. She was a stranger to him, and, if he was honest, dismissing her as a stranger had made it easier for him to accompany her on this fool's errand. It helped assuage his guilt at leaving Rumina and Tariq, and Mia in her hospital bed.

But now, after she had saved him not once but twice, such a dismissal felt dishonourable. He would find out more. He would ask her of her life and her family. He would ask of Greg's father. Was he dead, or had he simply cut ties with them in the way men did? And what of her people – her parents, brothers, sisters? Did she have any? Did they know where she was or what she was trying to do?

Suddenly he recalled the previous night. Carrie's expression on seeing that woman with the white hair. The sight of his own face on the TV moments later had driven it out of his head. Now, though, he should ask her about it.

The growl of an engine snapped him out of his thoughts. In the mirror he caught the reflection of a black four-by-four, cruising along like a shark. A shiver passed through him. He tracked its progress, keeping his movements to a minimum as though even blinking might alert them to his presence.

The engine note died abruptly, the vehicle stopping a couple of hundred yards down the street. From its flanks stepped two men wearing matching bomber jackets and sombre expressions. The jackets he recognised from the pictures on the television the previous evening.

FBI.

Heads bowed in conversation, they started walking toward the car. *Toward him*. Sajid swallowed, saliva thick in his throat. They could not be more than fifty yards away.

*Where was Carrie?*

They stopped suddenly, turning and heading down the driveway of the house next door to the shop. One of them rang the doorbell. Sweat began to prick Sajid's neck.

The door of the house opened. An old man stood there. White hair. Stooped gait. The attention of both agents fixed upon him. Sajid reached slowly for the door handle, pulling it gently till he heard the click of the release. Silently he pushed it open a crack, then froze. One of the agents had turned. He was looking this way, staring directly at Sajid. The car door quivered in his hand.

The agent turned back to the old man at the door. It was now or never. Sajid slipped from the car and made for the steps to the store, climbing them on uncertain legs, fearful that at any second he would hear them call out after him, tell him to stop, ask him who he was, what he was doing there. It was important not to run, or even to turn and look back, no matter how much he wished to do so. Finally he reached the top and pushed his way through the door.

Carrie was at the counter, her back to him, talking to an old white lady. The TV was on behind her, a news channel. It seemed no one in this country watched anything but sports and the news. Neither saw him enter and he saw no point in drawing attention to himself. Instead he lost himself among the aisles of produce.

The woman was speaking, a quiver of wariness in her voice.

'He's not in any trouble, is he? After last night, I don't know what to –'

'He's not in any trouble at all.' Carrie's voice, gentle, reassuring.

'So why're you looking for him?'

Carrie seemed to take her time replying. He ventured a peek from behind the protection of the shelves.

'He's my son.'

Sajid closed his eyes. When he opened them the old woman was staring at Carrie.

'I know him. Nice boy. Been in here a couple of times.'

The world seemed to shift around him. He watched Carrie fight to maintain her composure.

'When was the last time he came in?'

The woman gazed up at the ceiling in search of an answer.

'A few days ago.'

Through the window Sajid saw the two FBI men at the foot of the hill.

'Can you tell me where he's staying?' Carrie asked.

The woman shook her head.

"Fraid not.'

The agents had started up the steps. He needed to warn Carrie. They needed to leave.

Carrie thanked the woman, made to turn, then stopped. The agents were almost at the door. There was no more time. There had to be a back way out of this place. Sajid made for the counter and smiled at the old woman. 'Thank you for your time, madam,' he said, then grabbed Carrie by the arm and manoeuvred her toward his hiding place in the aisle.

'Agents,' he whispered. 'Outside. We need to get out the back.'

Carrie stared at him, then looked to the window.

'I need a minute.'

Had she lost her mind? The old woman clearly didn't know any more, so what was Carrie doing?

'But there's no time!'

Still she waited. Glued to the TV screen. He couldn't understand why. On it a picture of a young man in military uniform. Clearly not Greg and nothing to do with the supposed Sons of the Caliphate.

'Carrie, we need to go. They'll be coming in any second.'

She sprung to life, yet his relief died instantly as she headed for the shop door and flung it open. The agents were feet away, staring at them. To him they seemed like a different species, like giants hewn from granite.

Carrie seemed unperturbed.

'Excuse me, officers!'

*What was she doing?*

'Can I have a word?'

Carrie took out her phone and thrust it toward them as though it were a recording device.

'Emma Smith,' she said, '*Portland Mercury*. Can you tell me what happened last night?'

The agents seemed to stiffen.

'We're not answering any questions at this time, ma'am. There'll be a press conference later.'

'Can you at least tell me what you're asking folks?'

The man stepped back.

'Sorry, ma'am. Like I said, you'll have to save your questions for the press conference.'

The agents brushed past her, then past him in his baseball cap, without a second look, and into the store. For a moment, he just stood there. He felt Carrie tugging at his arm.

'Come on.'

She pulled him down the steps to the car.

'Get in.'

'What . . . what did you just do?'

'Cops,' she replied. 'Always happy to dish out the questions, less keen to answer 'em. We should get out of here. Won't take 'em long to figure out we're not the press.'

She started the engine and quickly reversed. 'Besides, we've got a long journey ahead and I don't know how much time we got left.'

'Where are we going?' he asked.

'Utah,' she said. 'A place called Clement.'

# CHAPTER 47

*Shreya*

Agents were dead.

The Bureau was compromised.

And Maria O'Connor was gone.

The room was airless. The temperature, several degrees too low for comfort. Not that the man on the other side of the table seemed to notice. His name was Pearce, or so he'd told her. A phantom in a grey suit and tightly knotted tie, who looked more forensic accountant than field agent; flown in from DC overnight to get to the bottom of the clusterfuck of the last twelve hours.

He looked up from his notes, pushed his glasses up the bridge of his nose and stared wordlessly at her, as though she were some specimen needing examination. She held his stare as long as she could, until her skin began to crawl, until her ears buzzed and the thousand pinpricks of discomfort grew to be too much, then dropped her gaze to the table.

Slowly, she'd told him everything: from finding Ripplebrook to losing Maria O'Connor; keeping her answers straight and to the point. But this wasn't a debrief; this was an interrogation and the worst, she knew, was yet to come.

'Special Agent Mistry, as I understand it, you received orders transferring you from the Bureau's LA office to San Diego. Is that correct?'

'Yes, sir.'

'And instead of going to San Diego, you contacted Washington and specifically requested to be allowed to come to Portland.'

'Yes, sir.'

'Why did you do that?'

'I wasn't due to report to San Diego till Monday. That gave me a few days – I thought I could be useful on this case.'

Pearce reached for a gold-plated pen that sat on the table and scribbled some notes on a yellow pad. He looked up and nodded.

'Let's talk a little about your *usefulness* to this case. Several witnesses have stated that you entered into a verbal altercation with your superior officer, Special Agent Taylor, on at least two occasions during the last forty-eight hours, actions which culminated in Special Agent Taylor removing you from the investigation, ordering you to leave Portland immediately and to report to San Diego by 8 a.m. this morning. Is that correct?'

It was more complicated than that. She should tell him so, but to explain it all – about the 224 and the 211 – would take too long. She needed to keep it simple.

'Is that correct, Special Agent Mistry?'

'Yes, sir.'

'And yet you disobeyed that order. Instead of making for the airport and leaving Portland, as you told Special Agent Taylor you would do, you in fact headed to this place, Ripplebrook, where you were found in the company of terrorists.'

She couldn't quite believe it. Was he suggesting she was somehow involved in whatever this was?

'No, no –'

'Agent Mistry.'

'I followed a hunch. It was my belief that the terrorists were based south of Estacada that led to the altercations with Agent Taylor. As soon as I realised I might have picked up the trail, I called it in.'

'Did you?'

Of course she did.

'Yes.'

'You're sure?'

She thought back.

'I tried to call Dan. I left a message on his cell.'

Pearce checked his notes.

'Ah yes, the message you left, which said, and I quote, "*Dan. It's Shreya. Call me as soon as you get this. I think I've found him.*" That's right, isn't it?'

'Yes.'

'You had just made what was potentially the biggest break in the case, one that if handled properly could have brought this whole thing to an end, and you made no mention of your location?'

She felt sweat trickle down her side.

'It wasn't . . . I . . . when I called, I wasn't sure he was exactly . . . When I tried calling again, there was no reception. I explained all this in my statement last night.'

'Yes, your statement to Special Agent Sullivan, who is now sadly deceased. We will talk about that. You mention that you were attacked and taken hostage by Maria O'Connor who ordered Yusuf Ghani to execute you; that Ghani took you to a barn near the building, tied your wrists and was about to kill you when he was shot dead by –' he checked his notes – 'Special Agent Kramer. Is that correct?'

She breathed a sigh of relief. This was safe ground. They couldn't think she was a traitor working with them. Ghani was about to kill her.

'Absolutely.'

'You're sure of that?'

'Yes.'

Pearce settled his glasses on his nose once more.

'You see, that's curious, because there's something I can't figure out . . . Who untied you?'

The blood sang in her ears.

'What?'

He looked at her as if it was the most innocent question in the world.

'You stated on record that Yusuf Ghani tied your wrists. My question is, who exactly untied you? Because neither Special Agent Kramer nor Special Agent Taylor recall doing so, and I can't find anyone else who does.'

And then she remembered. It was Ghani who'd loosened her bindings. He might have been letting her go. There had been no time to be sure. There was no way to explain that to Pearce.

'Agent Mistry. Who untied you?'

The room was suddenly stifling. She needed to keep it simple. She needed to count. Doubles. *One, two, four, eight . . .*

'I loosened them myself, just after Agent Kramer had entered the barn and shot the suspect.'

The lie caught in her throat and she coughed. *Sixteen, thirty-two, sixty-four.*

He stared at her.

'You loosened them yourself?'

*One twenty-eight, two fifty-six.*

*No.*

'Yes.'

He made another note, the gold pen scratching at the yellow pad.

'Let's keep going then. After you were found and examined by medical professionals, you were told to return to your hotel. Is that correct?'

'Yes.'

'And instead you ordered a junior officer to take you to the Bureau's secure facility where Maria O'Connor was being questioned, a facility whose location was classified and was then attacked some time after your arrival.'

The fog was descending, the words in her head sticking together.

'I only . . . I only asked. It wasn't an order.'

'You *asked* a junior officer. And how was that junior officer supposed to refuse?'

'I . . .'

*. . . Five hundred and twelve, a thousand and twenty-four . . .*

'Did you pass on the location of the secure facility to contacts of Maria O'Connor?'

'No! This is ridiculous! I *found* Ripplebrook. I led the Bureau to them. I was almost killed. Why would I have anything to do with terrorists? Any number of people knew the location of that facility. It was just a building in the dark to me. I still don't actually know where it is.'

Pearce made a show of writing his notes.

'But you knew the address of the safe house you were supposed to deliver O'Connor to. I understand Special Agent Taylor called you and told you.'

'That's true, but –'

'And shortly thereafter the vehicle you were travelling in was intercepted, run off the road and you *lost* Maria O'Connor.'

'I had no choice. She was holding a gun to an agent's head.'

Pearce nodded.

'Let's move on. What do you know about Sajid Khan?'

'Who?'

'The father of Aliyah Khan.'

*Where was he going with this?*

'Nothing.'

'You've never met him?'

'I don't think so.'

'What if I were to tell you that Sajid Khan flew into Vancouver two nights ago, and that a few hours later, a man matching his description was spotted crossing the US border.'

'You're saying Aliyah Khan's father is involved in this?'

'CBP officers gave chase but lost him. They believe he had an accomplice waiting on this side of the border. Now I ask you again, what is your relationship with Sajid Khan?'

This was madness. She'd never even met the man.

'I have no relationship with him. I don't even know who he is.'

Pearce reached for a blue file on the desk and pulled out a photo and slid it across the table.

She felt an electric jolt. A thousand thoughts crowded her head. She stared at the image; at the South Asian man: thin, greying at the temples. He looked tired, and old.

*Older than she remembered.*

She fought to maintain her composure.

*This was impossible.*

Pearce gestured at the image.

'This is Sajid Khan.'

*Khan.* She hadn't known his surname, just that he was Sajid, father of the girl she'd sat in the ambulance with, whose hand she'd held and watched over all the way from a protest march to a hospital beside the Thames. She'd sat in a waiting room with him and brought him tea and shared his grief.

It made no sense.

The room spun around her. She'd lost count. Needed to start again. Something simple. *Three, six, nine, twelve, fifteen . . .*

'I . . . It's not what you think. I only met him once. Just once . . .

His daughter, not Aliyah, her name was Munira . . . she was hurt at a demonstration in London. I was there.'

*Munira.*

*. . . Eighteen, twenty-one, twenty-four . . .*

Munira Begum. Not Munira Khan. It was the surname that had confused her, but she should have realised. Bangladeshi women sometimes took the honorific Begum as their last name. She didn't know why. Probably for the same reason Sikh women sometimes took the surname Kaur.

*Sometimes. Not always.*

The pieces fell into place. Munira Begum and Aliyah Khan. Sisters.

She didn't know exactly how long it was before Pearce let her go; exhausted, wrung dry.

Dan stood waiting for her, leaning against an ancient radiator, arms folded. His face was grey, like meat left out too long, his expression pained, and the circles round his eyes had graduated from dark smudges to distinct dark moons.

'You okay?'

'Yeah,' she told him. 'I'm sorry about Sullivan.'

He gave a sigh.

'I spoke to his wife. She's not good.'

She didn't know what to say. Deaths were awkward for her. Finding those words that offered solace to the bereaved. It was hard.

Dan filled the silence.

'How'd it go in there?'

She shrugged. 'I don't know. He kept insinuating stuff, putting two and two together and getting a conspiracy. It's like he thought I was some sort of traitor.'

'He's just doing his job, Shreya. And after last night, we're all under suspicion.'

'So what now?'

He stared at her. She wondered why, exactly.

'I'm afraid you're being suspended, pending further investigation. Orders from Washington.'

She looked at him blankly, unsure how to respond, conscious of the heat rising in her face.

'You should have told me, Shreya. If you'd told me, I might have been able to protect you.'

'Told you what?'

'That you know Sajid Khan.'

She took a step back. The image of Sajid Khan, gaunt, haunted, returned.

'I don't *know* him. I only met him once and never even knew his full name. You got to believe me, Dan.'

He shook his head. 'Doesn't matter what I believe. Like I said, the orders came from Washington.'

Faint praise indeed.

He seemed to sense her thoughts.

'Shit, way things are going, I'll probably end up joining you before the day's out. Soon as their new team shows up. They're sending down specialists from DC to take over. Do yourself a favour and get out of here before they arrive.'

He took her hand, led her to the window and lowered his voice.

'For what it's worth, you did a fine job finding that house in Ripplebrook, and you should know, you were right . . . There were other people in that house. Evidence Response pulled a bunch of prints. Looks like it was more than just our two girls from London that passed through that house.'

She stood up straighter. Outside, the rain hammered down on the windowpane.

'How many?'

'Six people as of now, not including contamination from you and one or two of the team last night.'

'Any names?'

'As of this time, two additional individuals have been identified.'

'That's positive.'

'No. It's a fucking disaster. They're both ex-US military. Special ops, just like O'Connor.'

He pulled out his phone.

'I shouldn't be showing you this, but we wouldn't have these if it weren't for you.'

On the screen, a picture of a white male: short hair; determined stare.

'This is Jack Corrigan. We believe he served in Afghanistan with O'Connor, part of the same ISA team tasked with information gathering. He matches the description of the man seen with Yasmin Malik at the mall in Burbank.'

*Another super-soldier.*

He flicked to a different photo.

'This one is Gregory Alexander Flynn. Native of Gainesville, Florida, he's a former engineer sergeant with the special forces. Two tours in Afghanistan. Seriously wounded in an ambush in Kandahar. Honourably discharged but seems to have had problems adapting since. Ended up doing time down in Ocala. Eighteen months for assault.'

'They don't sound like Islamists.'

'It's possible they were all recruited in Afghanistan, turned somehow and sent back as a sleeper cell.'

'You find anything Islamic in the house?'

'Not yet.'

'Isn't that odd?'

'Think about it, Shreya. They're the perfect agents with the perfect cover. Veterans with intimate knowledge of how our security services function. And who knows how big this truly is?'

A shiver ran through her. These people, whoever they were, had the intel and the firepower to attack a Bureau facility. If they could do that, they could do anything.

Ghani's words played in her head.

*'They have people everywhere.'*

More attacks were coming. More people were going to die. And she was suspended.

She left him to the timpani of rain on the window and headed down to the floor below. Washington knew that she'd met Sajid Khan. How, when even *she* hadn't realised? And suspending her? Even the most paranoid agents in internal investigations surely couldn't believe she was somehow involved with all this. *Could they?*

She thought of Aliyah Khan and Munira Begum.

Both daughters of Sajid Khan: grieving father, radical Islamist, the mastermind behind the Sons of the Caliphate? Sajid Khan: On American soil. Seeking revenge?

*Is that what this was about?*

Could that mild-mannered man from the hospital *really* have become a terrorist? But people changed, she knew that. Events changed them.

Yet something nagged at the back of her brain. It took five minutes of self-meditation and gentle rocking before it came to her. *Sajid Khan couldn't have known.*

The official version, the only version he would know, recorded Munira's injuries as caused by excessive force on the part of the British police. It didn't even mention the US protection detail. She only knew the truth because she'd seen it with her own eyes: witnessed the punch thrown by the agent, witnessed Munira's neck snapping back, her body folding, her head hitting the pavement.

Sajid Khan wouldn't know any of that because he hadn't been there. If he was seeking revenge, why would he seek it on American soil?

And yet he was *here*, as was Aliyah Khan, who had arrived with the girl who'd blown up the mall. Yasmin Malik who had been brought to the mall by a man called Jack Corrigan, an army veteran with a classified file, just like the woman with the white hair, Maria O'Connor, who'd called herself Miriam. Who else had been in that house? Where were they now? How did it all fit together?

She reached for her phone, pulled up Mike Raven's number and hit call.

'Mike.'

In the background she heard the thrum of a crowd. It sounded like he was in an airport.

'Shreya.'

'Mike, I need a favour. I need all the intel you can get me on Sajid Khan, father of Aliyah Khan. A file must already have been put together. See if you can get it for me.'

'Sure, Shreya, but –'

The noise, she realised, was not just coming from his end of the phone, it was also coming from somewhere in the building she was sitting in. Somewhere on the same floor.

'And Yusuf Ghani. Has his file been declassified by the Pentagon yet?'

'Nothing yet. Listen, Shreya. You need to switch on a TV. Right now.'

# CHAPTER 48

*Rehana*

The last few hours had been tough. Those pictures of Ripplebrook and the White House on the news, those halogen-hued helicopter shots, it felt like the end was coming, they'd be found and caught or shot, and that would be that. No revenge. No retribution. Just failure.

Fear pricked at her neck. There couldn't be much time left. How long before they were trapped? She just hoped they wouldn't find them before . . .

Jack brought the car to a stop on the outskirts of town and turned to her.

'You ready?'

She was ready.

'Okay then,' he said, and pressed down on the gas, rejoining the road south. She read the sign.

Port Arthur.

End of the road.

It looked like a ghost town. Boarded-up buildings jutting between empty lots like the last jagged teeth in a broken mouth. They drove down a deserted street, between an honour guard of stunted trees toward a water tank quietly rusting under a bullet-grey sky.

Where were the people? Why would Miriam send her to this town at the edge of nowhere?

They stopped for a red light hanging above a deserted intersection. Across the street a patrol car dozed, two officers inside like silhouette cut-outs. The car looked brand new, like a vehicle from the future. She felt exposed, naked, like they could see into the car and into her soul.

*Stay calm.*

He must have sensed her anxiety.

'Those boys ain't lookin' for us,' he said.

What did he know about it? What did he know about the South? Didn't he realise that out here, in the ass-end of nowhere, if those cops felt like it, the colour of her face was crime enough to get them pulled over?

The light turned green and he tapped the accelerator, driving slowly through the intersection. She shot a glance at the side mirror. The patrol car turning, following.

The road ran on, arrow-straight to the horizon, the car grinding over cracked grey asphalt. In the side mirror the patrol car continued to stalk, matching their speed, keeping its distance. She saw the sweat break out on his face. She pressed a button and lowered the window. The air smelled like gasoline.

The road opened out. The trees disappeared. A levee on one side now and on the other a bunch of low buildings. The patrol car veered off onto a side street and she breathed out.

The East Texas road map said they were close: a circled star beside the blue of the Gulf of Mexico.

*Two miles* . . . but already visible . . . a tangle of iron and steel; massive, alien-looking; a cathedral of metal spires belching flame and smoke into the air.

She imagined their bombs exploding; setting off a fireball that would destroy the refinery. People would have to notice that. The thought sent shivers through her.

He pulled off the main road, onto a dirt path that disappeared into the scrub.

He turned to her and reached for her hand.

'You okay?'

She bit her lip. Yeah. She was okay. She was going to do this. For Dad.

He got out, fetched the packs from the trunk, then got in the back. She looked on as he unzipped both rucksacks and got to work, checking wires, switching on the old-style Nokias. *'They're cheap, durable and the battery lasts forever,'* he'd told her, like he was some walking, talking *Anarchist's Cookbook.* *'Four phones in all. Two for each bomb. One to act as trigger, calling the other, which'll then act as detonator.'*

And then it was time to go.

She followed him. A ten-minute walk on a path that led to the perimeter fence. Another twenty to a spot hidden by trees.

'There,' he said.

A hole in the wire; a line carved with metal cutters. An aperture large enough for a person to crawl through. A job well done, too. You couldn't see the incision till you were right on top of it. She wondered who'd done it. He had hinted at the scale of it. *Good people, everywhere.*

He crawled through, then sat on the dirt and waited for her. Her breath was heavy. This was it. In five minutes it'd be done.

She wanted to say something to him, but he was on autopilot now, unzipping his pack and pulling out the hard hat and hi-vis jacket, the laminated pass that said nothing much but which would ease their path those last couple hundred yards.

'*People are sheep,*' Miriam had said. '*You'll be surprised how far hi-vis and a pass on a lanyard will take you.*'

She unzipped her bag, extracted and donned identical items, and then she was up and moving. Tall, straight-backed, like she owned the place. The storage tanks weren't hard to spot. Someone had helpfully thought to paint them red.

Her head buzzed. Was it fear or just the chemicals in the air? They were at the tanks now, him peeling off to plant his device, she setting down her pack, pushing it into position, pulling out her cellphone.

She sat back.

The air roiled and shimmered. The sky above her a chemical haze; a spiral clawing at the stratosphere. Not a bird in sight. Not a single living thing visible in any direction. Just metal and machinery and petrochemicals. It was good of Miriam to choose this target. The place deserved to go up.

'All set,' she said.

She stood and turned, expecting to see him, but there was no sign of him. He should've been right there, prepping his bomb beside the other tank.

She called out to him.

'Jack?'

The word was lost to wind and industrial roar.

Where was he? Had he left her?

Sweat on her brow. She rubbed at it with shaking hands, stumbling forward, rounding a corner.

'Jack?'

She ventured further, fear blossoming in her chest, and then she saw him, hunkered down, hidden between two tanks and hunched over his pack. She called his name but he didn't respond.

She moved closer.

'Jack. What's the matter?'

She was standing over him now. She reached out, put a hand on his shoulder.

The rest happened too fast. Jack swivelling, grabbing her arm, twisting it, throwing her to the ground. Her landing on her back, the shock rendering her mute. Why was he doing this? She tried to scream, tried to right herself. She reached for him – clawed at his face, anything. She needed to get up. If she didn't, he would kill her. That much was plain. She grabbed at his leg, dug her nails into the flesh of his calf. And then came the punch. That terrible punch that seemed to explode within her head, her stomach, her lungs all at once. Her limbs fell limp. In her mind she cried out, but her voice remained mute. She fought for breath that wouldn't come. Futile, empty attempts. Why had her body stopped responding? How? Another punch came. She closed her eyes against it, steeled herself against the coming agony but it was useless. A supernova flash of white before she was enveloped by deepest black.

When she came round it was to searing pain in her temples and her mouth full of blood. Her head a fog that cleared only slowly. She was on the ground, on her side, hands tied behind her. Against her head, the rough fabric of a rucksack. She tried to move, but it was useless. What had he done to her?

She opened her eyes to dirt, to a world upended, to the great curve of the red storage tanks feet away.

She called his name.

*Why? He wasn't coming back for her.*

She called out again.

'Somebody, help me, please!'

But no one was coming. She knew that.

Her heart thumped against her ribs. She fought to control her breath. A last stand against the dread that threatened her like a tide. She thought of her father and his final moments. The look in his eyes as the officers slowly stole the life from him. The fear he must have felt; fear that he had hidden because he knew she was watching. She would show the same strength, the same dignity. She would face her fate as he had. This was for him.

She fought the pain and struggled till she could look up. A view of the sky. How infinite it seemed. The rucksack at her head vibrated. She closed her eyes.

She would have liked to have seen birds one last time.

# CHAPTER 49

*Sajid*

The miles passed. The country changed. Pine forest to mountain pass to scrub and barren salt flat. And this, he knew, was a mere fraction of it. The land altered but the towns didn't. Not much, anyway; not as he'd expected. Everywhere the same small settlements: the one- and two-street towns, the low buildings, the large vehicles, the same weathered faces and the flags. Everywhere the flags, the Stars and Stripes hanging in variegated shades, in doorways and on flagpoles, painted on walls and pinned to garage doors.

'Why Utah?' he had asked her. 'Why this place, Clement?'

'The soldier on the TV,' she had answered. 'He was a friend of Greg's. They served together in Afghanistan. It can't be coincidence.'

He had looked up the story on her phone. Clement, Utah. The man was named Finn Ruck. Details were sketchy. He had been shot. By whom or for what reason was unclear, as was his condition. It worried him; a reminder of just how dangerous Aliyah's position was. Whatever she was mixed up in, whoever she was involved with, the stakes she was playing for were her life.

Yet dwelling upon it would not help Aliyah nor alleviate his fears. Instead he had turned his attention outward: at the country. Oregon and Idaho, and finally into Utah, while Carrie drove, flirting with speed limits and playing cat and mouse with patrol cars. What surprised him were the communities of caravans – *trailer parks*, Carrie called them – so many rows of white cubes, ten or twenty deep and dotting the land like aphids on a leaf. The flags were here too, more of them in fact.

'This is how people live,' she told him. 'A lot of us, anyway.'

'For the freedom?' he asked. Americans, he had found, were fond of that word.

She laughed. 'Ain't nothing free about them. You pay rent, and for water and gas and electricity and pretty much everything 'cept the air in the sky; that and the fact that if you're late with the bills, you're free to find alternative accommodation in the back seat of your car.'

A joke, he assumed.

'I don't know what it's like in England,' she said, 'but here there's plenty of folks fallen on hard times and been forced to live out of a vehicle. Whole families sometimes.'

She had left the radio on, and it provided a low background hum of commercials, news bulletins, guitar-heavy American music and relentlessly upbeat disc jockeys. He did not understand Americans. The smiles, the cheerfulness and the constant refrain for you to *have a nice day*. Were these kindnesses earnest gestures, or were they an attempt to mask contrary feelings? The abrupt ending of a song caught his attention. A news bulletin – not on the hour as the others had been. Reports of an explosion. He turned up the volume. A refinery in Texas.

'Oh God.'

Carrie pulled the car onto the dirt shoulder.

The reporter kept talking, his tone sombre, his words punctuated by the sound of trucks thundering past on the road; Sajid catching and digesting snippets. *Port Arthur . . . fatalities . . . a blow to refining capability . . . gas prices.* Anything and everything save the one question he wanted answered, and then it came. *Initial indications . . . terror attack . . . Sons of the Caliphate.*

Carrie threw off her seat belt and before he knew what was happening she had flung open her door and stumbled out, onto the verge, running, staggering into the scrub, falling to her knees.

He got out and ran to her.

She was bent over. The stench of vomit filled his nostrils.

He knelt in the dirt beside her.

'Carrie.'

'It's too late.'

'We don't know that.'

He reached out and placed his hand on her arm. She turned to him, her face twisted, asking what the hell he thought he was doing. She shook herself free of his grasp and stood up.

'This is your fault! You and that fucking *religion* of yours.'

He got to his feet but said nothing.

'Why? Why did this happen?'

And when he did not answer again, she began to pound her fists on his chest; each blow accompanied by a cry and the question '*why?*' until the punches became robbed of strength and the cries became sobs.

He put his arms around her and she cried into his chest.

'I do not think this was Greg and Aliyah,' he told her. 'They could not have made it in time from Utah. The distance is too far.'

# CHAPTER 50

*Shreya*

The pictures had been coming in for an hour. Apocalypse shot from a helicopter.

Smoke, jet black, billowing, blinding, spiralling skyward from a refinery reduced to a skeleton of twisted metal. And in among the smoke, tongues of thick, oil-fuelled flame that would burn for days.

Ghani was right. It was too late.

Her phone buzzed. Nikhil. She pressed cancel. Now wasn't the time.

She turned back to the TV screen. There would be bodies in there. She wondered how many. Men and women; lives ended by explosive force, or searing heat, or toxic, lung-burning chemicals.

The desire was to turn away, to switch off, to scrub your mind of the images and the thoughts, but you couldn't. It was impossible. The horror demanded that you look, that you bore witness.

She clutched at straws. An accident maybe? But already internal sources were talking of a coded message coming in from the Sons of the Caliphate.

Three days till the election.

This atrocity might even make Costa the favourite, and if he won, then God help us all.

Was this the work of Aliyah Khan, or her father, or one of the others who'd been at Ripplebrook?

The phone buzzed again. An unknown number.

This time she answered.

'Shreya.'

Mike Raven's voice.

'Mike?'

'I'm sending you the intel on Sajid Khan now.'

She thanked him.

'Any news on who was behind Port Arthur?'

'Yeah, they matched images from the refinery to one of the previously unidentified sets of fingerprints. A woman called Rehana Jones. Eighteen, African American from Columbus, Ohio. Got herself arrested at a BLM protest a few years back. Her dad died while being restrained by police.'

The name rang a bell.

'Jury cleared the officers. The girl seems to have converted to Islam.'

'Shit.'

'And there's something else you should know. There's chatter coming in from Tallahassee field office. Greg Flynn, another of those whose fingerprints they found last night; word is his mom's missing.'

'Missing?'

'She's his next of kin; lives out in the boonies in northern Florida. Tallahassee sent agents to check her out. House was locked up. She's not been seen for almost a week. Her employers say she took unpaid leave a couple of days after the bomb in Burbank. Told 'em she had an aunt near Madison who'd fallen sick. Said she needed to go up there and take care of her. Didn't say when she'd be back.'

'And?'

'Tallahassee felt it merited further investigation; ran her details through the usual databases. Customs and Border Protection has her passport going through Tampa International the same day.'

'Where'd she go?'

'London.'

'England?'

The pain in her head spiked.

'You're sure it's her?'

'We're awaiting video footage now. We'll run it through facial recog as soon as we can, but our working assumption is that Carrie Flynn was on a flight to London last Wednesday.'

She pinched at the bridge of her nose. 'I'm guessing it's too much to hope that she's come back?'

'That's just it. She *did* come back, but not through Tampa. She came in on the other side of the country; across a land border at a place called Sumas up in Washington.'

Shreya googled the place. A dot came up on a map. Close to Vancouver.

The mother of one of the guys who'd been in that house with Ghani and Aliyah and Maria O'Connor had flown to London and then returned across a land border close to where Sajid Khan had been sighted. *Sajid Khan . . . who had an accomplice . . .* But that was crazy . . .

'Mike, I need you to check something for me. Get hold of the passenger manifest for the flight Sajid Khan took to Vancouver. See if Carrie Flynn or anyone matching her description was on it.'

'You don't think . . .'

'I don't know,' she said. 'But we gotta check.' She hesitated. She had to tell him. He'd find out soon enough anyway. 'And, Mike, there's something you should know. I've been taken off the case and put on leave.'

There was silence on the line.

'Why d'you think I'm calling you on a burner?'

The file on Sajid Khan dropped into her inbox. She clicked it open and read.

Sajid Khan: immigrant; refugee from Bangladesh; medical student who'd fled to London after his family were murdered back home, 'victims of religious and political violence'.

Ironic that a man whose own life had been scarred by such forces should now seek to unleash it upon others. Her thoughts strayed to Yusuf Ghani. Wasn't he supposed to have fled similar things in Afghanistan? At least that's what she'd surmised from his heavily redacted file. Images filled her mind: of Ghani lying lifeless on the dirt floor of the barn. She recalled his expression. The sadness. Not what she'd expected of a jihadi zealot. Sajid Khan too had worn the same expression that night in the hospital three years ago. It didn't seem the face of a man who'd sacrifice his own daughter for jihad or just for revenge. She shook the thought from her head. This wasn't the time for sentiment. The guy had just crossed illegally into the country. Why else would he do that if he weren't involved in whatever was going on?

What was she thinking? She was off the case. This wasn't her fight any more.

Her phone buzzed. Nikhil again.

She should take it.

'Nik.'

'Shreya. Thank God.'

His voice sounded strained.

'Shreya. It's your dad.'

# CHAPTER 51

*Sajid*

The evening sun slipped between clouds and black hills. Sajid watched it reduce to a strip of red and gold on the horizon. The road wound on, relentlessly, interminably. Carrie drove now. It had taken time but she had accepted the logic of his statement: that whatever the truth of Port Arthur, his daughter and her son could not have been there, not if they had been in Utah the previous night.

But he understood her reaction – he hesitated to term it anything more precise. The stress she had been under these past days; the risks, the dangers; the hopes that soared on receipt of a whisper of information only to be dashed by each setback, each blow of bad news on the radio and the internet.

The news of Port Arthur had merely been the straw that broke her. Now she was silent. Maybe she regretted her words. Or maybe it was what she truly felt: that this was his fault, or Aliyah's fault, or the fault of his religion. He did not blame her. In darker moments had he not wondered if *Greg* may have been the one who had led Aliyah down this path?

He was overcome by a sudden urge to talk to her.

'Tell me about Greg.'

The mention of his name at least brought a glimmer of a smile to her face.

'He was a good kid. The nicest, kindest soul you could hope to meet. Always tinkering with stuff. Fixing things, making new things out of old junk. And when he wasn't tinkering, he'd be down at the animal shelter in Blue Springs helping out, coming home with every kind of busted dog or rat, fixing them too. And when some of them didn't make ... God. He was the best thing that ever happened to me.'

'You are close?'

It was a stupid question. He knew it as soon as the words left his mouth. She might ask the same question of him and Aliyah – so close that he had no idea she would lie to him and travel across the world to involve herself with terrorists. Yet Carrie did not react with the disdain he anticipated.

'We *were* close. But you know, kids grow up. People change. Shit happens. It'd be easy to blame his father. Owen was an asshole, and an angry drunk. Hardly ever around, and when he did come home, we wished he hadn't. It's my fault, I should've got the two of us out of there long before ... but sometimes you just keep going hoping things'll get better.'

'You cannot blame yourself. Often, things happen despite our best intentions.'

She turned to look at him, her face serious. 'Greg was almost fifteen by the time I finally got the courage. It was too late by then. He was ... he was a different kid. His grades went through the floor, and even if they hadn't, there was no money to pay for college, so he joined the army. Seemed the best shot at a future. He loved it. The army gave him – a purpose.'

She was opening up to him. Maybe now was the time to ask her the question that had been playing on his mind.

'Carrie,' he said softly. 'That woman. The one with the white hair. The one they arrested at the house in Ripplebrook. Who is she?'

She turned to him, her features suddenly hard.

'I don't know.'

'But you have seen her?'

Carrie turned back to the road.

'She just looks like someone I used to know.'

'Who?'

'No one. Just some lady who used to visit one of the people I care for.'

'But there was something more than just passing resemblance, wasn't there?'

For the longest moment, only the muffled hum of the engine and the sound of tyre rubber on asphalt filled the air. Sajid was content to wait out the silence.

'It was just a coincidence. Nothing more.'

He was not certain he believed her. He knew though, that right now, she would not give him anything else. He would try again later.

Carrie arched her back and rotated the joint of her bandaged shoulder.

'Let me drive,' he said. 'You should rest.'

For once she did not protest.

'We'll need to stop for gas soon anyway, and food.'

He cast a glance at the dashboard, the needle on the fuel gauge all but kissing the red line. A passing sign listed several options.

'Twin Rivers,' he said. 'Let's stop there.'

It was some twenty miles distant but he liked the name. He had grown up in a land of rivers: the thousand capillaries and distributaries of the Ganga and the Brahmaputra. Each had its own name: the Rupsa, the Parya, the Arial Khan, but really they were all just part of one whole, one mighty confluence that shaped the land and the lives of those who lived upon it. He imagined her Florida would not be that different. Heat and swamp and water and the ever-present threat from the elements.

Twin Rivers arrived with the moon, the clouds lifting to reveal star-dotted heavens. After a full day of driving the sight lifted his spirits. The night sky had always called to him, since he was a child lying on the flat roof of his father's house on those humid nights when it was too oppressive to sleep indoors.

Carrie stopped at a deserted gas station, at the pump furthest from a tired-looking cabin that passed for a payment booth. He waited as she stepped out and a blast of polar air invaded the warmth of the car.

Carrie filled the tank and then headed for the cabin, its windows adorned with a collage of fading red, white and blue bumper stickers, extolling the need to SAVE AMERICA and TAKE AMERICA BACK.

*Take it back from whom?* he wondered.

He recalled the graffiti he'd seen daubed on a London wall in dripping black capitals:

YOUR ENEMY DOESN'T TRAVEL BY DINGHY.
HE TRAVELS BY PRIVATE JET.

A truth rarely acknowledged. The dispossessed and the disenfranchised were always at the mercy of the rich, just tools to be whipped up by those in power to achieve their own ends. If he had learned one thing in life, it was that the rich stayed rich by making the poor fight among themselves.

Carrie returned and he took over at the wheel, heading on to the heart of town, a mix of small stores and fast-food joints, then kept going till he reached a lonely patch of dirt.

He killed the engine, fished out twenty dollars from the small wad of notes in his pocket, and despite her objections, insisted she take it. Once more he waited as she got out, turning to his own thoughts as she went in search of their dinner.

He thought of Rumina. Had the police found her? Had they questioned her about his flight from London? Guilt washed over him then settled like a stone in his breast. Her image forever tied to his feelings, to his failings as a father and a husband.

He would make amends. He would find Aliyah. He would bring her home – to her mother and her family – and then he would let Rumina decide the future.

It would be after midnight in London now. Would she be asleep, with little Tariq beside her? The thought of his boy nearly made him cry. When would he see him again? Had he merely mortgaged his son's future in the hope of rescuing his daughter?

His thoughts came crashing down around him, interrupted by the sight of three men rounding the corner, the noise of their conversation carrying over to him. Passing through a pool of street light, coats and hats wrapped tight, they made in his direction in the hurried, random way of men intoxicated by drink. He forced himself to relax. Drunks were generally fine if you avoided eye contact.

They came closer, their voices clear now: slurred words; jocular tones. He lowered his gaze. Within moments they would pass and he might return to his self-flagellation. They drew level with the car. It should have been fine. He should have just kept his head down. He would have, if one of them hadn't lurched into the wing mirror. Instinctively he looked up. The man was already uttering an apology as one of his comrades pulled him upright. But the apology died mid-sentence. The man stared at him.

'That's the guy!'

His friends ignored him, continuing to pull him away, but the man shrugged them off.

'I'm tellin' you, that's the guy!' He pointed at Sajid. 'The one on the TV!'

Alarms went off in Sajid's head.

One of his pals bent over to get a better look. Sajid turned away.

'Fuck!'

The man knocked on the window, a tap which became a thump.

Once more the fear returned. The close, claustrophobic, debilitating fear that he had felt back in the forest; the fear of what lay ahead. These men would break into the car; they would drag him out and –

'Hey, man! You that guy they're lookin' for?'

One of them was reaching for the door handle, yanking it.

'Fuckin' open the door, man!'

One of them was walking away, bending down, picking up something – a brick, or a rock. He was coming back, raising his arm, aiming at the glass between him and Sajid's head.

Sajid reached for the ignition but he knew it was too late. He closed his eyes and braced for the attack.

'Hey!'

Carrie's voice, ringing in the air like a clarion call.

'What the fuck d'you think you're doing?'

The men stopped. The one with the rock turned toward her.

'Guy in this car's a terrorist. The Feds are lookin' for him.'

'The fuck he is!'

Carrie was striding over now.

'You see a brown man and you boys just assume he's a terrorist. You drunk, ignorant fucks. That's my husband and he's as

American as any of you.' She reached the door. Sajid pressed the lock release. 'Now go home, you fucking shitheads.'

The men wavered. Carrie got in beside him, two paper bags in her hand. He turned to her, his head spinning in relief. She locked the doors, her eyes fixed on the men outside.

'Start the car, Sajid. Drive. Before they have a change of heart.'

# CHAPTER 52

*Shreya*

The wheels touched down on tarmac. Atlanta, green outside the porthole. A few thousand miles from the storms of Portland and yet her thoughts still a maelstrom. A rental car, hired from a guy in a tie and a half-sleeve shirt at a counter in the terminal and the longest ninety minutes on the freeway, speed limits be damned, till finally there it was, a hospital on the outskirts of Auburn. Nikhil waiting in an antiseptic anteroom, rising from a plastic chair. The cares of her family weighing on his shoulders, reflected in the lines on his face. An awkward embrace, befitting of ex-partners unable to escape each other's orbit for bonds of duty and family and maybe residual feeling.

'How is he?'

'He's stable. The doctors think he's through the worst of it.'

The smell of disinfectant in her nostrils.

'Can I see him?'

'It's one visitor at a time. Isha's in with him at the moment.'

Isha. The bridge that would always exist between them. The best thing they'd ever done.

'How's she taking it?'

'Pretty hard. You know how sensitive she can be.'

He led her down a corridor, past hospital staff in white uniforms and green overalls.

'He's in here.'

He stuck his head around a door.

'Isha, your mom's here.'

Shreya found herself struggling for breath.

The door opened. Isha stood there, eyes red, face smudged with tears. Shreya moved forward and hugged her, a tight embrace. To her surprise, she hugged her back. How long had it been? How long since the last time she had responded in this way and not with the forced, silent stiffness that seemed both protest and rebuke and which tore at Shreya's heart.

'He looks frail, Mom.'

She held her daughter tighter. 'He'll be okay,' she said. 'He's a fighter.' And even as she said the words, she doubted their sincerity. Truth was, she wasn't sure he had much left to fight for.

She left Isha with Nikhil and entered the private room.

Her father, eyes closed, wrapped within white sheets, hooked up to a machine recording all manner of stats: heart rate, blood oxygen, temperature, second by second. Isha was right. He looked so frail. The man who'd once swept her up above his head with one arm, now so small, so vulnerable.

She walked over and held his hand, the skin loose, parchment-thin. The eyes flickered and opened. No words. But a recognition in the weak smile and the lightest squeeze of the fingers and suddenly she felt something well up within her.

'Bapu,' she said. 'You gave us such a scare.'

She pulled up a seat and sat by him. There was so much she wanted to say: sorry, for not being there after Mom had passed; for leaving him in a home; for the situation with Isha and Nik; for her choices and the impact they'd had on him. She wanted to tell him she'd made those choices in good faith; that she thought it was her calling, that she was saving lives. She wanted to tell him that going forward, things would be different, that she would be here for him and for Isha. But the words remained stubbornly stuck in her head and instead she sat there, silently, with his hand in hers.

She didn't know how long it was before the nurse entered and ordered her, in the politest of terms, from the room. She gave her father's hand one last squeeze, then got up and made her way back to the waiting room, where Nik was sat in a chair, hunched forward, hands clasped together, lost in his own thoughts. He didn't see her till she sat down next to him. She should thank him, she realised.

'Thanks, Nik . . . for doing all this . . .'

He looked at her. Was he surprised to hear her say that?

'It's fine.'

'It's not. I . . . I should've been here.'

'You can't blame yourself, Shreya. The man had a heart attack. He's almost eighty.'

'Still. I should have . . . it's just that . . . with work and . . . this case . . . and . . .' The words dried up and suddenly a whole different sentence came to her. 'They've suspended me, Nik. They'll probably kick me out of the Bureau. Maybe Mom was right. Maybe I should never have joined. Maybe I should have put you and Isha first, but when I joined, I honestly thought I was doing the right thing and –'

'You can't think that way. You're . . . not like most people. You'd be miserable living the life your mom wanted for you. And you're damn good at your job. Doesn't matter what anyone else might think.'

*Anyone else.*

'Your folks okay?'

He scratched distractedly at an earlobe.

'Ah, you know. Same as always.'

Meaning they still hadn't forgiven her for the divorce; meaning they still wouldn't mention her name.

'And you?'

A tired smile. 'Keeping busy.'

There was more she wanted to ask him: about Isha, about their own situation, but the words wouldn't come.

'You look beat, Shreya,' he said. 'You should get some rest. There's nothing you can do here. I'll call you if there're any developments. You can stay at the house.'

*Their house. His house now . . . and his new girlfriend's.*

But Isha would be there.

It was tempting, but it would probably end in a fight and she didn't need that now. Besides, there were too many memories in that house, too many ghosts.

She reached out to put a hand on his, then stopped abruptly. That wasn't appropriate any more.

'It's good of you, but I'll stay at Dad's. I should really check on it anyway. It's been empty for almost a month.'

She stopped off at an all-night convenience store for a pack of Marlboros and a lighter – if this didn't merit a relapse, what did? – then drove home along quiet streets, past whitewashed churches and neat, well-watered lawns shaded by oak and smokebush and cypress. Each street unrolled like a memory, each block bearing witness to her childhood; streets she'd grown up on and which she'd been in such a hurry to escape.

Distance offered perspective though. Truth was she missed it, or at least appreciated it for what it was: as decent a place as anywhere to grow up as the daughter of white-collar Indian immigrants.

Maybe that's why she was so reticent about putting the house on the market. A last tie to her childhood. Selling it, an admission that her life here was over.

She pulled up to the house and parked in the drive. The front yard needed work; the garden her dad had nurtured for thirty years was missing its roses. The grass was dying. She walked to the front door, turned the key and reached for the light switch. The hallway hadn't changed in decades. Only the shoes lined up by the door were missing, as though she and her folks were out and would be returning soon. But the smell of the place betrayed the truth. It smelled of emptiness. It smelled hollowed out.

She wandered through to the kitchen, devoid of her mother's presence at the centre of it, kneading rotis or standing over a pot of something. The woman had spent a lifetime in here, Shreya's lifetime at least, if not her own, and she'd done it out of choice, not obligation.

Shreya turned on the little TV, still tuned to CNN as it always had been, so that her mom could fret about the world going to hell while making dinner. Pictures of black smoke over Port Arthur. Grainy images of a young African American woman.

'*That job will destroy your life, Shreya.*' Her mother's words. One of their final arguments. She pushed the memory away and thought instead of happier times; the three of them gathered around the dinner table with enough food to feed them all twice over. *American portions*, her father called them.

'*And why not?*' her mother would fire back. '*What was the point of the sacrifice in coming here if we cannot enjoy the benefits?*'

Mom had made the most of it, making friends: white and Black as well as Indian; recreating the meals from home, substituting American ingredients where the genuine Indian article was unavailable; raising a daughter as best she could, a hybrid child, a kid with shallow roots, fitting in nowhere.

And she'd died here, in this land she'd never wanted to come to but which she'd made her home.

Shreya should have appreciated the woman more. She should have made more of the time together.

Her phone buzzed. Unknown number.

She answered it. Mike's voice.

'Carrie Flynn *was* on the same flight into Vancouver as Sajid Khan.'

Shreya gripped the phone tighter.

'There's more. She hired a rental in Vancouver. It matches the description of the car that picked up Khan on this side of the border. We've got the plates.'

'Anything linking her to extremist groups of any shade?'

'The analysts are checking, but nothing so far. It's odd. If she's a terrorist she's a fucking dumb one. She's travelling under her own name and on her own passport.'

'You told Dan?'

'Not yet.'

She felt a pang of regret. She'd have to watch from the sidelines.

'Well, tell him now.'

'Will do, but Dan's not running the show any more. He's been pushed out. Replaced by a guy called Wyatt sent over from Washington.'

She hung up and walked over to the refrigerator. It was empty, save for a bottle of wine left over from God knows when. She'd go back to the convenience store later and pick up something more substantial, but for now, the wine would do. She took out the bottle, poured a glass and turned back to the TV.

Port Arthur replaced by a Costa press conference. She kept the sound off. A couple of weeks back he was finished. Ready to be consigned to the garbage can of history, but two attacks later, he was neck and neck. And Aliyah was still out there; Aliyah, Greg Flynn,

Maria O'Connor, Sajid Khan, Carrie Flynn and whoever else. There were more attacks coming. She knew it.

*Not her problem. Not any more.*

She picked up her glass and wandered through to the dusty-smelling den. Her parents' certificates, the key to their progress in this land of opportunity, stared out, framed and fading, on the wall. She sat down behind the desk, took a sip of wine and reached for a small photo – the three of them, smiling in front of the castle at Disney World. She must have been about fourteen. Beside it another photo: her father, in his early thirties, the day he became a US citizen, smiling in front of the Stars and Stripes.

She felt a wave of guilt well up. Her stomach empty, her emotions tattered.

# CHAPTER 53

*Greg*

He felt bad about leaving the Alfa. And not just because Finn's truck was a piece of shit. The car had been Sam Cotter's joy. It was the last link to him, and Greg had left it down a dirt road in Clement, Utah. It felt disrespectful.

They were somewhere south of Wichita, Kansas (state capital, Topeka); geographical centre of the contiguous forty-eight states, she'd told him; and he'd countered with home to Dorothy from *The Wizard of Oz.*

His knee was feeling better. Well enough for him to take the wheel again after she'd driven seven hours. She was teaching him the rudiments of chess – rooks marching in straight lines, bishops only on diagonals – when the news came through. A newscaster on the radio, relating the facts in a monotone:

*Port Arthur ... Oil refinery ... Dead and injured ... Sons of the Caliphate.*

So Miriam had found more bombs. It wasn't that surprising. This thing was bigger than just the few of them at Ripplebrook. Far bigger.

'Switch it off,' Aliyah told him. 'I don't want to hear any more news.'

Silently, he did as she asked.

It was minutes before she next spoke. 'It's Rehana,' she said, as though there were no doubt at all. No tears this time. Not like when he'd told her the truth about what had happened to Yasmin.

'Whatever Miriam's up to, it's working. Maybe we just hand ourselves in. They gotta see we ain't jihadis,' he said. 'Miriam can't have spies everywhere.'

'But she can,' Aliyah said, and he knew she was right. She reached out a hand and placed it on his, and the warmth of her touch began to soothe his angst. 'You know she can. Isn't that what you wrote in that letter?'

He looked across.

'What letter?'

'The one to your mum?'

An electric charge ran through him.

'How . . . how'd you know about that?'

'Last night, when I took the maps from the Alfa, I stowed them in your bag. This morning, when I pulled them out, I found a bunch of other pages with them. Your notes . . . the words you set out to your mum . . . the words about me. Is that how you feel about me?'

He began to flush. The words on those pages. He should've listened to his old man. *Never put nothin' in writing 'less you absolutely have to.*

He didn't know what to say.

She squeezed his hand.

'I don't deserve you, Greg.'

He mumbled something to the contrary, the words lost to the wind.

'Your mum. Did you send her a letter?'

'I did.'

'You took a hell of risk. If Miriam or Yusuf had found it . . .'

'Yeah but they didn't.'

'You were right though, about what you said about Miriam. She won't just give up. That's why we need to keep going. We need to get to Florida. We can figure out what we do when we get there.'

And so he kept going, despite his own doubts and because she wished it. Because he could think of nowhere better to hide. And because, as she'd told him back in Portland, she trusted him to keep her safe.

*

The lights of Memphis shimmered on the Mississippi. He'd always wanted to see the place: the city of B.B. King, though stealing in like a thief in the night wasn't how he'd pictured it.

'You need to stop, Greg.'

She was right of course. The pain was getting too much, like someone was sticking a blade into his knee, over and over again.

'I'm okay.'

'You're shaking.'

He hadn't realised. She pored over the map book of Tennessee, the pages dedicated to Memphis, and told him to take the next exit. He pulled off the freeway and headed for the lights of a neon-fringed street block and parked amid the anonymity of late-night clubs and all-night food joints.

Just taking his foot off the pedal felt like a mercy. He went through the ritual – the slow massaging of each muscle, each sinew. He noticed her staring and felt a pang of shame.

'There's a pizza place up there,' he said, a tad too quickly. 'What d'you want?'

'I want to come with you.'

She must have known that was a non-starter, but he didn't blame her. The truck was claustrophobic. Still, it was dark and they were the best part of twenty-four hours and a thousand miles from Clement.

'It's risky,' he said.

She'd picked up his baseball cap, pulled it over her hair and opened her door.

'It's my risk to take.'

He'd trust her. He took her hand and they headed toward the lights, making for a hole in the wall of a pizza joint – little more than a serving window surrounded by a crowd of clubbers mooching around on the sidewalk.

Aliyah sat on a low wall while he waited in line. He thought of his mom. Had she even seen the letter he'd sent? Did she have any idea of the shit he was in? He wondered if he'd ever see her again. What little he'd put in that letter was so awkward, so poorly expressed. He owed her so much more.

The line shuffled forward and a pale guy with a mullet and a stained apron took his order and then his cash. As he handed over a couple of pizza boxes, he seemed to stare, a glance that lasted a second too long. Greg felt a shiver run down his spine. He hurried back, the boxes warming his hands, trying to pick out Aliyah amid a gaggle of teens and a tapestry of shadows near the wall.

There she was. The baseball cap giving him a nod.

He walked over and handed her a box and she paid him with a smile.

'We should get back to the car.'

She opened the box, the scent of baked dough rising with the steam.

'Just a few minutes,' she said.

It was stupid. He knew it. A needless risk, but there was something tempting about it. The simple pleasure of just sitting there, eating a pizza with her. In another life, that might have been their story. Just the two of them doing the things regular folks did.

'A minute,' he said.

He sat down and she leaned into him. He felt the warmth of her arm against his. He opened his box and took out a slice.

'Tennessee,' she said. 'State bird?'

He didn't know. But that was pretty much part of the ritual now. He looked forward to learning something new.

'Mockingbird.'

'It's a sin to kill a mockingbird,' he said, though he couldn't remember why, or where he'd heard that.

A minute became five. He should have heeded his own warnings.

'Greg.'

The note of tension in Aliyah's voice roused him. He looked up. A bunch of guys, all loose jeans, tank tops and Vans, was staring at them. No, not them. *Him*. One reached into his pocket and pulled out a phone. He pointed it at Greg.

There was no time to think. He sprang up and forward, his weight on his good leg. His first punch knocked the phone from the guy's hand. The second knocked him to the ground nursing a broken nose.

He squared up to the others. Three skinny-ass skater dudes. Even with a fucked-up leg, he'd take those odds. He felt the adrenaline flowing. A memory of the old times. It felt good.

'What the fuck you think you're doin', pointing cameras at people?'

'Greg.' Aliyah's hand was on his arm. 'Leave it.'

He turned to her. More folks looking over. Others with their phones out.

*Shit.*

He pushed past them, pulling Aliyah in his wake.

A voice rang out behind him. 'That's them. Fuck! Someone call the –'

He never finished the sentence. Greg turned, grabbed him by his shirt and in one fluid motion rammed his skull into the guy's nose. He crumpled like a paper cup, his face exploding in a riot of crimson. He didn't wait for the guy to hit the deck before heading for the truck.

He flung open the door and got in, wrenching his knee in the process. He screwed his eyes shut against the pain. Shouts carried over on the wind. The beginnings of a mob. Aliyah jumped in beside him. People were getting closer. He turned the ignition, saw their faces as he pulled out, the flashes from camera phones. He pressed down hard on the gas.

He drove off, one thought filling his mind.

*They'd recognised him. Not just Aliyah. Him.*

# DAY 7

# *SUNDAY*

## CHAPTER 54

*Greg*

He should have torched the truck but he didn't have the time. Instead he removed the licence plates and pushed them deep into the belly of a dumpster. For a moment he considered dumping the rucksacks in there too, but the thought of them being discovered was too much of a risk. For one thing, his prints were on them. Instead he took the bags and left the pickup marooned in a back alley. Jacking another car might have been possible, but it was too big a risk.

His hair was black now, shaved down almost to the scalp. Aliyah's work, done quickly with scissors and dye bought from an all-night drugstore.

The night was cold, the temperature dropping as fast as his spirits. He led the way, hurrying through desolate streets, street-lamp orange piercing the darkness, animating the blues and reds of a hundred political posters plastered on derelict windows and corrugated walls.

He'd played football here once, back in the day: a game all but forgotten, but passing familiarity with the place instilled a degree of confidence. He knew where he was going. He knew what he was doing.

The bus terminal was an oasis of life amid the dead of night; a motley collection of students and sleep-deprived travellers waiting around, lounging as best they could on bolted plastic furniture and finding sustenance from a couple of old vending machines.

*Good crowd to get lost in.*

He pushed through the doors, Aliyah a few steps behind him, the brim of his cap pulled low over her face. The sight of a surveillance camera caused his heart to jump. He needed to stay calm. They looked different now. Almost unrecognisable from the pictures on the TV.

The screens said a bus for Atlanta was scheduled; a thirty-minute wait. Not long, but still an eternity to sweat through. He prayed the cops would still be looking for the car. The ticket booth was open, a world-weary African American man behind the counter. Greg avoided him and made instead for a row of machines at the edge of the concourse, buying two tickets and paying with cash. From Atlanta, he'd buy tickets to their final destination. It wouldn't leave him much; a hundred dollars at most.

*Finn's cash.*

The bus was idling at the stand. He handed a ticket to Aliyah, watched as she boarded, then waited a few minutes before getting on himself. Only with Memphis a brush of lights out the back window did he relax. Aliyah was seated a couple of rows in front. He closed his eyes and succumbed to fatigue, sleep rushing up on him like a wave, his dreams haunted by visions of Finn drenched in blood and his own face on a TV screen.

Atlanta arrived on the heels of the dawn, a kiss of gold falling low through the tinted windows, their arrival announced by a squeal of brakes and a hiss of air suspension. He looked toward Aliyah, already on her feet, reaching for her rucksack as other passengers struggled to life.

She was walking down the aisle before he managed to rise from his seat, coaxing his wayward joints without drawing attention to himself. Wincing against the pain, he grabbed his bag and limped forward along the aisle, down the steps, and into a daybreak of diesel fumes and engine noise.

He looked around for her and saw instead a patrol car lurking near the entrance. He pulled his eyes away and headed for the concourse, soon spotting Aliyah under a bank of screens announcing departure times. Beside them, a TV tuned to CNN: black smoke billowing up from Port Arthur; then a video of the president on the lawn of the White House, looking both grim and confused at the same time. The image changed, the blazing refinery replaced by stills of Aliyah and him. Head-and-shoulder shots placed side by side. A shiver passed through him, like seeing his own obituary in the papers. Another change: the candidates on the campaign trail. Costa spouting something, jabbing his finger at the camera; then Vice President Greenwood, sombre, more measured. *Wrong time for that.* Two days to the election and she was in danger of going the way of Hillary Clinton.

He made his way over, gesturing for her to follow, away from the screens and into the shadowed corners of the bus terminus. He headed for a pillar, dropping his rucksack beside it and lowering himself slowly to the ground on the far side, hidden he hoped from the cameras that scanned the concourse. Aliyah sat down next to him.

'There's an 8 a.m. coach to Gainesville.'

He looked at her.

'How'd you know that's where I was taking you?'

She smiled. 'That's where you grew up, right?'

He recalled telling her. One of those stolen moments in the barn back in Ripplebrook. He liked that she remembered.

*Two hours.*

A long time to be stuck in one place.

Sitting ducks.

He toyed with leaving the bus station; getting lost in the back-streets of Atlanta till departure time. But he didn't know the city and it was too early in the morning to find anywhere busy. And what if the police started checking the IDs of everyone coming back into the station? They'd be screwed.

'We should split up,' he said. 'Buy tickets, keep to different parts of the station and get on the bus separately.'

'I don't want to.'

He wanted to tell her to listen, to tell her that being together increased the risk to both of them. He just couldn't. The fear she'd been living with for two days now, ever since she'd first seen her face on the TV back in Idaho – of being recognised, reported; the stress of being the most wanted person in the country – he understood it now. It was stupid, he knew, but he needed the comfort of her touch.

'Fine. We'll hunker down here for now. I'll get the tickets.'

He began to rise, wincing as the pain shot up his leg. She placed a hand on his shoulder.

'*I'll* get the tickets.'

He fished out the creased bills from the pocket of his jeans and handed them to her, sitting back against the pillar as she disappeared. Across the way, a young mother was fighting a losing battle trying to feed gloop from a glass jar to a toddler, the kid pushing away the plastic spoon. The woman looked like she hadn't slept in a week, but still she persevered, cooing and coaxing till the kid complied and opened its mouth.

He turned away in time to catch an old guy looking at him. His heart stopped. The old guy looked away instantly. It was nothing, he told himself. Just one of those countless glances people gave strangers in public places. Still, Greg kept one eye on him. The guy crossed his legs: grey slacks and sneakers and a zip-up coat that was too warm for the climate but which didn't seem to matter to old folks. His eyes wandered the room before once more alighting on Greg.

He felt his skin crawl. He looked away, rubbing the side of his face with a hand. In the distance, Aliyah was heading back to him with the tickets.

*Dammit.*

The thing to do was act natural. Whatever suspicions the guy might or might not have, the worst thing Greg could do was draw attention to himself. He looked back. The old man was looking at his phone – an old-timey number by the looks of it – big keys and small screen. He forced himself to relax. The guy wasn't interested in him. He was just bored, and Greg was just jumpy.

Aliyah sat down next to him and handed him a ticket.

'Bad news. There's a delay. Engine trouble with the bus.'

'How long?'

'An extra two hours at least.'

Surely too long for their luck to hold. He should try again, should tell her to go sit somewhere else, but he didn't. If the game was up – if they were going to be found here, caught before they even got a chance to board the bus to Gainesville, caught and separated – then it stood to reason that he should eke out every precious second that was left to them.

He looked at her. The chain around her neck glinted in the light. The chain with its little pendant. The dove he'd made her. The same hands that had made those bombs for Miriam had fashioned that dove. He was glad. He loved her. It was enough.

The minutes crawled past, the terminus slowly filling. Locals and visitors mingling, merging, thronging, diverging like formations of starlings at sunrise. Ninety minutes more and he felt safer, the two of them, sitting at the base of their pillar, hidden amid the ebb and flow of people; their conversation lost among the general clamour.

She started teaching him about chess, again. Less about the movements of the pieces – more about the tactics.

'The beauty is in the manipulation. It's thinking ahead, making moves that force others into doing what you want without them even realising.'

Nine a.m. came and went, the screens stubbornly displaying no update for Gainesville. His leg was starting to ache. Too long in one position and it did that. Slowly he got himself to his feet. Aliyah'd been dozing beside him, the brim of the baseball cap pulled low over her face. She stirred as he rose.

'Where you going?'

'Nowhere. Just stretching my legs.'

His stomach growled.

'You want something to eat?'

'I'm okay.'

'We need to keep our strength up,' he told her.

A brightly coloured row of vending machines stood at the opposite end of the concourse, close to a corridor leading to the gates where the buses idled. He made his way over, just another traveller amid the crowd, and purchased plastic-wrapped Danishes and a couple of coffees. It might not be much, but it sure as hell was a lot better than the gruel Miriam usually served for breakfast.

*Miriam.*

Where was she now? Dead, he hoped, like Yusuf, but that was too much to expect. Folks like Miriam were professionals. Tough bastards. Hard to kill.

He headed back toward the pillar, the pastries in his jacket pocket and a coffee balanced precariously in each hand. He was about a hundred feet away when he saw them: two black-clad police officers, walking around, checking documents.

He stopped dead, feeling like his legs might give way. It took all his composure just to keep from dropping the cups. He took a breath, pulled himself together then set off again, circumnavigating the concourse, giving the officers a wide berth and arcing round back to Aliyah.

She looked up at him, smiled, then read the expression on his face. 'What is it?'

'Police. They're checking IDs.'

She got up and he left the coffees on the floor. 'Two male officers,' he told her. 'Get to the restroom nearest the gates. Hide in a stall. Stay there till they announce the Gainesville bus, then head for the gate.'

'What about you?'

He skirted the question.

'I'll meet you there.'

He watched as Aliyah crossed the concourse, keeping as far from the officers as he had. Once or twice he lost sight of her amid the bodies, finally picking her up as she reached the restrooms. He waited till he was sure she was inside, then looked to the cops. Seemed like they were seeking out couples. Young folks. White men. Darker women.

It gave him an idea.

The young mother was still across the way, still struggling to entertain her toddler. No sign of a daddy. He walked over and sat down next to her, giving her a smile. She replied in kind, though hers was fleeting. The toddler eyed him, then took up position behind the woman's knee. He pulled a face, then another, till the kid smiled.

He kept one eye on the cops, circling closer.

'How old is he?'

The woman turned to him. 'Oh, two in January.'

Greg made another face for the kid.

'He's cute.'

He pulled the Danishes from his pocket and offered one to the woman.

'It's kind of you,' she said. 'I'm fine though.'

'You sure? I only paid for one, but the machine seemed to like me and gave me two.'

The cops were close now. About fifty feet away.

The woman smiled, her tired face regaining for a moment the beauty of youth.

'Well, if it's no trouble.'

He passed her a Danish, then proceeded to open his own. He took a bite, and shot a glance at the cops.

'You going far?'

'Raleigh,' she told him. 'My folks' place.'

'They must be looking forward to seeing this little guy.' He gestured toward the kid. 'What's his name?'

By the time the cops came near, the three of them looked exactly like what he had hoped they might. Young, white parents with a kid, not even worth a second glance.

The announcement finally came over the loudspeaker, heralded by chimes and delivered in muffled, gritty tones.

'*6435 to Gainesville, gate number 8.*'

He said goodbye to the woman and the kid and wished them all the best. He stood up, gathered his bags and headed slowly toward the gates.

Gainesville.

His life coming full circle.

'*6435 to Gainesville, gate number 8.*'

Gainesville. End of the line.

He kept to the shadows, lurking near gate 8 till he saw her. She came over and squeezed his hand.

'You okay?' he asked.

'Yeah. Though I never want to spend an hour in a public toilet again. You?'

'Found myself a family and pretended to be a dad. Cops didn't even question me.'

She smiled at that.

They stepped forward, joining the queue through the gate and out into blinding sunlight. It took him a moment to adjust to the glare. Beside him Aliyah stopped. Two uniformed officers at the door of the bus, asking questions of folks and causing passengers to bottleneck. People pushed past them. She squeezed his hand. Seconds, more seconds. His shirt clung to his back.

Another bus pulled in. One of the officers peeled away ready to inspect the travellers it disgorged. His partner stayed at his post, besieged beside the baggage hold.

'Go, now,' he told her. She walked quickly, boarding while others blindsided the officer. The temptation was to follow her, there and then, but he stalled, then doubled back waiting agonising minutes till the last few stragglers said their goodbyes and ascended the stairs. The trickle of strays finally ended. The cop looked round, then walked off to vet another busload. Greg held fast. Interminable seconds punctuated by the pounding of his heart. The door began to close with a rubberised creak, and then he ran, head down, ticket in hand, pain snapping like fireworks through his knee. His vision clouded. He kept on despite the agony, even as he feared his leg might buckle under him. The bus engine growled to life. He threw himself at the door, thumping it with the sole of his palm. The driver looked down from his throne. Greg held up his ticket, his breath coming short and fast.

For a moment nothing happened.

Then he heard the pneumatic hiss as the door swung open.

He took a hold of the rail and hauled himself up the steps and received a shake of the head from the driver.

'Maybe don't leave it so late next time, kid.'

He collapsed into the first seat he found, next to a big guy with oversized headphones clamped over his skull. He tucked the duffel bag under his feet, then leaned back and took a breath, his shirt drenched and his heart still rattling in his chest. He looked down at his leg. It was vibrating, but the pain was ebbing to a throbbing ache. He wondered if he'd done himself permanent harm. Who cares? What mattered was keeping Aliyah safe. And getting her to Gainesville.

# CHAPTER 55

*Sajid*

New Mexico was far behind now. The twenty-four-hour news radio spoke of a sighting and the internet confirmed it. Credible reports of Aliyah and Greg in Memphis, Tennessee.

The revelations had thrown Carrie into introspection.

'Oh my . . . I think I might know where they're going.'

And so they drove. With renewed purpose. With renewed hope. Three-hour shifts, on and off, through the night and into the dawn. Utah, Colorado, Kansas, Missouri. It was Sajid's turn again. He was getting used to it, falling into a rhythm of sorts. Driving offered some steadiness amid his turmoil. His photograph, broadcast across the world. His name, maligned, slandered, portrayed as a terrorist . . . hunted. And with it all, the realisation that, finally, there would be no way out for him.

These were, he told himself, merely the logical outcomes of the path he had chosen. At least now, with his face up alongside that of his daughter, there was the chance that Aliyah might see it. That she might realise he was doing this for her; that she might reconsider what she was doing before it was too late.

The miles passed. The daylight ebbed.

'Sajid?'

Carrie stirred beside him.

'Where are we?'

'About thirty miles from Birmingham. You know, my wife has relatives in Birmingham – the other Birmingham, the one in England. We used to visit; take the coach from Victoria Station and stay for the weekend. Of course that was all before Mia's injury.'

He was not used to discussing Mia with anyone outside of the family, but now, with his fate all but sealed, it felt important to talk about her.

'Mia, that is to say Munira, and Aliyah are so alike. Both head-strong, like their mother. Neither of them ever listening to me. She was studying to be a lawyer, you know. Human rights. I told her, if you're going to be a lawyer, at least choose a branch of law that pays well but she wouldn't listen . . .' His voice trailed off.

He felt Carrie's eyes upon him.

'What happened to her?'

He took a breath.

'She was at a demonstration. Protesting against American policy in the Middle East. It was peaceful, but something happened. The police say the crowd began to throw rocks and bricks. They sent in horses and men with shields and batons. Mia was caught up in it. She was knocked to the ground . . . she . . . she hit her head. By the time they got her to hospital, the damage was permanent . . . what they call *persistent vegetative state.*'

She put her hand upon his arm. This time, he did not flinch.

'I'm sorry.'

'It was Aliyah who took it the hardest. She changed overnight. She used to be so outgoing, always smiling, always happy. I do not think she has smiled since. I felt as though I had lost both my daughters that day. It was partly why, when Aliyah told us she wanted to go to Japan, I let her, in spite of Rumina's objections. I thought it might help her to recover. You see what a foolish man I am?'

Carrie returned her gaze to the horizon. 'I don't see a foolish man. I see a man trying to help his daughter. I see a loving father.'

A sign flashed past. Twenty-seven miles to Birmingham. In the gloom he noticed the black-and-white patrol car lurking behind. Not the first of course. He had passed others in various designs in various states and each time he had felt his pulse quicken; each time he had checked the speedometer with the fear in his gut that he had accidentally transgressed, needlessly giving themselves away. Each time, however, the vehicle had remained thankfully motionless. Each time until now.

In the rear-view mirror, he watched its reflection roll forward, spitting dust as it joined the highway. He fought the urge to accelerate. The car drew closer.

'Carrie –'

His words were strangled in his throat by the sound of the siren. Carrie looked over her shoulder. Red and blue lights pulsed.

'Keep driving,' she told him.

He put his foot down, acceleration pushing him into his seat. The engine whined in protest. The gap to the police car grew, then began to diminish once more. It was no use. They were being reeled in. On a straight road, in a straight line, they would be overtaken in a matter of minutes. Reinforcements were probably already on their way. They would be cornered and caught.

He saw a turn-off, a dirt road into the trees.

'Hold on,' he said and sharply swung the wheel. The car skidded across loose ground. He feared they might flip over. He gripped the wheel tight, remembering the dirt roads of Chittagong, the words of his father's driver: *You need to speed up to get control.* He pressed down on the accelerator. The treeline was getting closer. He braced himself. At the last moment the tyres bit, regaining traction. He twisted the wheel. The car slewed, scraping a tree trunk before powering down the road.

He checked the road behind them for signs of pursuit. The seconds passed. His hopes soared. And then he saw them. The flashing lights of not one but two patrol cars. Carrie saw them too.

'Keep going!'

The road twisted, the car kicking up dust as he pushed it onwards while the gap behind them inexorably closed. He yanked the wheel, narrowly avoiding the limb of a tree. When he looked in the mirror again, one of the patrol cars had vanished.

He had no time to consider what had happened to it.

Ahead the road petered out, ending in a wall of trees and scrub. There was nowhere else to go. He slammed hard on the brakes, inertia throwing him forward. The car slewed round. He turned the wheel, hoping to find another route, a smaller road maybe, or even level ground, but there was nothing and then, ahead of him, in a cloud of dust, came the police cars, blocking off any chance of escape.

There was nowhere to go. Nowhere to run.

# CHAPTER 56

*Sajid*

He fumbled for the button on his belt release.

Outside: sirens and lights and the shouts of men.

'Carrie?'

The car door burst open; a gun thrust in his face. He went to raise his hands, but a voice yelled at him. He froze. More shouts, new voices, angry commands.

*'Get out!'*

*'Lie flat on the ground!'*

*'Hands behind your head!'*

Insults too. Expletives. Anger that suggested they would shoot him. Revenge for Los Angeles. Penance for Port Arthur. In this country, did they not kill black men for less? But he wished to stay alive; it was his duty to Aliyah, to his wife and other children. And to Carrie.

He felt hands on his wrists, yanking them down, wrenching

them behind his back. Electric pain spasming in his arms. He gritted his teeth, bit down to stifle any cry. He felt the steel of the cuffs.

There was no dread this time. Not like in London. Too much had happened to him since.

'What's your name, boy?'

He made to answer, his sentence cut short by a blow to the back of his head as the world blew up into pain once more and a torrent of expletives rained down on him.

He was bundled into the back of a vehicle, head covered with sackcloth, feet chained to the floor, his questions about Carrie met with orders to shut his damn mouth.

He closed his eyes and whispered a dua.

*In the Name of Allah. I seek refuge in Allah and in His Power from the evil of what I find and of what I guard against.*

No divine intervention expected; merely a calming and strengthening of his spirits.


They transported him.

He did not know where, the journey ending with him being manhandled out of the car, into a building and thrown into a cell.

There, a doctor examined him. Shone lights in his eyes and asked him questions. They photographed him and fingerprinted him. A stone-faced woman in a police uniform brought him a meal. She reminded him of Mrs Braithwaite back at the bureau de change. The same expression on both of their faces.

'It ain't halal,' she said, placing the tray with pre-wrapped containers before him.

He could have told her that he really didn't care. Instead he asked after Carrie, and received no response but the woman's retreating back.

He ate their food and drank their water. He wondered if it was drugged and decided it didn't matter. If they questioned him, he would only tell them the truth – that he was here to save his daughter.

He lay back on the metal bench, half expecting shrill voices to scream at him to get up.

*Isn't that what they did? Deprive you of sleep?*

But no voices came. His thoughts turned once more to Carrie, and then to Aliyah and his family. He had failed them all.

There came the scrape of a key turning in the lock. He saw the steel door open. As he pulled his aching body upright, an officer entered, broad arms, khaki shirt stretched tight over an ample stomach. The man applied silver shackles to Sajid's hands and feet and led him shuffling into a small room with a table and chairs and told him to sit.

He stumbled into a seat and stared at his cuffed wrists. Voices came from the corridor outside. The door flew open. He glanced up as a figure walked in. The breath caught in his throat. His heart pounded. This woman. It was impossible.

# CHAPTER 57

*Shreya*

The buzz of the phone roused her from exhaustion. Her first thought: that it heralded bad news from the hospital. But on the screen was a number, not Nik's name.

'They've arrested Sajid Khan and Carrie Flynn.'

Mike Raven's voice. He sounded nervous.

'Where?'

'Near Birmingham. Wyatt's sending a team over but they won't be there till close to midday.'

'Why so long?'

'Because they're currently needed in Port Arthur. Look, Shreya. Something's going on. Everything feels odd. Word is there's some power struggle going on in DC.'

'There's always a power struggle going on in DC.'

'This is . . . it's different. Wyatt's insisting no one talks to them before his own people get there.'

'What do you want me to do about it? I'm suspended. What does Dan have to say?'

'Shreya, Dan was the one who told me to call you.'

She sat up.

'Really?'

'I guess he thought you'd know what to do.'

She threw on her coat and headed for the door. What the hell was she doing? Her place was here, waiting for her dad when they released him from hospital, not tearing from Auburn to Birmingham in the middle of the night. But Nik was at the hospital. He'd call her if there were any developments. Nik – there once again to deal with all the trouble in her world.

She walked into the police station just after 8 a.m., craving caffeine or nicotine.

Sajid Khan looked like he could do with both, a bombed-out refugee, his face wearing the scars of what the officers said was a car crash but with bruises that bore the contours of a fist or two. He stared at her like he was in shock and she was a ghost. She reminded herself that he was a terrorist.

'You?' he said. 'But that's not ... You were with Mia in the ambulance.'

It took her a moment to make the connection. Munira, abbreviated to Mia.

'That's right.'

'Your name is ... Shreya, no?'

'Correct. Special Agent Shreya Mistry. I'm with the FBI.'

He seemed to have difficulty believing his eyes. She could sympathise. She'd felt the same on seeing his face in the photos Pearce had placed in front of her.

'They sent you to interrogate me?'

She answered with a nod. The lie was impossible. She got the formalities out of the way and sat down across the table from him.

'My friend, Carrie,' he said. 'Is she okay?'

'My questions first. Where's your daughter, Sajid?'

'I don't know.'

'Is she with Greg Flynn?'

'I think so.'

'What are they planning?'

'I don't know.'

'And you? What's your part in all this?'

'My part?' A shake of the head. 'I just want to find my daughter.'

'What?'

'I'm just trying to find Aliyah.'

'You travel halfway round the world and enter the country as a fugitive because you think you've got a better chance of finding Aliyah than all the resources of the US government?'

He leaned forward.

'You once told me that you had a daughter of your own. Would you do any less for her?'

She didn't want to think about that particular relationship.

'So tell me how you and Carrie Flynn ended up here.'

He paused, then embarked on a tale about Carrie Flynn turning up at his door in the rain, clutching a letter from her son; of a girl called Najmah and a message about Ripplebrook; of flying into Canada and smuggling himself into America; about reaching Ripplebrook just a few hours after *she* had; about a drive to Clement and then, after news of Port Arthur, south till they'd been caught outside of Birmingham.

She sat back, arms folded.

'You expect me to believe this? That you've miraculously fumbled your way here?'

'Is it any less plausible than the notion that I and Carrie are jihadis? Part of this Sons of the Caliphate nonsense? You know my story. You probably know that I fled Bangladesh to escape the mullahs. How could I then be a religious fanatic? As for Carrie, I'm not sure she even has a religion.'

'So why not just tell all this to the police? If you'd told us about Ripplebrook, we might have got there in time to save Aliyah.'

For a moment he just stared at her gravely.

'Forgive me, but as far as I'm aware, at least one person you found at Ripplebrook came out of that house in a body bag. Had she been there, what are the chances that Aliyah's fate would have been any different? I have already lost one daughter to the police. You really think I'd risk the life of another?'

She looked into his eyes. The guy still seemed to honestly believe that the British police were responsible for Munira's injuries. None of it made any sense.

She changed tack.

'Where were you heading?'

'Florida.'

'Why?'

'Carrie said it seemed logical. That Greg might attempt to find safety there.'

'Where in Florida?'

'First tell me if Carrie is okay.'

'She's fine. She'll be questioned shortly.'

'Can I see her?'

'That's not going to happen. Now tell me where in Florida.'

He again shook his head. 'I can't tell you that, not without something in return.'

She got to her feet.

'We're done here, Sajid. The next people that come through that door? They'll bleed you till there's nothing left, and then they'll throw you into a hole so deep you'll wish they'd shot you instead of arresting you.'

She headed for the door.

'Wait,' he said. 'What I've told you is the truth. I can prove it.'

She stopped and turned.

'Okay.'

'The letter which Carrie brought to London, the one from her son, she should still have it somewhere.'

'That's not proof of anything. It could have been written by anyone at any time. *You* might even have written it. You need to give me more. Otherwise I'm gonna send you back to that cell to wait for the anti-terror team from Washington to arrive. Every second you waste is time we could use to find your daughter. Whatever you know, you got to tell me and you need to do it now.'

He flinched.

'I don't know where Aliyah is. I don't know for sure that she is even with Greg Flynn. But if they are together, I can't believe they would do anything other than run and hide. And if they are, then I think there is one person who knows where they are heading.'

He lifted his eyes to hers and held her stare.

'Carrie.'

# CHAPTER 58

*Shreya*

The letter had been among Carrie Flynn's possessions. Shreya read it through twice, committing its contents to memory. Flynn's cell was a step up from Sajid Khan's: a mattress on top of the concrete shelf and a closed-off cubicle of a lavatory. The sort of cell they generally reserved for VIPs – like Epstein or one of the former president's lawyers.

Flynn herself looked like she'd seen better days, her arm bandaged and the fingers of a purple bruise creeping over the right side of her forehead. She sat up as Shreya entered. There was beauty in that face, a tired, weathered beauty. The sort that persisted in spite of the vicissitudes of life.

'Ms Flynn, I'm Special Agent Mistry. I need to ask you some questions.'

The professional thing to do would be to question her the way she'd questioned Sajid Khan. Slowly, methodically, repetitively. Except there was no time for that.

'Why'd you smuggle a jihadi terrorist into the country?'

The woman spat out a laugh.

'Is that what you think? Look at the guy. He's no more a terrorist than he is a fish. Whatever his daughter's involved in, it's got nothing to do with him.'

*His daughter.* It was a curious choice of words.

'And your son? He's involved too.'

Flynn gave a nod.

'Did he convert to Islam?'

There was that dismissive look again.

'He's *not* a Muslim.'

'You're sure?'

'Yes.'

'Because he'd have told you? Maybe in that letter he wrote you?'

The woman blinked. That was good.

'You wanna tell me why you helped Sajid Khan into the country.'

'I needed his help.'

'To find your son?'

'I take it you've read the letter. I knew I couldn't find Greg without him.'

'Sajid seems to think you might know where Greg and Aliyah are heading. Is that true?'

'I might have an idea.'

'Where?'

Carrie Flynn leaned back and folded her arms.

'They're not terrorists. They're just frightened kids. If I know my son, he'll be trying to find a place where they can hide. I'll make you a deal. You take Sajid and me with you and I'll lead you there.'

Shreya shook her head.

'I can't do that.'

'Then I can't tell you.'

Shreya rubbed at the pain at the base of her neck.

Time was running out. Wyatt's team would be here within six hours. She should tell them what she'd found and let them handle it … assuming she could trust them … a pretty big assumption given that Dan would hardly have sent her here if he were sure Wyatt's team were on the level.

'You need to give me something more, Carrie. Some reason to believe that everything you're telling me isn't just some fairy tale you and Khan have cooked up to save your kids. Otherwise, you and he will be charged, and the charge will be terrorism.'

Flynn stared at her, then looked to the wall and the sliver of light falling through the window slit.

'The woman. The one with the white hair. The one you pulled out of that house in Ripplebrook. I know who she is. Her name's Mary.'

The world seemed to shift beneath Shreya. Miriam, Maria, Mary. The same but different.

'How would you know that?'

'Because it's my fault she ever found Greg.'

*

Shreya told herself she had no choice. She needed to get Sajid Khan and Carrie Flynn out of there. Maria O'Connor, the woman who'd ordered Yusuf Ghani to kill her, who'd held a gun to Kramer's head, had also groomed Carrie Flynn, befriending her, more than a year before, in the home of one of the patients she cared for, claiming to be the woman's niece. Worming her way into Flynn's confidence, learning about her family, her son, wounded in Afghanistan, struggling to come to terms with civilian life, ending up incarcerated in Ocala. And then a month later he was free, released ahead of time, no explanation given nor requested; the woman disappearing soon after.

It was too convenient to have been coincidence. Maria O'Connor had secured Greg Flynn's release from a federal penitentiary. That took friends. That took pull.

A shiver ran down her spine. These people weren't jihadis. They were *inside* the security structures of the US government. They could get felons freed from prison and they could locate and attack an FBI black site. People like that would already know that Carrie Flynn and Sajid Khan were in custody, and that Flynn knew details about O'Connor's recruitment of her son. They would want to shut her up. If they could attack the FBI, they could easily infiltrate an Alabama police station. Maybe a hit squad was already on its way? Was that why the official FBI team was only due to get here after midday? Had they been deliberately delayed to allow an attack? With the election so close now, anything was possible.

There was no time to call Dan. She had to act. She strode into the sheriff's office like she owned the place, with the swagger befitting a big swinging dick of the Federal Bureau of Investigation and told him that *his* prisoners were now *her* prisoners. It still took the invocation of the august authority of the Bureau as well as the judicious deployment of several piquant threats before he agreed to release them, but in the end, that's what he did.

She signed the requisite forms and led Khan and Flynn to the car. From the trunk she took a couple of plastic ties, looping them through their handcuffs and securing them to the grab handles in the back of the car.

Khan said nothing, but Flynn didn't seem pleased.

'Is this really necessary?'

'It is,' she told her, 'unless you want to stay here and explain everything again to my less amenable colleagues from Washington.' She started the engine. 'So where we heading?'

Khan looked to Flynn.

'Northern Florida,' the woman replied.

'Not good enough. I need a place name.'

Flynn paused. An intake of breath followed by a heavy exhale.

'There's a trailer, outside of Gainesville. It was his dad's place. Greg used to go there when he needed to hide away from the world.'

'You want to give me an address?'

'Not for the moment. We wouldn't want your colleagues to get there before us.'

Shreya didn't argue. The woman had already told her enough.

She waited till they were on the road south toward Montgomery before she pulled over and got out. Calling Dan directly was a risk too far. It would implicate him, and he would be beholden to tell her to turn back. There had to be someone else; someone she trusted, someone who could claim, should the worst happen, that they were just passing on a message from a superior officer.

She tried Mike Raven, but none of his numbers connected. It unnerved her.

There was someone else though.

She brought up the name and pressed. This time the call went through.

'Kramer, it's Shreya.'

'Shreya? I heard what happened. I'm so sorry. If there's anything I can do . . .'

'I need you to get a message to Dan. Not Wyatt, only Dan.'

Silence on the line, punctuated only by the sound of Kramer's breathing.

'Go ahead.'

'Tell him we're looking for a trailer outside of Gainesville, Florida. It would have belonged to Greg Flynn's father.'

'Gainesville? Where are you, Shreya?'

'It doesn't matter. What matters is you tell Dan to find that trailer and get the whole Bureau combing the area round Gainesville.'

'Will do. And Shreya, whatever you're up to, be careful.'

\*

She made her way back to the car, started the engine and stepped on the gas. In the back, Sajid Khan and Carrie Flynn were silent. That was just as well as she didn't feel much like talking. Breaking them out of jail wouldn't exactly be career-enhancing, assuming she had any career left to enhance; but trusting them – believing their story – that was an even bigger risk and perhaps the biggest mistake of her life.

Less than twenty miles down the highway, her phone buzzed. She popped in an earpiece and took the call.

'Shreya?'

'Dan.'

'The fuck are you doing? I'm hearing that you've busted Khan and Flynn out of jail!'

'They're in my custody.'

'On whose authority? Hell, Shreya. This is insane. Wyatt's going nuts. He's talking about issuing a warrant for your arrest.'

'I'll explain later. Did Kramer pass on my message?'

'About Gainesville? Yeah, I just got it.' There was a pause on the line. 'There's something you should know, Shreya. The Veep's holding a rally there tomorrow. Final one of the campaign.'

'Greenwood? You think that's their target?'

She sensed hesitation.

'It gets worse. Costa has one in Daytona Beach. Looks like the whole election is coming down to Florida.'

'How far's Daytona from Gainesville?'

'Less than a hundred miles.'

Greenwood and Costa. Greg and Aliyah. All in northern Florida one day before the election. It was too much to be coincidence. Two rallies, two potential targets. A successful attack on either would tear the country apart.

'You gotta stop those rallies, Dan.'

# CHAPTER 59

*Greg*

'*Gainesville, this is Gainesville. Final stop.*'

Greg had been dreaming of his mother.

He opened his eyes to hues of a Florida sunset and fellow travellers rising for their bags. The guy beside him stared at him like Greg was keeping him from the rest of his life. Greg levered himself out of his seat to let the guy out, then sat back again and commenced the slow-motion callisthenics of his leg.

The door slid open, refrigerated air hitting panhandle heat. He got up, reached down for the duffel bag and hobbled off the bus and into the evening air. The humidity met him like an old friend. Hard to believe it was November, but then everything was fucked up these days.

He looked around. Travellers dispersing; vehicles and bodies idling nearby. Outside the ticket office, an old guy dozed on a bench beside the last payphone in the city. If there were police here, he couldn't see them. That at least was something.

Aliyah came down the steps. He gave her a nod then turned away, heading for the main road beyond the pooled light of the parking lot. He scanned the area beyond, a glance ahead – nothing more – in search of anything suspicious. He'd signal her with a scratch of his ear if he saw trouble and she'd disappear in the opposite direction.

But he saw nothing, kept his hand in his pocket and kept walking, crossing the street and heading north, away from downtown toward the hinterland of light-industrial sprawl, where the roads were wide and the rents were cheap. He knew these streets. He'd walked them, and he'd worked them, and he knew where to find what he needed.

The place was a few blocks up: a ramshackle chop shop past a used-car dealership and a few spare-parts franchises stocking Chinese knock-offs. It was where you came when you needed your wheels fixed and you weren't too concerned where the parts came from just so long as it was cheap. He'd worked there one summer, for a guy named Al who drove a beat-up old Lexus even though he was rolling in cash.

He'd learned a lot about cars that summer, and that Al's parsimony extended from his choice of car to the security of the lot, the only barriers against theft being an old lock on the chain-link fence and the hope that no one with any sense would waste their time robbing the place.

And that place hadn't changed, the small lot still rammed with crap and the overspill parked on the street outside. Those cars were easy to spot: usually just a collection of dust and rust, dents and dulled paintwork that pointed to a vehicle on its way to meet its maker.

He picked out several specimens outside the lot: a Ford, a Nissan and a Honda missing a wing mirror. Their keys, he knew, should've been in the shack at the back of the yard, behind the padlocked fence, but Al didn't exactly pay top dollar and the staff cut corners. Depending who'd been on shift at closing time, there was a good chance at least one of the vehicles would have their keys lodged behind the sun visor, or, if his old compadre Felipe had been on shift, then lodged behind the rear left wheel well.

He walked up to the Ford and tried first the driver's door and then the others. Locked. He knelt down and tried the wheel arch, his fingers searching rubber and the perforated metal of the bodywork and finding nothing. He got up and tried the other side just in case and with the same result. He moved on to the Honda and fared no better.

*Maybe Al had wised up with the security.*

The last was a grey Nissan Altima. Instantly forgettable. He tried the doors. Locked. He knelt in the dirt and checked the rear wheel.

*Bingo.*

He pulled out the keys, clicked the fob and the lights blinked in welcome. He got in, started the engine and drove back toward Tom Petty Park.

He didn't need a map now. He knew the country like a childhood song.

'How far is it?' Aliyah asked.

'Orange Lake,' he said. 'Not too far. It was my old man's place. He'd go down there to fish, or just to get away from me and Mom.'

'I'm sorry,' she said.

'Don't be. It was better for all of us when he wasn't around.'

He drove fast, stopping only for some provisions at a gas station near Rochelle. From there it was another ten minutes and he was pulling off the road and onto the path he remembered since boyhood. When was the last time he'd been here? Before Afghanistan; before everything. A fucking lifetime ago and yet it felt like yesterday.

A mile or so more and he'd be there. Three days and two nights.

From Portland to Gainesville. Then he'd take stock. Figure out their next move. Work out what he needed to do to protect her; what *they* needed to do to survive.

He saw it up ahead. A glint of metal in the moonlight. The squat square outline among the trees. He parked up behind it, out of sight of the road. Turned off the ignition.

Beside him Aliyah was staring out the windshield, curiously silent. He reached for her hand. 'We'll be safe here.'

He stepped out to the sound of cicadas and the smell of dew on the grass; the air still harbouring the warmth of day. He was a kid again, waiting for his dad to come down the step with the fishing rods, his mom smiling at the door. This was the place he'd been truly happy. At least for a while.

The trailer door was padlocked; the key would be under a brick behind the septic tank, where his dad had always left it.

'Wait here,' he told her as he headed off to find it, skirting around the side of the trailer and into the scrub beyond. In the daylight, it would have taken him seconds. Now, in the half-light, he inched forward, picking his way carefully over, making sure there was nothing to catch his leg or cause him to trip. He groped for the brick, eventually finding it a yard or two from where it should have been.

He knelt down to lift it, then stopped dead. A noise. Somewhere behind him. A rustle of foliage. The heavy fall of something. His heart pounded.

An animal, he guessed. A boar maybe.

*Keep calm.*

He turned back to the brick, lifting it, finding the key.

Another noise. Metallic this time. Then a scream.

*Aliyah.*

He scrambled to his feet, reaching for the gun Aliyah'd taken from Finn. The screams died. He raced back round to the front of the trailer and stopped dead.

There, in front of him, the car door flung open, Aliyah outside, standing stiff, her face a rictus mask. An arm round her throat, a gun at her head.

A voice he recognised. 'Drop the gun.'

And then another figure, approaching out of the darkness, snow-white hair shimmering in the moonlight.

'You didn't really think you could walk out on us, did you, Greg?'

# CHAPTER 60

*Greg*

'Greg.'

Miriam's voice, battlefield-calm. A gun in her hand, pointed at him.

*How did she know where to find him?*

'This is your last chance, Greg. Put the gun down.'

'Put it down, man.' Jack this time. 'Or Aliyah dies.'

He kept his gun trained on Jack.

'I do that and she's dead anyway.'

Miriam took a step to the side. *Outflanking him.*

'It doesn't have to be that way.'

He took a step back, keeping her in sight.

'Isn't that what you told Yasmin? And Rehana? What happened to them?'

Miriam shook her head.

'Yasmin's death was an accident. Rehana was killed by security at the refinery.'

*Lies.* They were all lies.

Jack brandished the gun.

'I'm gonna count to three, Greg. If you ain't put down your gun, I swear I'll shoot her. One . . . two . . .'

He tried to think. Tried to figure a way out of this.

'Final warning, Greg.'

He had no choice. Slowly, he lowered his arm to his side.

'Good boy. Now toss it over here.'

He bent down and did as ordered.

'And that fucking knife of yours.'

The blade went skittering across the dirt. Even as he rose, Miriam was on him, her gun in his back, pushing him forward.

Jack gave a familiar smirk.

'You look surprised to see us, Greg.'

Jack's expression changed, the smirk turning to glee.

'Shit! She didn't tell you, did she?'

*What was he talking about?*

'Tell me what?'

Jack gave a whoop.

'Gainesville. Your little girlfriend was always coming here.'

He said nothing. He could say nothing.

He looked to Aliyah. She stared back, expressionless. It couldn't be true. Florida. Gainesville. All this way across the country. It had been his idea. *Hadn't it?* He'd brought her here to keep her safe. Or had that always been the plan? For him to bring her here?

'Is that true?'

She dropped her gaze to the dirt.

Jack laughed. 'Seems you might not know her quite as well as you thought.'

His head spun.

Miriam pushed him to the steps and made him unlock the

trailer, the chain slinking snake-like to the ground, its padlock landing heavy in the dirt.

She forced him inside and pointed to the banquette.

'Sit.'

The place smelled like a tomb.

She took a lighter to a kerosene lamp, its glow illuminating Aliyah as she entered, Jack's gun at her back. He pushed her toward the bench and she landed almost on top of him. He reached out, caught her, steadied her.

Jack couldn't hide his amusement.

'Greg, boy. I warned you about her. I told you not to get involved. You think she's some innocent little girl? She ain't.'

He turned to Aliyah.

'When were you gonna tell him?' he heard Jack say.

'Tell me what?' He felt the panic take hold. The dawning realisation that he'd never been the one in control. He was like a rat in a lab experiment, thinking he had free will but all the time just reacting to their stimulus, going where they wanted him to go, doing what they wanted him to do.

What was it Aliyah had said?

*'The beauty is in the manipulation . . . making moves that force others into doing what you want.'*

But that couldn't be true. Aliyah wouldn't treat him that way. *Would she?* He felt her slipping away from him. Needed to try to get her back.

'Aliyah, whatever it is they told you, it was a lie. They're using you. Just like they used Yasmin. Just like they used Rehana. They found you and groomed you for their own reasons.'

Miriam gave a mirthless laugh.

'It still amazes me how dumb you are, Greg. How damn naive. You think I *recruited* Aliyah? You think I groomed her? It didn't happen. She *volunteered*, Greg. They *all* did. Aliyah, just like Yasmin and Rehana, reached out online and told me exactly what she wanted to do. I just provided her with the means and the opportunity. You do still want to go through with it, don't you, Aliyah? Isn't that why you came to Gainesville?'

He didn't understand. None of this was true. It couldn't be. Aliyah loved him. Didn't she? He looked to her for reassurance.

'Aliyah?'

Her face seemed to have grown waxen. She reached for his hand, her cold fingers interlacing with his.

'I need to finish what I started.'

It felt like the ground was opening.

'They killed Yasmin.' His voice was cracking. 'They killed Rehana. Whatever they want you to do, they'll make sure they kill you too.'

'It doesn't matter,' she said. 'If I don't, they'll kill me anyway.'

She turned to Miriam.

'You promise you'll let him go.'

A thin smile creased Miriam's lips.

'You go through with this and I'll make that promise. He's done what we needed him to do, got you here in one piece.'

And then it hit him. It was never just about him building their bombs. Miriam could probably have gotten half a dozen others to make them. But it was Gainesville and his connection to the place that had singled him out. He could get Aliyah to Gainesville. Jack was too busy dealing with first Yasmin and then Rehana. He could get her here and he could hide her till she carried out her mission. And then maybe Miriam would have ordered *him* to kill her. Is that what Miriam had wanted to talk to him about in her study, that morning after Jack came back? That other job she said she had for him? Had she sensed he wasn't ready? Did she suspect he wouldn't obey?

But in the end, he'd brought her here of his own free will, or what he had thought was free will. Had Miriam played him? *Games within games.* It was what Miriam did best. Had she adapted her plans and still got him to do exactly what she wanted? Or was this Aliyah's idea? Had she always intended to contact Miriam when she got here? His head spun.

But Aliyah was still trying to save him. He must mean something to her. He clung on to that.

He made to protest. Told them he wasn't going anywhere without her.

Jack let out a sickening laugh.

'Seems like we got a pair of star-crossed lovers.'

Miriam though was staring at the pair of them with what seemed like pride.

'Maybe there's a way for you both to come out of this alive?'

He felt his pulse quicken. Aliyah squeezed at his hand. It was a lie. It had to be. Just another and another. And yet in desperation, some part of him wanted to believe her. It was hope. A reed to be clutched at, and at least a stay of execution. And what was the alternative? A bullet in the head right here, right now? If death was certain, better it be tomorrow than today. Jack though looked like he might have other ideas.

'We should stick to the plan. We should –'

Miriam silenced him with a look.

'The best plans adapt to the circumstances. We can use –'

Her phone buzzed. She stared at the screen, then reached for the kerosene lamp. From the road came the growl of a car. Miriam killed the lamplight as the white arc of headlights strafed the windows.

'We have to go.'

Jack trained his gun on them.

'Get down. Both of you.'

Greg dropped to the floor, one arm instinctively pulling Aliyah close. Why? Why give a damn about her? After her lies. One chance, that's all he needed. One chance and he'd be out of there.

He heard the car draw closer, the sound of tyres crunching on grit.

Jack cursed. 'You said we had more time.'

'You will be quiet,' Miriam told him. 'Open the back window. Get 'em out now.'

The engine died. A solitary vehicle then.

Jack grabbed Aliyah's wrist, pulled her up and made for the rear of the trailer.

Miriam lifted a corner of the curtain covering the window. Took a glance at the white light of the headlamps outside. From the rear of the trailer the sound of a window being smashed out. Jack returned, looming out of the darkness.

'Get up. Don't make me fuck up that gimpy knee of yours.'

He got to his feet, made it to the rear of the trailer and joined Aliyah, Jack one step behind him. Outside a car door opened.

He felt the hard edge of the barrel of Jack's gun forced against his temple.

'You,' Jack said to Aliyah. 'Out the window and wait there. You make any other move and I blow his head off.'

'Fuck you, Jack,' she said, but still, she did as he ordered.

A shot rang out. It was close. Fired by Miriam, he thought. Then another. Then all hell broke loose. Jack pulled him to the window.

'You next, pal. Get out that window. And remember, you try anything and I'll shoot you in the fuckin' head.'

Greg manoeuvred himself up and over the ledge. One chance. That was all. He needed to time his jump, make sure he landed with his weight on his good knee. Jack read his hesitation.

'You tryin' to fuck with me?'

He lowered the gun, then smashed it against Greg's knee. He heard himself cry out in agony. Jack pushed him off the ledge. He was falling out of the window, landing brutally, shoulder first on the ground. He wanted to lie there; just lie there and die. And then he heard Aliyah. Felt her hands on his face.

'Greg. You've got to get up.'

Jack, his boots landing on the ground inches from Greg's head.

'Get up, dumbass.'

He hauled himself up with Aliyah's help. She placed his arm over her shoulder and dragged him forward, to the treeline and on; where to, he didn't know. Suddenly Miriam was there, running up behind them.

'Let's go.'

A car engine roared to life. Doors opened. He was bundled into the back. Aliyah beside him. And then the night took hold.

# CHAPTER 61

*Shreya*

There should have been backup. It should have been here, waiting for them. Dan should have gotten her voicemail, the one she'd left as soon as the Flynn woman had trusted her with the exact address. But there was nothing and no one here.

She tried calling. The line was bad.

'Dan. You get my message?'

His voice fought the static.

'... got it ... I'm on a plane ... we're en route to Gainesville. Sit tight. The cavalry'll be with you soon.'

'What about the local cops?'

'Wyatt wants it coordinated.'

'You told Wyatt?'

'He's in charge ... I didn't have much choice, but ... careful, Shreya ...'

She lost his voice to the ether and then the line too. She hung up and stared at the trailer through the trees, at the faint light seeping from its windows.

Carrie Flynn stirred. 'Why are we just sitting here? We need to go in there.'

'We need to wait for backup.'

The woman tugged against her restraints.

'What? No, that wasn't the deal. You wait for your friends, you go in there all guns blazing, you'll be handing them a death sentence. You promised us a chance to talk to them. We can end this.'

She shook her head.

'We don't know who's in there.'

Through the trees, she caught something. A shift in the shadows behind the window.

'Agent Mistry.' Sajid Khan's voice was measured. 'Please. Let us try.'

She tried to figure out a way of telling them the same thing using different words. She was not going to charge in there with two civilians in tow. She was going to wait for backup, as she'd been ordered.

And then the light in the trailer went off.

The Flynn woman noticed it too. 'They might be leaving. We got to do something, *now*.'

Shreya sat there, conflicted, considering her options, precious seconds passing.

'Agent Mistry, there's no time!'

Carrie Flynn was right. She turned and released the plastic ties that secured their handcuffs to the grab handles, then reached for her gun and opened the door.

'Stay here. I'll call you when it's safe.'

She closed the car door softly behind her. The air was too warm, too clammy. From all around came the rasping of cicadas, the croaking of bullfrogs. Horrible creatures. The trailer must have been about forty yards away. She set off, senses primed, through the trees, over crabgrass and dirt, the darkness enveloping, disorienting. With no light to aim at, it was hard to judge exactly where the trailer was. Slowly, though, its blocky shadow materialised less than twenty yards away. A twig snapped underfoot. She stopped dead, the breath dying in her throat.

She ducked down behind the nearest tree, heart pounding, blood roaring. From the trailer, the faintest of glows – too dim to be a flashlight. The illuminated screen of a phone, then. Something crawled up her gun hand. She shook it off and shivered.

*Pull yourself together.*

Deep breaths. In … out … in … out. Her mouth, cavern-dry, and from all sides the sounds of the bullfrogs.

She stood up and kept going. From somewhere the click of a car door. Behind her, she thought. Flynn and Khan disregarding everything she'd said. *Dammit.* She should never have released their cuffs from the straps.

The trailer was only feet away, seemingly dead to the world. She inched forward, the gun heavy in her hand. She thought of Isha and Nik. She thought of her dad lying in the hospital. What was she doing? She should have waited for the local police.

*Too late now.* The cinder-block step beneath the front door was dead ahead. She released the safety on the gun and took up position on one side. She reached out, fingers touching the steel handle, wrapping around it.

She pulled down gently and –

A flash of light, blinding her, the explosion of a gunshot, a hole blasted in the door inches from her head, splinters flying. She dropped to the ground, dazed. Another shot. Another hole in the door. Closer still.

A scream, somewhere behind her. Carrie Flynn, she thought. Her vision returned. She scrambled to her feet and ran for the trees. Behind her, a car engine fired to life. She turned, expecting another volley of bullets to punch through the night. Instead came voices, shouts rising above the hum of the engine. She rose, keeping low, and sprinted for the trailer once more, making not for the front this time, but the side. Somewhere doors slammed, tyres sputtered on gravel and then headlights arced round toward her. She ran, closing the distance to the dirt path. If they reached the road, she'd lose them again. She made it to the path, headlights in her face, blinding her. She raised her gun and fired. The car swerved, hitting her side-on, knocking her to the ground. A spasm of pain spiralled through her. She hit the dirt, just managing to keep hold of the gun, rolled and fired, only to see crimson tail lights skidding around the corner.

She sprinted back through the trees toward her own car. Carrie Flynn and Sajid Khan were taking cover close by.

'Get in!'

She jumped in and pressed the starter button, reversed into a cloud of dust then hit the gas and made for the road.

'Is it them?'

She ignored the question. She'd only seen a blur. Three or four occupants. A man in the driver's seat. A woman beside him. A woman with white hair. The tail lights disappeared amid the trees, then, in the distance, a glow of red – a road to the left. She turned the wheel and slammed hard on the brakes. The car slewed, and then she accelerated once more, the tail lights again beginning to draw closer. The distance began to narrow by the second. She pressed on the accelerator. Three hundred yards, two hundred. A shot rang out. The steering wheel bucked, then went live between her hands.

*A tyre. They must have hit a tyre.*

The car skidded, then yanked sideways on the dirt of the road. She spun the wheel, fighting to control the slide, braking hard, barely avoiding the stump of a tree and coming to rest beside a thicket.

# CHAPTER 62

*Greg*

He didn't know what had happened to the car behind them, nor had he much memory of the journey that followed, what with the blinding pain in his leg and the hurt in his breast. Aliyah had used him.

The car stopped. He looked up. A shack, surrounded by trees.

Jack dragged him out of the car and into the cabin.

He gestured to a door off the main room.

'In there.'

A shove on his back propelled him forward into what passed for a bedroom. In the glow of a naked bulb, he sat down on the bed, rusted springs creaking in complaint, and stared up at boarded-up windows.

Jack's voice: '*You too, princess,*' and Aliyah joined him, the door closing behind her; a key turning in the lock.

No other way in or out, unless he could loosen the casement

from around the window – impossible without alerting Jack to the noise.

Aliyah sat next to him on the bed.

'Greg.'

He didn't respond. Didn't even look at her. He didn't want to be anywhere near her.

'I need to tell you something.'

He grunted.

There was nothing she could say that could explain or make up for what she'd done. He should have left her back in Ripplebrook. Left her to Miriam and Jack and to her fate. It's what she seemed to want anyway. But he hadn't, and now they'd both pay the price. There was no way Miriam would let them live, no matter what she might say.

'You should never have come back to the house, Greg. I don't expect you to get it, but I need to finish what I started.'

He still didn't understand.

She put a hand on his arm, moved it lower till her fingers touched his own, caressing the rough blue ink above his knuckles.

'You know what happened to my sister.'

Sure he knew. He knew all about it: the protest, the police, the injuries that would never heal, the girl who was all but dead.

'I didn't tell you everything.'

She paused, as though struggling to find the words. Her voice wavered.

'That night in London . . . I was there. I was with her . . . I was with Mia at that demonstration.'

'But you said –'

'I lied. I lied to everyone. I was there and I wasn't supposed to be. Mum and Dad would have gone nuts if they knew, but Mia took me cos I insisted.'

'Why? You were a kid.'

'You wouldn't understand. Growing up Muslim in London, you grow up fast. Other people, white people, they look at you like there's something wrong with you, something suspicious. Like we're all terrorists. They don't see you as British, even though God knows you are, cos there's nowhere else you've ever lived. So you think fuck it, fuck them. Fucking hypocrites with their double standards. Dropping bombs on defenceless people, selling weapons to dictators, and then when innocent people fight back, *they* become the terrorists. You get pissed off by it all: the racism, the bigotry, the fucking dishonesty.

'She didn't want to take me at first. I was only fifteen, but I kept on at her till she said yes. I told Mum I was going to the library and then we took the Tube into town. It was like a carnival at first. Loads of people, all marching, waving placards, shouting slogans. We marched from Downing Street to the conference hall where all the politicians were meeting to discuss the violence in the Middle East and blocked the streets outside.

'Being part of that, it felt amazing. All these people – *good* people – marching for something. Trying to change things. Trying to make things better. For the first time I felt I belonged.

'But then it all went to shit. A car, one of those big limos with police outriders, pulled up. There was an American flag on its hood. Mia thought it was the American ambassador, but it wasn't. Suddenly it all just kicked off. People were pushing, trying to surround the thing. The police began to panic. They began lashing out, punching people, beating everyone back. That's when the fighting started. Mia and me, we were caught in the middle. Riot police on one side, guys throwing bricks and bottles on the other. She tried to get us out of there, but –'

Her fingers tensed.

'It was fucking chaos. There was no way back through the crowd. People were getting crushed. The only way out was to get to the police line. We pushed through. I thought I was going to die, but we made it to the front, close to the railings where the limo had pulled up . . .'

She paused and wiped at her cheek.

'Fuck it was horrible. Mia was arguing with the police to let us through. One of the security people must have taken pity on us; she cleared a space for us. We made it onto the pavement just as the car door opened. Three big men in suits got out, they formed a huddle and then out came this woman. Greenwood. Your vice president. I didn't know who she was back then. Her security guys were leading her into the building. Some protesters must have seen her because they broke through the police lines and went for her. I got knocked over. I remember looking up, seeing Mia, she was reaching down for me, trying to help me up. And then something happened. Her eyes closed and she collapsed.'

Her voice seemed to crack. She stopped, fighting back the emotion, he thought. Gently, he squeezed her hand.

'Aliyah . . .'

She shook her head.

'It wasn't the police that hit her. It was one of Greenwood's security guys. Mia wasn't attacking them. All she was doing was trying to help me. All she'd ever wanted to do was help people. And they destroyed her life for it. I watched her fall. I knew it was bad, even as her head hit the ground. I screamed, and then two of the men in suits were carrying me off, away from Mia . . .'

She looked at him and he saw cold hatred in her eyes.

'I remember Greenwood's face. She looked disgusted, as though Mia deserved it.'

She looked away. Cleared her throat.

'They threw me into the crowd. I tried to fight my way back to where Mia was but it was useless. I don't know exactly what happened next. Not really. Someone must have put me in a cab because

I remember getting home and rushing straight to the room we shared. I never told Mum and Dad. I never told them what happened. I never told them I was there. I fucking left her.'

Her whole body shivered. He put his arm around her.

'I know it's crazy, but I can't see any other way out of this nightmare. Yeah, Miriam'll probably kill us, but better to live another day than to die right here and now. And besides, I came here because of what happened to Mia that night. I don't give a shit about who the next president is, or any of the bullshit that Miriam spouted. But that two-faced bitch Greenwood is going to pay for what she did to my sister.'

# DAY 8
# *MONDAY*

## CHAPTER 63

*Shreya*

*She'd had them. She'd had them and she'd lost them.*

Maria O'Connor – Miriam – had been in that car, she was sure of it. She'd played it over, again and again, in her mind. There was little else to do. O'Connor, Jack Corrigan, they had been in that trailer. Aliyah Khan and Greg Flynn too, possibly. They had been in that trailer and then the light had gone off. O'Connor had known she was watching them.

And because of her *haste* another attack was coming. The question was where? The Greenwood rally? Costa's? Or both? If this was a jihadist thing, then Costa might be the more likely target, especially after his latest pronouncements on Muslims. But if it wasn't? The involvement of special ops personnel; the lack of comms chatter; the jihadi group that no one had heard of a month ago; the fact that attacks seemed to have resurrected Costa's campaign. If this *was* a right-wing conspiracy? A plot to put Costa in the White House? Then Greenwood would be the one in their sights.

Footsteps in the corridor outside. The cell door swung open.

'Why the hell didn't you just wait for backup?'

She looked up and sighed.

*Why hadn't the backup been there, waiting for her?*

'You look terrible, Dan.'

'So do you. Get on your feet, Shreya. I don't have time for your bullshit.'

She did as ordered.

'Wyatt's told the director, right? That both campaigns need to cancel the rallies tonight?'

'He's told him. And the director's told the campaigns of our suspicions. Both have elected to carry on with their rallies.'

She stared at him.

'That's ridiculous. It doesn't make any –'

'The race is too tight, Shreya. Too many people want them, need them to happen. Costa's team feels he's got the momentum. They think one more push and it'll get 'em over the line. As for Greenwood, she was banking on a buffer from the mail-in ballots, but it's all up in the air now.'

'Then he needs to *order* them to cancel the rallies.'

Dan gave a bitter laugh.

'Less than twenty-four hours till the polls open and you want the director to *order* the candidates to cancel their rallies. Have you any idea how that would make the Bureau look? How d'you think the attorney general's gonna react when he tells her the veep needs to cancel her last best hope of turning this damn election around? And Costa's people have already stated that if we stop his rally, he's gonna say we're trying to steal the election from him. Fuck, both sides'll claim we're trying to rig the vote. It'll be Comey and 2016 but on steroids. And what message does it send to the world? You might as well broadcast the fact that America can't even protect its election from a bunch of terrorists.'

'But there's a credible threat.'

'There's no *evidence*, Shreya! Nothing that points to an attack on the rallies. No comms chatter, no hard intel of any kind. You've got a hunch, okay, nothing more. And your word ain't exactly worth much right now. You know the lengths I had to go to convince Wyatt to let you out of here?'

'There's something bigger going on here, Dan. This isn't just some jihadi group. There's ex-military intelligence involved. They've even penetrated the Bureau for Pete's sake.'

He pushed her up against the wall and brought his mouth close to her ear.

'You need to be careful what you say. Wyatt already wants to charge you with aiding and abetting the escape of two terrorists.'

'They're not terrorists, Dan! They're just a couple of dumb parents who thought they could do our job. Dammit, we wouldn't have found out about Gainesville if it wasn't for them.'

'We'll see. For the moment they're being transferred to a hotel and placed under house arrest. As are you.'

'What?'

'You'll have access to your phone and laptop. You find anything out, you contact me immediately. I'll be with Wyatt at the Costa rally. If you're right, and they're planning an attack, then Costa is the more likely target. Either way there'll be a ring of steel round both venues. Police being bussed in from all over the state.'

'I can't be stuck in a hotel, Dan. I should be there, at the rallies.'

'It's the best I could do. Unless you'd rather stay here in this cell?'

\*

Shreya looked out of the hotel window. Helicopters danced in the distance. Below them, the O'Connell Center, lit up like the Fourth of July. Vice President Sarah Greenwood would be onstage in a little over an hour. In Daytona Beach, Chuck Costa would be doing the same.

And now Costa would win. She knew it. In times of fear, it was the fearmongers who won, the ones who appealed to anger, the populists who offered seductively simple solutions to complex problems. And people were scared now. You just needed to turn on the TV or the radio or check your social media to know that. Three attacks in the last twenty-four hours: two mosques and a Sikh temple into the bargain; because hatred didn't do nuance. She picked up her phone. Nikhil answered on the second ring.

'Shreya. Where are you?'

'I can't say, Nik. How's Dad?'

'He's stable. He's been asking for you. I told him you were by his bedside last night and that you'd be back later.'

She pictured the old man, lying there.

'Is Isha with him?'

'No, she's gone to that Greenwood rally with some of her activist friends.'

She gripped the phone tighter. She must have heard him wrong. 'What?'

'She was going to cancel, but your bapu told her to go.'

Shreya reached out, grabbing for the desk in front of her, steadying herself.

'Isha's in Gainesville?'

'Is that where it is? She'll be back late. I can get her to –'

'Nik, listen to me. We need to get a hold of her. Tell her on *no* account is she to go to that rally. Tell her to get the hell away. I'll call, but you try too. I gotta go.'

'Shreya? What's this ab—'

442

She hung up and called Isha's number, pacing the room as it rang and then went to voicemail.

'Isha, it's Mom. You must *not* go to the Greenwood rally today. If you're there, leave now. It's dangerous. Call me as soon as you're out.'

It would be okay. Isha would get her message. There wouldn't be an attack. The venue was locked down tight.

*Except she didn't believe it.*

An attack was coming. She knew it. It was a coup, orchestrated by people with links to the security services and moles inside the Bureau.

*'They have people everywhere.'*

She thought of Yasmin Malik, running through that mall, *away* from the crowd. The fear on her face. She wasn't a suicide bomber. She was a victim. A pawn in a bigger game. The girl at Port Arthur, a convert to Islam after the death of her father in police custody; and Aliyah Khan, mourning the loss of her sister in that protest march in London, when . . . *oh damn.*

Her collar burned. She called Mike Raven.

'Mike, you need to get a message to whoever's heading up security at the Greenwood rally. That's the target. I'm sure of it. They gotta close it down and get everyone out of there.'

She sensed his hesitation.

'Shreya, I'm just an analyst. They're not going to believe me without evidence. Why don't you call Dan and explain it yourself? He's on the ground there.'

'Dan's not with Wyatt at the Costa rally?'

'Change of plans, I guess. He's heading up security at the Greenwood event.'

The room began to spin. She reached out, gripping the back of a chair.

*Dan.*

Dan, who'd tried to send her to San Diego. Who'd dismissed her requests to search south of Estacada. Who'd gotten her kicked off the case. Dan, who'd been at the black site when it was attacked, who'd told her the address of the safe house in Portland to take Maria O'Connor to. Dan, who'd sent her to Birmingham to interrogate Sajid Khan and Carrie Flynn who had nothing to do with the attacks.

'*They have people everywhere.*'

She checked her watch. Greenwood would take to the stage in less than ninety minutes. She headed for the door, opening it a crack and finding the black-suited back of a security operative. Seemed a direct exit was out of the question. The window too was out. Seven floors up and locked tight.

*Dammit.* Then she saw it. The en suite; a door at the far end connecting to the adjoining room. She ran for it. Pulled at the handle. Locked. Long minutes passed as she picked the lock with quivering hands. Minutes she didn't have. Hands that all but refused to cooperate. But then she was through; the room beyond, empty save for ties and shirts draped over the bed. A businessman or a consultant probably. Still in meetings.

A pile of papers sat on the desk. She grabbed them and took them back to her own room. She had to hurry. She had to find Isha; had to get her out of there before . . .

She didn't want to think of the rest.

# CHAPTER 64

*Shreya*

She piled the bedding, sheets and pillowcases beside the door, pulled down the curtains and added them to the mound. The sheets of paper from next door would act as kindling.

Setting fire was a risk. What she needed was a distraction, not a disaster. There were innocent folks in the building.

She looked around. Her laptop was on the desk by the window. She sat down, brought up YouTube, and typed 'Screams'. And there it was. A six-minute soundtrack of screaming sound effects. Nothing else. Just people screaming.

*Eleven thousand hits.*

Thank God there were such people in the world.

She returned to the pile of linen and reached for her lighter. Didn't take long before the paper and textiles were aflame. On the laptop she turned the volume to maximum and hit play. The air filled with smoke and screams. She went through the bathroom into the adjoining suite and waited.

The guard must have heard the noise. Wouldn't he smell the smoke?

*Come on.*

Abruptly, the air convulsed to the tone of claxons. Fire alarms, followed by the swish of sprinklers.

Finally she heard it. The click of a lock. The swing of a door. The agent's footsteps. She opened the door, peered out, then ran for the stairwell.

Khan and Flynn were one floor down. A uniformed police officer was seated on a chair outside a door halfway between their rooms. With the beefed-up security at the rallies, maybe the Bureau just didn't have enough agents to place one outside of both Flynn's and Khan's doors. That was fine by her.

The guy seemed distracted by the sound of the alarm. She strode down the corridor. Dan had taken her gun but not her badge. The badge was generally the more useful of the two. She pulled it out and shoved it in his face.

'There's a fire in the building. I need you to help me get these two witnesses out of their rooms and to safety.'

The officer pulled out a keycard and unlocked the door. Shreya entered the room, then reached for his arm and pulled him across the threshold. Before he knew what was happening, she'd twisted it behind his back and used his momentum to drive him onto the floor. Her ribs burned. She didn't care. With one knee on his back, she reached forward and freed his gun from his holster.

Carrie Flynn looked at her as though she were a dream.

*

446

The roads around the convention hall were crowded with security vehicles and coaches unloading placard-bearing Greenwood supporters, off to the middle-aged equivalent of spring break.

'What happens if this doesn't work?'

Carrie Flynn, not restrained in the back of the car this time, but right next to her, in the front of a commandeered taxi.

That wasn't something Shreya wanted to consider. Isha was in there. She needed to find her.

'It will work,' she said. It *had* to work.

Behind her, on the rear seat, Sajid Khan remained mute. She caught his image in the rear-view. His face like that of a man off to the gallows, still praying for a last-minute reprieve.

Shreya waved her badge at a uniformed guard manning a security checkpoint.

The man scrutinised the pass for as long as it took him to read the letters FBI, before waving her through.

*Always go for the guys in uniforms. Never the suits.* The uniformed ones were less likely to question anyone holding a badge.

A second later they were moving, past the guns and into the grounds of the convention centre. Shreya descended a ramp and pulled into the underground parking lot.

'Centre of operations will be in the building's security office. Most likely it'll be down here somewhere. I need to get there. You know what to do.'

She walked them through to another security checkpoint and flashed her badge.

'These two have been vetted. They're cleared for the main hall.'

The woman scrutinised them. Sweat glistened on Sajid Khan's forehead. He wiped at it with the fingers of one hand.

The woman gave a nod.

'Okay. Carry on.' Flynn and Khan entered the elevator. She

waited till the thing was on the move, then turned and headed down a concrete corridor in search of the security office.

*

No one noticed her enter.

The room was dark, just banks of screens and desks manned by a small battalion of agents and the red light of a large digital display reading out the time. Dan stood at the middle of it all, his back to her, watching the monitors and their images from all corners of the building.

She found a corner away from him, disappeared into the shadows and looked up at the screens, at lines of smiling people, men and women with placards and kids in tow, waiting their turn to pass through the metal detectors. Beyond that, the cordon of plain-clothes FBI agents, waiting, watching.

On another screen the hall was filling up. Ten thousand seats. The faithful, taking their places in tiered rows and across the arena floor, facing a stage bedecked in red, white and blue and a banner reading GREENWOOD FOR PRESIDENT in six-foot-high letters.

She scanned the faces: for Aliyah Khan, for Greg Flynn and Maria O'Connor ... for Isha. Four among thousands, but what choice did she have? Maybe Sajid and Carrie would get lucky.

She caught a flicker on-screen: in one of the wide walkways leading to the main hall. A face among the throng of bodies heading in the same direction. For a split second it looked up at the camera. A glimpse. That was all she got, then it was gone, just another head in a crowd moving like platelets in the bloodstream.

*Isha?*

She moved closer. She needed to be sure. Another glimpse.

*It had to be.*

She headed for the door.

'Shreya?'

She froze.

'Are you fucking kidding me?'

She turned around slowly. Dan staring at her. What was that look on his face? Anger? Horror? She couldn't work it out.

Above her head, the ceiling began to vibrate. Rock music blasting in from the main hall, reverberating through a foot of concrete. She took a step back. Considered her options. If she turned and ran, would he have her shot? The bastard had given away the location of a Bureau black site. He was responsible for the deaths of fellow agents. If he saw her as a threat, he wouldn't think twice. She had to stop him. But how?

'Why are you here, Shreya?' An edge to his voice. She had to think fast.

'Wyatt's orders,' she said, even as her ears burned. 'He had a change of heart.'

A terrible lie, she knew, and he didn't seem to be buying it.

'Why wasn't I informed?'

'I can't say.'

He moved closer.

'Where were you going?'

'Up. To the main hall. I thought I might be more useful there.'

'You have something else to say, I think.'

She looked around. A room full of agents. His people.

'I don't think so.'

'Shreya –'

He stopped and pressed his hand to his earpiece.

Behind him, agents were on their feet, gathering around a monitor.

She craned a look at the screen.

*Oh God.*

# CHAPTER 65

*Sajid*

Metal doors parted. A mass of people stood before them in a cavernous antechamber; lines of bodies, snaking up to rows of metal detectors set up outside the hall.

'Wait in line,' Carrie told him. 'I'll be back in a minute.'

Before he could object she had wandered off. He shuffled forward, watching as she headed over to a row of concession stands, mugs, pins and other merchandise piled high on tables, returning soon after with two Greenwood for President T-shirts – white stars and red words on a blue background.

'Camouflage,' she said, handing him one and slipping the other over her head.

The lines snaked forward. Security guards waiting up ahead, manning metal detectors and rifling through bags. Not that different from what he was used to at Heathrow every morning. *Had been* used to. He would need to find new employment.

He marvelled at the people around him, at their enthusiasm. He struggled to think of similar rallies back in Britain. He could not recall ever seeing them. Not so large, anyway; definitely not so choreographed, or with such energy. The British, he felt, by and large saw political gatherings as they did a minor operation, to remove a boil or a cyst, say: a rather unsavoury business, which, if it had to be gone through, was best dealt with quickly and without fanfare. And while there was certainly something to be said for the enthusiasm and engagement of the American model, without trust or an informed electorate, did it not lead to tribalism? On balance, he thought he preferred the British way.

They reached the front of the line, Carrie going first, passing through the detector unmolested, waved on by a female guard with arms as wide as Sajid's whole chest. And then it was his turn: a detector manned by a white officer the size of a house. He held his breath and walked through.

No buzzer sounded. No lights flashed.

He breathed out, muttered a prayer of thanks and walked on to rejoin Carrie.

'Sir.'

A voice called out behind him. He stopped. He looked back. The security guard towered over him.

'Random search. If you wouldn't mind following me.'

He looked to Carrie. She seemed on the verge of making a scene – maybe she'd claim he was her husband, as she had done back in Twin Rivers. He prayed she wouldn't. He was a brown man living in a white society. 'Random' searches were a part of life. And what was it but a last throw of the dice by someone conditioned to see you as suspicious?

He shot her a glance, his face set in neutral, a calming expression he hoped she would understand, and realise that he had this under control. He moved to one side. The man patted him down, his hands the size of the rotis Rumina made.

'You local?'

The man's voice was affable, almost pleasant, as though this was the most natural of interactions. Sajid couldn't help but look at the gun at his waist.

'Just moved here recently,' Sajid told him.

'Where from?'

'Canada.'

There was a degree of truth in that at least.

The man finished his pat-down.

'You're clear. Have a nice day.'

Sajid gave him a nod.

He made his way to where Carrie stood waiting.

Music boomed from a multitude of speakers. American music: guitars and drums and shouting; a thumping beat that pounded his ears and shook his body. Carrie took his hand and they joined the crowd as it funnelled along.

'We need to make this convincing,' she shouted to him over a crescendo of noise.

They passed through the doors and into the auditorium, into megawatt brightness, two specks amid a sea of bodies washing up against a star-spangled stage. Carrie pointed to a row of seats in the tiered section to the left. 'We'll get a better view from up there.'

The music changed as they climbed to a couple of seats at the end of a row. He scanned the crowd: young kids, old women, black and white and brown, expectant faces. How were they to find anyone within this scrum?

He sat down beside Carrie, taking the seat next to the aisle, the noise reverberating under his feet. In front of him, a balloon bobbed from row to row.

The music faded and a man appeared, suited and booted and striding onto the stage like the ringmaster at a circus. He reached for the microphone and in that peculiar manner of announcers at boxing matches, launched into a full-throated welcome. The crowd cheered. It was politics as spectacle, he thought, and he paid the man's words little attention. What mattered were the faces looking up at him, the faces that applauded each slogan and cheered every attack line. The faces that roared in approval, first once, then again and again in rapid succession.

Sajid concentrated on them, peering row by row, face by face. An impossible task that had to be made possible. With everyone on their feet, the floor of the auditorium changed; morphing into a living, breathing organism reacting to stimuli from the stage. Cheers broke out; ripples of applause that started in one corner and spread, convulsing the whole.

Above his head, the music died. Onstage the suited man was standing aside, arms open, gazing adoringly into the wings. The cheers rose, deafening. Camera phones flashed. The music started again, presidential this time, and there, at the heart of it all, was Vice President Sarah Greenwood, smiling, waving, striding from the wings in a blue dress like a film star.

The crowd reacted in unison: clapping, cheering, following the woman's every movement as she took centre stage.

*All except one.*

It was her stillness he noticed; a woman, a few rows from the front, standing like a rock amid the crowd rippling around her. A fixed point in a sea of movement.

*Aliyah?*

He was on his feet, starting down the steps, two at a time, Carrie calling after him.

'Sajid!'

Another roar from the crowd drowned her voice. He ran now,

past rows of people, one after the other, his eyes fixed on the point where he had seen her. His vision blocked by a mass of humanity.

Carrie was behind him.

'Sajid. Stop!'

But he could not stop, not when it might be Aliyah. Not when she might be so close!

The floor of the auditorium shook to the drum of ten thousand people. He fought his way forward. She could not be more than fifty yards away. Backs blocked his path. He pushed through, his mind racing. Images of Yasmin Malik, caught on camera at the mall.

He was close now, so close. He did not even see the elbow that smashed into his face. It stopped him dead. The world cracked open. Suddenly hands were on him, forcing him to the ground, bodies on top of him, crushing the air from him, grabbing his wrists, wrenching them behind him.

He was screaming. Shouting. Incoherent.

*Aliyah! She was right there!*

# CHAPTER 66

*Shreya*

Shreya saw it on the monitors. Security officers surrounding Sajid, throwing him to the ground.

Dan was distracted, staring at the screens.

Shreya turned and ran bursting through the door and into the hallway, her mind filled with images of Sajid lying face down, hands behind his head. Had she been wrong to trust him? Had he been lying to her?

*Oh God.*

She turned a corner, almost colliding with an agent.

'Kramer?'

The agent looked at her like she was some sort of ghost.

'Shreya? I thought they'd locked you in a fucking hotel?'

'Long story.'

She turned and set off again, Kramer's voice ringing behind her.

'What the fuck's going on? You shouldn't be here!'

*No time to explain.* She sprinted up a set of stairs, conscious suddenly of the muffled roar of the crowd in the auditorium.

'Shreya! Wait!'

Dan's voice this time, booming down the corridor behind her. Her stomach lurched. Her legs all but buckling under her. The bastard was part of all this. How much blood was on his hands? And how much more would he spill before this was over?

*Screw you, Dan.*

She kept going, racing down a service corridor, the noise of the crowd growing, changing. The door to the auditorium up ahead. Two agents blocking the route. She pulled out her badge, brandished it at them like a holy relic.

'Move!'

She pushed at the door.

'Shreya! Stop!'

She was almost through when a pair of hands pulled her back. One of the agents pinned her to the wall, a hand at her throat. The other pointed a gun in her face. Dan appeared. Breathless. Sweating like a hog. Kramer was at the other end of the corridor. Staying back. Waiting in the distance.

'The fuck,' he breathed, 'is going on?'

A gun barrel forced against her temple.

*Was this how she died? Gunned down by fellow agents at the behest of a traitor?*

It would be easy enough to justify. He'd set her up. If she was dead, they could weave whatever narrative they wanted: disgruntled agent or jihadist convert. But there was Kramer to think of. Would he risk shooting Shreya in front of her?

*Kramer.*

Shreya's last throw of the dice.

'Kramer! I need you over here.'

Kramer ran over, confusion writ large.

Dan brought his face up close, obscuring Shreya's field of vision, blocking Kramer from sight.

'What the hell are you doing, Mistry?'

'I worked it out, Dan.'

'Worked what out?'

'You gonna tell them to shoot me?'

She couldn't read his expression.

'Don't fucking tempt me. Now what the hell are you doing? Why are you even here? And why is Sajid Khan in there being restrained by security?'

She wasn't about to tell him. What she needed was to lie, but the lie wouldn't come. Numbers, then. Numbers to calm her brain. Multiples of thirteen.

*Twenty-six.*

*Thirty-nine.*

'Shreya? Talk to me.'

*Fifty . . . two.*

Still nothing.

She struggled against the hands that pinned her, but it was like fighting a rock. Time was running out. She grasped at a partial-truth.

'Isha's in there somewhere. I need to find her, so either shoot me or let me do my job.'

She felt the weight of his stare; this man with whom she'd worked for years, but whom she hadn't known at all.

Dan turned to the agents.

She braced herself for what she knew was coming . . .

'Let her go.'

She couldn't believe it. Yet there was no time to work it out. She pushed through doors into an explosion of noise and light. Greenwood onstage, speechifying to massed ranks of the faithful.

*Where was Sajid?*

She ran along the front row.

A disturbance, halfway back, a ripple in the waves of people, an eddy of bodies out of sync with the others. Sajid, surrounded by agents, being dragged toward the rear of the hall, Carrie Flynn trying to stop them. Shreya sprinted for the centre aisle, reaching for her badge, shouting for the agents to let him go. One of them turned, raising his sidearm.

'Put it down!' Dan's voice, behind her. 'And let him go.'

*What was he doing?*

She reached Sajid's side.

'Aliyah!' he said. 'She's near the front.'

'Show me.'

She followed him, back along the aisle, his steps brisk, then faltering, as the crowd got to their feet and roared at something Greenwood had just said.

'Where?' she asked.

She saw confusion rend his face.

'I . . . I don't know. She was there, I'm sure. Five or six rows from the front.'

Shreya moved past him, counting the rows, *nine, eight, seven.*

*Six.*

She scanned the faces: black and white, young, old. Nothing.

*Five.*

The same process. Dan was behind her now. She needed to hurry.

*There!*

In the middle of the row beside a woman with a home-made placard.

*Aliyah.*

Emotionless. Eyes trained forward. Head unmoving. Dan saw her too. He was speaking into his cuff.

'Suspect spotted. Asian female. Row E. Possibly equipped with explosives. Get me snipers.'

She turned to him.

'No. Not yet.'

Shreya forced her way down the row, moving as quickly as she could. Behind her, Dan was ordering the people from their seats. Ahead, Aliyah must have noticed the commotion. She looked over ... staring Shreya straight in the eye. A second's confusion. Was it recognition?

The girl was getting to her feet, a loose coat over a dark blue police shirt. She swivelled around like a cornered animal, and there, at her feet ...

*Oh God.*

Shreya stopped dead.

A rucksack, black, bulging. A plastic phone in her hand. Finger over the buttons. Fear in her eyes. Fast, shallow breaths.

Shreya raised her hands, palms up, empty.

'My name's Shreya. And you're Aliyah, right?'

The girl said nothing, but her eyes glistened with tears.

'I can see you're frightened. I'm here to help. We can work this out.'

Around her, people were starting to suss that something was wrong. A woman screamed. Onstage, Sarah Greenwood continued, oblivious.

The girl began to panic, her finger poised above the buttons.

Shreya moved in, closing the distance between them so that they were only feet apart, palms still open, visible.

'Please! You don't need to do this. No one's going to hurt you. Whatever those people in Oregon told you, it's not true. They're using you. That's all. Please talk to me. How old ... how old are you?'

'Eighteen.'

'Eighteen. I got a daughter not much younger than you. She's here, in the audience somewhere. Listen to me, Aliyah. Your sister, Munira. She wouldn't want you to throw your life away.'

The girl bristled. A spark of fire in the eyes. Anger replacing fear.

'Fuck you. You don't know my sister!'

She was losing her. She heard Dan's voice.

'Get out of the way, Shreya!'

She ignored him.

*Sajid! Where was Sajid?*

She turned, saw him there. Surrounded by security.

Around them, the world convulsed. Greenwood had stopped mid-sentence, secret service agents running onto the stage, surrounding her, pulling her down. The crowd, panic rippling through them, toppling chairs, stampeding for the exits.

Suddenly Kramer was there, raising her revolver, aiming at Aliyah.

*Ripplebrook all over again.*

Shreya threw herself in the line of fire.

'Wait!'

Kramer's finger hovered on the trigger.

'Get out of the way, Shreya!'

Aliyah's finger on the buttons now, pressing down.

Sajid. He was her only hope.

'Aliyah! Your father's here!'

The girl looked up. Shreya moved so that she might see him; watched as shock rippled across her face, her fingers frozen on the keypad.

Shreya called to him, and then Sajid was walking over, hands raised, mouthing something to his daughter that she couldn't make out. He was standing beside her. Reaching out.

Aliyah backed away, her face contorted in confusion.

'Special Agent Mistry, step back now! That's an order!'

*No, Dan.*

Tears trickled down Aliyah's cheeks.

'You can't be here, Dad. That woman up there. She's the one responsible for Mia.'

'Aliyah, *maa*,' Sajid said. 'This is not the way.'

'Dad, you don't understand.'

He took a step toward her.

'Aliyah, you need to listen to this lady.'

She hesitated.

'No! Dad, you've got to go!'

She held up the phone.

Kramer pushed past, raising her gun.

'We're out of time, Shreya.'

'Wait!' she screamed back, launching herself at Kramer's arm, pushing the Glock away. 'Aliyah!' Sajid's voice. A strength to it; a determination she had not heard before. 'You must stop this. Mia would never want you to hurt people. And this boy, Greg. From what his mother has told me, he would not want you to die.'

The girl froze.

Shreya took her chance.

'Aliyah. I need you to let go of the phone and lift your arms. Can you do that for me?'

Slowly she did as ordered, raising her arms. She spread her fingers wide. The phone clattered to the floor.

Shreya shouted behind her. 'She's cooperating.'

Dan was beside her. 'Everyone out now!' He spoke into his mike. 'I need a bomb tech in here. Cut all comms!' He turned to her. 'There could be a remote trigger.'

Carrie Flynn stepped forward.

'Where's Greg?'

Shreya repeated her question.

'Aliyah, where's Greg?'

The girl looked at her.

'He's . . . he's not here. Miriam has him. Jack brought me.'

*Jack Corrigan.*

'Where is he now?'

'In here somewhere.'

'How'd you get in?'

'We were given police uniforms, passes.'

'By who?'

The girl shook her head.

'I don't know.'

Shreya remembered the footage of Jack Corrigan leaving the mall in Burbank, walking out calmly as a bomb exploded behind him.

*Jack Corrigan would already have a way out.*

She shut her mind to the chaos. *Passes and police uniforms.* They hadn't been frisked. No search of bags. No metal detectors run over them.

They'd most likely gotten in the same way Shreya had smuggled in Carrie and Sajid.

*The basement parking lot.*

She ran for the exit beside the stage and sprinted down the service corridor. The stairwell was filled with agents and police. She fought past and ran for the parking lot now choked with fire teams rushing in to secure the building. In the distance, a figure in blue heading the other way.

She set off after him.

The figure had stopped beside a pickup truck and pulled something from his pocket. Shreya drew her gun. The glow of a phone illuminated his face.

She closed the distance and raised her gun.

'Freeze!'

He looked up. His fingers flexed over the screen.

'Drop it, Corrigan, and raise your hands!'

He shook his head.

'I press this button and a thousand people will die. Now here's what you're gonna do –'

She didn't wait for him to finish. She fired. A double tap, just like on the training courses, just like Kramer had done with Yusuf Ghani, and Corrigan went down, the phone skittering across concrete.

She ran forward and knelt beside him.

'Where's Greg Flynn?'

But Corrigan was already dead. Beside him lay his phone. She picked it up and read the message on the cracked screen. CALL FAILED. NO NETWORK COVERAGE.

# CHAPTER 67

*Shreya*

She rose slowly to her feet, a hollowness overwhelming her. First time she'd killed someone. Shouldn't it have triggered something? But it was as though her every emotion had been scooped out. Killing Corrigan had elicited nothing in her. Something in her head should've screamed stop. Yet it hadn't. She'd just squeezed the trigger and ended his life.

Was she in shock? Or was this something else? Was it because Isha was here somewhere? Was that why she'd shot him out of hand without listening to him? Was she, on some level, scared he might set off the bomb and end her daughter's life?

The world around her seemed to fall away. She was outside it. A spectator, looking in on herself. Suddenly she was surrounded. Black uniforms and green coveralls. Shouts and sirens. A hand touched her shoulder, breaking the spell.

Dan.

The shock of seeing his face, feeling his touch, hit her like a wave of ice water. He was a traitor.

*Wasn't he?*

But then why had he given the order to cut all comms? If he hadn't, Corrigan might have managed to set off the bomb. She didn't understand.

'Shreya. You're with me.'

She followed him, dazed and mute, back to the ops centre. He sat her in a chair.

*Corrigan was dead. She had killed him.*

The room felt like it was shaking but then she realised it was her. It was coming from her.

Someone had supplied Jack Corrigan and Aliyah Khan with police uniforms and passes. Someone had gotten them through a ring of steel with a bomb. *She'd assumed it was Dan.* He was in charge, transferred suddenly from the Costa rally. But what if she was wrong? He could have had her shot. Instead he'd let her into the auditorium. And he had cut the comms to the building.

None of it made sense.

On the monitors, scenes of crowds being ushered to the exits.

*Isha.*

She got to her feet.

'My daughter's down there. I need to find her.'

'Sit down,' he told her. 'I'll put out a message. If she's in the building, we'll find her.'

She looked him in the eyes. Yes, she was . . . shit . . . at reading people, but this time she felt sure. There was no deceit in his expression. He meant what he'd said. He'd find her daughter. Guilt washed over her. Dan might not be a traitor after all. But if not him, then who?

'We need to question Aliyah Khan,' she said. 'Someone on the inside got her into the building. We need to find out who.'

'Kramer's dealing with it.'

'And Greenwood?' she asked.

'Safe. Milking the publicity as we speak. Courage in the face of death, all that shit. She'll be on her way to the airport soon.'

He came and stood next to her. From his pocket he took a packet of cigarettes, tapped one out and lit it. He lifted it to his mouth with a shaky hand and took a drag.

'You did good, Shreya.'

She didn't feel good. She felt useless. Her conscience weighed heavy. She should tell him. She should apologise for having suspected him.

'Dan –'

But he was distracted; touching his earpiece; getting a message. His expression wavered. He looked down at her. It made her uneasy.

'What?' she said. 'What's happened?'

'The bomb. The one Aliyah Khan was wearing. The explosives team's initial assessment is that the thing was crude. A fraction of the explosive power of the ones used in Burbank and Port Arthur. The blast range would have been minimal. She'd have been lucky to kill anyone beyond ten feet. From where she was sitting, the chances are she'd never even have injured the veep.'

She looked up at him. That made no sense. Why go to all that trouble? Why risk everything, penetrating the security around Greenwood just to set off a crappy device killing only herself and a few supporters? If this was a plot to get Costa into the White House, how would that help?

'We need to question Aliyah Khan,' she said.

'Sir?'

An agent walked up to Dan.

'A call on the satellite line. LA field office. Analyst by the name of Raven. He says he needs to speak to Special Agent Mistry, urgently.'

Dan gave a nod.

She got up and took the handset.

'Mike?'

'Shreya. I think we got a problem. Yusuf Ghani. The unredacted version of his service record's just come in. He was an intelligence asset for the military. His EB-4 Green Card – the officer who signed off on the application later left the army and joined the FBI. It was a Lieutenant Susan Kramer.'

*Kramer.*

But that was impossible.

'What?' Dan's voice, a million miles away. 'What is it?'

She didn't answer.

Kramer was an Afghan vet. She'd told her as much. But she'd saved Shreya's life. *Hadn't she?* Suddenly Kramer's words came back to her; the night Maria O'Connor had held a gun to her head.

'*I did what I had to.*'

Had she killed Ghani because he could identify her?

She'd known the address of the black site. The safe house too. And the trailer in Orange Lake – she would have been with Dan when she'd divulged the address.

*Kramer. Not Dan.*

She turned to her boss.

'It's Kramer. She signed off on Ghani's Green Card. She knew him. She brought him to America.'

His face turned ashen.

'That's not possible.'

'She's working with them, Dan. That's why they've always been a step ahead of us. She killed Ghani to stop him revealing her identity. She knew where O'Connor was being questioned in Portland. She's got to be the one who got Jack Corrigan and Aliyah Khan into the building tonight, and . . .' The words all but died in her throat. '*She's got Aliyah.*'

470

Dan was already heading for the door, speaking into the mike clipped to his lapel.

'I want *all* the exits sealed . . . Find her.'

*

The digits on the clock glowed red. Ten minutes gone. The convention centre locked tight. If Kramer had Aliyah, if they were still in the building, then it would only be a matter of time before they were cornered and found.

The doors opened. She looked up in hope. Two suited agents pushed Sajid Khan and Carrie Flynn into the room.

Dan had the satellite phone pressed to the side of his head.

'No sign of Kramer or Aliyah Khan.'

She felt sick.

At least Greenwood was safe. Costa too.

She stared at the row of monitors with their live feeds still coming from inside the hall, empty now, scattered with placards and detritus like bodies left on a battlefield. Aliyah had been sitting a good twenty feet from the stage. If Dan was right about the size of the explosive, the blast would never have reached Greenwood.

Dan had Wyatt shouting in his ear, reducing him to stuttering mere *yes sirs* and *no sirs*.

She checked her phone. No signal. Comms still cut off. A sudden chatter behind her. The agents at the monitors. One of them walked over.

'Agent Mistry, you should see this.'

She got up and followed him. A hush had descended, the others suddenly silent now, staring at her. The agent gestured at a screen, but she was already looking at it. A grainy black-and-white image. A girl in the centre. Seated on a chair. Hands and legs tied.

Her stomach lurched.

*Isha.*

'Where is that?' she asked.

'Level minus 2, lower basement, area C5.'

A sign had been placed on the floor in front of Isha, fashioned from a Greenwood placard.

'Zoom in on that.'

The camera panned in.

AGENT MISTRY. COME ALONE.

# CHAPTER 68

*Shreya*

She pushed through the double doors. A cold, concrete tomb lit by flickering strip lights; a deathly silence punctured only by the metronome drip from a pipe somewhere. Half the FBI behind her on the other side of that door. Enough men and materiel to start a small war. On this side: nothing, save for the sole figure two hundred yards away, restrained to a chair.

She wanted to run, to throw caution to the wind and sprint over to her daughter; to take her in her arms and get her out of there. But that would be suicide. Instead she walked slowly forward, boots echoing on the cement floor, feeling for the reassurance of the gun at her waist.

The distance closed. Isha's face coming into focus. Tear stains running down her cheeks.

'Mom?'

Once more she fought the urge to rush forward.

'Don't worry, baby. I'm here.'

'That's close enough.'

Kramer's voice, echoing from the shadows. And yet there was something different about it. It sounded raw. She tried to get a fix on it.

Kramer stepped out from behind a pillar, her gun trained on Isha, and walked over to the girl.

'First Aliyah, now your daughter. I seem to be collecting little Asian girls.'

'Where is Aliyah?' she asked.

Kramer smiled.

'You don't need to worry about that.'

'Let my daughter go, Kramer. She's got nothing to do with this.'

The agent shook her head.

'Was it you who figured it out?'

Shreya nodded.

'I thought as much. Hell, Shreya. You're too smart for your own good. If you'd just been a little slower. If you hadn't had the building locked down, I could have been out of here and there'd have been no need for any of this.'

She gestured to Isha.

'So here's what's going to happen. You're going to get me and your little girl a car and safe passage out of here. And once we're out of here and far enough away, I'll let her go. I give you my word.'

'And Aliyah?'

'I told you not to worry about Aliyah.'

'You know that's not up to me. Neither Dan nor Wyatt is gonna sanction it.'

'Well, you better make sure they do, because otherwise your daughter here is gonna be the first to die.'

The bile rose in her throat. Fear and anger, combining, metastasising into something: a feeling that enraged her and hollowed her out at the same time. She fought it down. What was needed now was ice-cold determination. For once though, dispassion was hard to muster.

'And if you make it out of here, then what? You know the Bureau'll hunt you down. All this for what? To try to get Costa into the White House? Was that really worth the deaths of so many innocents?'

Kramer blinked.

'You really don't understand, do you?'

'Understand what?'

'Maybe you will, one day. Right now, you've got five minutes to get me that car and safe passage, before I blow your daughter's head off.'

This time the rage got the better of her.

'You harm her, and I will kill you.'

She headed back through the doors, Dan waiting on the other side like an expectant father, cigarette burning down to his fingers.

'Well?'

'She wants a car and safe passage. Says she'll release Isha once she's far enough away, but she won't say the same for Aliyah. We need to give her that car. If we don't, she'll kill the both of them.'

Dan sucked on the dregs of his cigarette.

'Wyatt's on his way over from Daytona. He'll be here soon.'

She ran a shaking hand through her hair.

'We don't have time to wait for him, Dan! We need to do this, now!'

The seconds ticked by. Shreya tasted sweat salt on her lip.

Wyatt's voice came over the speakerphone.

'It's out of the question.'

'Sir, there's a hostage's life at stake.' Dan's voice. Rough, close to breaking.

'And what happens when the press get hold of it? One of our own agents – a terrorist – and then you want to tell them we let her get away? We can't just cave in.'

475

'And what if they find out that we let a teenage girl die needlessly when the veep was already out of danger?'

Silence on the line. Dan pressed on.

'There are still terrorists out there, sir. We can track the car. Maybe Kramer'll lead us to the others; to Maria O'Connor and Greg Flynn and whoever else is involved.'

'And what if you lose her?' Wyatt's voice, static charged. 'It's too much, Dan. It's too risky.'

'I think it's our only option . . . sir.'

She headed back toward the ops centre; her legs, unsteady; head in a fog. Fear weighted every step. This was on her, now: Isha, Kramer, Aliyah. All of it. Wyatt had made the call, Dan had convinced him, but they'd done this for her, because of her. And now the burden of it all rested on her shoulders.

The corridor seemed to close in on her. Nausea gripping her stomach; panic in her chest; her breathing suddenly shallow, coming in fits and starts. Fighting for air, she stumbled to the wall and shut her eyes.

How could she have been so wrong? She should have seen through Kramer. She should have figured it out. Instead she'd accused Dan. Maybe they were right, all of those people in the Bureau who called her a screw-up. She *had* screwed up, and now Isha was paying the price. She crumpled to the floor and finally the tears came, each drop born of anger and grief and so many regrets.

But there was no time for self pity. She had to keep going; had to do her job. For Isha and for Aliyah. Slowly her breathing settled. The tears eased and she wiped the last of them from her face.

She got back to her feet.

Sajid Khan and Carrie Flynn were being held in an office down the hall. She owed them an explanation. By the time she entered the room, her face bore no trace of emotion.

Khan was seated on a couch, Flynn pacing the room; both under the dispassionate gaze of a golem of an agent. Khan looked up expectantly as she entered. Flynn stopped pacing.

'Have you found my boy?'

Shreya shook her head.

'No ... and I'm afraid there's worse news. Aliyah's ... been abducted.'

Flynn stared at her.

'Abducted?'

Sajid Khan looked like he was having trouble taking it all in. He got to his feet.

'How is that possible?'

'At this point, I can't answer that.'

Carrie Flynn bustled over, and for a moment, Shreya thought she might launch herself at her.

'Can't or won't? After everything we've gone through. How the fuck can this be happening?'

Shreya raised a placatory hand, for all the good it did.

'I'm asking you to trust me. We'll figure this out.'

Carrie Flynn gave a snort of derision.

'That's easy for you to say. Have you any idea what we've been through?'

She shouldn't have told them. It was unprofessional. She should have kept it to herself, but in that moment something snapped. She told them. Of Isha and the agent who was holding her hostage; who wanted a car and a way out or she'd kill her daughter.

Sajid Khan walked over and took her hand, much as she had taken his, three years ago in a London hospital.

'We are truly on the same side now.'

*

In the ops centre, Dan was orchestrating proceedings like the captain on the deck of a submarine.

'Where's the car now?'

'Moving north on the 441. Pursuit vehicles holding back but within five hundred yards.'

'Keep tracking.'

He spoke into his lapel mike.

'Go through her laptop and whatever else you can find. We need every detail of her life, asap. Phone records, bank records, everything.'

Shreya thought only of Isha. If she got out of this, would she recover? Would she ever be the same girl again? Her daughter's life altered irrevocably, and it was her fault. What would she say to Nikhil? Would either of them ever be able to forgive her? Would she ever forgive herself?

The agent monitoring the drone footage of the car turned from his screen.

'She's stopped.'

Shreya strained to look over his shoulder. Dan's voice from beside her.

'Show me.'

The light was fading. The picture, grainy. Just tail lights visible under a bridge.

'Send one of our vehicles past,' he said. 'Slow but don't stop. I want to know what's going on.'

Shreya's stomach twisted. The waiting, the not knowing; it was always hard, but this was different. This was Isha's life on the line. The seconds ticked by. Eternity in the space of two minutes. Static on the intercom, displaced finally by a voice.

'Vehicle is stationary . . . No occupants.'

Shreya closed her eyes.

Dan was shouting.

'I want all assets converging on that car. I want the net closed.'

*Too late*, Shreya thought. Kramer was too good an agent. There would have been another car waiting. They'd have been in and out in ten seconds. She looked at the screen, her worst fears coming true. Her daughter, lost to her, in the hands of killers.

The car was stopped just off the junction of the 441 running north–south, and the 222 running east–west. The possible radius was already about ten square miles, she guessed, and growing by the second.

Kramer had lied to her. Why not just let Isha go? She'd outlived her usefulness. Why hold on to her?

Was this personal? Was this some sort of payback aimed at her? Was this because she felt she'd been forced to shoot Ghani? No. Kramer was a professional. She was too objective, too dispassionate, too focused to be swayed by motives of revenge. She'd held on to Isha because she might still have worth. A bargaining chip, but to bargain for what? It was over.

*Wasn't it?* Something felt wrong. Out of place. The pieces. They didn't fit. Too many kids. Too many pieces still in play. 'No.'

Dan turned to her. 'What? What is it?'

'It's not over.'

'What?'

'These are ex-special forces. The best of the best. Leaving Aliyah alone; arming her with such a pathetic bomb. They wouldn't have been that sloppy.'

He shook his head.

'Shreya, we'll get these guys, and we'll find your daughter. But we foiled a major attack tonight. Greenwood's okay. She's already heading to the airport.'

No. That was too simplistic. There was something more going on. She needed to figure out what, and fast. Isha's life depended on it.

She stared at the monitor, at the map of the roads round Gainesville.

*The airport.*

Only a mile from where Kramer had abandoned the car.

Kramer's words. *'You really don't understand.'*

'Greenwood's on her way to Gainesville airport?'

'Yup.'

'And Costa?'

'What?'

'Where's he?'

Dan shrugged. 'Quickly, Dan! Where is he? We need to know!'

'Heading back to DC too, I guess. Wyatt closed down his rally as soon as he got word of the bomb here.'

She looked at the neon digits of the clock. Three minutes since they'd lost Kramer. Three minutes and counting. Time running out. What was she missing?

'Where's Costa's plane? Daytona Beach?'

Dan shook his head.

'It's at Gainesville. I saw it this morning when we landed.'

Both planes, at the same airport, at the same time. Shreya closed her eyes and recalled that night in Portland. The attack on the black site.

*'Shit.'*

'What?'

'They weren't targeting Greenwood *or* Costa at the rallies,' she said. 'They were herding them.'

# CHAPTER 69

*Greg*

The car had drawn up, high beams lighting up the night.

It should have been Jack and Aliyah. Instead, three figures had exited: a woman, youthful, but stone-faced, leading Aliyah and some other girl at gunpoint. The doors opened and the woman forced the others in first. Miriam had the car moving before the woman had even closed the door.

He turned in his seat. Aliyah looked shook up. The girl beside her looked catatonic, her expression like that of civilians he'd seen caught in crossfire. He reached back for Aliyah's hand and squeezed cold fingers.

'Where's Jack?' Miriam asked.

'Dead,' the woman said.

He realised he'd seen her before. That day in Estacada when Aliyah had run off. As for Jack, it took a moment to process the news.

481

*Good. The bastard deserved to die.*

Miriam gestured to the girl.

'And who's that?'

'A little insurance. You don't need to worry about it.'

Miriam took a sharp left and he saw the signs for the airport.

'You get this done, Greg, and you and Aliyah can disappear. New names, new identities. It's all ready.'

He gave her a nod.

Miriam pulled up at the security checkpoint and flashed a pass. A young-looking guy examined it, then lifted the boom and waved them through.

She drove on and stopped close to the airstrip.

'You know what to do.'

He did.

Two planes, two bombs.

He got out and walked across the tarmac, rucksacks slung over his shoulder and airport ID clipped to his blue overalls. He approached the security check and took his place in line. The guards were taking their time, scrutinising every face and every badge. He felt the familiar knot of tension in his stomach; forced himself to breathe: long inhalations, longer exhalations.

The line snaked forward. A bearded guard checked his ID while he kept his eyes on the ground. He headed south-west, the details etched in his memory, hugging the walls of a hangar, passing through a service entrance into the terminal and turning right.

The door was five hundred yards away; two heavyset security men lounging on a bench beside it. He gave them a nod and walked past as though he'd done it a hundred times before. Beyond was the stairwell, just as Miriam had said it would be. At the bottom, the exit to the parking lot, the ground support vehicles lined up neatly in a row.

*'The catering truck will be at the far end. Keys under the sun visor.'*

The truck was there; a couple of tarp-covered crates sitting on its hydraulic platform. He walked over, lifted himself onto the platform and pulled back the cover of the first crate. Inside were two trolleys, foil-topped food containers in one, bottled beverages in the other. He opened the side of the first, removing the items from the bottom row, making space for one of the rucksacks.

He unzipped one and took a look at the device. Primed and ready. Certainly large enough to blow a hole in the fuselage of a private jet. He had to be careful. There might be surveillance. He did what he needed to do, then zipped up the rucksack, pushed it into the hollow and replaced the meals. He moved on to the second rucksack, the second crate, and repeated the process. Replacing the covers, he jumped down and headed for the cab. The door was unlocked; the key where Miriam had said it would be. Inside, on the passenger seat, sat a clipboard, its front page a form of times, and flight details and signatures. He looked at his hand before gripping the wheel, thought it should be shaking, saw it wasn't, and so he turned the ignition and drove.

Aircraft were parked along the tarmac. Two stood out, tended by fuel tankers and ground crew. He found Costa's first, a twitchy security detail surrounding it. Secret service, he guessed. Black suits and ties like they'd stepped off a film set. Behind them, blending into the night, were more men with bigger guns and body armour; watching; waiting.

He drew up close. An agent approached the cab. Greg lowered his window and handed over the clipboard. The agent checked it over. Greg held his breath. He needed to stay calm. He needed to pass this test or it was over. The agent looked up from the paperwork and stared hard at him. He felt his entrails turn to ice. It wasn't working. The agent seemed to see through him. And then came the slightest of smiles. The guy waved him through.

He wasn't sure what had just happened, but he didn't hang around to find out. With a nod, he pressed down on the gas and drove on, parking up close to the fuselage as a white-shirted steward descended the steps to meet him.

'Hope you brought plenty of booze.'

The guy jumped onto the hydraulic platform and Greg pressed a button. The truck bed came to life with a metallic buzz, rising till it was in line with the door to the cabin. The steward extended a ramp from the platform to the plane and then wheeled the trolleys, one by one, from the container into the galley.

Another few minutes and the job was done. He lowered the platform and moved on to Greenwood's plane, going through the whole thing again with another security detail and another flight attendant, a woman this time, who cracked the same joke.

He drove back to the terminal, passing the lights of a motorcade heading the other way. Three vehicles and police outriders, all cutting across the apron.

*Greenwood or Costa?* It didn't matter now.

He parked the truck back in the lot and checked his watch. Eight minutes to go. His leg hurt. Miriam would be waiting with Aliyah at a service entrance near the edge of the airfield. Timing was everything. He needed to get Aliyah away before the bombs went off.

He walked back to the terminal, a hitch in his step, past staff and security personnel heading the other way. He kept his head down as a group of armed officers rushed past.

A gaggle of folks were gathered under a TV. A photo of Jack filled the screen. The image changed again, a shot of the motorcade he'd just seen, pulling in to Gainesville airport, but he wasn't watching any more.

Jack, Yasmin, Rehana, Yusuf. All dead.

He wasn't about to let that happen to Aliyah.

# CHAPTER 70

*Greg*


The car was waiting on the slip road at the end of the runway. Miriam in front, Aliyah in the back, illuminated in the glow of the vanity light.

Miriam opened the door and stepped out.

Greg stopped a few feet away.

'You get it done?' she asked.

He gave her a nod.

'Shame about Jack,' he said, looking for a flicker of emotion from her; anything that might suggest she mourned his passing.

'He's a martyr to the cause,' she said.

'Like Yasmin and Rehana and Yusuf?'

'We all find our causes, Greg. Even you.' She gave the barest and most frightening of smiles. 'They had their causes; something they were ready, if maybe not willing, to die for.'

'And me?' he asked.

She held the smile.

'Your cause is right here, isn't she?'

He felt his blood rising.

'You used me. All those folks in that mall. They're dead because of what you made me do.'

She stared at the planes on the tarmac.

'Collateral damage, Greg. Didn't you cause some of that yourself back in Kandahar?'

He didn't have time for her bullshit.

'I've done my part. Now let Aliyah go.'

'What's the hurry? Plenty of time to start your lives. You're about to go down in history. Shit, you probably deserve a medal.'

She pointed across the runway at another group of vehicles; flashing lights speeding across the asphalt.

'Shouldn't be long now.'

The motorcade was pulling to a stop, secret service agents fanning out. Miriam walked back to the car, opened the door and took something from the seat. The first plane began to roll forward, taxiing toward the runway.

Miriam turned, a black box the size of a phone in her hand.

He took a breath. All the talk of new lives and new identities, it was bullshit. He knew that. Miriam would kill them just as surely as she'd killed Yasmin and Rehana. He'd only have one chance to stop her.

Miriam was looking out at the runway. He followed her gaze: watched the second motorcade disgorge its passengers. Figures climbing stairs into the plane. The door closing. Engines firing. The plane lurching forward. Suddenly the expression on Miriam's face changed, ice-cold equanimity faltering. He saw it too. A commotion out on the runway. A vehicle careening toward the runway.

Miriam cursed.

'Looks like we're going to have to speed things up a little.'

The whine of engines rent the air. The first plane began to race down the runway. Seconds later it was airborne. The other with its lights on, figures visible in the cockpit, began to taxi.

It accelerated, the noise of its engines rising to a deafening crescendo. It hurtled forward, almost straight toward them. The vehicle which had appeared was tearing along a service road and onto the apron, skidding to a halt ahead of the onrushing jet. Agents were running toward it, pointing weapons. The tone of the plane's engines changed, roaring as the aircraft took off, missing the roof of the car by mere feet.

Miriam raised the device in her hand. She waited, precious seconds.

'High enough,' she said.

She pressed down and he heard the cataclysm of explosions.

# CHAPTER 71

'Where the hell are my comms!'

Dan's voice echoed behind her.

Shreya headed for the door, bursting through, running down the corridor till she reached the office where Khan and Flynn were being held.

'You two, come with me.'

The parking lot was a sea of police tape; a cordon sanitaire around the scene of Jack Corrigan's demise. Yellow ribbon for a soldier who was never coming home. Her car sat just beyond.

'Get in,' she said as she flashed her badge at the forensics team and told them to get the hell out of the way. She reached for the glove box, pulled out a gun and passed it to Sajid. 'You might need that.'

He stared at it dumbfounded.

'I would not know what to do with it.'

'I would,' Carrie said.

He passed her the gun as Shreya started the engine and headed for the exit, carving a path through a throng of vehicles.

'Where are we going, Agent Mistry?'

Sajid's voice, still restrained after all that had happened to him. That was a marvel in itself.

'The airport. I think that's where they're heading.'

Ten minutes of racing through night-time traffic. The longest ten of her life. Isha out there, in the hands of a killer. Is this what Khan and Flynn had been living through? Sajid Khan was right, they were equal now. There was solidarity in that.

The white lights of town gave way to the orange sodium of the airport. A security checkpoint coming up fast. A dozen gun-toting men in helmets and black uniforms standing round it like this was Somalia or something. She flashed her badge and yelled at them to raise the damn boom gate, then stepped on the gas.

*Terminal or airstrip?*

She made for the airstrip, swerving past refuelling trucks and baggage carts. She rounded the last building, a row of private planes up ahead. One was taking off; another was taxiing toward the runway. Greenwood or Costa? It didn't matter.

She gunned the car forward, along the slip road, onto the runway, bringing it skidding to a halt in the middle of the tarmac, just a hundred yards in front of the jet.

She heard the scream of engines.

*It needed to stop. It had to stop.*

Vehicles were hurtling down the airstrip behind it: police, fire trucks, secret service SUVs.

'Get out of the car!'

The doors behind her opened, Flynn and Khan falling onto the tarmac, running. The deafening whine of the engines, the smell of aviation fuel filling the air. The jet hurtled toward her and then it was airborne, passing over the top of the car, all but clipping the antenna on its roof.

Secret service men were descending; vehicles were drawing close; men with guns getting out and charging toward her. Where were Carrie and Sajid? She couldn't see them.

She got out of the car, badge in hand like a shield that might protect her. Black suits around her, shouting for her to get down on the ground. She was trying to warn them, pleading with them to contact the planes, to get them back on the ground, but no one was listening.

They were on top of her now, forcing her to the tarmac, pulling her arms behind her back. She was shouting at them, screaming, begging them to listen. She felt the hard edge of a gun shoved in her back.

She closed her eyes, and then came the explosions.

Greg felt the force of the blast ripple through the tarmac; saw the yellow flames leap into the night. He hadn't expected the blast to be so strong; the catering truck a flaming wreck, ripped asunder by both bombs exploding in its cabin. Just where he'd left them.

*Fuck you, Miriam.*

The woman let out a cry.

'No! What the fuck did you do?'

He didn't wait for her to work it out.

He lunged forward, aiming a blow at her face. Miriam was reaching for her gun, her hand halfway up by the time she detected the blow. She made to parry and the gun fell from her grip. He dived for it, wrapping his fingers round the handle as she made to stomp on his head. He struggled to his feet, turning to find his target, though she saw him coming and aimed a boot at his knee. He heard the crunch of his bones before he felt the wave of pain surging over him. He collapsed back to the concrete, still grasping the gun, Miriam's hand locked onto his arm. He pulled her forward and she fell to earth, trying to wrestle the gun from him. They grappled and rolled for what felt like seconds, minutes. The gun. He was turning the gun toward her. She looked down and kicked again. His knee. He braced for the pain but it was too late. It surged through him like electric current. This time the joint was shattered. He knew it. Nausea welled up like a tsunami: a hot, sickening, all-encompassing wave. His strength was failing, leaching away. The gun barrel turned back toward him.

Shreya opened her eyes to flames in the distance.

A truck, not the planes, destroyed.

*Isha! Was the girl among the wreckage? Please God. No!*

She struggled against the agents who held her down. A command was shouted across and they released her. One held a hand to an earpiece.

The comms were back up, she guessed.

She got to her feet amid a chorus of shouts. The agent with the earpiece gestured to the others.

Another explosion ripped through the air. A fuel tanker next to the burning truck had just gone up in flames. And there, in its glow, she saw them. Two figures. Silhouetted. One pulling the other toward a row of aircraft hangars.

She checked her gun and ran.

The darkness of the hangar's shadow was immediate. Ahead, the figures were already stepping into the light of another hangar, shadows slowly resolving into bodies: Kramer to the rear, Isha ahead. Shreya ran on, lungs burning, closing the gap, reaching the hangar, catching her breath, drawing her gun.

Kramer was at the far end, searching for an exit. Finding nothing.

She raised her weapon.

'Kramer!'

The agent spun round, yanking Isha toward her, pointing her Glock at the girl's head. Shreya saw the terror in her daughter's eyes; the tracks of tears on her face. Once more the anger welled up. 'Isha. You okay, honey?'

Kramer answered for her.

'She's unharmed.'

The agent looked older, somehow. Solemn. Determined.

'Let her go.'

'I can't do that. Not yet.'

Shreya swallowed, her throat dust-dry; her finger tight on the trigger. What she wouldn't give for just one clean shot. She had to keep Kramer talking. Eke out an opportunity.

'It's over, Kramer. Both planes are away. The candidates are safe. But Jesus. Trying to assassinate both of them? Why?'

'System's broken, Shreya. Country's going to shit. All this fucking polarisation. Things need to change before it's too late.'

'So what is this? A coup?'

'Not a coup. A second revolution. A reset. Imagine it, the political system, fixed, working for the people again. Giving kids like your daughter a chance at a future.'

*Isha.*

The fear spiked within her.

'Let her go, Kramer. She's not part of this.'

The agent paused for a moment. Something flickered in her eyes. A look of disgust on her face.

'You think I'd hurt your daughter? Don't you see, Shreya? I'm not your enemy. I'm a patriot. Just like you.'

Shreya spoke softly. 'Then please, Susan. Let her go.'

Kramer smiled. 'I think that's the first time I've heard you use my first name. I'll make you a deal. You lay down your gun, kick it over there. You let me go and I'll let her live.'

Shreya kept her gun aimed. It was a trick. It had to be. Kramer would wait for her to lower her gun and then shoot both of them. The agent seemed to sense her thoughts. She shifted the Glock away from Isha's head, pointing it straight up into the night.

'You need to trust me, Shreya. I could've killed you on half a dozen occasions, but I didn't. I'm not going to do it now.'

Trust. How was she to trust a woman who'd played her? Who'd lied to her from the start. She tried to read Kramer's face. Gleaned nothing.

It came down to a straight choice, like left or right. Take a risk or play it safe.

She chose left.

She lowered her arm and placed the gun on the ground, then kicked it away and looked at Kramer, nerves taut, heart pounding in her chest. She held her breath.

Kramer gave her a nod.

'I wasn't sure you'd do it.'

'You said you weren't my enemy. Now prove it.'

She released her grip and then Isha was running. Running toward Shreya. Falling into her arms. Sobbing into her chest. Shreya held her tight.

She turned back to Kramer. The woman was watching them; her face utterly inscrutable to Shreya. The gun still in her hand.

Shreya breathed.

'Let me take you in.'

There was something there – in Kramer's eyes, in the corners of her mouth. What was it? Anger, or anguish? She couldn't tell. Shreya Mistry – so good at getting inside a person's head; so pathetic at reading their faces.

Kramer shook her head.

'I know too much. There are too many good people involved. I won't betray them.'

Shreya felt sweat at her neck.

'Ghani. Was he a friend?'

Kramer didn't flinch.

'He was a good man.'

'And yet you killed him.'

'Some things are bigger than friendship.'

From behind she heard shouts. Secret service? FBI? It didn't matter. The perimeter was being sealed tight.

'You know they won't let you escape.'

'I know.'

Kramer's gaze faltered.

Shreya closed her eyes and hugged Isha tight. Kramer's voice suddenly intruded on her introspection.

'I'm sorry, Shreya. There's no other way.'

She looked up and let out a cry, a hopeless, powerless lament, which died in her throat as Kramer pressed the gun to her own temple and fired.


Around Sajid the world was ending.

Explosions ripped through the air. Airport trucks reduced to a twisted wreck of flame and metal. He heard Mistry shout. The men who had been about to shoot her were now helping her up.

Carrie was beside him, and then she started running.

'Greg!'

He called after her. She ignored him and kept running, away from him, toward . . . and then he saw. Two figures locked in violence beside a car. He too began to run. The figures ahead of him solidifying. A man and a woman. Greg and that woman with the white hair. The one whom he'd seen on the television being taken from the house in Ripplebrook. And then, *Aliyah*! She was there too, coming out of the car. The woman was getting to her feet, turning, striking Aliyah with something. He watched his daughter fall to the ground.

He heard himself cry out. Pain, anger, suffering, all in that one primal roar.

He ran on, reaching Carrie, passing her, remorselessly closing ground. He was close now; close enough to see that the woman held a gun. The boy on the ground was trying to rise, grappling for it, trying to pull it from her, and then he was screaming in agony. She aimed a kick to his leg, then lifted the gun, aiming at his head. Aliyah was rising, trying to stop her. Sajid ran, like he had done all those years before, on that night in the rain of Chittagong. With a yell he threw himself at the woman.

He saw her turn, raise the gun, aim the muzzle at him. He heard the shots and then the world came up to meet him. Nothing. He felt nothing at all. His body divorced from his mind. More shots rang out. The woman stumbled and fell before him. He saw the blossom of crimson spread across her chest like the carnations that once grew in his father's garden. He saw Carrie, her arm outstretched, the gun in her hand. He saw boots run forward, guns raised. He saw Aliyah, her hands to her mouth. Running toward him. Kneeling beside him. Cradling his head. Tears streaming. Yelling silent cries into the night.

He heard nothing now, yet he saw everything. He saw the chain around her neck, the small silver bird taking wing upon it. He saw the boy, Greg, stumble after her. He saw Carrie. He saw her take his hand yet he could not feel her touch. He saw the tears on her face. He wanted to tell her . . . to thank her . . . she had saved his daughter, but his throat was dry and the words would not form. He closed his eyes and saw Tariq and Rumina and Mia. He saw his mother and his father, and then he was running toward them, through the rain, through the forests of his homeland.

### THE END

# ACKNOWLEDGEMENTS

*Hunted* started life back in 2019 as an idea inspired by a transatlantic telephone conversation with Josh Kendall, who would go on to become the US editor of this book. It has taken over three years to write and to get right. The journey wasn't always easy and I'm indebted to those who had faith in me and those whose strength and support saw me through the difficult times.

In particular to my wonderful editors: to Jade Chandler for seeing the potential in this book, to Kate Fogg for getting me through the hard yards; to Josh Kendall, with whom every conversation is an education, for setting me down this road in the first place, and for his belief and guidance; and to the force of nature that is Katie Ellis-Brown, for her wisdom, her energy, her encouragement and for showing me the way when I was lost. I am truly blessed to have had you all on my side.

I'm indebted to the wider team at Harvill Secker/Vintage, especially to assistant editor, Sania Riaz; Mia Quibell-Smith, and Bethan Jones for all the wonderful publicity they garner; to Sophie Painter, Lucy Upton and Carmella Lowkis for the online marketing; to Caitlin Knight and Nat Breakwell for taking the book to the world; to Dan Mogford, for the wonderful UK cover; to Hannah Telfer, Faye Brewster and the wider team at Vintage for all their support.

Thanks also to Richard Cable and Liz Foley who have nurtured and guided my career since the beginning. I couldn't have asked for better bosses.

In the US, my thanks go to the team at Mulholland, especially Liv Ryan, Karen Landry, Lena Little, Bruce Nichols, Craig Young, Judy Clain, Danielle Finnegan, Lauren Hesse, John Leary and Meg Mugelino, and also Michael Pietsch for championing the social power of crime fiction.

I'm grateful to Honor Spreckley and the whole team at Rogers, Coleridge and White, and especially to my agent, Sam Copeland who, ten years ago, took a chance on me and changed my life. If being talented and handsome were crimes, he'd be serving a life sentence.

Thank you too, to all the booksellers, bloggers and reviewers who've championed and supported my work and the work of so many other writers. In times of trouble, good fiction is a source of comfort, and we writers are honoured by your dedication and love for books.

A special thanks to my early readers: Steve Cavanagh, Lee Child, Mick Herron, Val McDermid, Adrian McKinty, Ayisha Malik and Ruth Ware. Thank you for your advice, your encouragement and your suggestions. I know the book is better because of you.

Thanks too to my friends The Red Hot Chilli Writers: Alex Khan, Ayisha Malik, Imran Mahmood, Amit Dhand, and of course, my partner in podcasting, Vaseem Khan. Thank you for your *bakwaas* and your 'glass of water related insights'. Except for Ayisha, you were all absolutely useless.

Thanks also to Anna Mazzola, Laura Shepherd-Robinson and Adrian 'Buncle' Scottow, for their wit, their charm, and their ability to drink champagne like it was going out of fashion. And thanks to Colin Scott and to my brother and sister writers in the crime fiction community. Who'd have thought there could be such camaraderie in what is supposed to be a solitary activity?

And finally of course, thank you to Sonal, for putting up with this bin-fire of a husband. Thank you for your love, your infinite patience and your infinite grace. I lucked out the day I met you.

# CREDITS

Vintage would like to thank everyone who worked on the publication of *HUNTED*

**Agent**
Sam Copeland

**UK Editor**
Katie Ellis-Brown

**US Editor**
Josh Kendall

**Editorial**
Jade Chandler
Liz Foley
Sania Riaz
Kate Fogg
Liv Ryan

**Copy-editor**
Katherine Fry

**Proofreader**
Fiona Brown

**Managing Editorial**
Rowena Skelton-Wallace

**Contracts**
Emma D'Cruz
Gemma Avery
Ceri Cooper
Rebecca Smith
Anne Porter
Rita Omoro
Hayley Morgan

**Design**
Dan Mogford

**Audio**
Nile Faure-Bryan

**Digital**
Anna Baggaley
Claire Dolan
Piers Irvine

**Inventory**
Georgia Sibbitt

**Publicity**
Mia Quibell-Smith
Amritpal Bhullar

**Finance**
Ed Grande
Lee Tuck
Jerome Davies

**Marketing**
Sophie Painter
Lucy Upton
Carmella Lowkis
Yazmeen Akhtar

**Production**
Konrad Kirkham
Polly Dorner

**Sales**
Nathaniel Breakwell
Malissa Mistry
Caitlin Knight
Rohan Hope
Jade Perez
Neil Green
Jessica Paul
Amanda Dean
Andy Taylor
David Atkinson
David Devaney
Helen Evans
Lewis Cain
Phoebe Edwards
Justin Ward-Turner
Amy Carruthers
Charlotte Owens

**Operations**
Sophie Ramage

**Rights**
Jane Kirby
Lucie Deacon
Lucy Beresford-Knox
Rachael Sharples
Beth Wood
Maddie Stephenson
Agnes Watters

Abir Mukherjee is the bestselling author of the award-winning Wyndham & Banerjee series of crime novels set in 1920s India. His books have been translated into fifteen languages and won various awards including the CWA Dagger for best Historical Novel, the Prix du Polar Européen, and the Wilbur Smith Award for Adventure Writing. He also co-hosts the popular Red Hot Chilli Writers podcast which takes a wry look at the world of books, writing, and the creative arts, tackling everything from bestsellers to pop culture.

Abir grew up in Scotland and now lives in Surrey with his wife and two sons.

Website: abirmukherjee.com
Twitter, Threads & Instagram: @radiomukhers
Facebook: AuthorAbir

# Award-winning mysteries from
# ABIR MUKHERJEE

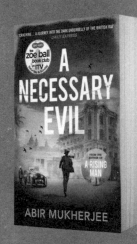

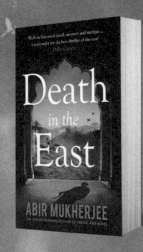

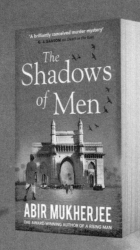

'Abir Mukherjee is doing something uniquely different in the crime genre...breathtaking'
PETER MAY

'Exceptional historical crime'
C. J. SANSOM

## Out now in all good bookshops